"Jill Jones creates characters that ring with truth, weaving them into a plot rich and full, tempting the reader with the lure of legend and romance. Taut suspense propels the turn of each page, and heightens the sensual discovery of love . . . spellbinding."
—*Reader to Reader Reviews*

"Ms. Jones charts new terrain in her writing with this mesmerizing romantic suspense. It's a page-turner from start to finish and impossible to put down until the satisfying climax."
—*Old Book Barn Gazette*

"Dangerous secrets and ancient rituals make a spellbinding backdrop for this new tale of romantic suspense by the awesome Jill Jones. THE ISLAND makes for top-notch reading."
—*Romantic Times*

CIRCLE OF THE LILY

"An incredible accomplishment by one of the top authors on the market today."
—*Painted Rock Reviews*

"Her clever and compelling plot twists will keep . . . readers riveted."
—Amazon.com

THE SCOTTISH ROSE

"THE SCOTTISH ROSE seamlessly blends the elements of romance, time travel, adventure, and danger with truly spectacular results."
—*Romantic Times*

"Exciting, absorbing, one of the top books of the year."
—*Affaire de Coeur*

"A book to treasure . . . a unique page-turner, sure to win a favored place on bookshelves."
—*The Belles and Beaux of Romance*

MY LADY CAROLINE

"An imaginative storyteller, magnetic story—a blend of past and present that you'll find delightful."
—*The Literary Times*

"A truly remarkable story."
—*Publishers Weekly*

"A bewitching ghost story . . . This is an author to watch!"
—*Romantic Times*

EMILY'S SECRET

Winner of the prestigious "Maggie" Award from Georgia Romance Writers

"A magnificent novel!"
—*Affaire de Coeur*

"A totally unique premise that lingers in the heart long after the final page is turned."
—*Rendezvous*

"An outstanding debut by a highly talented new author. Snap up this delightful and visionary tale ASAP!"
—*Romantic Times*

"Beautifully written and compelling . . . I loved it . . . A must read!"
—Heather Graham

"Lovely! It's the book I've always wanted to write."
—Marion Zimmer Bradley

"A great debut for a talented new author."
—Jasmine Cresswell

"Wonderful!"
—Barbara Erskine

Bloodline

Jill Jones

St. Martin's Paperbacks

This is a work of fiction. Only the characters of J. K. Stephen, Prince Albert Victor Edward (the duke of Clarence), Dr. William Gull, and members of the Royal Family surrounding Queen Victoria are historical; all other characters herein are fictitious, and any resemblance they may bear to persons living or dead is entirely coincidental. The events described herein concerning the murders committed by the perpetrator known as Jack the Ripper are historically accurate as best as can be determined from in-depth research. All other events are entirely fictional.

BLOODLINE

Copyright © 2000 by Jill Jones.

ISBN: 0-312-97412-4

Printed in the United States of America

St. Martin's Paperbacks edition / June 2000

St. Martin's Paperbacks are published by St. Martin's Press, 175 Fifth Avenue, New York, NY 10010.

10 9 8 7 6 5 4 3 2

For my daughter, Brooke Shannon Cundiff,
with love and thanks for your enthusiastic and generous
support of my work, and for your ideas that brought special
dimension to this book,
and for my new son-in-law, Chuck Cundiff,
whom we welcome into our family with all our hearts.
May your lives be blessed with
love, peace, joy, and abundance.

ACKNOWLEDGMENTS

I wish to thank Mr. Peter Blau, for sharing his Sherlockian expertise, and Special Agent Marie Dyson, profiler with the Critical Incident Response Group Unit, a division of the FBI's National Center for the Evaluation of Violent Crime at Quantico, Virginia, for lending authenticity to this tale. I am also indebted to David Abrahamsen, M.D., F.A.C.Pn., author of *Murder and Madness, The Secret Life of Jack the Ripper*. Dr. Abrahamsen's insight into both the crimes and the minds of the criminals who committed them was critical to the development of this story.

Thanks to Patricia McLaughlin for helping me locate sites for the book in and around Washington, D.C., and to my critique partners for helping work out the bugs.

I wish to thank my daughter, Brooke Cundiff, for her special research into the old Ripper murders that brought exciting new ideas to the story, and my husband, Jerry, for his creative support and all the wonderful meals.

Thanks to my editor, Jennifer Enderlin, for her encouragement and editorial talent, and to Denise Marcil, for opening new avenues for me.

. . . this new strange year of three eights that could never be written again . . .
Her Royal Highness, Queen Victoria

Though this be madness, yet there is method in't.
William Shakespeare
Hamlet II, ii

In famous London City, in eighteen eighty-eight,
Four beastly cruel murders have been done . . .
Some say it was old Nick himself,
Or else a Russian Jew.
Some say it was a "cannibal" from the
Isle of Kickaiboo.
Some say it must be Bashi-Bazouks,
Or else it's the Chinese
Come over to Whitechapel to commit
Such crimes as these.
From the tabloid press in the autumn of 1888

Author's note: Excerpts of poems written by J.K. Stephen are indicated by an asterisk (*). All other material attributed to him, including the diary, is fictional.

Bloodline

Prologue

The book was old. Very old. And very secret. So secret, in fact, no one but himself knew of its existence. Others had seen it, but they were either dead now, or had forgotten, attaching no importance to it when it was first unearthed from an old chest in the attic of his family's home. He alone knew the precious secrets it contained, written in fading ink upon yellowed pages. Secrets of love and betrayal and death. Secrets that reached past his mind and flowed into his soul, filling him with a painful joy and an apprehension of his yet unfulfilled destiny.

One day, he would effect that destiny. One day, he would consummate that painful joy. One day . . .

One

Victoria Thomas stared into the eyes of the killer and thought she might be sick. She gripped the railing that stood between them and kept her eyes locked on his, determined not to blink, refusing to let him see her fear.

Men like this lived to see the fear in the eyes of their victims. It empowered them to paralyze their prey with terror. It made them potent again, and filled them with desire.

For them, instilling fear was foreplay to the bloodlust.

Victoria straightened, mustering control, although a sheen of cold sweat slickened her skin, and she had to fight to keep her breathing even. His eyes filled with hatred when she did not succumb to the terror. Hatred, and rage. Clearly, he wanted to kill her, as he had the others. Would kill her, given the chance.

But she would not become his victim.

And neither, she vowed, would anyone else.

She summoned a strong voice and turned her attention to the judge who had requested her testimony in this, the penalty phase of the killer's trial.

"Your honor, William Coleman killed five young women in cold blood. He planned their deaths, he stalked them, and he took pleasure in watching them die slowly and painfully." She shuddered involuntarily. Coleman was possibly the cruelest killer she had ever encountered. He had cut the tongues from his victims so they could not cry out, then slowly and methodically dismembered them while they were alive. If she never caught another killer, she would be satisfied that at least she had taken this man out. And her testimony now was critical to keeping him out. He mustn't ever be allowed in society again. If she had her way, he would die. She forced herself to continue, trying to appear calm, keeping her testimony professional and clinical.

"William Coleman must never walk the streets again. He is not insane, for he knew full well what he was doing at the time, and that it was wrong. But he is psychopathic, and in my opinion, he can never be rehabilitated."

"Could you explain further, Ms. Thomas?" the judge asked.

Victoria knew this particular judge was a proponent of capital punishment, and that he was asking her to give the jury a strong reason to return the death penalty. She was with the judge. She must make them understand that the death penalty was the only way to guarantee he would never kill again. "Yes, Your Honor." She turned to face the jury. "A killer like William Coleman is driven by a fantasy that can never be fulfilled. With each murder, he is satisfied for a while, but the fulfillment does not last, and he is driven to kill again. His need to kill is so deeply embedded in his psyche that it becomes the driving force of his life. He can't *not* kill. If he were ever paroled, he would kill again and again until he was caught."

Victoria saw the horror on the faces of the jury and believed she was succeeding in convincing them. Thank God. Sending men like Coleman to death row was the one reward that made her job bearable. These bastards deserved to die. Unfortunately, not all of her cases ended so satisfactorily. Some killers not only escaped capital punishment but eventually managed to be paroled. She had put a few such killers behind bars and had been incensed to learn of their release. Outraged that the system would return them to society where they would likely kill again. And more than a little worried that they might seek revenge against her.

She tried not to think about that. It was part of the job, came with the territory. She couldn't let fear stand in her way.

The judge's voice broke into her thoughts. "Could you please be more specific, Ms. Thomas?" he prodded.

Victoria drew in a deep breath and exhaled heavily. She appreciated that the judge was pushing her to convince the jurors they had no choice but to demand William Coleman's death, but she was emotionally exhausted from this case, and the judge's question pushed her to the edge of her endurance.

"Since he bragged about what he had done and told me he would kill more women when he got out of jail," she said, pausing to let her words sink in, "I could draw no other conclusion after delving into Mr. Coleman's psychological background. He was raised by his older sister, who he claims badly mistreated him and who he came to hate, although after his divorce, he moved back in with her. He told me he did that because he had decided to kill her, saying he wanted to 'tear her limb from limb.' But the sister died of natural causes soon after, leaving him frustrated in his intent and unable to fulfill his fantasy of killing her.

"His hatred of her grew, intensified by his perception that somehow she had died on purpose to thwart him. He had to punish her. But she wasn't available, so he abducted young women who looked much like his sister had when he was a teenager and under her domination. He took a job as the high school custodian, chose his victims carefully from among the student population he saw every day, and murdered them instead. Because he never killed the true object of his hatred, he never succeeded in fulfilling his fantasy. He never will. But he will keep trying. As you heard in earlier testimony, after we caught him, we found a list of future prospects. There were over twenty names on it. If he is not permanently removed from society, it is probable that he'll return to the area and pick up where he left off, and the lives of those women who were on his list would be seriously at risk."

It took the jury only a short while to decide the fate of the murderer, and when the foreman read their vote for the death penalty, a thunder of applause and cheers resounded through the tense courtroom. The judge banged his gavel, shouting for order, only adding to the pandemonium. But the relief in the room was palpable. With this man behind bars, these people could feel safe once again in their quiet community.

How could anyone ever feel safe? she wondered as she left the courtroom. This man was just one among many, a growing brotherhood of sick, ruthless killers who preyed primarily on women. Some were not just killers. Some, like William Coleman, were butchers, who took pleasure in defiling female flesh with a knife. What kind of society are we, she thought, to have created such monsters?

And what would it take to stop them?

Stopping them was her job, and Victoria worked hard at it. She knew she had the reputation of being among the best in the business. In addition to her extensive knowledge of the workings of the criminal mind and her years of experience in homicide investigation, Victoria relied on her keen intuition as well to help in her quest. It had been her intuition that had led to the arrest of William Coleman.

While other profilers were convinced the killer was a much younger man—most serial killers are in their twenties—she'd had a gut feeling this murderer was much older. Because the victims had all been students at the same high school, the investigation had centered around the male students and younger faculty members. On a hunch, Victoria had insisted that the police put a tail on older faculty members . . . and the custodian.

They were watching him when he stopped and offered a ride to the girl who could have become victim number six. A dark-haired girl who looked very much like the other victims. The police had followed his car to the house once inhabited by his sister and rescued the girl, who was struggling against him as he led her from the garage to the house. Her hunch had saved the girl's life. And caught the killer.

Victoria hurried out of the courtroom, eager to put the case behind her. She stepped out of the gloomy building into the bright October sun, feeling as if an enormous burden had been lifted from her shoulders. She was exhausted from this lengthy case and in need of some time off. But she sighed and ran her hand through her hair, thinking of all the other cases that were pending and in need of her attention. She was tired, but she could never rest until she had given all she had toward stopping these killers. For the victims. For their families.

Most of all, for her sister, Meghan, who had not deserved to die at the hands of such a killer, but had nonetheless. A killer who had never been found. Looking into the eyes of William Coleman during this trial and hearing the detailed testimony of his butchery had brought back all the dark, sickening memories of Meghan's murder. Trials such as this always brought back the horror of her sister's death and renewed the anguish and grief she had struggled to bury over the past seven years. Her throat tightened, and she blinked away unbidden tears. Taking a deep breath, she looked out into the sunshine and forced those memories back into the nether reaches of her mind, where they hid but never quite went away.

Victoria spotted the vehicle that awaited her and dodged shouting reporters and aggressive photographers as she dashed toward it. A man opened the door for her, and she slid into the backseat and the anonymity that she craved.

"You look like hell." Her boss and mentor, Mike Mosier, handed her a soft drink as the driver swerved away from the curb and maneuvered through the heavy traffic.

"Thanks a lot." She sipped the cold sweetness through a straw and felt the sting of the carbonation against her dry throat.

"Bad, huh?"

Victoria leaned her head back against the seat and closed

her eyes. "The pits," she murmured, thinking it a gross understatement. "At least with the death sentence, he's not going anywhere anytime soon."

"You did a great job on this case, Victoria."

"Thanks," was her only reply. She appreciated Mike's compliment, but she wasn't in the mood for small talk. She was just glad the whole thing was behind her. She hated having to testify. It always made her feel naked and vulnerable. She was a very private person, and she did not like the publicity that inevitably accompanied her appearance at these sensational trials. She endured it only because she believed that in the long run, her work made a difference.

Intellectually, she knew she could never rid the world of the monsters, but emotionally, she felt she had to try. For every such sicko she helped put behind bars, women's lives would be saved, women who would never even know they might have become his victims. She couldn't bring Meghan back, but she had vowed she would do everything in her power to prevent the senseless deaths of others. Exhaustion was a small price to pay.

"You need a vacation." Mosier's voice broke into her thoughts.

"What are you, a mind reader?"

"It doesn't take a psychic to know you're pushing it too hard, Victoria."

Victoria sighed. Yes, she'd been pushing it hard. And yes, she needed a vacation. But she wasn't taking one. "Can it, Mosier. You know that's not an option. There's just too much—"

"You're no good to us if your brain's fried and you can't keep your eyes open."

Her brain did feel as if it were fried, scrambled as well. Her eyes burned behind closed lids. Her muscles were stiff with tension, and a headache threatened at her temples. The idea of a vacation beckoned her seductively even as she discounted the possibility. "Mike, I can't. You know all that I have on my plate right now."

"You've had too much on your plate for months. You're

going to get sick if you don't slow down. Take a couple of weeks to decompress from this thing."

"A couple of weeks!" Victoria couldn't imagine being away that long. Her desk would be piled high. But Mike was adamant.

"The world isn't going to stop if you take some time off, Victoria. Nothing is so pressing at the moment that it can't wait, or that the rest of us can't cover it. Take a vacation."

"But . . ."

The car turned onto I-95 and headed toward the FBI Academy at Quantico that was home to the National Center for the Analysis of Violent Crime, NCAVC, the division for which they both worked. With exaggerated authority, her boss flipped out his badge. "That's an order."

Later that evening, Victoria sipped a chilled fumé blanc and checked her watch, annoyed. She could count on Trey for a lot of things. Unfortunately, being late was one of them.

But tonight it didn't really matter, she reminded herself, trying to relax. She was in no hurry, and this was one of her favorite restaurants. There was something comforting in the hum of dinner conversations as they rose and fell around the notes of the music emanating from a baby grand at the back of the room. The soothing ambience created by the rose-colored tablecloths and soft candlelight combined with the wine to at last take the edge off the day.

Beneath the table, Victoria slipped one shoe off and wiggled her toes. She was in the process of repeating the maneuver with the other tired foot when she looked up and saw Trey's handsome face break into a wide smile as he spotted her from the hostess stand. She waved, and he headed in her direction.

"It's about time," she chided when he reached the table. She took his hand and raised her cheek to his brotherly kiss. He wasn't really her brother, but she thought of him as one. She and Meghan and Trey had grown up together, their families being close friends, and he'd always been her "little brother."

"Bad traffic," he replied, handing her a single, long-stemmed, peach-colored rose. "Forgive me?"

"How come you have to be so damned charming?"

He took the seat across from her and signaled the waiter for a drink. "The charm is inbred, don't-you-know."

She laughed with him, but sardonically, remembering the strict rules of their upbringing, the discipline they had endured as children growing up in high society families. Because of who they were, because of their bloodlines and heritage, more would always be expected of them than the average person, Victoria's mother had reminded her two daughters, ad nauseum.

Trey had fared no better. The only child of Victoria's father's law partner, Trey was James Winston Delaney III. It was Meghan who had given him the nickname Trey, meaning "the third." She'd told him he didn't seem much like a James, certainly not a Winston, which was his mother's family name. Trey had not taken offense. On the contrary, he was pleased. He readily embraced anything that would annoy his parents, James II and Marilyn, who meant well but who demanded much of Trey without giving much in return.

The waiter served his double scotch on the rocks. "Cheers," he said, raising his glass. "To what do I owe this unexpected pleasure?"

In the past few years Trey had become the darling of D.C. society, at least among the women, and she was glad his social schedule wasn't so full that he couldn't make it for dinner on such short notice. "My boss."

"Since when does the agency pick up a dinner tab?"

"The tab's mine," she told him. "My boss wants me to take a vacation."

He looked at her, perplexed. "So what does that have to do with me?" He paused, then added with an affected Ricky Ricardo accent, " 'Splain me, Lucy."

Victoria laughed. One of Trey's most endearing qualities

was his quick wit and keen sense of humor, although there had been times when she hadn't appreciated his adolescent practical jokes. His humor could be black at times, too. And biting.

But in the dark weeks following Meghan's murder, his attempts at levity were all that had held her together at times. He had suffered terribly from the tragedy, too, but he had helped her get through with his ready smile and an occasional attempt at a joke. Victoria guessed it helped him deal with it, as well, although she knew he had never really gotten over it. He and Meghan had been very close friends. Trey had been away at law school on the night of the murder, and she knew he blamed himself for not having been there for Meghan.

"Mosier thinks I've been working too hard," she offered in explanation, "and suggested I take a break. I guess he's right. So I've decided to go to a symposium in London that's being sponsored by a chapter of that Sherlock Holmes group I belong to."

"Ah, yes, the Sherlockians." Trey sipped his drink and eyed her quizzically. "You choose the damnedest forms of recreation, Tori."

Victoria bristled. She hated to be called Tori, her childhood nickname. Trey was the only one who got away with it, mainly because with him, her protests fell on deaf ears.

"For your information," she said curtly, "Sherlock Holmes was the world's first true profiler."

Trey laughed. "Sherlock Holmes is a piece of fiction. But whatever . . . I still want to know what your vacation has to do with me. You want my permission or something? Go, by all means."

"I didn't invite you here to get your permission," she snapped, thinking maybe she shouldn't have invited him at all. But she needed him. "I want to know if you'd . . . like to come along."

Trey looked startled, then his eyes narrowed. "Why?"

Victoria didn't want him to get the wrong impression. She was not romantically interested in him. Never had been. He was five years her junior, Meghan's age, and she felt nothing except sisterly toward him. "I'm not asking you to go as a date," she said sharply. "I just don't like going to these things alone. Sometimes guys, well, they get too friendly, if you know what I mean, and when it's a professional gathering, or even pseudoprofessional, like this one is, it's hard to put them off without offending them. If I'm with someone, it's not an issue." Funny she should be asking him for protection of sorts. She'd always been the protective one in their relationship. The big sis running interference for both him and Meghan.

"A bodyguard?" He looked down at his chest. Trey was well built, but neither large nor muscular. "I don't think I'm quite the type."

"No, silly. Not a bodyguard. An . . . an escort. I've seen the society columns. You seem to be a one-man escort service for half the good-looking single women in D.C. Won't you do it for an old friend?"

The following Thursday afternoon, Victoria rushed down the stairs when she heard the cab driver honk in the parking lot in front of her apartment. She couldn't believe it, but she really, really was going to take a short vacation. And she was excited about it.

Since Mosier had insisted she take some leave, she had spent an inordinate number of hours on the Internet chatting with other Sherlockians who would be attending, and she anticipated an intriguing weekend at the conference. The main speaker was supposedly Britain's foremost expert on the topic that had attracted her to attend. Mike was right. She needed this break, and she appreciated his tenacity in insisting on it. She made a mental note to bring him a tacky souvenir from London.

As the taxi pulled up to the departure area at Dulles, she saw Trey waiting for her and felt a small surge of relief. She hadn't known for sure he would show up. She could have, would have, gone alone, but she didn't want to. He'd held out to the very end, not committing, claiming that he couldn't see spending a weekend with funny old men wearing deerstalker hats and smoking long curved pipes. She'd pointed out that there were likely to be women there, too. "Perhaps you'll meet some smashing duchess or baroness," she'd said, hoping to tempt him, but to no seeming avail.

"Thanks for coming," she said, giving him a warm hug.

"You knew I would." He took her bag and paid the driver. "I just like to yank your chain once in a while, for old times' sake."

On the plane, they settled in for the overnight journey. Trey ordered a double single-malt whisky and contented himself with thumbing through the airline magazine until the movie came on. Victoria picked up a book she'd started reading earlier. She laid it in her lap when the evening meal was served, and Trey caught a glimpse of the title. *"The Complete History of Jack the Ripper?"* He looked up at her with an uneasy expression. "I thought you were supposed to leave all that crap behind." He took a dinner tray from the flight attendant and passed it over to her. "Aren't you supposed to be on vacation?"

"Oh, didn't I tell you?" She paused, ripping open a package of crackers. She had withheld this particular bit of information from him on purpose. He did not share her enthusiasm for crime detection, and since Meghan's death, he had been put off by anything having to do with violent crime. Perhaps it was unfair of her to have asked him to be her escort, she realized suddenly. But it was too late. She gave him a cheery smile. "Saturday's presentation is called 'The Unsolved Case of Jack the Ripper—Where Was Sherlock When We Needed Him?' "

The gathering on Saturday morning was everything Jonathan Blake had feared it would be. The large meeting room in the hotel was packed with men and women of all ages, some of the men wearing deerstalkers and sporting Holmesian-style pipes, all eyes bright at the prospect of spending a weekend dabbling in crime.

Jonathan hated public speaking because he didn't consider himself very good at it, and he regretted he had allowed himself to be talked into this. But as the Commissioner at New Scotland Yard had pointed out to him, it was a great opportunity to accrue some good public relations for the Metropolitan Police. And when the commissioner wanted good PR, no one argued.

Still, he could have begged off. He was in the middle of several investigations, and he would have much rather been working on those cases than hand-holding a bunch of dilettantes. However, Jonathan knew he was the most qualified person in the Criminal Investigative Division to present the program that had been requested of the Yard by a group that called themselves "Sherlockians." They wanted an expert to discuss the world's greatest unsolved mystery, the identity of Jack the Ripper, and Jonathan was known as one of England's foremost "Ripperologists."

Sometimes when he considered his passion for this ancient and likely unsolvable case, he thought he must be off his head. But he was in good company, for the world was filled with armchair detectives, scholars, and nutcases, all of whom were set on naming the infamous killer, or promoting their pet theories as to his identity if the truth could not be had.

Looking out across the sea of eager faces in the rows of chairs that faced the head table where he sat, he decided he was no better than they were. Their passion was for a fictional sleuth, his for a long-dead murderer.

Funny what people did to entertain themselves.

A woman with straight blond hair and owlish glasses hurried toward him, an eager smile on her face. "Thank you so much for coming, Mr. Blake," she said breathlessly as she reached the table and dropped a pile of papers at the place next to him. "I'm Janeece Fairchild, the chairwoman of this little event." She thrust her hand at him. "We've spoken on the telephone."

He shook her hand and summoned a better humor. "It's my pleasure to be here." It was only a small lie, after all.

"Oh, it's going to be a fabulous weekend, I just know

it. We have so many distinguished guests. I just learned that Victoria Thomas is here. She's an expert profiler with the FBI, you know."

"I'm afraid I haven't—"

But she didn't hear him as she continued to inventory the roster of impressive names, none of whom Jonathan had heard of. ". . . and even Lord and Lady Chastain. He's a member of Parliament, you know." She broke off suddenly and looked at her watch. "Oh, dear, I must stop this rambling. Are you ready? It's time."

Jonathan nodded. He would never be ready, but oh, well. He was stuck with the assignment. Might as well get it over with.

"Let's do it."

Two

Victoria sat two rows from the front and watched as the good-looking Englishman rose and came to the podium after a lengthy and impressive introduction by the event coordinator. He toyed with his tie, as if he were uncomfortable, then cleared his throat.

"Ladies and gentlemen," he began, lowering his head slightly toward the microphone. "I bring you greetings from New Scotland Yard and the commissioner of the Metropolitan Police Service. This illustrious institution has a long and proud record of service to the queen and the people of Britain, and we are committed as much to the prevention of crime as to its resolution."

Victoria stifled a yawn, hoping his presentation would be more exciting than his introduction. Otherwise, with her jet lag, she might sleep through it. Then she saw him grin almost mischievously.

"Actually, the Yard asked me to make this presentation today not knowing that I plan to tell the story of one of its most dismal failures."

A titter of laughter ruffled through the audience. The grin broadened and was punctuated by a dimple in his left cheek. It was the sexiest grin Victoria had ever seen, a grin she was certain could charm the socks off the queen herself. To her consternation, her stomach did an unexpected somersault.

Inspector Jonathan Blake oozed boyish charm as he continued. "My only request is that no one send a recording of this program to the commissioner." He paused again, then added, "I do value my job."

The laughter was more solid this time, and Victoria could see that Jonathan Blake and his little grin had captivated the rest of his audience, as well. She settled back in her chair and crossed her arms. Well, charm had its limits. She'd come a long way to hear England's foremost expert on the Ripper murders. She was ready for him to get on with it.

"The world may never know the identity of the man whose pseudonym has become synonymous with murder of the foulest kind," he said, the grin vanishing. "Jack the Ripper. But why is he so famous? His killing spree was short and confined. He is credited with murdering only four, possibly five, women within a period of less than ten weeks, although a few other still unsolved murders are sometimes attributed to him."

Only four or five women. Victoria shuddered. How could he say that so lightly?

Inspector Blake went on. "Now, the murder of five women is deplorable, but compared to some of the crimes committed in today's society, his do not seem to warrant the notoriety that has been attached to his deeds. Certainly the crimes of other killers, such as Son of Sam and Jeffrey Dahmer, were far greater in scope and equally as dreadful, if not more so, and yet when we think of serial killers, the first name that comes to mind is Jack the Ripper. Why so?

"The reason is threefold, in my opinion," he continued. "First is the very nature of the crime itself. Never before in recorded history had anyone killed in such a cold-blooded manner, completely without motive. The women were all prostitutes, destitute and alcoholic. They were the very dregs of society. They owned nothing, so there was nothing to steal. They had no power or connections, so we can rule out blackmail and revenge. There appears to be no rational reason for the brutal slayings."

Madmen need no reason, Victoria thought grimly, put off by his calling those poor women the dregs of society. Had he no compassion?

"The second reason for the notoriety of Jack the Ripper is the media," he went on. "I said a moment ago that never before in recorded history had such horrendous crimes taken place. We don't know for a fact that such murders had never been committed. The key word here is 're-corded.' Before this time, very few serial killings were written into the history books. But in 1888, the year of the murders, yellow journalism was at its zenith. Everything was sensationalized to the hilt in order to sell newspapers." He paused and looked out across the audience, then grinned and said, "Some things never change."

Unsettled all over again by that grin, Victoria squirmed in her seat while those around her laughed at his poke at the media. He was right in many respects, of course, but in the States at least, the media had become one of law enforcement's most powerful allies in helping to locate and identify criminals, and a part of her found his disparaging remark unnecessary.

Blake proceeded. "The newspaper stories of the murders brought the horror to readers in gory detail the likes of which had never been known. That alone might have been sufficient to create the legend that surrounds these killings. But the murderer, seeking notoriety, used the newspapers to insure his immortality when he sent the first of his famous correspondence to the Central News Agency. It was dated September 25, 1888, and it was signed, 'Yours truly, Jack the Ripper.' Catchy name. Descriptive. And above all, memorable. Now the papers not only had bloody murder to report, they had an appealing name to use in connection with those murders. Jack the Ripper."

Jonathan Blake gave a short, almost derisive laugh. "The murderer would have done well in the advertising business, thinking up memorable names and slogans, for this one stuck and has been notorious for over a hundred years."

Victoria grimaced, thinking Blake's aside out of place

in a serious presentation. Then she reminded herself that this was not a professional seminar. She had come here to learn more about what she considered to be the most fascinating case of all time, but it was also supposed to be a fun getaway weekend, an intellectual lark filled with debate and speculation in an atmosphere such as one might expect at a murder mystery weekend party. She tried not to be so critical of the speaker. He wasn't doing such a bad job. She needed to quit behaving like such a type A.

Victoria glanced at Trey, who sat to her left, and saw from his body language—arms and legs crossed, eyes glazed—that he didn't give a damn about Blake's speech one way or the other. She sighed quietly. It was no small measure of their friendship that Trey had sacrificed his weekend to come here and endure all this. She owed him, big-time.

Before refocusing on the speaker, she gazed around the room, studying the other attendees and wondering with whom she had chatted on the Net. The room was filled with men and women of all ages. She guessed she'd likely communicated electronically with the younger set, but one never knew.

Behind her and slightly to her left, her gaze met that of a young man who stared at her openly and unsmiling. He was not bad-looking, with wavy chestnut hair and the broad torso of a body builder, but there was something about him that gave her the creeps. Something about his eyes . . .

Don't be silly, she scolded herself. There was no reason for her to feel that way. But she was unnerved, because her intuition warned her to keep her distance from him, and her intuition was rarely wrong. Uneasy, she returned her attention to the speaker.

"The third reason for the killer's continuing celebrity, I believe, is—" The inspector was interrupted mid-sentence by a portly man with a ruddy face, wearing a worn houndstooth jacket, who stood up and harrumphed at the speaker.

"With all due respect, Mr. Blake, those Ripper letters

were a fraud. I have it on the best authority. You see, sir,
Jack the Ripper is alive and well and living in Kent."

Jonathan had expected eccentricity from the people gathered here. Only eccentrics attended such functions. But the
man who challenged him was clearly over the edge, and he
wasn't sure what to do about it.

This was the part he disliked most about public speaking. Interruptions like these always threw him off. He had
been doing fine until now, even elicited a few laughs, and
had begun to relax. Now he felt his shoulder muscles
tighten again. Taking a deep breath, he recalled what the
PR trainer had taught them at the Yard about handling
hecklers.

"I appreciate your information, sir," he replied with
forced equanimity. "I'd be interested in speaking with you
afterward. Perhaps you have information that might be
valuable to the Yard." He hoped he sounded earnest. He
was supposed to be showing respect for the man, despite
his absurd folly. But he also hoped fervently the old boy
wouldn't seek him out after the speech.

The audience had laughed at the man's ridiculous claim,
then rustled with embarrassment. Now Jonathan heard what
sounded like a collective sigh of relief, and the heckler,
mollified, resumed his seat with a nod.

Jonathan started to return to his notes when his eye
caught the gaze of an attractive woman sitting across the
aisle from the heckler. She seemed amused at his discom-
fort. Wishing she'd trade places with him, he struggled to
pick up the thread of his presentation

"As I was saying, the third reason Jack the Ripper remains so notorious is simply that he was never caught.
Some say he was a Polish Jew from Whitechapel named
Kosminski who had a reputation for hating women. Others
suspected Michael Ostrog, a Russian doctor and a convict
who later was put in an insane asylum as a homicidal maniac. A third favorite was Montague John Druitt, a young
doctor from a good family whose body was found in the

Thames in December after the murders had ceased.

"Our own favorite mystery author, Sir Arthur Conan Doyle, submitted that Jack the Ripper was really Jill the Ripper and put forth the theory that the killings were the work of a mad midwife. And of course, there is the pet theory that the Ripper was Prince Albert Victor Edward, the duke of Clarence, grandson to Queen Victoria and the future king of England. In the 1980s, a diary surfaced, supposedly written by the Ripper, and the name of James Maybrick, a merchant from Liverpool, was bandied about for a while as the murderer, but the diary is now believed to be a hoax.

"The fact is that, in spite of all investigation and speculation, the identity of Jack the Ripper remains a mystery."

An hour and a half later, after wading through the details of the murders and the difficulties faced by the police at the time, Jonathan stepped down for a lunch break. From the enthusiastic applause, he gathered he'd at least managed to hold his audience. His relief at being out of the spotlight was short-lived, however, as he was immediately surrounded by members of the audience, all asking eager and surprisingly intelligent questions.

With the exception of the heckler, it would seem he had misjudged these people, Jonathan thought. He'd expected eccentric dilettantes. Instead, he found himself facing educated, erudite enthusiasts, some of whom knew a great deal about sleuthing. Suddenly, he hoped he hadn't offended any of them with his rather elementary presentation, and he made a mental note to elevate the tone of his speech after lunch.

He saw Janeece making her way through the crowd, and he gave her a broad smile. Perhaps she would disentangle him from the crush. But she had someone in tow.

"Inspector Blake," she said in her breathy manner, "I want you to meet someone." She thrust a small, quite attractive although obviously vexed woman at him. The same woman whose eye he had caught earlier. "This is Victoria Thomas, the FBI profiler I mentioned. Ms. Thomas, may I introduce Detective Inspector Jonathan Blake?"

Victoria Thomas looked nothing like his notion of an FBI agent, certainly not like someone in the seriously gruesome business of criminal profiling. She was petite and feminine, with a delicate bone structure that sculpted her face into lines of classic beauty. A pale silk blouse softened the lines of the expensive-looking claret-colored suit she wore. Her dark brown hair was arranged in a sleek but attractive twist on top of her head, as if in an effort to lend height to her slight but most appealing figure.

Jonathan cleared his throat. The weekend had suddenly become more interesting.

Then he looked into her eyes. They were the color of dark honey, with flecks of emerald embedded in the amber, and they fairly shimmered with irritation. He guessed she didn't like being herded along by Janeece Fairchild. For that, he couldn't blame her. He offered his hand. "Ms. Thomas. Welcome to London." The cool slimness of her hand in his had a surprisingly unsettling effect on him.

"Thank you, Mr. Blake," she said, withdrawing her hand after a brief but firm handshake. "It was an . . . interesting presentation."

It sounded on the surface like a polite compliment, but Jonathan wasn't sure. He was always suspicious when someone used the word "interesting" as a descriptive adjective. Something could be interesting without being particularly good.

"I appreciate that," he said, choosing to believe she had meant it in a positive way. "It means a great deal coming from someone with your knowledge and background."

She gazed up at him, a hint of sardonic humor in her eyes. "I wouldn't think you'd put much stock in what a profiler thought. I take it from your presentation this morning that you consider scientific method the only valid approach to criminal investigation."

Her words were softened by a smile, but he heard the challenge behind them. Jonathan was caught off guard by her thinly veiled hostility, and it surprised him. He hadn't meant to offend her or anyone else. He was only presenting things the way he saw them. He didn't want to enter into a debate on investigative styles at the moment, but he felt compelled to defend his beliefs.

"Yes, scientific method is the most infallible approach to solving a crime. Facts don't lie, Ms. Thomas. They are not vulnerable to the mistakes that happen when human emotion gets in the way."

"Facts are sometimes hard to come by without the use of human emotion. In my work, for example, intuition is invaluable, Mr. Blake. Sometimes facts are only uncovered by following your instincts. Even Sherlock Holmes knew that."

Jonathan became aware suddenly that the group that surrounded them had grown quiet, and tension was thick in the air. He was actually grateful when Janeece broke in.

"Well, I'm sure you must be famished," she said to Jonathan. "Lunch is ready, and I've made arrangements for Ms. Thomas and Mr. Delaney to join us. You can continue your conversation there. Follow me."

Only then did Jonathan see the man standing just behind Victoria Thomas. Although taller than she, her date/lover/husband/who-knows-what was not a large man, yet he had the look of hidden strength about him. With dark hair and eyes against a very fair skin, he was both striking and handsome. Well, her date/lover/husband or whatever could have her. Victoria Thomas was wound too tight for him. The incident reminded Jonathan of why he remained a confirmed bachelor.

He had no wish to continue his conversation with the American woman, but he turned and followed the indomitable Janeece to his fate. Just get through the day, he told himself, and try not to piss anyone off.

Three

King's College, Cambridge
Ninth May 1883

From this day forward, my life will never be the same. Heretofore I have cowered in the shadow of that great Devil I must call father and have forced myself to pretend affection toward the Whore who is my mother. Together, they have made my life a living hell. No matter what I have achieved here or at Eton, it has never been enough. No matter how hard I have tried to please them, they have made it clear they believe I am not good enough to claim the bloodline of the almighty Stephen family.

But with this remarkable turn of events, they cannot help but acknowledge my merit at last, for today I have been retained to direct the studies of Prince Albert Victor Edward, the future king of England. I, J. K. Stephen, will serve as tutor and mentor to His Royal Highness, and despite the difficulties of which I have been forewarned, I will not fail. This new trust vindicates me and proves me worthy of my heritage. It is I, not the Devil and not the Whore, who will move freely amongst the royals. It is I who will hold power unlike any that despicable pair has ever known. Bugger the Devil and his undisguised scorn. Bugger them both. Henceforth, my life belongs to the Prince.

In spite of her annoying attraction to Jonathan Blake's boyish good looks and easygoing style, Victoria had grown
increasingly testy during the course of the morning, for it
became clear that he was nothing but another by-the-books
cop like the one who had botched the investigation of her
sister's murder. She deplored his repeated insistence that
strict scientific method was the only valid approach to
crime detection. She supposed one could call psychology a
science, but Blake wouldn't agree. According to what she'd
heard him say today, if evidence couldn't be touched,
tested, and mechanically analyzed, it did not belong in an
investigation.

So she was not happy when after the program, Janeece
sought her out and insisted she meet Blake, and now she
was being forced into his company for lunch. His speech
and condescending attitude toward any nonphysical approach to crime detection—her very stock-in-trade—had
put her in a bad mood, and she wasn't particularly interested in making further conversation with him. But being
a good Southern girl, she didn't want to appear rude, so
she took Trey's arm, and they made their way to where the
luncheon had been set up. She hoped Janeece would not
seat her next to the inspector.

"I just know you two will have a lot to talk about,"
Janeece said, beaming and indicating they were indeed to
sit next to each other. "And Mr. Delaney, it would be my
honor if you would take the seat next to me."

They were at a large round table at the head of the room,
but none of the rest of the seats seemed to be reserved.
Victoria was startled and not totally thrilled when the gentleman who had made the absurd statement about Jack the
Ripper being alive and well and living in Kent asked if he
could take the seat next to her.

"Name's FitzSimmons," he said cordially, extending his
hand. "Reginald Smythe FitzSimmons. Of Kent," he added
with a twinkle in his eye.

His manner put her at ease, and Victoria liked him immediately. She suspected his interruption of Jonathan

Blake's speech had been nothing more than a playful prank on the part of the old man, maybe to bring the cavalier detective down just a notch. "Please, sit down," she said.

Others joined them, one of whom was obviously a friend of Jonathan Blake's. "Good to see you, old boy," the man said, extending his hand to the inspector. "Read any good books lately?"

"Hello, Roger," Jonathan replied, standing to shake his hand. "I didn't know you were part of this gang of Sherlock Holmes fanatics." She saw him grimace suddenly and glance her way with an apologetic grin. "Sorry. I didn't mean to offend. Now, or earlier," he added pointedly.

Victoria found it difficult to hold on to her pique, and she wished suddenly she hadn't been so petulant toward him. The man was entitled to his beliefs, as narrow-minded as they were. And he was, after all, the expert she had come to hear. Why was she being so uptight?

"No offense taken," she replied, relaxing and giving him a smile. "I *am* a fanatic." Damn, she wished he wasn't so good-looking.

He introduced his friend as Roger Hammersmith, a London dealer in antiquarian books and letters. To her surprise, it appeared that Jonathan Blake was one of his best customers. She would not have pegged him for an intellectual type.

Victoria was dismayed when the young man she'd seen staring at her earlier took a seat directly across the table from her. Maybe it was his build that perturbed her. She'd never been comfortable around overly muscular men. She wished he'd chosen to sit at another table. But it seemed he had sought her out intentionally.

"Aren't you Victoria Thomas, the FBI profiler?" His eyes were like blue ice, his accent American.

Victoria shivered. "Yes," she replied, so put off by him that she was tempted to move to another table. She didn't know how she could feel this way about a total stranger, but she had long since quit trying to ignore her gut instincts. And they were screaming at her to get away from this man. "How did you know my name?"

He leaned beefy arms on the table and stared at her unblinking. "My name is Billy Ray," he said slowly in a strong Southern accent. "I'm from Virginia. I saw your picture in the newspaper stories about the Coleman trial. Guess you're pretty proud of sending him up the river."

A chill ran down Victoria's spine at the almost taunting tone of his voice. "Coleman sent himself up the river by murdering those women, Mr. Ray. All I did was see that justice was done."

"You must be pretty good at getting a judge to believe you. I hear you've managed to put away quite a number of guys. When I read you were on Coleman's case, I knew he didn't stand a chance."

Victoria didn't like it that the man seemed to know so much about her. "How do you know who I've helped prosecute?"

"I follow all the big murder trials. It's . . . sort of a hobby." He leaned toward her and added with rather childish enthusiasm, "You're really famous, you know."

Damn.

Victoria clenched her hands together beneath the tablecloth. Just what she needed, a groupie. She was suddenly very thankful Trey had come along. She forced a small smile.

"Thank you, Mr. Ray. But I'm on vacation right now and trying to be invisible. Just one of the crowd." She tried to be polite, but her tone was cold, her words clipped. She might as well have told him to bug off. But if he was offended, he didn't show it. He just continued to stare at her, as if he were trying to memorize her face.

Suppressing another shudder, she chose to ignore him and turned her attention to the couple who were approaching the table. He was a tall, gaunt man of about sixty years, she shorter, younger, softer, and much rounder. Watching them, Victoria thought with wry amusement that they looked like a walking number 10. They were Alistair Huntley-Ames and his wife, Elizabeth, Lord and Lady Chastain. Distant relations of the Prince of Wales, the man explained, not haughtily, but not without pride, either. His wife gave him a fleeting, almost scornful look, but it vanished as she took her seat, and her face assumed a blandness that somehow saddened Victoria.

One chair remained vacant at the round table, between Jonathan and Lord Chastain, and at the last minute, a heavyset woman who appeared to be in her early forties dashed over to the table. "Oh, my, oh, my," she said, her breath coming in short gasps. "I can't believe it. Is . . . is this chair taken?" She looked hopefully and longingly at Jonathan Blake, and Victoria bit the side of her mouth to stifle a snicker. Glancing across the table, she caught Trey's amused grin.

Jonathan stood and helped the woman into the seat, and Victoria thought the poor thing might swoon. Obviously the detective's charm had worked on her. "I'm Adele Quigley," she said after catching her breath a moment. "I'm a librarian."

"Do I detect an American accent, my dear?" asked FitzSimmons genially, helping himself to two of the cold dinner rolls and butter.

"Pittsburgh," she replied, never taking her eyes off Jonathan. "Oh, I just can't believe my luck. That was practically the only seat left in the whole room, right next to our speaker." She emphasized the last word with a delighted little squeak. "You can't imagine how much I enjoyed your presentation this morning," she told him. "But I'm confused by something."

"And what would that be?" Jonathan asked.

Victoria poured a cup of the hot tea that had been steeping in a little metal pot. Maybe it was just his British manner, she told herself, but damned if Blake's reply to the woman hadn't sounded imperious. As if he were offended that she hadn't clearly understood his sterling presentation.

"You said you were going to tell us the story of Scotland Yard's most miserable failure," Adele told him.

Jonathan passed her the plate of rolls, and she took the largest. "Actually, I'm in the middle of that very story," he replied, awarding her a smile. "You'll hear the other half this afternoon. The Ripper case was far and away the worst debacle in the history of Scotland Yard, old or new. Everyone from the top down bungled things at every turn. The crime scenes were not secured, and so much evidence was likely overlooked or destroyed. Autopsies were not held in a timely manner, which meant decay had set in, possibly obscuring some important data." He must have seen Adele Quigley's face blanch, for he quickly apologized.

"Pardon me. I know we're about to have lunch, but the truth is, bodies don't last forever, and they provide primary evidence for forensic studies. I realize that investigative technique was primitive in that era and that they did not have the scientific tools available to them that we have today, but the main problem, as I see it, is that the police allowed emotion to get in the way of fact. They reacted to pressure and panic."

Victoria felt her hackles rise ever so slightly, but this time she held her tongue.

"Could you explain, Inspector Blake?" asked Lord Chastain.

"The Ripper murders raised a huge outcry. Everyone from the queen on down demanded that this maniac be captured immediately. In my opinion, the police allowed pressure from the media and the hysteria of the people to send them into an unnecessary panic in their search for the murderer. As a consequence, they reacted from emotion, not intellect, and let the Ripper slip through their fingers."

"Are you saying you would have acted differently given the circumstances?" Victoria couldn't help it. She had to call him on his self-righteous pronouncement.

"It is hard to say how one would act in such a situation," the detective admitted. "I know pressure from the outside can drive the police to make mistakes. But I believe if they had adhered to higher professional standards in all areas of the investigation, things might have turned out differently." Jonathan Blake looked around the table and added with his compelling grin, "Where was Sherlock when we needed him?"

Across the table, the disturbing young man named Billy Ray appeared to listen to Jonathan with interest. But Trey rolled his eyes, and Victoria gave him a slight nod. This man was so full of himself.

Reginald FitzSimmons cleared his throat. "If you are such a scientific investigator," he said, "with all due respect, you must admit that the letters supposedly sent to the Central News Agency were a hoax and a forgery. Macnaghten indicated in his memoirs that he even knew which bloke from the media sent them in order to stir up more sensation."

Victoria was impressed by the old man's knowledge of the case. Sir Melville Macnaghten came late into the investigation, but wrote one of the few firsthand opinions on it early in the century.

"A very good point," Jonathan replied, unruffled. "Scotland Yard and the press received a number of letters that were pure hoaxes. But the truth of the matter is that two of the letters, or rather the first letter signed 'Jack the Ripper' and the bloodstained postcard, have never been discounted as being authentic. And then there's the incident with the kidney."

"Kidney?" Adele Quigley's eyes widened.

Jonathan appeared to realize suddenly that he might have gone too far in suggesting unpleasant details at the luncheon table, for he looked around uneasily at the others. Victoria waited with hidden glee to see how he would sidestep the matter. To her amazement, he didn't.

"I'll be talking about these things in this afternoon's presentation, but briefly, a third communication was received shortly after the letter and postcard, but this time, the Ripper sent his correspondence to Mr. George Lusk, a civilian who was chairman of the Mile End Vigilance Committee."

"But what does that have to do with a kidney?" Adele asked, her eyes shining with morbid fascination.

"What was sent to Mr. Lusk, along with a note, was . . . one half of a human kidney."

"Come on," Trey growled. "We're about to have lunch."

"Indeed, Mr. Blake," sniffed Lady Chastain.

Victoria agreed, thinking the inspector had truly overstepped the bounds of good taste, but she said nothing. She found it rather amusing, in a macabre sort of way, and waited to watch Jonathan Blake bury himself.

"I apologize," Jonathan said, sounding sincere. "We should wait until later—"

"Oh, no," Adele pressed. "Was it . . . was the kidney from one of those poor murdered women?"

Jonathan paused, now looking seriously distressed. He nodded slightly. "Yes," he said in a low voice, "it was."

The wait staff arrived at that moment, bearing trays of steaming hot dishes. "Oh, at last," Roger Hammersmith exclaimed, obviously relieved to be able to change the subject. "What have we here?" he asked as the waiter placed one in front of him.

"House specialty, sir. Steak and kidney pie."

Four

Sandringham, Norfolk
Fourth June 1883

After meeting today with the Prince, I must admit to these pages my trepidation in the matter of his education. I must not fail, and yet, all that his former tutor Dalton relayed to me appears to be true. He seems to be distinctly dull-witted and absentminded, a tabula rasa, as he is called behind his back—an empty mind. It is Dalton's opinion that he simply cannot learn.

And yet there is something behind his dark eyes that reaches into my soul and makes my heart ache for him, for in him I sense a kindred spirit. According to Dalton, the Prince's father makes fun of him, calling him "Collars and Cuffs" in disparaging reference to the high collars and wide cuffs he wears in an effort to disguise a too-long neck and arms. Having been the brunt of my own father's derision, I can guess how this fragile boy must suffer. Perhaps it is this mutual anguish that will bind us together and allow me to succeed where Dalton and others have failed.

As he listened to the inspector's presentation later that afternoon, he followed the story closely, keeping an ear out for mistakes, for he'd read the true account a thousand times in the old book and knew by heart what had really taken place in Whitechapel over a hundred years ago. It had first been nothing more than a fascinating tale, until he began to feel the pull of his ancestor's emotion, instilling in him a sense that one day he must follow in his footsteps.

He straightened in his chair as a profound notion suddenly struck him, nearly taking his breath away. "One day" was now. It was no accident that he'd been summoned to this symposium. He was being called to his destiny at last.

It was an unsettling notion, although exciting. Nervous perspiration dampened his skin, and his heart thundered in his chest. His destiny. Was he ready? He had read and memorized the words of the master. He had practiced the skills, but only once. Did he have what it would take to step into the very substantial shoes of a legend?

His mind raced as he considered the challenge. Yes. It was unquestionable. His time had come. Tonight, here in London, in Whitechapel where it all began, he must take up the knife and assume the legacy of the man whose tormented life paralleled his own in so many ways. The work had brought consolation and relief to the master; perhaps it would bring an end to the anguish and despair that had been his hidden companions for as long as he could remember.

By the end of the afternoon, Jonathan was ready for a stiff drink, but he didn't dare seek one in the hotel lounge. As he passed by, he could see it was packed with symposium attendees. Although he had given them a complete and intensive crash course in Ripperology, and in spite of the dozens of questions he had fielded afterward, their appetite for information seemed insatiable. He knew he would be accosted if he showed up in the bar. He felt bad, too, about the incident at lunch, and he didn't relish the thought of running into those poor souls again. No one had touched their savory pie except him.

Entering an elevator, he considered skipping the dinner and costume ball that evening, for he was hungry only for the quiet sanctuary of his own small flat. PR was far more demanding than police work, he decided. He was beat. He'd made the presentation. He'd done his duty. The commissioner would never know if he cut out now.

Just as the elevator doors began to close, he saw a slender woman in a deep red suit walk into the lobby and search the various seating areas as if looking for someone. Unexpectedly, his heart took a tumble. Victoria Thomas. He was surprised at his reaction to her. He remembered her scarcely concealed hostility toward him before lunch, and he was certain he had mortified her with the kidney incident. She'd made it clear she didn't like him much. But all afternoon during his presentation, his gaze had returned repeatedly to her. He couldn't help it. He didn't understand his attraction to her, but it was there and it was real.

She turned and began to walk toward the elevator, and without thinking he stuck his hand between the doors, sending them open again.

"Going up?"

She hesitated a moment, then smiled tenuously and nodded. "Yes. Thank you for holding the elevator. Sixth floor, please."

An awkward silence stretched between them as they began to ascend. Jonathan looked up at the lighted panel indicating the floor numbers as they passed, trying to ignore the seduction of the light floral scent that surrounded her. He glanced in her direction to see that she too was staring at the panel. "Have you ever noticed how people in an elevator never speak? They just stand there and watch the numbers."

She smiled. "That's true. I didn't mean to be rude. I enjoyed your presentation this afternoon, Mr. Blake," she said. "Very detailed and engrossing. Are you sure you haven't deduced who committed the crimes?"

Jonathan took this as high praise coming from her. He hoped she was sincere. During the afternoon session, he had tried hard not to dwell on the importance of scientific method, in deference to his respect for her kind of work. Criminal profiling wasn't for him, but he knew many excellent professionals in the field who used it with good results.

"I have my pet suspects, just like everyone else." The doors opened, but suddenly Jonathan was not ready to let her go. "Who are yours?" he asked, following her out of the elevator.

"Well, professionally speaking, I'd have to go along with John Douglas's profile on him."

"Who's John Douglas?"

"One of the pioneers in profiling with the FBI," she replied. "He thinks it was someone from the area, an asocial loner who hated women, who was probably raised in a family with a domineering, perhaps alcoholic mother and a weak or absent father."

"Sounds like a stereotype to me."

She scowled. "Of course it is, in a way. Profilers look for patterns, similarities in behavioral traits among perpetrators of sexual crimes, and a great number of them fit this type."

Jonathan didn't want to offend her again, so he dropped further protest, although he thought the traits she'd listed were nothing particularly unusual or revolutionary.

"You said 'professionally.' Do you have another opinion . . . personally?"

She gave him an amused look. "I've always been partial to the theory that the prince did it. It's the most romantic hypothesis at any rate. But I doubt if you have room for such romanticism in your own investigation."

Jonathan didn't respond to her little barb, because what she said was true. "It's a tantalizing theory, that there was a royal cover-up, but there's not a shred of hard evidence to support it," he said. "In fact, there is no hard evidence to support any of the major speculations."

She cocked her head to one side. "Then I guess we'll never know for sure, will we?"

"Not unless something new turns up."

"Like what?" She looked skeptical.

Jonathan had never told a soul about his continuing

search for that evidence. His colleages already thought him daft for his obsessive interest in the Ripper murders. But suddenly he felt compelled to reveal his folly to this woman, a virtual stranger.

"I . . . ah . . . have a standing order at Roger Hammersmith's bookshop for anything that might be relevant to the subject. Roger buys entire libraries from England's old estates and noble families," he said, feeling a little foolish. But he went on. "I'm hoping that one day, the missing police files might surface. Or an authentic diary. Something that could be forensically tested that would lead to a definitive identification of the Ripper."

"Missing police files? You think they were deliberately removed? I thought you said today they were lost when Scotland Yard moved its premises to New Scotland Yard."

"I gave the official line."

Victoria looked intrigued. "What are you implying? Do you believe there was a cover-up?"

"I don't believe anything until I have proof."

"Of course not."

"But I do believe it is suspicious that those particular papers disappeared."

"Be careful. You're bordering on speculation." Her lips parted in a smile, and Jonathan was overcome by an urge to reach out and touch them. But he didn't.

"Speculation based on fact," he went on, trying to ignore the disturbing effect she was having on him. "There are other papers missing that might have some bearing on the case, as well."

"Oh?"

"The prince was in very ill health during the time of the murders," he said. "Syphilis. But although the physician to the royals, Dr. Gull, kept meticulous notes about other family members, there seems to be nothing in his records to indicate he treated Prince Albert Victor Edward for anything other than an early bout with typhoid fever."

"What does that have to do with the murders?"

"Victims of syphilis, in the final stages, go insane. I'm

not saying the prince was Jack the Ripper. All I'm saying is that his medical records are missing, as well as the police records. Don't you find that an odd coincidence?"

"You're speculating again. If there was some kind of a cover-up, don't you think those papers would have been destroyed?"

He found it odd to be talking so easily to her. Normally, he was shy around women he didn't know well. "I suppose you are right," he admitted. "But I just can't seem to give it up. I think one day, those papers, or something definitive, is going to show up in some long-forgotten file, or in a chest stored in someone's attic or a cache buried behind a barn."

"Now who's being romantic?"

"Well, yes," he said, suddenly abashed. "I suppose I am." He hadn't meant to act like an overeager schoolboy. He looked at his watch. "I'm sorry to have kept you so long." Liar. He wanted to detain her longer, but he feared he might make an ass of himself. "I must go now. I have some telephone calls to make on one of my cases."

"Not me. I'm under strict orders not to call in." Another smile lit her lips, tilting the edges upward in the most tantalizing manner. "My boss ordered me to take this vacation, so I guess I'd better follow his wishes."

"Sounds like a great sort of boss," Jonathan replied, watching those lips. "But attending a Jack the Ripper symposium seems an odd notion of a holiday for someone in your line of work."

She laughed. "My boss didn't know about that part. But in truth, this weekend's event is relaxation of a sort for me. The crime is in the past, not something I'm pressured to solve in order to stop a killer. With this, I can just enjoy playing with the possibilities, even if it is a crime that can never be solved."

"Maybe."

At that moment, the doors to the elevator opened again, and Trey Delaney emerged. "There you are," he said to Victoria, taking in the pair of them with his dark gaze. "I see I've fallen down on the job," he said, placing an arm possessively around her shoulder. "Sorry. I had an errand to run. Everything okay?"

For the first time, Jonathan saw Victoria's composure slip. She acted as if she were a little embarrassed to be caught alone with him, and he wondered uncomfortably if Trey Delaney was the jealous type.

"I'm fine," she said. "We were just talking about the possibility of finding new evidence to prove the identity of Jack the Ripper."

Delaney gave Jonathan an appraising look. "What kind of evidence?"

Jonathan had no interest in confiding in this man as he had just done with Victoria. What was their relationship? he wondered. He downplayed his answer. "It's unlikely that any evidence will ever surface, but it would be interesting if those missing police records I mentioned today turned up. Or an authentic diary."

Trey laughed. "Fat chance. I hardly think Jack the Ripper was the type to keep a diary." He turned to Victoria. "Come on. It's time to get ready for the big bash tonight."

Victoria hesitated, then looked up at Jonathan, her amber eyes wider than he'd seen them, her expression softer. "I'd be interested in discussing this further with you. You are coming to the costume ball, aren't you?"

Victoria was disturbed by the strength of her attraction to Jonathan Blake. Even this morning, when she'd been irked by what she perceived to be his condescending manner, she'd felt it. And it grew stronger during the afternoon session, when he repeatedly looked in her direction. Just now, in the corridor of the hotel, even though their conversation had been purely academic, her insides had been turning little flip-flops.

She had no room in her busy life for romance, she warned herself. And she wasn't interested in a weekend fling. Still, she couldn't shake thoughts of him as she donned the elegant costume for the gala ball.

Victoria hadn't tried on the dress she'd rented in D.C.; she'd been in too great a hurry. She hoped it was presentable. She raised it over her head, and in a rustle of satin and velvet, the rich golden garment fell over her shoulders, its skirts tumbling to her ankles. She blinked when she looked in the mirror. It fit her like a second skin. "Oh, dear," she murmured.

Always careful in her manner of dress, Victoria avoided anything that could be considered sexy. She thought it unprofessional. The only things she owned that were sexy were certain pieces of her favorite underwear that nobody saw but her. But this costume was more than sexy. It was *way* sexy. On the hanger in the costume shop, it had looked like it came from the wardrobe of a perfectly proper Victorian lady. But on her body, it projected a completely different image.

It had a high lace collar, but the open pattern of the lace was unlined at the top of the bodice, and it dipped in the front to a dangerous vee just at her cleavage, revealing curves she normally kept hidden. Velvet and satin took over at that point, cleverly cut to accentuate the roundness of her breasts and the narrowness of her waist. Behind was a large bustle that made her doubt she would be able to sit down, but which showcased her derriere in a surprisingly appealing manner. Victoria had thought the Victorians were prim and proper. The costume designer must have taken some license with this dress.

"Oh, dear," she said again, wishing she'd chosen something more demure. But it was too late now. It didn't much matter anyway, she told herself. She was with Trey, and he probably wouldn't even notice. But the image of Jonathan Blake stole into her mind again, and she suspected he *would* notice. An unfamiliar sensation rippled through her, a mix of excitement and anticipation, and she was too honest to deny that she wanted him to notice.

Twenty minutes later, as she was arranging a coil of dark hair in her final attempt to look like a member of Victorian society, she heard a knock at the door. She opened it to find Trey in full period costume looking as dapper as any young noble of the time ever could. Dapper. And sexy. Funny, she'd never noticed Trey was that good-looking.

"Damn," she uttered, ushering him in. "You're a real lady-killer tonight." She took in every inch of him, from the high round hat to the white spats and elegant walking cane. She should have known a costume ball would strike Trey's fancy, for he had never dealt well with reality. He was sweet, but irresponsible, and lived his life as if it were some kind of game.

His eyes traveled approvingly over the length of her body, as well. "Your mother would wash your mouth with soap," he remarked, kissing her on the cheek. "Been around the cops too long." He eyed her again. "You're a knockout yourself, Tori. You look real sexy in that. Now I know why you wanted an escort. I'll have my hands full tonight keeping the men away."

Heat rose in her cheeks. She didn't want Trey to think she was a knockout. Or sexy. Those were inappropriate descriptions coming from someone in a brother/protector role. She reached for the wrap that went with the outfit, and Trey draped it over her shoulders.

"That's a good idea," he said with a slanted smile. "I don't want to have to work too hard tonight."

The Sherlockian society had chosen this hotel as the venue for the conference because of its authentic Victorian ambience, and as she descended the stairs with Trey, Victoria had the peculiar sensation that she was stepping back into the golden age of the queen whose name she bore. Gas lamps, not electricity, illumined the mirrored corridors, shedding a magical glow on the richly polished mahogany of the furnishings. They strode over ornate Oriental rugs which she suspected had been there since the hotel was built over a century before. The sumptuous decor was embellished with large and lush tropical greenery, hothouse plants that would not survive naturally in any English garden.

Around them, others in period costumes strolled toward

the ballroom, where dinner and dancing awaited. There was a kind of magic in the air, an excitement that came with playing at being in another time. Victoria recalled that weekend fling she'd thought she wasn't interested in, and wished suddenly that she was with someone other than Trey. For in spite of her earlier inclinations, she itched for an evening of wicked romance.

"Ah, Ms. Thomas." A man's voice startled her from her reverie, and she turned to see Reginald FitzSimmons headed her way, a plate of canapés in one hand and a glass of champagne in the other. "You look stunning, my dear."

She grasped Trey's arm a little tighter, but relaxed when she saw the portly man was more interested in the prawns on his toast than in her bosom. "Thank you," she replied, glancing around nervously to see if anyone else might be ogling her. To her distress, she saw the muscular young man who'd sat at her table at lunch, dressed not in costume but in jeans and a tight-fitting polo-style shirt, leaning against the wall nearby, arms crossed, staring at her.

Billy Ray.

Victoria instinctively drew her wrap closer and turned away. What was with that creep? Why was he watching her?

Five

Sandringham, Norfolk
Twenty-ninth July 1883

Although I have yet to inspire my charge to attempt any serious study, we have spent long and not unpleasant hours together. He is a gentle soul, timid and easily influenced. I must tread carefully, however, for I find I am attracted to him in the most inappropriate manner. His large, heavy-lidded eyes are almost sensuous, and his smooth face, clean shaven except for a small moustache, waxed and turned up at the ends, beckons me to caress it, as I once caressed the faces of my boys at Eton. I have fought to bury those unnatural instincts since arriving at Cambridge, allowing them to surface only in the safety of the brotherhood of the Apostles, but when I am with Eddy, they stir to life again. I must guard against these feelings, for they could lead to my instant downfall and disgrace should Eddy learn of them and report me to the Queen.

Only on these pages can I record the appetites that torment me, and in so doing enjoy some temporary respite from the guilt and anxiety that shadow me when I think of the Prince in these terms. I find solace in words—

My heart exists in empty desolation,
Its joy suppressed by those who would not understand

The loneliness and dreary isolation
That is the fate of one who'd love another man.

Jonathan had almost decided to pack up and leave when Victoria surprised him by asking if he were planning to attend tonight's gala. If he didn't know better, he would have sworn there was an invitation in her eyes. Wishful thinking, old boy, he told himself as he tied his cravat. In spite of her unlikely profession, Victoria Thomas reeked of upper class. Women like her didn't fall for detective inspectors from Manchester.

He hadn't stayed because of her, he told himself. He'd stayed because Janeece Fairchild had told him that he was to receive a gift of appreciation from the society, which was to be presented at dinner. He would be conspicuous by his absence if he didn't attend. He'd hired a costume for the affair, so he decided he might as well use it. As for Victoria Thomas, he doubted she'd seek him out. She was just being polite, probably her way of apologizing for her somewhat contentious behavior after the morning session. Jonathan planned to sit through dinner, smile and do his good PR thing, and skip out before the dancing began.

Those were his plans. Until he saw Victoria enter the ballroom on the arm of Trey Delaney. Suddenly, there was no one else in the room.

Only her.

She didn't see him at first, and he stared at her openly, unable to tear his gaze away. She was a vision in lace and velvet, the essence of sensuality. His skin grew warm, and he felt a disturbing masculine need begin to build.

Jonathan vaguely heard Janeece Fairchild ask him a question. He attempted to turn his attention to her, but he was totally distracted. "I beg your pardon? I didn't catch the question."

He had to work to focus on his answer, for his mind, his heart, his body, were screaming for him to go to Victoria Thomas.

This was madness. He wasn't very good with women.

What made him think she'd look twice at him?

He glanced across the ballroom at her again, and this time their gazes locked, and all of Jonathan's earlier plans evaporated.

"Excuse me, ladies," he managed, and extricated himself from the circle of women who had waylaid him the moment he entered the room.

Her gaze never left his as he approached, and Jonathan thought she was the most beautiful woman he had ever seen. He didn't care that she was with another man. He only knew that he had to go to her, or die.

"Good evening, Ms. Thomas," he said, the words sounding distant and formal in his ears.

"Please call me Victoria." Her voice was softer than he remembered, husky almost.

"Victoria, then. You look lovely tonight." He saw her blush slightly, but she didn't blink when she acknowledged the compliment. The color of her dress deepened the gold in her eyes. He must look away before she drew him into their depths. He must pull himself together, or he truly would make an ass of himself.

"Champagne?" Reginald FitzSimmon's voice broke the spell. Jonathan looked up and saw his erstwhile heckler detaining the waiter who was circulating with liquid refreshments.

"Ah, yes, please." He needed something to quench his fires. He raised the flute to Victoria.

"To Victoria. Long live the queen."

"Hear, hear!" FitzSimmons rejoined, clicking his glass to Jonathan's. "I say, with these splendid costumes, one could believe we were back in that age. I almost expect the old girl to make an appearance tonight."

Jonathan joined in the ensuing laughter, but was once again under the spell of the only Victoria he wished to see tonight. Struggling, he turned to Trey, desperate to learn what his relationship was with Victoria Thomas.

"I didn't have a chance to speak with you at lunch, Mr. Delaney. Tell me, are you with the FBI, as well?" he asked, trying to get a bead on the guy. He assumed they were not man and wife. They had different last names and wore no wedding bands, although that meant nothing in this day and time. Trey seemed unaware of the rare gem at his side. Was the man blind?

"Good Lord no," Delaney replied emphatically. "That's Victoria's thing. Me, I can't stand the sight of blood."

Victoria broke in. "Trey is a good friend, Mr. Blake, whom I conned into accompanying me to this event. I didn't tell him until we were on the plane what the weekend was all about."

"I see," Jonathan said, but didn't. "Good friend" could mean many things. What kind of good friend jumped on an airplane, not knowing what he was getting into? A rich good friend for one thing, he decided. Was he Victoria's lover? The thought nearly made him ill.

"I see people are beginning to be seated," FitzSimmons pointed out. "Shall we find a table?"

As happens often at such affairs, Jonathan found himself seated with much the same group that had been together at lunch. Trey and Victoria took their seats, but unfortunately Roger Hammersmith slipped into the one on the other side of Victoria. Jonathan wanted to punch him out. Instead, he politely took the chair next to Janeece Fairchild, who plopped down beside Roger. Next, the Huntley-Ameses fell in, Elizabeth looking decidedly bored. Missing were the muscular young American man and Adele Quigley, who were replaced by two striking young French women who completed the circle. They were not wearing costumes, but were dressed instead in chic and rather daring couture creations—from Paris, they told the others. Jonathan noticed they immediately captured Trey's attention.

After enduring endless questions from Lord Chastain during dinner, Jonathan was almost happy to leave the table to receive his gift of appreciation from the sponsoring Sherlock Holmes Society—his very own deerstalker hat and brier-root pipe. He himself wasn't much of a Sherlockian, but these would be humorous mementos of this most remarkable day. As he made his way back to his seat, the orchestra struck up the first dance number of the evening, and Jonathan saw that Trey was engrossed in animated conversation with the French lovelies. His stomach tightened, and he made a bold decision.

"May I have this dance?" he asked, tapping Victoria lightly on the shoulder. The smile she gave him stirred the fires all over again. He deposited his gifts on the table and led her to the dance floor, willing his fingers not to tremble. "Will your date give me a black eye later?" he asked as he drew her into his arms. He thought nothing had ever felt as delicious as her body next to his.

"He's not my date."

"Your husband?"

"Nope. Not even close. He's what I said he was, just a good friend." She added with a twinkle in her eye, "I'm glad to see he's met those two." She nodded toward the French duo. "They're more his type. I'm afraid he finds me kind of a drag." She briefly explained the relationship between herself and Trey, leaving Jonathan awash with both relief and terror.

She was unattached, available, and in his arms. God help him.

From the corner of his eye, he watched Victoria Thomas step onto the dance floor with the man who had been the speaker today, watched how her body, clothed in that obscenely revealing dress, leaned into his. Her face was raised to his, and she wore the seductive smile of a whore. He'd seen that smile before, on his mother's face, when she wanted something from a man.

At the thought of his mother, a slow, hot rage began to coil in his gut, and the anguish he tried so hard to suppress surfaced with a vengeance. He hated her for what she had done to him, making him less of a man than others. He hated all women, who like his mother were controlling, manipulative whores. Victoria Thomas was no different, he thought, just more hypocritical. One moment an ice queen, the next a bloody whore.

The rage flooded his body, tensing his muscles, heating his blood. He took a deep breath, struggling for control. And then he remembered. Tonight, he would no longer suffer the humiliation of impotency. Tonight, he would take his revenge. Tonight, he would go for blood.

Victoria had to work to keep from melting in Jonathan's arms. Her skin fairly burned where he touched her, and being so close to him was turning her on like crazy. She should never have allowed him to draw her onto the dance floor.

She glanced over Jonathan's shoulder at Trey, but found no hope for rescue from that quarter. He was too busy entertaining the French women. Damn him, she thought, but knew it wasn't Trey's fault she was falling for Jonathan Blake like a schoolgirl. Neither was it Trey's responsibility to save her.

Jonathan had wasted no time in probing her about her relationship with Trey, and she didn't think it had to do with his worry about getting a black eye. He was a male on the hunt, and she was his prey. A shiver ran through her. She must be careful tonight, very careful. Her body wanted him, and it seemed her mind had no say in the matter.

The slow dance ended, and the band turned to a faster number. Jonathan released her from his embrace, but they did not leave the dance floor. Instead, they began to move in time to the upbeat music. She saw Trey escort both of the French girls onto the dance floor, one on each arm, and she had to laugh. It was so Trey. D.C.'s most eligible bachelor. He knew the effect he had on women, and he played it to the max. She only wished he weren't so irresponsible. She worried about his myriad liaisons. She felt that they would someday get him into serious trouble.

In only moments, Trey and the French women had stolen the show, dancing in exotic frenzy as a trio. The rest of the dancers stood aside to watch the spectacle. Victoria was mortified when Trey began to make blatantly seductive moves, first toward one woman, then the other, for to her horror, their dance was having a disturbingly erotic effect on her. Standing so close to Jonathan in the crowd, her sexual desire for him flamed into the danger zone. In a panic, she excused herself and fled to the powder room.

Patting her face with a damp paper towel, she glanced at her flushed complexion in the mirror. What the hell was going on? This was not like her. She'd never let herself become so unglued by a man in her entire life. A man who this morning she didn't even like very much.

Victoria was more than a little scared. Scared of her desire, and burning with it at the same time. It didn't take a rocket scientist to know he felt the same. The evidence had brushed against her when they danced, even though he'd tried to hold her at a distance. It was a wasted effort, for their bodies seemed determined to meld.

Where was this going to end? There was only one logical conclusion, but Victoria was no tramp. She would not jump into bed with Jonathan Blake, no matter how badly her body betrayed her. She had to take her leave of him. Immediately.

She swept out of the ladies' room, intending to return to the table to pick up her wrap and evening purse, say her good-night to Jonathan, and return to the safety of her room. But as she walked briskly down the corridor, someone fell in beside her.

"In a hurry?" he said.

Startled, Victoria turned toward the voice and found herself facing Billy Ray. Her heart sank. "Uh, yes, actually I am."

He stepped in front of her, halting her progress and backing her into the wall. "I was hoping we'd get a chance to talk," he said in a lazy drawl that set Victoria's teeth on edge. "I'm real interested in the Coleman case."

"I'm sorry, Mr. Ray, but—"

"Call me Billy," he said, extending one arm over her

shoulder and leaning against the wall, effectively pinning her to the spot.

Victoria's pulse raced as she considered how best to extricate herself. "My . . . uh . . . date is waiting for me. Perhaps another time."

"Are you afraid of me, Victoria?"

She raised her chin. Hell would turn to ice before she admitted that she was very much afraid of him. "Is there a reason why I should be, Mr. Ray?" she replied coldly. She loathed the sound of her given name coming from him, and she'd be damned if she lowered herself to address him in such a personal manner.

"I bet William Coleman is afraid of you," he went on, not answering her question. There was a glint of malice in his eyes. "Why'd you have to do that to him?"

Victoria was stunned. "Why do you care about William Coleman? He's nothing but the lowest kind of slime."

She saw his jaw clench. "You think you know so much," he growled. "But you know nothing. William Coleman is a decent man."

"Who brutally murdered five young women?"

"You're mistaken about that. You've put the wrong man in prison."

Victoria knew better, but she didn't argue. She had to get away from this crazy. "Please, I have to go now."

Slowly, he drew away from her. "Sure," he said, dropping his arm to his side. "We'll talk about this another time."

The hell we will, she thought and turned to leave. To her profound relief, she saw Jonathan turn into the corridor.

"There you are," he said, hurrying toward her. "I was beginning to get worried about you." He saw Billy Ray and frowned. "Is everything all right, Victoria?"

"Yes," she lied. "Fine. Thank you." But she immediately linked her arm in his and steered him toward the exit. "Please, just get me out of here," she said in a low voice when they were out of Billy Ray's earshot.

"Is he a friend?"

"No, just a creepy curiosity seeker. He's interested in one of the cases I handled." She paused at the entrance to the ballroom and turned to Jonathan with a wan smile. "Thanks for coming after me. I wasn't in any real danger, but I was having a little trouble disengaging myself. I guess it shook me up a little. I think I'd better call it a night."

His expression changed from worried to disappointed. "It's early yet. Don't leave. I won't let him get near you again, I promise."

The wise woman in her knew it was time to leave, for Jonathan's sex appeal was working its magic on her all over again. But it was early, not even eight-thirty, and she didn't particularly relish spending the rest of the evening watching British sitcoms on television.

"I suppose I could stay just a bit longer . . ."

He didn't give her time to change her mind, but led her directly back to the table. The adrenaline rush from her unpleasant encounter with Billy Ray had left her shaky, and she was actually glad to be in the company of a lot of people. She hoped she could manage to avoid him for the rest of the weekend. The guy was bad news.

The band was on a break as they returned, and the conversation around the table was focused on Jack the Ripper. "But it could not possibly have been the duke of Clarence," Lord Chastain was arguing as they took their seats. "That's preposterous. Prince Albert Victor Edward, or Eddy as they called him, would have been surrounded by people at all times."

"Improbable, but not impossible," Jonathan joined in. "Even princes have private lives. Eddy had syphilis, and he might have had spells of madness that drove him to kill. I admit that is pure conjecture, but as Ms. Thomas has pointed out to me, sometimes one must use one's instincts to get to the facts."

Victoria didn't know which startled her more, his statement or that he reached for her hand beneath the table. He gave her one of his heart-melting grins and squeezed her hand, and her insides turned to mush. It should have been

Trey who rescued her in the corridor; that was the reason she'd asked him to come in the first place. But a part of her was glad it had been Jonathan.

"It does seem unlikely that he could travel all the way from Windsor to Whitechapel, kill those women, and make it home again undetected." This from Roger Hammersmith. "That is some distance to cover."

"Maybe ze story about Dr. Gull is true," piped up the young French woman whom Trey had called Chantal, surprising everyone. "I read that he was suspected at one time. Maybe he was ze facilitator and transported ze prince to ze East End to do his dirty work, then brought him safely home by private carriage."

Victoria blinked in surprise. She would never have expected such an intelligent pronouncement to come from her, and she wondered suddenly who these two were. They were dressed like French hookers, but if this one was a hooker, she at least had a brain. As if he read her confusion, Trey leaned over and whispered, "They're med students from Paris. And history buffs."

She gave him a skeptical glance, but he just grinned and shrugged. One thing was clear, however. As her escort, Trey considered himself off duty.

"From what I've read, I think we can discount Dr. Gull as an accomplice," Jonathan told the young woman. "But the prince could have arranged for his own transportation. He was good friends, I understand, with Lord Somerset, the superintendent of the royal stables."

Reginald FitzSimmons snickered. "Very good friends, I understand. They were both caught at the male brothel in the Cleveland Street scandal."

"What was that?" Victoria asked. It was obvious these people knew a lot more about the case than she did.

Jonathan explained. "The prince was a homosexual. In those days, homosexuality was severely punished. Look at what happened to Oscar Wilde. Eddy was caught in a police raid on a known male brothel, but he was immediately released, and the incident was hushed up by royal command."

Victoria thought about that a moment, then said, "Well, if they would cover up something like that, think to what lengths they would go to cover up his serial killings."

Those gathered around the table grew quiet. "Good point," Jonathan said. "If we just had—"

"Hard evidence," she said, stepping on his words and giving him a wry grin.

"What is it like, zis Whitechapel area?" Nicole, the other supposed med student, asked.

"Nothing like in those days," Roger replied. "It was a slum of the very worst kind. Now, it's just an inner-city neighborhood, not really very far from here."

"Let us go zere," Chantal said, her eyes bright.

"When?" Trey looked dismayed.

"Tonight. Right now. Zis band is a bore."

Jonathan withdrew his hand from Victoria's, leaving hers feeling cool and empty.

"Not a good idea," he said. "Even though I suppose it is safe enough, we shouldn't go down there dressed like this. We'd be accused of slumming."

"Which we would be," Roger pointed out.

"Nonsense," FitzSimmons huffed. "It's perfectly safe. I could go for a pint of something besides champagne. Let us be off for the Ten Bells."

"Ten Bells?" Victoria was not at all sure she wanted to participate in what sounded like an ill-advised adventure.

"Well, it used to be the Ten Bells. It's a public house in the East End. Now it's called the Jack the Ripper pub."

"All right!" Chantal said, drawing her arm down in a very American-style gesture.

Jonathan looked at Victoria, and she just shrugged. "I'm game if you are," she said. As long as they went as a group, she supposed they would be safe enough. Safer than if she stayed here and chanced to run into Billy Ray again. Safer as well on a personal level, for if she stayed here with Jonathan Blake, she might well end up in his bed.

Six

The unthinkable has happened, and I am awash in both joy and terror. Today, in the privacy of our new quarters in Neville's Court, Eddy told me a story that exposed his secret inner anguish, then revealed to me the dark longings that lodge within his breast, longings that match my own in passion and despair.

While on a world tour, which his father insisted he must take, he was forced to sleep with a native whore in the West Indies. He wept when he described his shame in succumbing to the woman's seduction, and how he felt so unclean afterward it made him ill. It was then he told me that he could love no woman and that he harbors feelings for me that mirror the desire that has been building in my heart for him. He told me of his love in an outpouring so tender and simple, I wept to hear it. Yet I cautioned him against letting our true feelings be known. I pray in his simple mind he comprehends the consequences of our relations becoming public knowledge.

My beloved prince is sweet and vulnerable and tries hard to please me, and I am a compassionate master. I know his weaknesses, but unlike his pig of a father, I do not demand what he cannot give. Instead, I guide him where he can succeed. I show my love in this way and

*hope to engender within him a loyalty so strong he will
never leave me, for he is my world now, my life. I will
never betray his love as long as I live.*

The early-autumn night was chill and damp with a heavy
fog enshrouding the streets of London. What used to be the
Ten Bells public house was now both the "local," the drinking establishment for the working man in the neighborhood,
and because of its name, a tourist destination. When the
merrymakers from the convention spilled out of the two
taxis they had hired to bring them here, Jonathan reluctantly
went to the front door of the pub and peered in. He shook
his head. "This is a mistake," he said to Victoria. "There
don't appear to be any tourists here tonight. Only locals. I
think it would be the better part of valor if we got right
back into those taxis and returned to the hotel."

"Oh, don't be such an old stick, Inspector," said Reginald FitzSimmons. "I frequent this place from time to time.
It's not too rough a crowd."

Chantal and Nicole, like decorative bookends at Trey's
side, pushed past them. "We've come all this way to do,
how do you say, ze Jack ze Ripper zing," Chantal said.
"I'm going in."

Behind them, Jonathan escorted Victoria, who hugged
her wrap tightly over the bodice of her gown. They were
followed by the others, all of whom had chosen to come
along, surprisingly even Elizabeth Huntley-Ames, although
she looked thoroughly unhappy. Her husband, Jonathan had
noted, had been openly enjoying the view of the long legs
that extended from beneath the outrageously short skirts
worn by the two French beauties and the outline of breasts
revealed by their tight sweaters. He had no doubt Elizabeth
had noted that, too.

Inside, the air was blue with cigarette smoke. The pub
was filled mostly with men, although there were some
women among them. When Nicole and Chantal made their
entrance, the boisterous chatter subsided as the regulars
scoped out the newcomers. But when the rest of the group

entered, dressed as if they'd just returned from the Victorian age in H. G. Well's time machine, the place went completely silent. Jonathan placed a hand protectively at Victoria's waist.

"I don't like this," she whispered to him.

"Neither do I. We'll only stay a little while," he promised.

But Reginald FitzSimmons was right at home. "What are you staring at, man?" he blustered at a rather bemused-looking patron. "You've seen stranger sights, I'm sure." He headed for the bar. "Ansel, a round for the house, please," he said in a voice loud enough for all to hear. At that, a communal cheer went up and the noise level returned to normal. Jonathan wondered what FitzSimmons did that he could afford such a generous gesture, but he obviously knew the barkeeper, and the man didn't bat an eye at the order.

There were no tables available, so the group gathered along a stretch of the wall where a wooden plank served as a bar. FitzSimmons brought him a pint of stout and handed Victoria a half-pint of a light-colored ale. "Used to be my second home," he said, "before I moved to Kent." He raised his glass. "Cheers."

"You lived around here?" Alistair Huntley-Ames sounded incredulous.

"Oh, no, no, my good man. But I've always been haunted by this neighborhood, and what went on here a hundred years ago. Jack the Ripper could have stood on this very spot and quaffed a pint or two before picking out his *victime du jour*," he said with a mischievous gleam in his eye. "You know, the site where he butchered his last victim is not far from here."

"Butchered?" Elizabeth stared at him aghast and brought a pudgy white hand to her throat.

"Oh, yes, my dear," FitzSimmons told her, warming to the story. "Just like the good inspector described this morning, only it was worse than his most polite telling of the matter." He nodded in Jonathan's direction. "Unlike the

Ripper's other victims, who were homeless, Mary Kelly had a small room, and she took her client home, where he not only killed her, but because of the privacy it allowed him, he engaged in a bloody orgy that must have lasted more than two hours. He cut her throat so deeply it nearly severed her head. When her remains were discovered the following morning, she had been disemboweled, skinned, and disfigured in every grotesque way imaginable, and her body parts were lying on the bed and a nearby table. Everything, that is, except her heart. It was removed and never found."

Jonathan cringed. What FitzSimmons said was true, but he wished the man would be a little less graphic. He was speaking of the murder of Mary Jane Kelly, a young prostitute who had had the misfortune of meeting up with the killer somewhere close by. Maybe in this pub. It was possible.

He could see FitzSimmons had scared the living daylights out of Elizabeth. She was as pale as the frock she wore. Victoria wasn't much better when she turned to him. "Could we leave now? I . . . this . . . is just too much." To his shock, her eyes were brimming with tears. Perturbed and perplexed, Jonathan wished they'd never come along. Things were much more interesting on the dance floor.

"Of course," he replied to Victoria, and turned to Huntley-Ames. "I believe your wife is rather distressed," he said. "Ms. Thomas and I are going to hail a taxi. Will you join us?"

Lord Chastain shot his wife a disgusted look. "I suppose. Elizabeth, you simply have no sense of adventure."

The look she shot back could have killed. "You may stay, Alistair. I'm sure I will be safe with Mr. Blake and Ms. Thomas."

"And I'd never hear the end of it," he grumbled, downing the last of his beer.

Trey, Chantal, and Nicole decided to go off in search of some hotter action, leaving Roger, Janeece, and FitzSimmons to rehash the gory days of yesteryear. As the taxi pulled away from the curb, Jonathan caught sight of a brawny young man in the circle of light beneath a street lamp across from the pub. He couldn't be sure, but he thought it was the man who'd given Victoria a hard time earlier in the evening. He glanced at her to see if she'd noticed him, but she seemed to be intently studying her hands that were clasped in her lap. He said nothing, for he didn't want to alarm her. Besides, the fellow had as much right to come here as they did. He guessed many of the conference-goers would make their way into Whitechapel before it was over.

The atmosphere in the taxi was frigid as tension stretched between Alistair Huntley-Ames and his wife, and Jonathan didn't attempt to make small talk with them. He was more concerned about those tears he'd seen in Victoria's eyes and wondered what had triggered them. She didn't seem the type to become so upset over graphic descriptions. She must have seen many gruesome crime scenes in her line of work. He said nothing, but took her hand, which was as cold as the atmosphere in the cab.

When at last they arrived at the hotel, they left the Huntley-Ameses to their private concerns, and Jonathan felt sorry for them both. They reminded him of his parents, mismatched and miserable after the glow of young love had worn off. They were one reason he'd remained single for the entire thirty-five years of his life. Who wanted to live like that?

They bade good-night to the unhappy couple, and Victoria turned to Jonathan.

"Thanks for getting me out of there. That's two rescues in one evening. I'm sorry I'm such a dud." Her heart was heavy, but not because she'd caused them to leave the pub. For some reason she could not fathom, FitzSimmons's graphic description had brought back her own horrific visions of how Meghan's body had been defiled. She was surprised at herself, because in her work, she had seen many dreadful sights, and they hadn't fazed her. Why to-night?

Jonathan laid a hand on her shoulder. "You're not a dud by any stretch," he said, tilting her head up slightly with his other hand. "Do you want to go back to the dance, or would you rather have a quiet nightcap with me in the lounge?"

She noticed he didn't give her the option of saying good-night, which was what she ought to do. The magic of the evening was ruined. "I'd probably better go," she said, but he slid his hand along the length of her arm, and her body responded with the same disturbing sensations as before.

"Don't. Not just yet. There's a fireplace in the lounge, and I heard they have devilishly divine Irish coffee. It's only half past ten."

Victoria gazed at him, aware that his hand was still on her arm. Very aware. She was chilled from the night air and the haunting memories, and she shivered. Suddenly she did not want to be alone.

"One drink."

They found a settee near the crackling fire, and the warm glow of the flames raised her spirits. The Irish coffee lived up to its reputation, sending fluid warmth to her insides, where it mingled with another kind of warmth generated by the man sitting next to her. He wasn't touching her. He didn't have to. Just his presence seemed enough to warm her from the inside out.

"Want to tell me about it?"

His question interrupted her rather disturbing thoughts, and she blushed slightly. "About what?"

"What brought the tears back there in the pub? Were you afraid?"

Her inner glow was doused instantly, and Victoria stiff-ened. It was none of his damned business. She still could barely talk about Meghan's murder with close friends and family. To speak of it to someone who was virtually a stranger was unthinkable. "It . . . was nothing."

"I'm a better detective than that," he pressed gently, and

began to massage the back of her neck. At his touch, Victoria's usually staunch defenses began to crumble. Still, she fought to keep that nightmare to herself.

"It's not something I want to talk about. Or think about, for that matter."

Jonathan did not reply. He simply worked on releasing the tension in the muscles at the back of her neck. Gently. Quietly. Victoria wished he could work out that other, deeper pain that she'd carried with her for so many years.

"My sister was murdered." The words were out before she knew they were coming. "Seven years ago. It was a brutal slaying. Her body was butchered in a similar manner to what FitzSimmons described as having happened to Mary Kelly. It . . . it brought it all back, that's all." Her throat was so tightly constricted she could barely manage the last words, and hot tears burned her eyes.

Jonathan's hand paused in its ministration. "*That's all*? Good God. I'd like to throttle that old man." He leaned forward so he could see her face, and brought his hand around to cup her chin. "Oh, Victoria, I am sorry. I'm so sorry."

Victoria looked for the pity she usually saw in the faces of those who knew, pity she hated. But instead she saw compassion. Still, she was too private a person to accept it. "Don't be. It wasn't FitzSimmon's fault," she said. "He didn't know. And it's been a long time. I should be over it by now."

"It's not something one gets over easily."

Victoria wondered if he knew what an understatement that was. No, it wasn't easily gotten past. Not with therapy. Not with time. Not with the work that drove her so hard to prevent other brutal crimes. "I saw her body just after it happened." Where did these snatches of the story keep coming from? Victoria did not mean for them to surface. She had no wish to expose her still-raw wounds to anyone.

"My God. Why? Were you asked to identify it?" Jonathan removed the mug of coffee from her shaking hand and set both of their drinks on a nearby table. Then he took her hands. She raised her eyes to his.

"I . . . I'm the one who found her."

"Christ."

"She'd gone to a motel room, to meet a man. We didn't know that, of course, until after she disappeared. When we discovered the next morning that she hadn't come home that night, I went to her room and found her diary. She'd written about her plans for the liaison, and where they would meet. The only thing she didn't write was the man's name."

She began to worry the skin on his fingers with her thumbs. "Meghan got a little wild, I guess. Our parents had always been so demanding. She was a rebel, or at least a rebel wannabe. This was her way of getting back at them, I suppose. Anyway, I knew her pretty well, enough to know that by that time, she would probably be ready to be rescued. I . . . I went to the motel she'd noted in her diary and showed her picture to the manager, who remembered her. When no one responded when we knocked on the door, he let me in with his key. She was . . . she was . . ."

Victoria's world turned bloodred, and she crumpled against Jonathan, not caring that she was making a spectacle of herself. For some reason, she'd allowed him to open that Pandora's box, and she did not have the strength to shut it again. Instead, she let all the nasties out, where they attacked her heart and mind and spirit with a vengeance.

Memories of the blood that was swashed throughout the room, the sight of her sister's mutilated body, the smell of death, pervaded her senses, and she choked on them. Her stomach turned and blinding tears spilled from her eyes again. And again she had not the strength to suppress them.

Instead, she leaned into the warmth of Jonathan's arms and the harbor of his embrace and cried. Cried as she had not cried since that awful time. Cried as her stomach wrenched and her eyes ached. Cried until the pain grew numb, and the memories hid themselves away once again in the darkness.

Only then did she withdraw from his arms and realize to her horror not only that she'd broken down in the arms of a man she hardly knew, but that she'd done it in a public place. "I've got to go," she said, sniffing into the handkerchief he'd given her during the flood. "I'm . . . I'm so embarrassed."

"Don't be," he said gently. "No one saw you. This place emptied out a while back."

"I probably ran them off," she said with a small laugh.

"It was closing time at the bar. Come on." He took her elbow and helped her to her feet. "Let's get you to your room."

Victoria's head was light and her sinuses soggy as she rode the elevator with Jonathan. As had happened earlier, neither of them spoke. They just stood quietly watching the numbers on the lighted panel above them as they were lifted to the sixth floor. Gone was her earlier hot passion, washed away by her grief, leaving her spent and drained.

"Got your key?" Jonathan asked as they stepped into the corridor.

She reached into the small bag she carried and brought it out, handing it to him with shaky fingers. She did not know if he expected to be invited into her room. If he did, he was in for a disappointment. She could easily turn him away now. She was no longer sexually vulnerable to him. At least not tonight. Those old horrors had seen to that.

He did come in, however, and she didn't protest.

"Will you be all right?" he asked, looking into the closet as if he thought the bogeyman might be hiding there. The only bogeyman stalking Victoria was the haunting memory she'd just tried to wash away with her tears. Surprisingly, she did feel a little better for having done that, although she found her behavior in a public place appalling.

"Sure. I'll be fine. I really do apologize . . ."

He came to her, standing an arm's length away. He

placed his hands on her shoulders. "Do you have night-mares?"

His question, and the tender concern in his voice, took her by surprise. "I used to, all the time. They've faded over the years though, thank God."

"You may have one tonight, thanks to Mr. Fitz-Simmons's bringing all this up for you again. I'm in room 708. Call me if you need me. Will you join me for breakfast?"

Morning seemed an eternity away, and the thought of food was repulsive at the moment. But she nodded. "Not too early."

"Nineish?"

She nodded again and gave forth a small hiccough.

"I'll give you a call," he said. He gazed at her for a long moment, as if contemplating something, then lowered his lips to her forehead, brushed it with a gentle kiss, and was gone.

Victoria stared at the door as it closed behind him. She hadn't wanted him to stay, but a part of her wished he had. For his kiss, so chaste and tender, had lit a tiny glow deep within her, a glow that if fanned ever so slightly, would burn hot once again.

No, it was better he was gone.

It had not been as difficult as he had anticipated. Not difficult at all, once he surrendered to his destiny. When he did not fight it, his consciousness melded with the master's, and the work was accomplished with a natural ease and flow. He became one with the night, and the knife, and the blood.

She had been an easy mark. A woman alone on a dark street. A whore, no doubt. But he had not even accosted her. He had simply approached her silently from behind, strangled her, laid her down and laid her open. A simple exercise, too simple almost, not as satisfying as he had expected. It was over in five minutes. The master's design, executed with perfection. He had not a spot of blood on him when he finished. The souvenir secured in a bag in his coat pocket, he'd wiped his knife on the woman's skirt and hidden it away in its most ingenious little hiding place.

It had been an easy kill, but it was only an exercise. Practice for the play that was to come. Already he needed more. Already he grew hard thinking of the blood, thinking of the game, thinking of the women who would die . . .

Seven

Trinity College, Cambridge
Ninth September 1884

I am bereft. My beloved prince has been taken from me, if only for a short while, and my days without him are long and empty. He has gone to Sandringham with his mother, who insisted he join her there for a fortnight of some banal frivolity. He did not wish to go, but he was not strong enough to withstand her demands.

Eddy fares no better at the hands of his mother than I. MotherDear, as he calls her when in public, selfishly manipulates his life, breezing in when the fancy strikes, demanding his full attention and love, and then blowing away again without so much as a faretheewell, leaving him bewildered and forlorn. She does nothing to protect him from the open ridicule I have witnessed among the court. I hate her and wish she would leave us in peace.

Perhaps it is as well he is gone, though, for tonight I happened into a pub and heard a raucous and obscene song that referred to me as the "Bastard Stephen" and to Eddy as the "suckling." Enraged, I challenged the cowards who were singing it to stand and fight, but they slunk off into the night. The incident sickened me, for I realized that we have not been as discreet as I had hoped in our affair.

Leaving the pub, I wandered for hours along the dark-

*ened streets of Cambridge, wanting to choke the life out
of those singers, wanting to be with Eddy, wanting to kill
MotherDear who has the unfair power to separate us. In
the past, when rage was upon me, or black despair, I
found comfort in blood sport, for spilling the lifeblood of
quail or boar served to ease the anguish, at least for a
time. I taught Eddy this means of assuaging the demons
that torment us, and we have often joined together in the
hunt.*

*This night, I could not settle for the blood of bird or
beast. Only the blood of a woman would quell my rage
against MotherDear for taking my Prince away. On those
dark streets, I happened upon a whore eager to sell her
puss for a small sum. I paid it, but it was not her puss I
wanted. I wanted her life. I had no weapon upon me
other than my great hands, which I nearly used in my
madness, but when she raised her skirts to reveal the disgusting thing, I turned in abhorrence and ran until my
feet carried me to my doorstep and the darkness of my
lonely room. I tremble still with the rage. I wish I had
killed her . . .*

> *I should not mind
> If she were done away with, killed or ploughed.
> She did not seem to serve a useful end
> And certainly she was not beautiful.**

If she had suffered a nightmare, Victoria did not remember
it the next morning. She had slept well and awoke refreshed. She stretched lazily, trying to remember where she
was and what she was supposed to do today. The conference would reconvene at ten, she remembered. Today's
program would be on a lighter note than yesterday's. The
morning session would feature two movies shown back-to-
back in which Sherlock Holmes endeavored to solve the
mystery of Jack the Ripper. In the afternoon, a play in
which Sherlock would come face-to-face with Jack the Ripper, written by one of the London Sherlockians, would be

performed. The evening was to be a roundtable discussion of whether Sir Arthur Conan Doyle, creator of the world's most famous sleuth and a contemporary of Jack the Ripper, had missed the mark completely when he was asked to look into the Ripper case, or if he had known more than he ever revealed.

She would enjoy all of the events, Victoria thought, but wrinkled her brow, thinking there was something else she'd planned to do. And then she remembered. Jonathan Blake. She had agreed to meet him for breakfast. Sitting up, she looked at the bedside clock. It was nearly nine. Good grief. Hadn't they agreed on nineish for breakfast?

Rushing to the mirror, she saw that she looked even worse than she had feared. Her eyes were still swollen from her crying jag, and her hair was a tangled mess. She couldn't let Jonathan see her like this. Going to the telephone, she dialed his room to tell him she needed more time. The phone rang six times before it was answered by the voice-mail system. She replaced the receiver. She found it curious that he wasn't there. Was he already on his way to her room?

Damn.

Victoria thought he'd promised to call her first. She grabbed a hairbrush and attacked the thick brown curls and had made some small measure of progress when the phone rang.

She jumped, startled, but answered it on the first ring, her heart racing. "Hello? Jonathan?"

"This is the concierge desk. We have a message for you. Is this a convenient time to deliver it to your room? We were asked to wait until nine o'clock."

A message? Her pulse slowed. "Of course. I'm awake." She hung up, perplexed, and donned her robe.

The message arrived moments later. She took the envelope and gave the young man a tip before closing the door. She tore open the envelope. The note inside was written on hotel stationery.

"Dear Victoria, I'm sorry but I won't be able to meet

you for breakfast. Something has come up, and I had to go to the Yard. I'll try to break loose later in the day and come by the hotel. Please give me a rain check. Jonathan."

Victoria did not want to admit the depth of her disappointment. Since he had not tried to take advantage of her vulnerable state the night before, she'd decided she might be safe enough around him, if she could keep her own desire in check. Now, it looked as if she'd spend the morning at the movies.

Oh, well.

She showered and dressed, paying more attention than usual to her hair and makeup, knowing it was for Jonathan's benefit, in case he showed up. If his job was anything like hers, he might not be able to get away, but she sincerely hoped she would see him later in the day.

Checking her image one last time in the entry-hall mirror, she opened the door to leave and noticed a small package on the floor next to the wall just outside the door. It was a square white box tied with a wide red ribbon. Had it been there when the bellhop had delivered Jonathan's message? Maybe it had accompanied the note, and he'd set it down to knock on the door and forgot to give it to her. Her stomach did that same strange little dance it had done yesterday when she'd first seen Jonathan's smile. He must really have wanted to see her again to send a present in apology, she thought, bending to pick it up.

She pulled the ribbon loose and raised the lid. Whatever was inside was hidden by fluffy white tissue. She took it to the desk and lifted the entire contents out with the paper, which fell away when she placed it on the flat surface. Victoria's eyes widened, and she covered her mouth with the back of her hand to stifle a scream.

Before her lay a small zipper-style plastic bag containing something soft, red, and wet. Something that looked horrifyingly biological, like an animal gland one might purchase at a butcher shop. Tucked into the tissue was a note, written on hotel stationery:

"Yours truly, Jack the Ripper."

* * *

The sun slitted in through a crack between the drawn curtains, striking him right in the eye and awakening him from an erotic dream. It took a moment for him to remember what had taken place the night before, but when he did, to his amazement, his cock hardened. A slow smile crawled across his lips. He was a man once more. He rolled over in his bed and felt peaceful for the first time in as long as he could remember.

Victoria kept her eyes on the grisly little packet that sat on the desk in front of her as she reached for the phone. Her hands were shaking so badly she could hardly press the numbers. She managed to dial room 708, then remembered that Jonathan wasn't there. He'd been called in to Scotland Yard. Scotland Yard. How could she reach him there?

She found a telephone book in a drawer and looked up the listing for the agency, only to find there were many numbers. What division was he in? She dialed the main number, and after long minutes, she was connected to his line. To her dismay, it was answered by voice mail. Hastily, she left a message for him to return her call as soon as he could.

Hanging up, she fought back the nausea at the pit of her stomach. Was this a prank? Who would have done such a thing?

She took a deep breath and tried to remain calm, tried to think like an investigator, not a victim. What should she do? Call hotel security, for one thing. But her knees were weak, and she wished she wasn't alone. Suddenly, she remembered Trey, and relief washed through her. Thank God he had come with her. She needed him now as she hadn't needed him in a long time.

Taking care to replace the plastic bag in the box exactly as she'd found it, in case it would be needed as evidence, Victoria carried it gingerly down the hall to Trey's room. She'd call hotel security from there, but at the moment, she needed his presence to steady her. She pounded loudly on his door and heard a muffled "Just a minute." Moments later, a tousled-looking Trey stuck his head around the door.

"What do you want?" he growled. She could tell he was naked, at least above the waist.

She didn't care if he was stark buck naked. She was desperate. "Trey," she said, pushing through the door. "Let me in. Something's happened . . ."

It was then she heard the giggles. She froze. Oh, cripes. He wasn't alone. She'd forgotten the French women. Wondering which one he'd ended up with, she jerked her head toward the bedroom, and was shocked to see not one but both women in Trey's bed. Chantal giggled again and gave her a little wave.

Her face flamed, and she turned to Trey, who stood wrapped only in a towel, eyeing her with a look that told her she should have minded her own business. "You didn't!"

He shrugged. "Don't tell Mother," he said with a sardonic smirk.

"Good grief, Trey. I can't believe it."

"Whatcha got there?" he asked, changing the subject and poking his nose toward the box she clutched tightly.

Victoria stared down at the box, then looked at Trey, then at Chantal and Nicole.

"Uh . . . nothing," she said, feeling sick all over again. "It's nothing." Damn him. How could he let her down like this? "Forget it," she snarled at him and turned on her heel to leave. "You make a damn lousy bodyguard," she muttered as she passed him. "You're fired."

Back in her room, Victoria took a bottle of spring water from the small refrigerator and guzzled the whole thing, as if the cool water could wash away her fear and confusion. She felt hot tears threaten and blinked them back furiously. Damn him! Damn the son of a bitch. She'd never been angrier at Trey in her life.

But Trey was not her primary problem at the moment. The little white box taunted her from atop the desk. At last, she picked up the phone and dialed hotel security.

Moments later, the short, balding manager appeared at her door, his face as white as the bed linens. With him was a uniformed guard. "I'm told we have a problem here," he said, and Victoria explained to him what she had told the guard.

"Are you certain it contains . . . uh . . . animal glands?" he asked nervously.

Irked, Victoria picked up the box and held it out toward him. "Want to see?" Did he think she was making this up?

"No . . . uh, no thank you," he stammered. "I believe you. Maybe we'd better call the police."

The police. Yes. One policeman in particular would do.

As if summoned by the gods, Jonathan knocked on her door only moments later. "I picked up your message on my car phone. What's wrong?"

"Oh, thank God," she said, grabbing his arm and yanking him into the room. He was unshaven, and his face looked haggard, as if he hadn't slept. His eyes narrowed when he saw the two men in the room.

"What's going on, Victoria? What's happened?" It was his turn to take hold of her arms, and she saw alarm in his eyes.

"It . . . it's probably nothing, just a prank, but I had a rather bizarre little present left at my door this morning. I was just talking with Mr. Adams here to see if we could sort out where it came from."

"A present? What kind of present?"

She nodded to the white box on the desk. "A rather meaty one, if I do say," she replied, wishing her attempt at levity would lift the rock in her stomach.

Jonathan went to the desk and opened the package just as Victoria had done earlier. When he saw what was inside, he went white.

Jonathan had answered the phone a little after one A.M. to be informed by his supervisor that a woman's body had been found less than two blocks from where he and the

others had gone on their little adventure to the Jack the
Ripper Pub. With a deep sense of foreboding, he'd dressed
and headed out into the night in a car that had been sent
by New Scotland Yard to take him directly to the scene of
the crime.

When he saw the victim, his stomach had turned. She
was lying in shadow on the pavement, her skirts raised
above her knees, her legs apart. Her throat had been deeply
slashed, and her abdomen ripped open. Blood puddled beneath her, its metallic odor tainting the air. Jonathan
thought he was going to be sick.

It wasn't the blood that distressed him. Or the horrific
wounds. He'd seen it all before. It was the killer's MO that
rocked him to the core. His style. For it was the style he
had only yesterday described to the Sherlockians gathered
in the old hotel.

The style of Jack the Ripper.

He'd spent the early hours of the morning leading the
investigating team, making sure the crime scene was secure,
taking care that no one contaminated any possible evidence.
But a profound misgiving knotted his stomach.

Had he in some way been responsible for this woman's
death?

It was just too coincidental that on the night after a symposium about Jack the Ripper such a murder as this would
take place. He strongly suspected the killer had sat in his
audience earlier in the day. Taking notes, so to speak.

Later at the morgue, the coroner compounded his fears.
"It was brutal, but swift," he'd said after examining the
body. "Reminds me of the old Ripper murders."

Now, standing in Victoria's hotel room, looking at the
contents of the package she'd received, his fear turned to
horror.

"I want to speak to every bellhop who was on duty this
morning," he said to the hotel manager. "I want to know
who delivered this. Go collect them. I'll meet you in your
office in fifteen minutes."

When the men hurried out, Jonathan double-locked the

door behind him and turned to Victoria. "Hopefully we can get to the bottom of this quickly," he said, "but until we do, it would be best if you stayed in your room. Don't let anyone in, except me, of course."

"Don't be silly, Jonathan. I didn't come all the way to London to stay in a hotel room. This is just a prank. I will not be held hostage by some practical joker."

But Jonathan suspected this was not a practical joke. He hesitated, not wanting to share the awful possibility with her. There was no need to worry her prematurely. He wished he could haul her pretty ass to the airport and put her on the first plane back to D.C., where she would be safe. But he knew she could not leave now. Not if what he suspected turned out to be true.

And if it did, he would brook no argument from her concerning her safety. He'd take every measure he could to protect her, even if he had to throw that same pretty ass in jail. For she was in terrible danger.

"Perhaps it is only a joke," he said as calmly as he could. "But—"

"But what?"

"Nothing. I'd just feel better if you'd stay here until we find the culprit."

"There's something you're not telling me. You're making too big a deal of this." Her eyes sparked in golden challenge, and her perception reminded him of what she did for a living.

Maybe he was making too big a deal of it. He hoped so. Maybe she was right, and it was just a sick joke. But the coincidence was too great.

"Jonathan," she almost shouted in her exasperation. "What is it?"

He heaved a sigh and rubbed the back of his neck with one hand. "There was a murder last night. In the Whitechapel area. The MO was . . . reminiscent of the Ripper murders."

"Oh, God," she murmured. He saw by the look in her

eyes that she'd instantly arrived at the same conclusion he had. "Someone from the convention."

"Could be. I don't believe in coincidence," he said.

"But what does that have to do with me and the little present that was left at my doorstep?"

Jonathan stared into those deep golden eyes and knew she wouldn't let up until he told her everything. She was a detective, the same as he. She trusted her instincts, and it was only a matter of time until her intuition put two and two together.

"I was with the coroner during his examination," he said quietly. "Besides murdering and mutilating the victim, the killer also . . . took a portion of her liver."

Eight

London
Twenty-second August 1885

    *I should have known our happy days could not last,
but I had dared to dream that when Eddy had served his
time at Cambridge and at last matriculated, I would become his companion and guide in the larger world. Yet
the Pig Prince and MotherDear, no doubt urged on by
the old Whore Queen, have wrenched my beloved Prince
from me and are demanding he assume the royal duties
of his father, who is more interested in poking whores
across the Continent than he is in fulfilling his obliga-
tions as Prince of Wales.*

    *Eddy writes that he is filled with terror at what is
thrust upon him, but I am helpless to come to his aid.
Can they not see he is not yet ready for kingship? Do
they not understand that without me, Eddy will never
manage in their world? The insufferable ingrates! It was
I who brought him through scholarship he never grasped,
I who gave him the appearance of success. It must be I
who leads him now, or we shall both perish. The agony
of it all splits my breast and fills me with that dark and
dangerous rage I find increasingly difficult to control.*

Victoria's lunch sat untouched in front of her, but Trey
scarfed his as if he hadn't been fed in a month. "Double

sex must take a lot out of you," she remarked dryly. He
raised his head, startled.

"I can't believe you said that. You're usually such a
prude."

"Maybe it's time I got over that."

"You'll never get over it. You were born that way."

Victoria's spine stiffened, but she did not argue. He
might be right. She'd always been conservative. But she
didn't want to think of herself as a prude. And yet, she
couldn't conceive of behaving the way Trey had the night
before.

"Are you free to go?" she asked, knowing he had already
been interviewed extensively by the police, who were rou-
tinely questioning every person who had attended the symposium. Those with tight alibis were given permission,
encouraged even, to go home. The police had their hands
full and didn't need a bunch of curious armchair sleuths
hanging around to hamper their efforts. Most of the attendees, however, were eager to leave. The copycat Ripper
murder had badly shaken everyone.

Yesterday, the murders perpetrated by the killer known
as Jack the Ripper were a thing of the past, safely examined
from the distance of over one hundred years. This morning,
the murder and mutilation of a streetwalker in Whitechapel
was in their collective face.

"They say I can leave anytime," Trey replied. "Thanks
for vouching for me and the girls."

Victoria winced. It had been embarrassing to tell the
police what she'd seen when she went barging into Trey's
room, but she'd had no choice. At any rate, he and the two
young women were off the hook. His playmates had already left for Paris.

"Are you coming back to the States with me?" he asked.

"I can't. Jonathan said Scotland Yard wants me here, at
least for a while, because of that awful little present that
came my way."

Trey's face darkened. "Isn't that dangerous? Are you

sure the good detective doesn't have other motives? Seems to me he's got the hots for you."

Victoria blushed in spite of herself. "He does not. Does your mind never come out of the gutter?"

"Prude."

"Shut up."

Trey leaned toward her. "Really, Victoria, you shouldn't stay here. It's dangerous. There's a madman on the loose, and somehow he has pulled you into his nasty little game."

"Madmen are my business," she reminded him, trying to sound unconcerned, although in truth, she was totally unnerved. Jonathan had reported back to her that the liver piece had not come from a calf. It was taken from the body of the woman who was murdered the night before.

"Madmen who send you body parts? I'd be on the first plane out of here. Honestly, Victoria, I don't understand how you can deal with stuff like that so calmly. After Meghan—"

"Don't go there, Trey."

He broke off and shook his head. "You're in danger here."

"So stay with me. You can have your old position back, although I can't say you did such a hot job for me as a bodyguard."

Trey gave a bitter-sounding laugh. "Didn't look to me like you wanted me on duty once you laid eyes on the inspector."

Victoria shot him a withering look. "Didn't look to me like you wanted to *be* on duty once you spotted the Frenchies."

He shrugged. "So we both got what we wanted."

No, they didn't, she suddenly realized, but didn't want to go there, either. "So are you going to stay?"

"I can't. I haven't told you this, but I'm starting a new job this week."

Victoria blinked in surprise. Trey with a real job? Trey doing something responsible for a change? "Why, that's wonderful. Congratulations! What will you be doing?"

"It's a sales position. An old friend asked me to take the job, so I'm doing it as a favor to him . . ." He cleared his throat and continued. "Not because I need the money or anything."

Victoria grinned at this, wondering if Trey, the perceived rich young playboy, had managed to run through his trust fund. "Of course you don't need money. Still, I'm proud of you for helping your friend out. What will you be selling?"

"It's hard to explain. It's a kind of technical service. I'm not real clear on exactly what it entails, if you want to know the truth. I'm supposed to go out to the West Coast next week for training. That's why I can't stay here any longer. I want a few days between this trip and that to catch my breath. There's only so much jet lag this old bod can take."

Victoria gazed across the table at her long-time friend, awash with relief and joy at this news. Until now, Trey Delaney had lived like Peter Pan, unable or unwilling to assume any real responsibility in life. He had gone to law school at the insistence of his father, and his parents expected him to become a junior partner in the law firm headed by his father and hers. But after Meghan's death, Trey told his parents he needed some space, some time to "find himself." He dropped out of school and disappeared into the wilderness of the Washington State rain forests for nearly a year. Marilyn had been beside herself with worry, for he had not contacted his family for many months. She'd thought he was dead.

But Trey came home eventually. He was different in some ways. Quieter, more subdued. He bought a town house in Georgetown but refused to go back to school and made no attempt to find a job. He seemed content to live off his trust fund and party as hard as he could. His parents were furious, which only aggravated their already strained relationship. Within a year, articles began to show up in the society columns, linking Trey with many young women of D.C. society. That should have appeased Marilyn somewhat, for she'd always wanted him to marry well, but in-

stead, it only made things worse, because it was obvious
Trey had become a notorious playboy.

Paybacks are a bitch, Mama, she thought.

Still, the big sister in her had always wished he would
grow up and do something more substantial with his life.
Maybe that time had at last arrived.

"When's your flight?" she asked. Trey looked at his
watch.

"Five. Guess I'd better get packing." He laid a twenty-
pound note on the table for lunch and stood up. "Sure you'll
be okay?" he said, touching her hair lightly.

"I'll be fine," she assured him, hoping it was the truth.

Jonathan entered the hotel restaurant where they sat,
anxiety written all over his face. When he spotted Victoria,
that anxiety changed to annoyance. He strode briskly toward them.

Trey grunted. "Your replacement bodyguard just showed
up, and he doesn't look very happy," he said, kissing her
cheek lightly. "Good luck." He left, nodding at Jonathan as
he passed and picking up a toothpick at the cashier's desk
on his way out.

"I told you to stay in your room." Jonathan almost barked
at Victoria as he took a seat across from her, frowning
fiercely.

"Who the hell are you to tell me to stay anywhere?" she
bit back. "Don't talk to me like I was a naughty child."

He took a deep breath. "I didn't mean it that way, but
. . . Victoria, you of all people know the danger you might
be in. We're dealing with a very sick mind."

"I've run across a few of those before."

"I suppose you have. But not one, I daresay, who sent
you a chunk of human liver."

She glared at him with those golden eyes. "Jonathan, I
appreciate your concern," she replied at last, her voice less
angry, "but I can't stay locked up while you sort things out.
This is my business, in more ways than one. Let me help."

"You can't help if you're dead."

"I'm a big girl. I can take care of myself."

Jonathan's scowl deepened again. This woman was as strong-willed as a race horse, and he knew it was pointless to expect her to huddle behind her hotel room door during a murder investigation, especially one that involved her. There was only one way he could think of that he could keep an eye on her.

"Very well," he said without enthusiasm. "You can come along, but only unofficially. I must ask you to stay in the background."

"I can do that," she said, then added mischievously, "but it won't be easy."

He gave a sigh of surrender and glanced at her untouched meal. "Are you finished? You haven't eaten a bite."

She was out of the chair like a shot. "Not hungry. Let's get on with it."

Jonathan did not plan to really involve her in the investigation, and he hoped she would keep quiet and let his men do their work in the manner in which they had been trained. It was one thing to pay lip service to psychological profiling, which he admitted he had done yesterday in an effort to appease her. But it was quite another to taint his scientific approach with what he considered mumbo jumbo.

"They're interviewing in one of the conference rooms," he said, striding down the corridor on long legs, making it necessary for her to take almost two steps to his one. He did not slow his pace. If she wanted to get involved, she would just have to keep up.

Inside the room, two of his best CID men were interviewing Adele Quigley, who sat on the edge of her chair, twisting her hands. Her frightened expression softened when she saw Jonathan.

"Oh, Mr. Blake. I'm so glad to see you. Oh, this is simply awful. Terrible. I . . . I can't believe it's happened. I've told these men where I was last night. I went directly to my room after dinner, when the dancing started." She paused, looking embarrassed, and Jonathan felt sorry for her, thinking the reason she left the party was for lack of a partner.

"They're just doing their job," he assured her. "Do you have any way to prove where you were?"

She shook her head. "Only my word. Surely you can't think I had anything to do with that murder? That's preposterous"

"Yes, it is," Victoria broke in. She turned to Jonathan. "You're wasting your time and hers. She's not a suspect."

"Every conference attendee who can't prove where he or she was at the time of the murder is a suspect."

"She doesn't fit the profile, Jonathan. This is the work of a sexual killer. Nearly one hundred percent of sexual killers are men. Men with strength and stealth."

Jonathan was furious at her intrusion, but when he looked at Adele Quigley's stout build and flabby muscles, he had to admit she was an unlikely candidate. "Put her on the C list," he told his men. "And make sure you verify her contact information in the States, in case we have reason to investigate her further."

When interviewing potential suspects, Jonathan's team used an alphabetical method of sorting them out. The A list was comprised of prime suspects, those who had motive, or means, or opportunity, or all the above, and others who had been seen in the vicinity of the crime within six hours of the incident and who had no provable alibi. The motive, means, and opportunity of those on the B list was less certain. This list contained those who hadn't been seen in the vicinity in the hours surrounding the crime but who were known to frequent the area and who were also without a confirmed alibi. Also on the B list were those with spousal or family alibis only.

The C list was for those who had no known connection with the crime scene, but who for one reason or another might be involved. In this case, having attended the Sherlockian conference was enough to put every attendee on the C list for starters. The D list was for those whose alibi was airtight, confirmed by at least two nonrelated parties.

Jonathan turned to the librarian from Pittsburgh. "You may go home, Ms. Quigley," he said more gently. "If we need further information from you, we will be in touch."

She scurried from the room like a frightened rabbit let out of a trap.

"How many left?" Jonathan asked his men.

"That was the last. Except for the two we can't find."

"Can't find? Who are they?" Jonathan's hopes soared. If the killer was among the participants at the symposium, it was likely he was one of the two who had now disappeared.

"Let's see," said one of the officers, thumbing through the list. "There's a Reginald Smythe FitzSimmons, and an American, Billy Ray. FitzSimmons was not a guest at the hotel. Ray checked out early this morning."

"I knew it," Victoria uttered. Jonathan wheeled around.

"What? Do you know something about either of these guys?"

"Only what my instincts tell me."

Jonathan resisted the urge to roll his eyes when he saw how pale her face had become. "And that is . . . ?"

"First of all, it's not FitzSimmons. He's physically too large. An Orson Welles type simply can't get the business done quickly and cleanly enough. But Billy Ray—"

"He's the chap who cornered you last night in the corridor, isn't he?" Jonathan asked, suddenly thinking it very likely he could be their man. He agreed with Victoria that FitzSimmons's body type precluded the hard physical work of such a murder. But Billy Ray was a muscle man. He had the physique to have performed the murder. He'd frightened Victoria last night, and he could imagine him playing the devilish prank of sending her the liver.

"Yes," she answered his question. "He's aggressive, and . . . I don't know, there's just something about him that gives me the creeps."

In spite of his suspicions about the man, Jonathan had not found Billy Ray to be "creepy." What was "creepy" but an irrational emotional reaction? There was no room for that kind of conjecture in his investigation. "That doesn't make him a killer, Victoria," he said, playing devil's advocate.

She whirled on him. "You listen to me, Mr. Blake. I will not suffer your condescension against a tool that has been invaluable in solving more than a dozen murders in the United States—my instincts. You may not believe in psychological profiling and intuitive approaches to crime detection, but they work, and I have the track record to prove it. So get over it and listen. This man could very well be your killer. He does fit the general profile. He's young. Most sexual killers are in their twenties. He told me he follows all the big murder cases, which means he's obsessed with murder."

Jonathan was shocked by her outburst, but he had no intention of letting her temper throw him off. "That still doesn't make him a killer," he protested.

"No, it does not. But it makes him more likely to try his hand at it than someone who never thinks about murder."

"Okay, okay." Seeing the fire in her eyes, Jonathan decided he'd better back off and listen to what she had to say, if for no other reason than to calm her down.

"I would put money on it that he's a loner, a bully, that he frequents porn sites on the Internet and gets his jollies from cutting the tails off cats."

"That's the profile of a sexual killer?" Jonathan tried not to sound sarcastic.

"Each case is different, of course," Victoria said, pacing to the window and back. "But in almost every instance, the sexual killer is a young male with low self-esteem, usually the victim of some kind of abuse in a broken or dysfunctional home who blames the rest of the world for his unhappiness. Usually we find out that he has been dominated or controlled by someone during childhood, and believes himself to be a victim. Sometimes he will act out his anger by starting fires, or torturing animals or small children. Often he is attracted to pornography, although he hates women in real life."

"And you think this is an accurate profile of Billy Ray? What if he just wanted to copy the Ripper for notoriety?"

Victoria came up short, her face livid. "You know it can't be a totally accurate profile of Billy Ray. I don't have anything to go on other than generalities. But he's a suspect, and I intend to try to get enough information on him to see what he's like. And when I do, I bet you'll see he fits many of the above criteria. And yes," she added, "he could have done it for the notoriety. To be somebody important. That's another aspect of this type of personality."

"And he could not have done it at all," Jonathan pressed. "It could be that he's just a fellow who gives you the creeps."

"Then where is he?"

Victoria hadn't been so pissed off since the day Lieutenant Grizzell had informed her family that the McLean police had come to a dead end in their investigation of her sister's murder. They claimed to have followed up every lead, examined every clue, and had come up with nothing. It was as if the killer had vanished in thin air, they said, as if that explained their failure.

Victoria knew better. She'd stayed in close contact with the police during the investigation, and she'd overheard rumors that Grizzell had "misplaced" certain materials vital to the case, to wit, the crime scene photos and virtually all the original notes made by the investigating team. He'd tried to re-create what he could, but if it ever became known in court that the records on the case were pieced together from memory, they wouldn't be worth the paper they were printed on. In Victoria's opinion, the idiot was an inept, unprofessional cop who called off the investigation to cover his butt.

Although the case had never officially been closed, at Grizzell's recommendation neither the local police nor the FBI had pursued it further. That alone was appalling enough, but worse had been her parents' reaction to the decision. Her father, Lloyd Hamilton Thomas, was a powerful D.C. attorney and could have pulled all kinds of strings to keep the investigation alive, she believed. But her mother, Barbara Wentworth Thomas, had suffered terribly, not only from the death of her younger daughter, but also from the sensational press that followed the murder. Although Barbara was a pillar of society, she was also an extremely private person. Victoria guessed that in one respect, she was like her mother—both valued their privacy. Barbara had borne her grief in dignity within the intimate circle of their wealthy, long-time friends, but she could not bear the exposure of the media. When the police gave up, so did she.

Fuming, Victoria had gone to her father, who had surprised her by standing by his wife's wishes in the matter. "Victoria," he'd said, and she could almost hear his patronizing tone of voice, "I've spoken at length with the chief of police, and with my contacts in the FBI. They are in agreement that unless some new evidence is uncovered, this killer may never be caught. I've been an attorney for nearly thirty years. I've seen a lot of things go down. Some good. Some bad. I hate this as much as you do, but the fact is, some people get away with murder."

Some people get away with murder.

Over her dead body.

That day, Victoria had moved out of her parent's mansion and into a small apartment, and like Trey had done before her, dumped her plans for a career in law. She had another destination in mind.

Her first stop was a Ph.D. in criminal psychology, financed by her trust fund. After graduating, she applied to the FBI Academy, to her mother's complete and utter horror. It simply wasn't done by a well-bred young lady like herself.

She didn't give a flip about her breeding at that point. She wanted a resolution to Meghan's death, and if the police and the FBI couldn't or wouldn't pursue the issue, then she would do it on her own, as soon as she learned how.

Fascinated by the workings of the criminal mind, Victoria proved to be a talented and creative investigator. After three years in the field, she applied for and was accepted for special training as a profiler. After two more years under the mentorship of Mike Mosier in the NCAVC, she became a full-fledged member of the team that fought crime using psychology, instinct, and intuition rather than relying solely on facts and figures.

And she'd been damned good at it, so good that now at thirty-three, she was one of the most respected profilers in the business.

But all that had not brought her one step closer to finding her sister's killer. She had managed to access the agency's files on the case and had examined every aspect of it. And she, like the rest, had arrived at a dead end.

Even so, intuitively she knew they had all missed something. Killers didn't just vanish into thin air. One day, she would have her answers. She would never give up until she learned the truth. And in the meantime, she would do everything in her power to stop other madmen from indulging their bloodlust.

Victoria turned to Jonathan's men. "Have you checked this morning's flights to the States? Billy Ray may have hopped a plane. But if he didn't, and if he's the killer, I think we can expect more of what we got last night."

"We haven't checked the airports yet," one investigator replied, looking distressed. He shifted his glance to Jonathan. "Would you like us to do that, sir?"

Jonathan glared at Victoria, and she knew he resented her usurping his authority. "We will conduct this search in an orderly manner," he told them all, his voice dangerously calm. "You said we have spoken to everyone who was at the Sherlockian symposium?"

"Everyone but these two," his man confirmed.

"What does the A list look like?"

"The A list includes a fair number of symposium attendees, the group that went to the Jack the Ripper Pub last night," he said, turning to a list made on a legal pad. "It originally included FitzSimmons, Roger Hammersmith, Janeece Fairchild, Lord and Lady Chastain, James Winston Delaney the Third, Chantal Duprès, Nicole St. Germain, and . . ."—he looked up apologetically—"yourselves."

"What about Billy Ray? I could have sworn I saw him outside the pub as we were entering the taxi."

"Could be. But nobody we've interviewed has mentioned seeing him there. Shall I add his name to the list?"

"Absolutely," Victoria interjected. "Jonathan saw him in the area, but he probably didn't go inside."

"Who has been eliminated from that list?" Jonathan wanted to know.

"Delaney and the French women, for starters," he said, and Victoria thought she caught a glimpse of a grin straining from behind his straight face.

"I know about them," Jonathan said brusquely, obviously hiding his own embarrassment. "Who else?"

"Lord and Lady Chastain vouched for one another, but that only slipped them to the B list. Ms. Fairchild placed a phone call from her room at half past eleven, which we checked out with the person she called. It was her mother, but we put her on the C list anyway."

Victoria laughed. "It wasn't Janeece. It wasn't any of the women who were here. I guarantee it."

"Why do you say that?" Jonathan wanted to know.

"Because psychotic women don't kill like this. Men take their rage out against others, whereas women turn it inside. They become self-destructive. They're likely to be alcoholic, drug addicts, or suicidal. That's why I'm certain it wasn't a woman."

"It wasn't Roger Hammersmith, either," Jonathan said, looking at the yellow pad. Then he added dryly, "He's over forty, overweight, and not alienated enough to fit the profile."

Victoria gritted her teeth at his patronizing tone. "Good call, Inspector. What list does he go on?"

"C-list him," Jonathan instructed. "And ourselves, as well. Technically, neither of us has a provable alibi."

"Inspector . . ." one of the men groaned.

"Do it. We have a protocol for a reason." Then he turned and began to pace. "Obviously the killer did return to the hotel, even if he wasn't a guest. He came back to deliver his little present to Ms. Thomas's door. That happened sometime before nine o'clock this morning, since the bell-hop who brought my note to Victoria around nine said he noticed the box sitting in the hallway at that time. I suspect it was dropped off much earlier, probably before dawn. Not many people are stirring that early in the morning, so there would be less chance of being seen. But surely somebody, the night clerk or a housekeeper maybe, might have noticed a man carrying a wrapped gift at that odd hour. Ask around and see if you can learn anything." He gave his men descriptions of both FitzSimmons and Ray, turned to go, then paused.

"Dust Billy Ray's rooms for prints. And . . ." he added with an upward twist of his lips, "check this morning's flights out of both Heathrow and Gatwick. Let's see if Mr. Ray has flown the coop."

Nine

London
Sixteenth August 1886

Tonight I have reclaimed my beloved Prince after nearly a full year of wretched separation. I have been frantic to find some means of reestablishing the power over him I once enjoyed, but it has been difficult, as I am no longer welcome at Windsor.

My scheme took months to devise, months I spent in mortal pain as my desire for the Prince went unrequited. I took to the hunt to ease the pain, and during one particularly savage foray, I recalled Eddy's fascination with blood. It was then a plan began to form in my mind that I was certain would bring him back to me.

I practiced for months before contacting Eddy. I wanted it to be the perfect hunt. I prowled the lanes and alleys of what was to become our new hunting grounds, the slums of Whitechapel, to learn the lay of the land, the pattern of the constables, and the ways of the whores. At last I felt ready to proceed. I arranged for a message to be delivered to him, asking for a tryst. My heart pounded as I waited at the appointed site, and the pain in my loins became almost unbearable. He had withheld himself from me for almost a year. Would he come?

I was rewarded for both my boldness and my patience. He arrived exactly at the hour I had requested, and as I *joined him in his carriage, he wept with joy to see me. He swore he had been held a virtual prisoner at court and was only able to meet me this evening through an accidental set of circumstances. I scolded him for his weakness and asked if he did not love me anymore. He vowed his love for me and begged forgiveness, saying he would do anything to prove his devotion. I told him I wanted to go for a hunt and made him promise he would go with me and ask no questions.*

His driver left us at the nearest Underground station, and we took the train for Whitechapel. Eddy was clearly frightened at the prospect of entering such a cesspool and could not understand how it was to be our hunting grounds. I wanted him to be afraid, for only then would he be in my power. He must learn to depend upon me once again and not succumb to the demands of those who do not love him as I do.

We reached the stinking warren and slid into the deep shadows that hide the filth and disease of the place, and waited. Eddy still did not comprehend the nature of our hunt, and his innocence filled me with eager anticipation. I had planned the deed, practiced it in theory, but had never consummated it. Tonight, it would be completed. Tonight, a whore would die.

We did not have to wait long. A ragged woman came out of the Ten Bells across the street, wobbling drunkenly into the dark lane, singing pathetically. "That's our prey," I whispered to Eddy and was rewarded by a look of shock in his eyes. I slipped my dagger from its sheath inside the head of my cane. "Watch carefully," I instructed him. The whore led me to a darkened courtyard, where she expected me to participate in the lewd business that was her trade. Instead, I raised my knife and brought it down swiftly, driving it into her neck. The fear in her eyes in that instant when she realized what was happening hardened my passion, and when her blood spurted from the gash in her neck, my body shuddered in

*ecstacy. She crumpled to the ground, another heap of
garbage amongst the filth.*

*With shaking hands, I wiped my dagger on her skirts
and turned to see if Eddy had indeed followed to watch.
He stood not ten yards from me, his eyes shining in fascination as he stared at the corpse, and I knew I had won
him to me forever.*

He groomed his nails and reflected on the events of the
weekend. It could not have been more perfect. A stroke of
luck? He did not think so. Rather the summons of destiny.
He had known the call would come but had not expected
that it would be accompanied by such a perfect set of circumstances.

Nor had he expected to feel such gratification in the
deed. It returned his power. A thrill shuddered through him.
He would never lose his power again. Never give it up to
any woman. This was but the beginning. The whore was
nothing but a token, a pawn in a greater stratagem than
even the master ever dreamed. He laid the nail file aside
and lit an old pipe, wishing the smoke weren't so rough-
edged. But the master had smoked this very pipe, and the
time had come to employ everything of which his legacy
was comprised.

The game board was already forming in his mind. He
had studied the master's words and works carefully, and
now at last he understood the shape and form of his destiny,
the path of his power. He looked at the map that lay open
before him and slowly, with great care, drew a symbol over
the face of it and considered his next move.

Jonathan obtained Billy Ray's address in the States from
the hotel computer, but since FitzSimmons had not been
registered at the hotel, there was no address on file. After
checking the telephone directory and coming up with no
listing, he turned to Victoria. "Surely he had to give his
address when he registered for the conference."

"Janeece will have it," Victoria said.

Using Jonathan's police credentials, they obtained the number of her room from the front desk. Janeece Fairchild answered their knock with a strained look on her face. "You just caught me in time," she said, ushering them into her room. "Your men said we should all just go home, and I must tell you, I think that's a capital idea." Her voice quavered. Behind her, clothes and symposium materials were strewn on the bed, and a suitcase stood open and ready to receive them. "This is just a dreadful business. It will be the ruin of our Sherlockian society, I fear."

From her records, Jonathan and Victoria gleaned FitzSimmons's address, thanked their erstwhile hostess and left.

"Where to now?" Victoria asked.

"FitzSimmons said that Jack the Ripper was alive and well and living in Kent." He held out the paper with the address on it. "He gave an address in Kent. I suppose that's as good a place to start as any."

"You seriously think FitzSimmons is our Ripper copycat?"

"It seems unlikely, for the reasons you gave earlier, but . . ." He shrugged.

Jonathan waited outside Victoria's room while she changed into more comfortable clothing and shoes. He wished she weren't so stubborn and would stay sequestered in her room until they caught the killer. He didn't really want to take her on this quest. It could be dangerous. But he had to remind himself, this woman had graduated from the FBI Academy. As feminine as was the veneer, underneath she was hard as nails. And he expected she'd seen as much violence as he had, maybe more. From what he could discern, crime in the U.S. seemed more prevalent and more ruthless than in the U.K. Still, he was uneasy about taking a woman on what might turn out to be a dangerous mission.

She came out dressed in crisply pressed jeans and an oversized green chenille sweater. On her feet she wore sneakers and thick socks. "I know this isn't very professional, but as you said, I'm not officially on the job. Is this okay? I'm about to freeze in this damp weather."

This was a different Victoria than either the primly suited professional or the alluringly gowned party-goer of yesterday. And in a way, more appealing than both. More real. More approachable.

Damn.

Jonathan huffed out a breath. "Fine. You look fine. Do you have a raincoat? The forecast is rather dismal, I'm afraid."

The drive to Kent was uneventful if soggy. Seated next to him in the small car, Victoria gazed out the window at the passing scenery.

"Everything's so green," she observed. "I expected to see fall colors."

"You'd see that in the north. Here, it's more maritime. Cool and wet, but not all that cold." Jonathan glanced across at her and was annoyed by the distinctly sexual sensation that came over him. He'd thought he had rid himself of those feelings earlier when she'd lashed out at him like a mad hornet. Now the sting was gone, and the disturbing feelings were back.

"Are you from around here?" she asked.

"No," he replied, but not offering further information. He didn't particularly want to go into his background. Not that he was ashamed of it, but he knew she was from a different social stratum than he was. A much loftier social stratum. She hadn't told him specifics about her background, but her style and demeanor spoke volumes. She was one class act.

"Where, then?"

Jonathan kept his eye on the road, wishing she'd give it up. But she was an investigator. If she wanted this information, she'd get it sooner or later. "Manchester," he said at last. "My father was a steel worker, until times got bad."

They rode for a while with only the sound of the wipers breaking the silence between them.

"How did you get into law enforcement?" she asked.

"I broke the law."

She laughed. "That sounds like a story: Tell me."

Her earlier steely attitude had disappeared, but Jonathan didn't know whether to be glad about that or not. She was entirely too likeable as she was at the moment. He'd never spoken of his past with anyone in his present, and he wasn't sure he wanted to now. But as he'd discovered yesterday, it seemed easy to tell her difficult things.

"When I was a teenager, I got caught up in a gang. We didn't really break the law, I guess, but we pulled some pranks and got involved in some petty vandalism. The leader of the gang wasn't from our neighborhood. Ernie was the son of a wealthy merchant family on the other side of town, but he got a thrill out of slumming."

He paused, his face warm, wondering what she must be thinking. She didn't speak, so he went on. "One day Ernie dared us to pull off a burglary. That's when I bailed. I don't think it was because I was such a good guy. I was just scared of getting caught. But Ernie and my friends did it without me. They robbed a store and were caught red-handed. The police sent my friends, the poor kids, to jail, but Ernie, the rich kid, went free with little more than a reprimand. It was a lesson in reality, I suppose, but at the time, I was outraged. I decided right then I would join the police and rectify the injustices of the world."

"And have you?"

Jonathan laughed without humor. "You know better than that. The Yard is pretty clean, but there is always going to be corruption. As they say, money doesn't talk, it screams, and as long as there are people like Ernie's father willing to use their money and influence to cover up their sons' crimes, there will be payoffs."

Victoria gazed out the window again and after a while let out a long sigh. "I guess you're right," she said. "Even my father once told me that some people get away with murder."

* * *

The address given by Reginald Smythe FitzSimmons turned out to be an abandoned warehouse. "There's got to be some mistake," Victoria said, diving back into the relative warmth of the car. As they explored the area, looking for some sign of the old man's habitat, they had splashed through puddles and unsuccessfully fought off the rain with lightweight coats and only one umbrella between them, until now they were both thoroughly cold and wet.

"He's a liar," Jonathan said simply, starting the car and turning the heat up. "A liar, and maybe a murderer."

"I wouldn't bet on it."

"I wouldn't discount it, either. Why would he register a phony address if he didn't have something to hide?"

Victoria had no answer. She did not think FitzSimmons was a likely murderer, but she had to admit, his behavior had reached beyond eccentric. She recalled his claim, made in front of a roomful of witnesses yesterday, that Jack the Ripper was alive. Had he been referring to himself? Had it been a plea for someone to stop him?

"Where to now?" she asked Jonathan.

"Someplace we can get a cup of tea and warm up before heading back."

"Dear me, how very British," she teased.

He turned to her with a grin. "Don't knock it. It's an institution that's held this country together for centuries."

That grin. Dear God, she'd forgotten its power over her. She hadn't seen that grin since early last evening, before she fell to pieces in his arms. Jonathan hadn't had much to grin about since the murder, she supposed. It was just as well, since that look seemed to render her witless. "Tea sounds good," she managed, tearing her gaze from his handsome face. Otherwise, she feared she might lean across the seat and kiss it.

They found a small tearoom on a side street with a parking space nearby and made a dash for its cozy warmth. Inside, the smells were incredible, and Victoria remembered she hadn't touched her lunch. Jonathan suggested she try the "cream tea," and she thought she might die of pleasure when the freshly baked scones, heaped high with butter and fresh whipped cream, passed her lips.

"Highly civilized tradition," she murmured, licking her fingers in an unladylike manner. "No wonder you Brits perpetuate it." She looked up and found Jonathan staring at her in a most unsettling manner. "What?"

"Don't do that."

"Don't do what?"

"Lick your fingers like that."

"Am I embarrassing you with my bad manners?

He hesitated, then said, "No, you're turning me on."

Victoria blinked, not certain she had heard him right. Then her cheeks began to burn, and another fire kindled somewhere lower in her anatomy. "I beg your pardon?"

Jonathan had the good grace to look abashed. "I . . . I'm sorry. I don't know where that came from. Please forgive me."

Victoria tried to be shocked. Offended. Insulted. But she found his honesty disarming. In just a few words, he'd acknowledged the attraction that had played between them during most of the course of yesterday evening. It had gone into temporary remission during their heated exchange concerning the murder investigation earlier in the day, but she'd felt it growing again in the close confinement of the car on their trip to Kent.

"Is that a bad thing, that I'm turning you on?" she replied, wondering where her bold words were coming from.

Jonathan lowered his hand to lightly brush her fingers, which had remained in midair, and Victoria fairly sizzled.

"Only if you think so," he said, his gaze penetrating hers.

Her heart was pounding furiously. What in blazes was she doing? She didn't know how to play these games. But she sure as hell knew where they would lead.

Was that a bad thing?

She moved her hand away, but not in rejection. Instead, she dipped her forefinger into the whipped cream again and touched it to his lips.

The feel of his tongue against her finger was almost more than she could bear. He licked slowly, until he had removed most of the cream, then sucked gently on her finger. Victoria's body raged with desire. "Now we're even," she said breathlessly. She saw him swallow hard.

"We'd better get back to London," he said, his voice now husky.

"Don't they rent rooms in Kent?"

Victoria had never done anything so outrageous in her entire life. Or wanted it more.

"I'm on an assignment," he reminded her as he kissed her fingertips.

Victoria thought she might melt right there on the chair. "It's late," she murmured, "and besides, you've done all you can do for the time being."

He gave her the grin that was her undoing. "You have a point. Let's go."

Twenty minutes later, they had secured a room, locked the door, and closed the world behind them. Victoria was in his arms like lightning and was scorched by his kisses. Hunger stirred in her belly. She had never known such hunger, and it was not for food.

"Jonathan . . ." She breathed his name as he slipped the sweater over her head. Together they fell across the bed, not bothering to turn down the bedclothes. Fingers wrestled furiously with buttons and hooks and zippers until at last they were free. There was no time, or need, for foreplay. Jonathan was as hot for her as she was for him. She opened to him and cried out as he thrust inside her.

"Oh, God, oh, yes," she moaned, arching into him, wanting more. He gave her more, and more, and more until she thought she could stand it no longer. Her world began to collapse in on itself, and she was flooded with a sensation so exquisite it brought tears to her eyes. She could feel the pulse of Jonathan's release even as her body wound down in a rhythm of its own.

Spent, they lay quietly, breathing heavily, sweating in

the cool room. And Victoria began to come back to her
senses. What had she done?

She tried to feel mortified, but didn't. Worked at being
ashamed, but wasn't. Instead a bubble of laughter rose in
her throat.

"What is it?" Jonathan asked, his lips moving against
her ear.

"This morning," she said between short gasps for air, "I
told Trey it was time I got over—"

"Over what?"

"Being a prude."

Jonathan rose up on one elbow and stroked her breast.
"Prude," he said, "is not a word I would ever use to describe you."

Jonathan could not believe what had just happened. Yesterday he hadn't even known Victoria Thomas. Today,
they'd just coupled like two rabbits in heat.

And he'd thought she was wound too tight for him.

He'd definitely read her wrong. Victoria Thomas was as
natural a lover as any woman could be.

Lover.

He'd never had a lover. Not really. A few short-term
relationships, but none in which he'd considered his partner
a lover. Why had he used that term with Victoria?

The notion scared him.

Gazing down on her body that was stretched luxuriously
beside him, he thought again she was the most beautiful
woman he'd ever seen. Her skin was perfect, flawless. In
their moment of passion, her hair had tumbled loose from
its clip and lay in rich curls around her head. Her nipples
stood erect in rosy brown invitation, and he accepted. He
heard her intake of breath at his touch, and felt himself
growing hard again.

This time, their lovemaking was slow, sensuous, and
tender. They'd turned down the covers and afterward snug-
gled together as they listened to the patter of rain on the
windowpane.

"This is crazy," Victoria murmured, kissing his neck.

"Insane," he agreed.

And it was. But there didn't seem to be a damned thing either of them could do about it.

"We should go back to London," she said.

"Yes," he agreed.

"Tonight," she said.

"Yes," he agreed.

"Now," she said.

"No."

And they didn't.

Early the next morning, Jonathan at last headed the non-descript gray coupe toward London. Victoria sat in silence beside him. He guessed she was in the same state of shock as he was. Neither had dreamt when they first met just where they would end up, and by the light of day, it was awkward and unsettling.

Halfway to London, his cellular phone rang. He lifted it from its cradle in the car.

"Blake here."

"Where the hell are you?" a familiar voice shouted, and Jonathan winced. It was his supervisor, Richard Sandringham.

"I . . . ah . . . drove down to Kent yesterday to check out that lead. It took longer than I expected, so I decided to stay overnight." It wasn't exactly a lie, but he felt a little guilty just the same. "Turned out to be a phony address. We might be on to the killer, though, if we can just find him."

"How long will it take you to get here?"

Jonathan heard the anxiety in his voice. "About another hour. Why? What's up?"

"We just received a letter, couriered over from the *Times*. This doesn't look good, Blake."

"Letter? What kind of letter? From whom?"

"It was sent to the newspaper, but they shot it over to us immediately. Let me read it to you."

As the words reached his ear, Jonathan was filled with trepidation.

"Dear Boss," it read. "You thought I was through, didn't you. Ha. Ha. I will never finish my work. I will kill into infinity. Yours truly, Jack the Ripper."

Ten

He opened the old volume with the tenderness of a mother touching her newborn babe. He caressed the ancient pages, turning them one by one, as he had done so many times over the years since he'd discovered the book hidden away for more than a century among a collection of ancestral memorabilia. The words written here, and the story they told, spoke to him as if the author were whispering in his ear. He felt the pain behind the tale and understood the frustration of the man of yesterday whose blood flowed in his own veins today. The author of these words had, like him, suffered at the hands of women, had lost his power. But he had discovered a way to regain it, and he'd passed along his secret to his descendant.

How strong were the ties of bloodline. How powerful the forces of heritage. Tomorrow, he would take up where his ancestor had left off, and in following his footsteps, would hold power unlike he had ever known.

He had much work to do, but tonight, he wished only to worship at the shrine of the master. He fondled the ring of braided hair he had found between the pages of this book. It had been a gift to his ancestor from someone who loved him very much. His throat tightened, and he wondered . . what would it be like to be loved?

*   *   *

In Inspector Sandringham's office, Jonathan and Victoria examined the letter that had been sent over from the London *Times* before turning it over to the forensic lab.

"This is the same kind of stationery that he wrote the note on that came with the gift of the liver," Victoria pointed out. "Hotel stationery. I guess this sort of seals it that the killer was at the conference."

Jonathan agreed. "Where else would he come by it? But FitzSimmons was not an official guest at the hotel."

"He could have stolen it off a housekeeping cart," she said.

"Or we could be wrong about both him and Billy Ray. Maybe the killer is someone who works there."

"That's possible. He could have been the waiter who served our steak and kidney pie," she remarked dryly. "From the way the note is worded, I'd say the subject is delusional and might actually believe himself to be Jack the Ripper. Maybe he heard about the symposium and signed on at the hotel as a busboy or other menial laborer just to see what was going on, and the events triggered his urge to kill."

Jonathan made a note to see if any newly hired employee had been on duty during the event. "He's a bold one, at any rate."

"Just like the real Ripper," Victoria remarked. "Going for notoriety."

"In which case," Jonathan added slowly, "he's likely to copy the Ripper's other actions."

"To the letter," she agreed. "How soon did the original Jack strike after his first murder?"

"One week."

"That soon?" She laid her hand on his arm and looked up, her golden eyes clouded with dismay. It wasn't just professional concern he saw there, but rather something much deeper. "We have to stop him, Jonathan. I know you don't like the media, but couldn't we put out police drawings of the two suspects?"

Jonathan hedged. "I don't want to do that just yet. For

one thing, as we just said, it might be that neither of them is our man. I want to check out the possibility that it was a hotel employee. But even if that doesn't pan out, it's premature to post drawings of FitzSimmons and Ray. Only one of them can be the killer. The other would probably take offense at seeing his face on a wanted notice."

"Tough," she retorted. "So he raises a little hell. At least we'll know where he is and by coming forward, he'll clear himself."

"This isn't the States, Victoria," Jonathan said patiently, irritated with her torpedoes-be-damned attitude. "We have our protocols, and one of them is not to invite litigation." He could see she was not happy, but then, this was not her case. Damn it all, he wished he didn't have feelings for her. It complicated an already difficult investigation. If he trusted she would stay safely out of things in her room at the hotel, he would not have brought her in on it. But he knew better than that.

"So, what do you suggest?" she asked bitterly. "Shall we just wait around and see who gets the next knife job?"

Jonathan clenched his fists but held his tongue. "Come on. We have work to do."

By the light of day, the Jack the Ripper Pub looked like any other local workingman's drinking establishment on a busy street corner in London. The only thing sinister about it was its name. And the fact that it was just two blocks from where the copycat Ripper murder had taken place on Saturday night.

Jonathan put his hand at Victoria's waist and opened the door for her, thinking about the dramatic events that had taken place since their first visit here. A woman had been brutally murdered nearby. A grim mystery was afoot. And he'd had a one-night stand with Victoria Thomas.

A one-night stand. He didn't want to think of it in those terms. It hadn't seemed like that at the time, and it sounded so . . . coarse. But after their rather nasty little exchange earlier, he was uncertain where they stood, and feared their attraction had been but a temporary aberration.

Inside the pub, a few patrons lunched on typical tavern fare, and the publican busied himself restocking his shelves with clean glassware. Jonathan recognized him as the same man who had been on duty the night of the murder and approached him for questioning.

"Oh, I know FitzSimmons," he said in answer to Jonathan's query. " 'E's 'armless enough. Th' old bloke comes in from time to time. Kind of 'ung up on th' Jack the Ripper murders. Knows a lot about them, seems to me. What is 'e, some kind of professor?"

"We don't know what he is," Jonathan replied. "We only met him on Saturday. He's disappeared, and since he was last seen here on Saturday night, we wondered if you can remember if he said anything that might help us find him."

" 'E was in rare form that night, 'e was," the man said. "Regaled th' house with Ripper stories. Th' others who came in with 'im left after a bit, but 'e stayed late. 'E was pretty high by the time he decided to leave, so I called 'im a taxi."

"What time was that?" Jonathan asked.

"A little before eleven."

"He didn't return to the hotel," Victoria said. "Do you know where the taxi might have taken him?"

"I didn't escort 'im t' th' car, m'am. 'E was tipsy, but 'e could still walk. I don't know what address 'e gave th' driver."

Jonathan thanked the man and got the name of the taxi service. Back in his own car, he dialed the number on his cell phone, and in moments had his answer. He replaced the phone in its holder and turned to Victoria.

"The driver's record shows that he only took Fitz-Simmons two blocks before he demanded to be let off. Victoria, it was within steps of where the murder took place and around the time the coroner thinks that poor woman was killed."

"I can't believe it," Victoria cried. "I just can't believe Reginald FitzSimmons is our man. Not only does he not fit the profile, he was drunk!"

"You kind of like the old boy, don't you?" Jonathan said, touching her cheek lightly. He shouldn't have done it, but he somehow couldn't help it. He didn't like the strained atmosphere that had stretched between them since they'd left the Yard.

Victoria jumped as if she'd been burned. "Don't do that."

"Why? Are you mad at me?"

"No."

"Prove it," he said, laying his hand on her shoulder.

"Jonathan," she groaned, but turned toward him. "Don't start this again. Not here. Not now."

Relief flooded through him. The hungry look on her face told him she wanted him as badly as he wanted her. Maybe it hadn't been a one-night stand after all.

"Oh, be that way," he said, removing his hand and giving her a grin. "But I'm disappointed. I thought we might stop by the hotel for a nooner."

"Pervert."

"Prude."

"I am not!"

Jonathan wanted nothing more than to take her in his arms and remind himself once again how very unprudish she was, but he restrained himself. It was enough to know there was still promise in the air.

"I have to go in to the Yard for a while," he said.

"I want to go back to the hotel."

He leered at her. "Change your mind?"

"Quit that. No, I'm a little tired, and I'd like to take a bath and change clothes."

It wasn't an unreasonable request. "Will you do as I say and lock yourself in your room until I'm free again?"

She gave him a pained look. "I'm supposed to be on vacation," she reminded him. "Maybe I'd like to go see the queen or something later this afternoon."

"Then maybe I'd better assign a man to you. Or better yet . . ." He paused, eyeing her lecherously. "I could take you into protective custody. We could find a safe house for you, where I could ravish your body anytime I wanted."

"You really are a pervert," she shot back, but then gave him a wicked smile. "I like that in a man."

At last Victoria agreed to his terms. Not because she was afraid that Jack the Ripper was going to come after her, she assured him, but because after she refreshed herself, she had some work she wanted to do.

"What work? I thought you just said you were on vacation."

She sighed and gave him a rueful smile. "It's just the way I am. My work is my life. Better get used to it if you want to hang around me."

It sounded almost like an invitation, and Jonathan decided he would give it a try. "What are you going to do?"

"Your guys believe Billy Ray is still in England, because no one by that name has taken any flights out of here since the murder. But I have a hunch—"

"Here we go again."

"Hush. I think it's possible he might have used an alias, or skipped through the Channel tunnel to France and left from there. Have your guys considered those possibilities? I think he could have gone back to the States. I want to call Mosier and sic him onto Ray. I just have a feeling he's our bird."

Jonathan didn't take offense at her stubborn persistence. Or her intuition. He was beginning to learn they were just part of her "ways." Besides, he had to admit, she might be right.

He didn't let her off in front of the hotel but insisted on walking her to her room, and he waited until he heard the door lock slide into place before leaving again. He wished she would move to another hotel, but as Victoria pointed out, if the killer was stalking her, it wouldn't matter where she stayed.

In his office, Jonathan found a pile of message slips on his desk. It would take him an entire day to return all those calls, he thought glumly. He hated returning phone calls. Thumbing through the notes quickly, he paused when he came to one from Roger Hammersmith. Curious, he picked up the phone.

"Roger, Jonathan Blake here. What's up?"

"I have a package for you I think you might find very interesting."

"A package? What's in it?"

"I don't know."

Jonathan frowned. How could Roger think it would interest him if he didn't know what was in it? "Well, open it."

"I can't. I promised not to."

"Who sent it?"

"Can't tell you. Trust me on this one, old boy. You won't be sorry, I'll wager."

"I'll drop by the bookstore this evening. How late will you be open?"

"Sevenish. I'm closing early tonight. I have an . . . uh . . . appointment."

By the way Roger said it, Jonathan suspected he had a hot date. Good for him. He'd been a widower far too long. Unlike Jonathan, Roger needed a woman to look after him. He'd been getting a little seedy of late, Jonathan thought.

"Very well. See you before seven."

Jonathan hung up the phone and considered what it would be like to have a woman in his life on a permanent basis. He'd always harbored a repugnant stereotype of married life. Husband and wife stuck together by a long-ago vow, hating each other, bored out of their minds. It was a picture of his parents that he'd carried with him all his life. They were gone now, and he hoped they'd found happiness in the afterlife, because they'd been pretty miserable in this one.

Somehow, Victoria Thomas didn't fit the image of his mother, however. He simply could not imagine her as a sullen housewife. He couldn't imagine her as a housewife at all. A thought occurred to him, and he brightened. Maybe she didn't go for the marriage thing, either. Nobody said a lover had to become a wife.

Then another thought cast a dark shadow. Nobody said a lover was permanent, either. Victoria lived thousands of miles away. When she left England, she would leave him.

Jonathan wadded the rest of the messages in his fist and threw them onto the desk. He ran his fingers through his hair.

Christ, this was all he needed.

Victoria waited a few minutes, then opened the door and peeked into the hallway, half expecting to find Jonathan Blake lurking there to see if she would behave and stay in her room. A part of her hoped he would be, but it was better that he had gone on his way. Otherwise, she suspected she might weaken and go for that nooner.

Going back into her room, Victoria threw the dead bolt. As annoying as Jonathan could be where his work was concerned, she could not deny her feelings for him. And she had no doubt those feelings were reciprocated. It was disturbing. She was unaccustomed to anyone caring quite so much about what she did. In one respect, she found it stifling, but on the other hand, it was kind of touching to have a man so concerned about her welfare.

And what a man. She glanced at the bed, thinking what might have happened there if he had stayed. God, what a night they'd spent together in Kent. Victoria tingled all over just thinking about it. What was with her? She'd become like a sex maniac in Jonathan's arms. She simply couldn't get enough of him. No wonder she was so exhausted today. Yawning, she wondered when Scotland Yard would give her permission to return to the States. If she and Jonathan kept this up, she would die of sleep deprivation.

Noticing the message light was blinking on the telephone, Victoria dialed the concierge, who informed her a note had been left for her. They would send it right up.

So reminiscent was it of Saturday's scenario that Victoria checked the floor in the hallway when the bellboy brought the envelope, just in case another goody had been left there for her. To her relief, there was nothing.

The envelope was large and square. It had not come in the mail, but rather had been hand-delivered to the hotel. The concierge had found it on his desk and did not know who had put it there. She tore it open. Inside were two pieces of paper. One appeared to be from a cheap tablet of lined paper. The other looked formal, official, and old.

"What on earth?" Her hands trembled as she took them to the small desk and flicked on the light.

"Things are not always as they seem," read the words neatly printed on the lined paper. "You are in grave danger. Beware."

Victoria's skin grew clammy, and the hair stood up on her arms. She glanced at the door to make sure she had indeed locked it. Maybe Jonathan's overprotectiveness wasn't so ridiculous after all.

She looked at the second note. "Sir, Our worst fears appear to be sustained. This must not proceed. Take action immediately as discussed." It was signed simply, "V.R."

Feeling slightly nauseous, Victoria slumped into a chair and put her hand to her mouth. Her other hand shook slightly as she held the warning note and reread it. Had the murderer sent it? Victoria knew that some killers literally cried out to be caught, and it wasn't unheard of for an intended victim to receive a warning in advance of the attack.

She did not know what to make of the second letter at all.

Victoria leaned back and closed her eyes, trying to remain objective. There was no doubt in her mind that a full-fledged Ripper copycat murderer was at large. The MO of the killing, the signature style of the Ripper, the delivery of the liver, and the letter sent to the newspaper all pointed to someone who knew the old case very, very well.

But this warning letter didn't fit, as far as she knew. The original Ripper hadn't been known to forewarn any of his victims. Perhaps this wasn't from the killer after all. But who could have sent it? And why to her?

Her knee-jerk reaction was to call Jonathan immediately.

He hadn't had time yet to arrive at the headquarters of New Scotland Yard. It would be easy for him just to turn around and . . . what? Rescue her? From what?

Victoria stood up and tossed the two messages onto the desk, disgusted at being such a ninny. She would not be held hostage by her fear. If the creep was out there waiting for her, she wanted to confront him. By daylight, of course. She considered a course of action that might flush him from the shadows and get him to reveal his identity without endangering her or anyone else.

She looked at her watch. It was just past one, London time. Mike wouldn't be at work yet. But a man in his position was at work twenty-four seven anyway, in the office or out. She couldn't wait all day. She had other things to do. Reaching for the phone, she placed the international call.

Ten minutes later, after listening to Mike's tirade about her choice of vacation activities, she managed to calm him down enough to give him the specifics of the case, and asked him to instigate a search for Billy Ray. With false confidence, as she said goodbye, she assured him she would be perfectly safe.

She had barely hung up the phone when it rang again. "Hello?"

"Tori?" Trey's voice sounded as if he were in the next room, not across the ocean.

"Trey? Where are you?"

"Home. Where you ought to be. Are you okay? Have they caught the killer yet?"

She heard the open concern in his voice and was grateful for it, even though it was unnecessary. "It's very sweet of you to call, Trey. No, we haven't caught him yet. But we're working on it."

"What's with this 'we' stuff? Are you involved in the investigation?"

"What do you think? I couldn't just sit around eating bonbons while Scotland Yard goes after the killer."

"Why don't you just get your sweet ass on a plane and come home? You're in danger there."

Victoria grinned. Trey kidded her about using low language, but he was pretty good at it himself. "I can't. Not until Scotland Yard releases me. It's because the killer sent the . . . uh . . . liver to me. Besides, I think I can be of help in the case."

"You're sick, Victoria," Trey growled. "You're obsessed with murder. And you're too damned hardheaded for your own good."

Sick? Obsessed? Hardheaded? Her temper flared. "It's my job, Trey," she retorted. "I'm not sick or obsessed. It's what I do for a living."

There was a long pause on the line, then he said softly, "Okay, okay. I'm sorry. Just be careful. And give me a call when you get home."

"Thanks. I will. And good luck on your new job."

She hung up and stared at the phone, surprised at Trey's sudden protective attitude toward her. It had always been the other way around. She thought about what he'd said, that she was obsessed with murder. She wanted to deny it, but her entire life did seem to revolve around brutal killings. The notion made her shudder. Maybe Trey was right. Maybe she was becoming obsessed. Maybe she should convince Scotland Yard that it would be better for her to return home than to get further involved.

But she knew she could no more back off now than she could fly.

Dismissing the idea, she considered again whether to call Jonathan. He should know about the latest "special delivery" right away. But she knew that if she told him, he would take measures to protect her, and she would then likely become a virtual prisoner of Scotland Yard. For her own safety, she granted. But she would be unable to move about freely. And she had other ideas about that.

That phone call could wait.

Victoria took a quick shower and slipped into fresh clothing, eager to put her plan into action. Scrounging among the brochures and pamphlets she'd gathered about the sights to see in London, she came up with a map that marked the underground stations and tourist destinations. She donned comfortable walking shoes and her all-weather coat, stuffed the map in her handbag and headed for the door. She would purchase an umbrella if necessary, one with an extra heavy handle, she thought grimly, in case she needed a weapon.

Outside, the air was cool and damp, but it was not raining. Victoria stood for a moment at the street corner, getting her bearings and listening to the pounding of her heart. She wasn't frightened, she told herself. She was just aware. The killer could be nearby, and it was her plan to get him to reveal himself if she could. What she'd do then, she wasn't sure, but she didn't think he would make a move against her in broad daylight with people all around.

Her hope was simply that she would "accidentally" encounter someone she recognized from the conference. If someone was stalking her, he might show himself in a casual, seemingly innocent, encounter, just to play with her. Perhaps, if her nerves didn't fail her, she could engage him in conversation and learn something that would later lead to his capture. She fully expected the person to be Billy Ray.

Crossing the street along with a crowd, she glanced behind her. No portly gentleman. No bodybuilder. Nobody she recognized. Still, she was tense as she walked the two blocks to the tube station and descended into the dimly lit underground. It too was filled with people, but she was uneasy. Hits were made in places like these regardless of the crowds. But she doubted that the Ripper copycat would strike here. It wasn't his MO, she reminded herself. His kind of slime lurked in the midnight darkness of lonely streets and preyed on the homeless and helpless.

Nonetheless, when she arrived at her destination, Victoria was glad to return to the surface. She walked briskly to the ticket booth of the attraction she'd come to see. The Tower of London. Now a major tourist draw, the ancient stone fortress had seen more than its share of terror and death. For centuries, prisoners had been incarcerated here, tortured, beheaded, and piked, sometimes for no reason other than that they were on the wrong side of the political fence.

Again seeking safety in numbers, Victoria joined a group gathered around one of the tour guides. Were the killers of yesteryear so different from the man she sought today? she wondered, looking up at the crenellated structure. Killers were killers. But those killers of old *had* been different, in one important respect. They were killers with motive. The Ripper copycat and others like him killed for the pure pleasure of it.

Suddenly, out of the corner of her eye, Victoria caught sight of a familiar face. Someone from the Sherlockian weekend had joined the group. The person spotted her and did not hesitate to edge through the crowd and approach her.

"I thought you were instructed to go home," Victoria remarked, surprised but unafraid.

Adele Quigley shrugged. "I was. But I would have had to pay a premium to change my airplane ticket. Besides, this was the vacation of a lifetime for me. I had prepaid everything and planned to spend a full week, and I decided not to let what happened scare me away. I moved out of the hotel into an inexpensive guest house in Earl's Court, and I've been sightseeing ever since. I've been to Buckingham, Westminster, Harrods, all over London on the underground. But you can bet," she added as the group began to move toward the Tower, "I won't be going back to Whitechapel."

Eleven

King's College, Cambridge
Sixth October 1887

It has been many months since I last saw my beloved Prince. I have to work to control the rage that burns inside me at the notion that he is being deliberately kept from me. I do not deserve this treatment, for I was and am Eddy's only friend. He has managed to smuggle messages to me these past miserable lonely months, and a mourning bracelet that he wove from hair plucked from his head. They are all that sustain me.

My days are empty, but my nights are filled with powerful, seductive dreams. In them, I am threatened by women. Sometimes it is Lady Stephen who shows herself to me, at other times more common whores. I am ashamed to admit it, but sometimes it is the image of my little cousin Virginia who raises her skirts to me. I am compelled by these women to thrust myself inside their vile cunts, whereon they consume me. They tear my flesh away and emasculate me. But I am stronger than they. I must be stronger to survive. In these dreams, my cock becomes a rapier, and even as I submit to their obscene demands, I take my revenge. I slice into them, riding them mercilessly, until they are slain and lie bleeding beneath me.

"There's nothing. No weapon. No fingerprints. We did not find a hair, a fiber, or any foreign bodily fluids on the victim." Jonathan listened as the coroner reported the results of the autopsy on the victim who had been murdered in Whitechapel. "The killer must have worn a space suit and swallowed the knife."

Jonathan swore under his breath. He'd been hoping for some kind of evidence from the crime scene that he could use to compare DNA with that of Reginald FitzSimmons. If they ever found him. The old gentleman, if he was the killer, was no slouch. He knew a great deal about the original Ripper and apparently had managed to copy him in every respect, including vanishing without a trace.

"What's the report from the neighborhood canvass?" he asked the investigators on his team. "Did anyone see anything?" The portly FitzSimmons would be hard to miss.

"If they did, they're not talking," one of his detectives told him. "Everyone is terrorized down there in the East End. Afraid this is going to be a repeat of that bloody autumn."

"What did forensic come up with on the letter that was sent to the *Times*?" Jonathan was growing increasingly exasperated at the nothingness they were presenting him.

"The handwriting and ink are the same as on the note delivered with the . . . uh . . . liver. Unfortunately, as before, there were no fingerprints on the *Times* letter. Our experts think both were written by a male, someone who was in a state of high excitement. He is probably left-handed but turns his paper as if he were right-handed. The ink is from a common ballpoint pen, and it's smeared slightly from the top down. Of course you already know, like the first note, this one was written on stationery from the hotel where the Sherlockian meeting was being held. The odd thing is, the letter was postmarked Saturday evening. It could have been sent before the murder took place."

Jonathan's head jerked up. "What?"

"The letter was mailed at a post office near the hotel

sometime before midnight Saturday. The murder was committed around eleven P.M."

Until now, Jonathan had been unsure whether the real killer had written the second note, using hotel stationery because it was handy, or if someone from the conference, upon hearing of the murder, had decided to jump into the action for a lark and sent a phony note. Someone young and brash who would do such a thing for the excitement of it. Billy Ray came to mind.

But now he knew better. Whoever had committed the murder had it planned all along. Maybe he'd come to the conference with this in mind.

A male in a state of high excitement.

FitzSimmons? Somehow the image didn't fit. The old man, although mentally keen, seemed too plodding. Had it been Billy Ray? He certainly had the muscular build for it. And as Victoria had pointed out, he was attracted to murder and followed all the big murder cases.

Billy Ray? Reginald FitzSimmons? Or someone else altogether?

FitzSimmons and Ray. FitzSimmons and Ray. They remained his prime suspects. And neither was anywhere to be found. Maybe Victoria was right. Maybe they should circulate their pictures in the media.

His phone rang, and he picked it up. "You've got a call on line one," the receptionist said. "She says her name's Elizabeth Huntley-Ames, Lady Chastain. Sounds upset. Want me to ring her through?"

Lady Chastain sounded more than upset to Jonathan. "It's . . . oh, Inspector, it's terrible, and I was wrong not to tell you in the first place."

"Tell me what?"

A sniffle, then silence, then . . . "It's so embarrassing."

"You can speak to me in confidence, Lady Chastain. I am privy to many secrets." Jonathan's voice was calm but his curiosity was raging.

"It's . . . it's Alistair. He's been cheating on me for some time now. He goes out in the evening, and sometimes does not return until dawn. If I confront him with it, he goes into a rage. I'm sick of it, I tell you. Sick of it!" Her tirade ended in a little hiccough of a sob.

"I'm sorry to hear this," Jonathan replied, wondering what Huntley-Ames's philandering had to do with him. His division did not handle domestic disputes.

"I didn't quite tell your men the truth the other morning when we were questioned at the hotel, because I was afraid Alistair might harm me afterward. But I've been thinking about it, and I decided I had to call you, because . . . I'm afraid that he might be . . . the killer."

Jonathan stared at the wall of his office. "I see," he said for lack of something more intelligent. He was stunned. Lord Chastain was an MP, although not particularly powerful in the country's political structure. Still, he was a highly unlikely suspect. But stranger things had happened, and Jonathan had learned not to discount anything. "What brought you to that conclusion?"

"The night of the murder, after we left you, we went to our room, but a short time later, when he thought I was asleep, he dressed again and went out. He . . . he didn't come in until after four A.M."

Jonathan thought it more likely that Huntley-Ames had a mistress than that he was a Ripper copycat murderer, and he suspected Elizabeth had had enough time to fret about her husband's blatant infidelity the night of the murder to make this call in revenge. He smiled at the woman's artifice. He would not have thought she had it in her.

"Did you find blood on his clothing or belongings?" he asked.

"N—no. But I didn't look. At the time I had no reason to suspect him of . . . of . . . murder. Alistair is finicky about his clothing, and he hung everything neatly in the closet when he came in. He packed his own things when we left."

Jonathan let out a breath. "Are you willing to come in and make a statement?" As expected, she hesitated.

"You don't know Alistair. He gets mean when he's angry. I'm afraid—"

"Without your statement, our records show he has an alibi because he was with you. If we should indeed discover that he was the murderer, you become an accessory to the crime by covering for him."

There was a long silence on the line. Then she hung up.

It was a stretch to take the woman's story seriously, but whether he believed her or not, Jonathan was concerned about what Elizabeth Huntley-Ames had told him about her husband's bad temper and penchant for violence. He would interview Lord Chastain again, but there were ways to do it without letting him know his wife had made this call. Jonathan turned to his assistant.

"Move Lord Chastain back to the A list."

Victoria jumped when she heard a knock on the door, even though she was expecting Jonathan. She had returned to the hotel from her "sightseeing" adventure only a few minutes before, and when she'd picked up the single message that was waiting on her voice mail, she'd heard his most unhappy voice scold her for not being there and inform her that he was on his way over.

"Who is it?" Victoria was not taking any chances.

"It's me. Jonathan."

She opened the door a crack and peeked out, and her heart did the now expected little flip-flop. "Solved any crimes today, Inspector?" she said as she opened the door fully.

"Where the devil have you been?" He was inside in an instant, and in the next, she was in his arms.

"Got tired of working," she said, her heartbeat racing, "so I went sightseeing." He smelled of October rain and man, and she wanted him in bed again.

He took her head between his hands and kissed her. The kiss was anything but gentle, as if he had to prove to himself she was solid and real. "Why the hell can't you play it safe, just for a little while?" he murmured, searching her eyes with his.

"I was perfectly safe," she whispered, encircling his

body with her arms and pressing into him. She felt his erection against her belly and pressed harder. He drew in a sharp breath. "Damn it, Victoria, what am I going to do with you?"

"Make love to me, Jonathan. The door's locked, and everything else can wait."

And it did.

"You've got to stop doing that," he said later, cradling her in his arms. "You're making me crazy."

"Me? You're the one who started all that kissing stuff."

He was quiet for a long while. Then he said, "Now about today—"

"Don't start it, Jonathan." She pulled away slightly. "I am perfectly capable of taking care of myself. FBI, remember?"

He sighed. "You *have* made me crazy. When you didn't answer the phone, all kinds of terrible things went through my mind. I know we're just getting to know one another, so to speak, but honestly, Victoria, if anything happened to you—"

"If anything happened to me, what?"

His look was both forlorn and perplexed. "It would break my heart."

Victoria's own heart lurched at his admission. She lay very still, watching this man struggle with obviously unfamiliar emotions. Emotions with which she too struggled. What was happening here? Was this just about sex? Or was it something more? It was too hot, too heavy, too fast.

Too scary.

She rolled away. "Nothing's going to happen to me." *Except that I might lose my heart to an Englishman.* "I went to the Tower, and guess who I met up with? Adele Quigley, of all people. I'd have thought she would have taken the first plane back to Pittsburgh. Makes me wonder who else didn't leave town."

She slipped on her robe, and Jonathan drew on his pants. They sat on opposite sides of the bed, looking at one another in silence. Jonathan was so handsome Victoria feared she might succumb to his sexual appeal all over again. "You stay there," she said, desperate to regain control over her wayward desire, "and I'll sit over here." She went to a chair across the room next to the desk.

"We have to talk. I called Mosier," she said, hurrying to get down to the business at hand. "I've filled him in on the situation here, including my involvement in it. He went through the roof when I told him about the liver being left outside my door, and he insisted I come home right away. Then I told him where the liver came from, and he about split a gasket. He doesn't like it, but I'm signed out until Scotland Yard releases me.

"I gave him what I know about Billy Ray," she continued, trying to stay focused on the murder case and not on the breadth of Jonathan's shoulders, "including a physical description and the address we got from Janeece. He's put somebody on it. If Ray is back at home, we should know it soon." She let out a breath. "What's happening on your end?"

He told her that the two Ripper notes had proved a match. "And our prime suspect list now has three names on it."

Victoria was as surprised as Jonathan had been about Lord Chastain's supposed nocturnal activities on the night of the murder. "Do you think she's lying?"

He shrugged. "I have an appointment to talk to him at his office later this week. I decided against letting him know Elizabeth blew the whistle on him, at least for now. She claims he's abusive, and I don't want to make matters worse for her. I'll just tell him we're reinterviewing those who went to the Ripper pub that night."

"Abusive?" Victoria raised a brow and gave it some consideration. "Actually, I can see it, now that you mention it. He belittled her in front of the rest of us, and you could tell theirs is not the most loving of relationships. Elizabeth seems in many ways like a woman whose spirit has been broken. I'm surprised she had the courage to call you."

"Maybe it's her little revenge. It might not be true at all."

"Things are not always what they seem," Victoria murmured, "which brings me to this." From the desk, she picked up the envelope that had been delivered to her earlier and tossed it to Jonathan. "This was waiting for me when we returned this morning."

She watched the blood drain from his face when he read the first note, and her nerves tensed.

" 'You are in grave danger. Beware.' " Jonathan read the words aloud, then looked across at Victoria, worry etched in every handsome line of his face. "I can't believe you went out after you got this."

"I can't hide here forever, Jonathan. Actually, I was hoping whoever sent the note might be nearby and reveal himself. It could have come from the killer, but it could also have been sent by someone else, someone who is honestly trying to warn me. Maybe someone who knows who the killer is but doesn't want to come directly out with it."

"Lady Chastain?"

Victoria raised her brows. "Now there's a thought."

Jonathan studied the note for a long moment. "I can't say for certain, but this doesn't look to me at all like the handwriting on the other two notes." Then he turned his attention to the other paper that had come in the mysterious envelope, and Victoria saw his eyes widen in astonishment. "This accompanied the warning note?"

"Same envelope. Obviously different authors. Got any idea what it is?"

Holding the paper gingerly by the edges, he turned it over, held it up to the light, turned it back to the front side, and studied the message again. At last he shook his head. "I can't say for sure. I'll have the lab examine it, as well as the other note. But this looks to be much older. The paper is heavy, the ink's faded to red-brown. Inks used at the turn of the century did that, but it's also possible to artificially age modern inks. So this is either a relic of that time, or an excellent forgery."

"Who is 'V.R.'?"

This time, he was slow to answer. "This is pure conjecture, and you know I don't like that," he said, "but it could be . . . Victoria Regina."

"Queen Victoria?" Twentieth-century Victoria was astounded. "You don't mean it."

"I'm not saying she wrote it, but whoever did might have meant to give the impression that it was penned by her."

Victoria's mind began to race as possibilities whirled through it. "Let's say, just for grins, that it is an authentic note from Queen Victoria to—someone. How did the author of the other note, someone obviously from this age, get his hands on it? Or hers? And why did that person send it to me?"

She looked across the room and saw that Jonathan was staring a hole through her. "What?"

"Pack your bags. I need to get these things to the Yard right away, and I'm not leaving you here alone again."

"Where are you taking me? To that 'safe house' you were talking about?" The thought was not all that unpleasant, considering what he'd promised to do to her there.

"No. You're going home with me."

Jonathan dropped the two mysterious messages at the forensic lab with orders to rush their examination. It only took a moment to confirm that the handwriting on the warning note Victoria had received did not match that on the modern-day Ripper messages. As for the older correspondence, he was completely mystified, both as to its age and content as well as why it had been included in the envelope and sent to Victoria.

One thing was clear to him, however. He didn't understand how or why yet, but Victoria was somehow involved in the murderer's scheme, and he believed her life was in danger. Maybe it hadn't been the smartest move to insist she stay at his flat, for they both knew the other danger that awaited them when they were alone together, but he'd felt it was the only choice at the time. Now he wasn't so sure. It was a delicious danger to have her so close, but he could not allow their relationship to get in the way of the investigation. His mind was already only half on the job.

He made a mental note to ask Inspector Sandringham to help him find another, safer place for her to stay. Maybe with that American who had recently joined Scotland Yard, Jack Knight and his new wife. Or maybe they should just let Victoria return to the States. She'd be safe there, at any rate.

When he returned to where she sat waiting for him in the reception area, however, he thought both were bloody wretched ideas. He wanted her no place else but with him.

"When will they have something?" she asked, standing to greet him. This evening she was half business, half casual, wearing a dark blazer over matching slacks and a colorful scarf over a feminine blouse. She looked sharp. Sophisticated. Beautiful. What did she see in him? he wondered.

"I put top priority on it, but it may take a day or two. Come on. I promised Roger to be at his place before seven."

The Rabbit Hole Antiquarian Bookshop was a tiny store wedged between a travel agency and an ice-cream parlor on a busy street in London. The windows looked as if they hadn't been washed in this century, and the clutter inside was equally mucky, but Jonathan loved the place. Treasures were to be found here, especially when one was friends with the owner.

"Jonathan! Come in." Roger's voice boomed from behind a stack of books piled high on a counter toward the rear of the store. "We've been waiting for you."

To his surprise, Janeece Fairchild poked her head around the books and gave them a little wave. "Well, I'll be damned," he said under his breath. "So that's what he was doing at the Sherlockian thing."

Victoria gave him a fleeting grin. "Did he know her before? Maybe they met there. Either way, they looked as if they were getting kind of cozy at the dance."

Janeece hurried toward them as best she could down a narrow aisle, looking owlishly at home among the books. "Oh, Inspector, Ms. Thomas, it is so good to see you again. Roger is being very mysterious about this little package he has for you." She shook Jonathan's hand, then Victoria's.

"Quite a place, isn't it?" she said, sweeping an arm out over the room and its piles of dusty books. "I just love it. Roger's quite a bibliophile. I heard about him from a friend and came in to see if he could perhaps keep an eye out for material pertaining to my famous distant cousin, Virginia Woolf. I've heard I am related to her, and I'm trying to trace my lineage back to see if it's true." She wiped a finger across a book jacket and made a face. "Roger's not much of a housekeeper, I'm afraid. I've volunteered to spruce the place up when I have time."

Roger joined them. He was middle-aged, with a pleasant round face and thinning hair. He looked somehow happier than he had on Jonathan's previous visits, and Jonathan guessed Janeece was the reason. In his hands, Roger carried a thick manila envelope. "Sorry we're in such a rush tonight. We have tickets for the theater and thought we'd grab a bite beforehand. Care to join us?"

But Jonathan had other plans for the evening. "Thanks. But we've a lot to do ourselves. Rain check?"

"Of course. Now, down to business." He held out the envelope and studied it before handing it over to Jonathan. "The person who asked me to give this envelope to you has also asked to remain anonymous. That person told me that this is just a small sample of what can be made available to you, provided it is returned to me in three days. I do not know what it contains, but I can assure you, it came from a most remarkable source." Without further comment, he handed over the package.

Jonathan wanted to open it on the spot, but if the donor insisted on such secrecy, he thought it better to wait until they reached the privacy of his flat. "Thanks. I'll see what

we have, and get it back to you in three days. Have fun at
the theater."

Outside, a light drizzle had begun to dampen the chilly
air. "Let's go home," Jonathan said, taking Victoria's hand
and hurrying toward the parking garage where they'd left
his car. He unlocked it and held the door for her, thinking
it strange that he was taking a woman to his home. He'd
rarely done that before. His quarters were his refuge, and
the only woman allowed in was the housekeeper, Mrs. Dunstan. But it seemed natural that Victoria should be going
there with him.

Natural? Jonathan shuddered, and blamed it on the cold.

His flat was in an old town house that had been renovated and subdivided into five sets of living quarters, one
on each floor. His was on the second floor. He pitied the
poor buggers who lived on the fifth, for all the residences
were accessible only by stairs.

"A very tall house," Victoria remarked as they parked
on the street in front of it.

"And no elevator. I hope you find it comfortable. It's
not exactly the Ritz."

She covered his hand with hers. "Are you sure this is a
good idea?"

The sizzle hadn't diminished. "No."

"I can go back to the hotel. I'm sure I'd be safe enough
there."

"No." This time he was emphatic. "You're staying with
me."

"This isn't totally about my safety, is it?" she asked
softly.

And Jonathan realized she'd cut to the heart of the matter. He'd pretended that it was for her safety, but he had to
stare the truth in the face. He'd brought her here because
he wanted her here. In his home. All to himself.

"No," he replied after a long moment. "No, it isn't, Victoria. The thing is, I don't know exactly what it is about."

"I think I have a clue," she said with a short laugh.

"It's . . . it's not about sex, if that's what you're thinking."

"Actually, I was." Her voice was low and husky. Sexy.

"Victoria." He said it somewhere between a groan and a plea.

She removed her hand. "Okay, okay. Let's go in and see what's in that package."

But Jonathan knew it wasn't the end of that discussion.

Twelve

Victoria shared Jonathan's apprehension about her returning with him to his flat. Each time she was with him, it grew harder to maintain any semblance of objectivity. It appeared the night of wicked romance she'd wished for had become first a little weekend fling, and then something that had gotten out of hand altogether. And she wasn't quite sure what to think about that.

Jonathan's flat was clean and attractive, although modestly furnished. "No frills" came to her mind. Jonathan deposited her suitcase in the small foyer. "Welcome to my humble abode," he said.

Victoria surveyed her surroundings. There were several doors off the foyer, all closed except the one to her left. Through it she entered a living area that included a wooden table and four chairs, unadorned by tablecloth or cushions. A worn but comfortable-looking sofa faced a fireplace with a wonderful old marble mantel above it. Two upholstered chairs were placed on either side with a low table in between. The walls were adorned with prints of traditional English artwork, mainly hunting scenes.

The most remarkable aspect of the room, however, was the bookshelves. They filled the entire far end of the room, bracketing the window that overlooked the street, and extending along both side walls for at least six feet. They were laden with books of all shapes and sizes, some stacked sideways on top of others.

"You must be Roger's best customer," she remarked, both surprised and impressed.

"Some people play the ponies. I buy books."

"Have you read them all?" she asked, going to the shelves and turning her head to read the titles. There were classics, both in fiction and non. How-to books. Cookbooks. True crime. History. Travel. Even some in foreign languages.

"Not all. But most. Sometimes I buy a book just because I want to own it."

She turned to him, thinking what a package he was. Lover and literati all rolled into one. Something akin to joy swelled inside of her, a feeling of immense happiness and pleasure, and she had to work not to fling her arms around him. Instead, she took a deep breath and said, "So, shall we see what's in Roger's mysterious package? Or is it marked for your eyes only?"

"It's not marked at all," he noted. They went to the table, where he unlaced the old-fashioned tie that held the envelope closed, and carefully slid the contents onto the table.

The papers were yellow and brittle with age. Printed at the top of each page were the words "Metropolitan Police, Criminal Investigative Division."

"These look similar to the kind of forms we use for our official reports," Jonathan remarked, picking up one of the sheets.

"They look old to me," Victoria added, her pulse picking up a beat. "Is there a date on them?"

Jonathan let out a low whistle. "A very interesting date. This one is marked '1 September 1888.' "

"You're kidding. Wasn't that the day after the first Ripper murder?"

"Yes, it was. Or at least the first attributed to him." Jonathan picked up the first sheet and read aloud.

" 'Unidentified female found dead approximately 3:40 A.M. on 31 August 1888 in Buck's Row near the Board School by PC John Neil 97J. Body examined by Dr. Llewellyn, who determined life extinct. Time of death estimated no more than thirty minutes before, due to severe injuries to the throat. Body was moved to the mortuary in Old Montague Street, where I, Inspector John Spratling, discovered additional injuries, to wit: her abdomen had been cut open from breastbone to pubis and her intestines were exposed. Llewellyn in his postmortem examination noted bruising about the face and lower part of the jaw. Possible cause: pressure of fingers. Due to the small amount of blood at scene of murder, Llewellyn now suspects strangulation, not incisions, was the cause of death.' " He stopped reading aloud, but his eyes ran over the rest of the report.

"What does it say?" Victoria wanted to know.

Jonathan raised his eyes. "It's a description of the injuries. Graphic, but if you want . . ." He held out the paper to her.

She shook her head, remembering how FitzSimmons's detailed description of the last Ripper murder had affected her. "I don't need to know the details," she told him. "But what do we have here? Could these be—"

"The missing police files?" Jonathan shook his head. "I don't know. There's nothing here that strikes me as new ground. It could be our killer is playing with us again."

Heads together, they scanned the rest of the reports. There were five of them, dated from 1 September to 15 September 1888, each containing details of the murders of Mary Ann Nichols and Annie Chapman, first two victims officially attributed to the Ripper during that bloody autumn.

"Where do you think Roger got these?" Victoria asked. "It seems too coincidental that they would surface the same day I was sent what might be another artifact from that time."

"I doubt they are real," Jonathan replied. "And I don't think it is a coincidence at all. I think our killer is having fun with us, showing off, so to speak. Letting us know how knowledgeable he is about the murders."

"He's going to strike again." Victoria shivered. "Soon." She knew it would happen as well as she knew her own name.

"If he is trying to replicate history," Jonathan said, "then I expect our copycat will strike again next Saturday night in Whitechapel."

"Jonathan," she said urgently, "we have to stop him."

"Inspector Sandringham's already on it. He kind of thinks like you," he added with a little grin. "I forgive him for it, though."

Victoria ignored him. "What do you mean, he's on it?"

"He expects the killer to make another move on Saturday, unless we find him between now and then. He's assigned more officers than you would believe to the area starting at sundown."

"I just hope that's good enough," Victoria said, filled with foreboding. "As I recall from your presentation, Whitechapel was crawling with cops once they realized there was a maniacal killer on the loose, and it made no difference whatsoever."

"That was then and this is now. We're a little more sophisticated these days. They'll be using infrared viewers and radios, and they've implemented a curfew. If he does try it, he'll find it dicey."

Victoria failed to be reassured. "Can't we speed things up in your forensic lab? If those letters I received today were from the killer, there might be something in them that will lead us to him before Saturday."

"I doubt if they've had time, but I'll check." Jonathan picked up the phone and dialed the lab. It was late, but he knew the dedication of the team in that department. "Any fingerprints on those two specimens I dropped off earlier?"

Victoria saw him shake his head and felt her own disappointment. She had hoped the tools of modern investigation, not available to the police in the days of the original Ripper murders, would identify this killer before he had a chance to strike again.

Jonathan murmured responses to what he was being told,

then said, "Thanks for getting to it so quickly. I know you have a lot going on. I'll be by in the morning. I've come across some other rather interesting items for you to take a look at. Carry on and call me if anything interesting turns up."

He rang off and turned to Victoria. "They're already well into their examination of the two messages you received today. No fingerprints, and as I suspected, the handwriting on neither matches that on the new Ripper messages." He sighed and ran his hands through his hair, glancing at the old CID reports on the table. "No sense in taking these in tonight. They couldn't get to them until tomorrow anyway."

Silence fell between them. There was nothing more they could do on the murder investigation tonight. Now they had to face their personal dilemma.

What to do about them.

Victoria read the ambivalence in his eyes that she felt in her heart. She wanted him. He wanted her. But neither was ready for the intensity of emotion that had unexpectedly surfaced along with their desire. It was too much, too soon. And in a way, it was as frightening as the events that swirled around them.

"I'll take the sofa." Jonathan thought it was the decent thing to offer, although he no more wanted to sleep alone on the couch than eat a bug.

Victoria gave him a rueful smile. "You know that's not going to solve the problem."

"What is?"

"What's the problem? Or what's going to solve it?" she asked quietly.

Jonathan wasn't certain exactly what the problem was, but he thought it might have something to do with life structures being altered. "We need to talk about both," he said, "but let's do it over something to eat. I'd cook something, but there's not much in the refrigerator. There's a great Indian-style takeaway around the corner, however. Could you go for a little tandoori?"

They walked through the thickening shroud of fog and drizzle to the restaurant, picked up their food and a couple of beers to go with the spicy meal, and returned to Jonathan's flat twenty minutes later. Neither had said more than was necessary to transact their business.

"Smells divine," Victoria remarked as they took the food out of the bag. "I didn't know I was so hungry." Spreading the low table by the fire with newspapers, they laid out the cartons. Jonathan brought plates, mugs, and utensils from the kitchen, then turned on the gas logs and poured the beer into the mugs. These things were important, he told himself—these preparations, the meal, the drinks. But that was bullshit, and he knew it. All it did was postpone the inevitable. It was time to face reality.

"So where were we?" he asked, taking a seat on the floor next to her.

"The problem," Victoria said, struggling to cut a piece off the bright red tandoori chicken.

"Use your fingers. It's the only way." She did, and he regretted making the suggestion, for watching her lips engage the chicken leg did nothing to solve his problem.

"As I see it," she said, dabbing at her mouth with a napkin when she finished, "we have a simple case of undernourished libidos. From what you've told me, there haven't been many ladies in your life, and I haven't had a real date in years. It makes sense that . . . well, all those libidinous urges that have gone unfulfilled for so long would now surface and beg for attention."

Jonathan laughed out loud. "You sound like one of those nutty psychologists on television talk shows," he said.

"I am a nutty psychologist."

He grinned at her. "Okay, tell me then, professor, why are those urges surfacing now? Between you and me?"

Her gaze found his and locked onto it. She wasn't smiling. "I don't know, Jonathan. And frankly, it scares me. I find you attractive and all that, but I'm not one to jump into bed with a virtual stranger. And yet I did."

"I seem to recall having done some of that same kind of jumping," he said. The memory of their stolen hours in Kent rekindled his barely controlled longing for her. She looked exquisite in the firelight. She had removed the blazer and scarf, and the softness of her blouse and the glow of her skin invited his touch. Her eyes seemed to darken as he gazed at her, and he guessed she was fighting her own desire, as well.

"So," she said slowly, lifting her mug to her lips, "have we defined the problem?"

"It's a theory I could live with."

"Then how do we solve it?"

The answer was obvious. But it wasn't an easy solution. Because it raised all kinds of other problems. Still, Jonathan knew nothing else would suffice, at least for him, at the moment. He moved closer to her, but did not touch her. His solution might not be hers.

"We could feed the hungry libidos until they are satiated, and then maybe they'll go away."

He saw her swallow. "Or we could try to starve them out," she said, her voice hoarse.

"Didn't work before. They came after us with a vengeance." He lowered his lips until they were almost touching hers. She did not move away.

"How hungry do you suppose they are?" she murmured, raising her head slightly.

With his foot, Jonathan edged the table away from them. He drew her onto the sofa and found her lips once again. "Ravenous," he said as he crushed her against him.

Victoria was beside herself with desire as Jonathan's lips touched hers. Good God, where was this going to end? Her behavior was appalling, but there seemed to be nothing she could do about it. When she was around Jonathan, she was out of control. It frightened her even as she answered the call of whatever-it-was that seemed to draw her to him like the proverbial moth to the flame. A hungry libido? Perhaps that was part of it. But there was something more, something deeper than unmitigated physical lust. It had something to do with completion. Fulfillment. The end of a journey she had not known she was on.

Later, her hunger for him sated momentarily, she lounged against Jonathan's body, luxuriating in their nakedness.

"Cold?" he asked, cradling her in his arm.

"Not yet. It'll take me some time to cool down after that." But moments later, the chill of the room settled around her, and she shivered.

"We'd better get some clothes on," Jonathan said, shifting his weight and sitting up.

"Or turn up the fire." Victoria didn't know where these naughty thoughts kept coming from. But the truth was, she didn't want to get dressed again. Already she longed for the feel of Jonathan's body against hers.

She watched as he slipped on his slacks, regretting that her view was obstructed. He had great buns, and the rest of him . . . Well.

"Come on," he said gently, prodding her from the couch. "I'll get your bag for you." They returned to the small foyer, where he snagged her suitcase and led her into the single bedroom of the apartment. She dug into the bag, found her robe, and slipped it on.

"You can forget the couch," she said, noting he had a double bed. "I wouldn't want you to get cold."

Jonathan came up behind her and encircled her with his arms. "You're chilled, aren't you?"

His body heat warmed more than her skin. "You Brits don't know beans about effective heating."

He nuzzled her ear. "Maybe not. But we have hot water. Would you like to warm up in a bath?" Jonathan asked. "This place has got a great tub."

"Great" was the operational word here, Victoria thought when Jonathan showed her the bath. It was huge.

"Looks like there's room enough for an army," she commented.

"I've never tried that, but I'm sure there's room enough for two."

"Jonathan!"

"I'm still hungry."

She turned to see that disarming grin on his face and knew that she was lost all over again. She sighed.

"Do you have any bubble bath?"

The water nearly reached the top of the tub once they got in, and it felt delicious. He hadn't come up with any bubble bath, but they'd used some shower gel to raise a head of foam on the surface. They sat facing each other, one at each end of the mammoth tub, the most distance they'd put between them in a couple of hours. Jonathan smiled at her, sheepishly it seemed.

"Comfortable?"

"Yes," she said, "and no."

His face clouded. "What's the matter?"

She squirmed. "This is embarrassing."

"What is? Taking a bath together? Seems to be a little late to go all prudish."

She splashed water in his direction. "I'm not prudish!" Her cheeks burned, and she sank lower in the water. "Or maybe I am." Her mother's image loomed before her eyes. Barbara Wentworth Thomas would not be happy if she could see her daughter at the moment. But then, Barbara Wentworth Thomas hadn't approved of much she had done since Meghan's death. "It's just that . . . hell, Jonathan, this time last week I didn't even know you."

"Thank goodness it's this week," he said, taking one of her feet in his hands and beginning to massage her toes. Her belly tightened at his touch, but she didn't pull away. "What's the matter?" he asked gently. "Is your libido feeling guilty?"

Guilty? She supposed she did feel just a little bit guilty. She'd been taught that "good girls" didn't do things like she'd done with Jonathan the past few days. Especially with strangers. Guilt wasn't something she was accustomed to, either. She'd always been the good daughter, for the most part, going along with her parents' rules and wishes, until Meghan's death, when she'd bailed on her mother's desire for a "proper" marriage and her father's plan for a junior partner. They hadn't liked it, but neither had they thrown her out of the family. Victoria put the brakes to her runaway thoughts. What the hell was she doing thinking about her parents at a time like this?

"It's not that. It's just that . . . well, I've never felt like this toward a man."

His hands paused. "Like how?"

She didn't like being pressed in a direction she found distinctly uncomfortable. "You know, there's a real pushy part of you I don't like."

"Show it to me and I'll cut it off."

He laid her foot along the crease of his groin, where it nestled softly against his genitals.

Victoria took in a sharp breath. "That's not the part I meant."

"Good God, I hope not. I'd have to rethink my offer." He picked up her other foot and worked on it. "You were saying?"

"I was saying . . . I don't know quite what to make of us."

"Me either." He ran his fingers between her toes, scrunching bubbles where their skin met. "Do we have to make anything of us? Other than that we're two consenting adults with hungry libidos?"

A shard of disappointment cut through her. He was right, of course. What had she expected? A marriage proposal? She wasn't even interested in that kind of thing. But she'd hoped she was more to him than just a good lay. Obviously, that wasn't the case.

Suddenly, she felt naked and vulnerable. She had behaved deplorably. She'd allowed him to see her in a way no other man had, and she regretted it down to her toenails, which she now withdrew from Jonathan's grasp. She sat up in the tub and hugged her knees to her breasts. "Maybe it would be best if I go home," she said, feeling miserable. "Whose decision was it that I had to stay on anyway?"

"Victoria, what's wrong? What did I say?"

She reached for the large towel he had set out for her on a nearby chair. "It's nothing you said, Jonathan. It's my own stupidity. I have a life. A career. And I need to get on with it."

Stepping out of the tub, she covered herself with the towel and went into the bedroom, where she dried off hastily and slipped into her clothes before Jonathan had time to get out of the water. By the time he came into the room, wearing only a towel wrapped around his waist, she had her suitcase shut and in hand.

"Where are you going?"

"I don't need a bodyguard, Jonathan. You and I both know why I came here. Well, we did our thing, and now it's time for me to go."

Thirteen

King's College, Cambridge
Fourteenth June 1888

    I have been estranged from Eddy since his frightful and foolish foray into the East End alone last February, where he stabbed a whore with a clasp knife. He lost his nerve and ran, leaving her alive and possibly able to identify him. For the first time, I comprehended the colossal mistake I made in introducing him and his simple mind to the deed, for he gave no forethought to the consequences. It was his good fortune she died later of other complications and never identified her attacker. In my fury, I banished him from my quarters, but have regretted it ever since.

    Today my wish for reconciliation was granted. My beloved Prince has just departed after stopping for an unexpected visit on his way to Sandringham. He dismissed his entourage with uncharacteristic authority and entered my rooms with an unusual air of confidence. It pleased me to see him in such high spirits, for when I saw him last, in the dark days of February after his dreadful error, he was a simpering fool.

    This visit, he said, was to apologize for hunting without me. He lost his confidence at this point and fell to his knees, begging my forgiveness. I was gladdened and relieved to learn I still controlled his heart and, to some extent, his actions. He seems to understand the terrible risk he took, and yet he fears in the future he might not be able to control himself. The bloodlust torments him as unmercifully as it does me, and he begged me come to London and join him in a hunt. We have arranged it for the Bank Holiday on sixth August. It fills me with un-speakable joy that in spite of our estrangement, I still own his heart, and he remains in my power.

Jonathan swore he would never understand women as long as he lived. One minute things were going swimmingly, so to speak, and he had every expectation the libido-feeding might go on long into the night. The next minute, Victoria was pissed and on her way out.

"Wait," he said. "It's late. You have no place to go. And I think you owe me at least an explanation before you fly out of here."

"There's nothing to explain," she said. "I just changed my mind, that's all. Or else, my libido is sated."

"That's nonsense," he said, going to her. "You said you don't know what to make of us. Well, neither do I. If you're looking for an answer to that, I can't give it, Victoria, be-cause I don't have one. Do you think this is any easier for me than you? I'm a bachelor, for God's sake, a confirmed bachelor with no plans for a woman in my life, ever. Then you come waltzing in and my whole world tilts upside down. I can't think. I can't work. When I'm around you, I'm as hot as a teenager, and as helpless. I ought to stay as far from you as I can manage, but I can't." He broke off, thinking if she left he would die. "Victoria," he said. "Don't go."

The phone rang.

"Don't go," he said again, holding up his hand as if that would somehow stop her. "That . . . that might be the lab." If nothing else, maybe she would stick around to see if they'd come up with anything. He rushed past her into the living room where the phone continued to ring insistently. He picked up the phone set in one hand and the receiver in the other, hoping his towel wouldn't slide off. "Blake here." He turned to see if Victoria had gone, but she stood in the doorway, watching him, suitcase still in hand.

It was Hensen at the lab, and he was excited. He'd just finished running some tests on the old note that had been sent to Victoria, along with the warning. "I'm quite certain the paper is authentic to the late eighteen hundreds," he told Jonathan. "I collect samples of papers from different times for our files, and I found an identical match in the royal stationery collection from the year 1888."

"The royal stationery collection?" Jonathan had not known the Yard had any such resource.

"Yes, sir. It's . . . sort of a hobby of mine. I get a little obsessed with my work, I suppose." Hensen sounded both abashed and proud. "I have made it a point to gather dated letters, legal documents, and other written artifacts from history for this very purpose, to provide materials in case we needed them for forensic comparisons. This kind of paper, sir, was used by Queen Victoria for her personal correspondence."

"V.R." Jonathan murmured, astounded.

"It could be a forgery, but I'd wager a week's pay that's Her Royal Highness's initials written here. As for what the message means, I haven't a clue."

"You're due a bonus for this one, Hensen," Jonathan said, ringing off and raising his eyes to meet Victoria's gaze. "Our man at the lab says he's dead certain that old note you were sent today was written by Queen Victoria."

Victoria let the suitcase fall to the floor with a heavy thud. "He's sure?"

Jonathan explained how his man had arrived at that conclusion. "He could be wrong, of course. But he's an expert in the field when it comes to forensically verifying correspondence."

"What does it mean, Jonathan?" She came toward him, and he suddenly remembered that all he wore was a towel.

"Let me get some clothes on, and we'll talk about it."

He touched her arm before leaving the room. "You're not going anywhere, are you?"

She gave him a smile that bespoke surrender. "I'd already changed my mind before the call."

They talked long into the night, sitting at opposite ends of the sofa in front of a warming fire. They talked about the curious old note. They talked about the mysterious warning letter, and the letter sent to the *Times*. Even about the delivery of the human liver. They talked about the old Ripper murders, and killers in general, and what drove them to kill. For the first time, Jonathan realized the depth of Victoria's commitment to her profession, and why she had become a profiler in the first place. It wasn't only because of her sister's death, although that had sparked it. It was about understanding the mind behind the killing. It was about knowing the killer better than the killer did himself in order to stop him.

Bottom line, it was about saving lives. Although they disagreed on technique, in the end, they were after the same thing.

"Do you think you could pull together a profile on our killer?" he asked, surprising himself.

"Do my ears deceive me? The scientific-method-only cop asking for a profile? Don't patronize me, Jonathan."

They had remained at a safe distance for as long as he could stand it. Sliding across the sofa, he put his arm around her shoulder. "I'm not patronizing you. I would really appreciate your help." What surprised him even more was that he meant it. How could it hurt? Maybe she'd come up with something . . .

She drew her head back and looked at him long and hard, as if trying to decide whether to believe him or not. Then she gave him a slow smile. "Very well. I'll start tomorrow." She touched his chest. "But now, isn't it time for bed?"

He lit his pipe and looked at the game board. Although he had intended to follow the master's timetable, he found he could not. He had more to do than the master. A larger territory to work. So he had created a timetable of his own.

Also unlike the master, he chose a different kind of whore for his work. Where the master cut the dregs from society, the apprentice chose to slice away at society itself, those hypocritical whores.

He'd selected his starting point carefully, for there was a pattern to follow. His victim, however, was a totally random selection. She was an easy mark as she left the opera house and walked alone down a side street to her car. He'd watched from the shadows across the street, waiting, on fire with the bloodlust. The bitch was dressed to kill, so to speak, in white satin. Perfect. The blood would look exquisite against it.

As she dug in her purse for her keys, he crept up behind her. From the way she swayed unsteadily on her feet, he guessed she'd been drinking. He touched her shoulder, and she whirled about in surprise. Seeing him, she smiled. An instant later, when his hands encircled her neck, her smile turned to surprise, and then to horror. It was the horror that made him hard.

The kill was swift and silent from there. He simply choked the life from her. But unlike the last place he'd worked, this street was not a safe enough place to finish his job. Others would come this way soon when the opera was over. She must have been bored and left early. He didn't blame her. He hated opera.

When she went limp, he dropped her onto the pavement, took her keys, and opened the back door. He slid her onto the seat and tucked her feet in, making sure he had both shoes. There must be nothing to indicate that she had died on that spot. It wasn't part of the master's plan to move the whore, but he had no choice.

He drove to a secluded park, parked, and took her body out of the expensive foreign car. He laid it across the wide hood, where the engine's heat would warm her, then went to work, feeling the power welling in his loins.

He finished quickly and stood back to admire his work.

He wondered if the police would notice that the incision resembled a music note. Before leaving, he took a small Polaroid camera from his pocket. Aiming it at his masterpiece, he snapped off a shot and waited while the film developed. He smiled. Too bad the master had not had a way to record his work. This was historically important.

Satisfied that the flash had supplied sufficient light, he took another picture, then walked quickly off into the darkness of the night.

The next day, Victoria and Jonathan turned what he believed to be phony police records from 1888 over to Erik Hensen, telling the examiner he must have them back in twenty-four hours. In just under that, Hensen returned them, authenticated. "Where the hell'd you get those?" Hensen had wanted to know, his eyes bright with curiosity.

Victoria had bit her tongue, knowing she could not give the secret away.

"I can't say just yet. If we're lucky, there'll be more where this came from," Jonathan answered the man enigmatically, not telling him they were about to return the priceless treasures to their anonymous donor. "I'd appreciate it if you don't mention this to anyone until we see what else turns up."

After making careful photocopies of this first batch, he and Victoria paid another visit to the Rabbit Hole Antiquarian Bookshop, where he reluctantly handed them over to Roger.

"I hope to God this guy wasn't lying about providing us with more documents," he told Victoria as they left. "I would never let these out of my hands unless I thought it would lead to others that will shed more light on the truth of those old murders."

Victoria spent the next few days in a conference room near Jonathan's office, working on the case from a criminal psychologist's point of view. She hoped he wasn't just throwing her a bone, giving her something to do to keep her out of his hair. Whether he believed in the value of profiling or not, she knew its worth, and she was determined to prove it to her hardheaded Englishman. She was glad of the opportunity.

It was difficult, however, because there was so little to go on. She'd seen the crime-scene photos and read the coroner's report, but the forensic exam was not yet complete. And as far as victimology went, there was even less for her to work with. The dead woman's family had not come forth to claim her, and she apparently had few friends. She did not believe, however, that the victim had known the killer. From the physical evidence, it appeared she may not even have been aware of the killer until he reached to strangle her from behind.

Jonathan had provided her with a laptop, which she used to communicate with Mike and the others back at Quantico. Mike had called her every day, as well, not only to keep her informed on their search for Billy Ray, but also to check on her well-being. He was upset because she'd become involved in the case when she was in personal danger. It wasn't what he'd had in mind when he'd insisted she take a vacation.

She didn't feel endangered, she assured him, working in the offices of Scotland Yard and spending her free hours with Jonathan. And her work was less than demanding. So far, it had consisted mainly of collecting and entering what data she had on the case, and spending hours trying to get her mind wrapped around the mind of the killer.

Why here? Why now? Why this victim?

It was nearly two o'clock on Thursday afternoon when Jonathan popped his head in the door. "Ready for a break? I'm starving."

Victoria was concentrating so deeply it took a moment for his invitation to register. "Uh, sure," she replied, "let me just check one more thing here." She finished downloading the case study she was using as a comparison, then put the laptop to sleep. "Lunch sounds great," she said, turning to him, and her heart skipped a beat.

Damn. She wished she didn't harbor such feelings for

him. This whole affair was impossible. And soon it would come to a screeching halt.

"I know the perfect place," he said, taking her arm. But he wouldn't tell her where they were going. "It's a surprise."

A few minutes' ride on the underground and a short walk brought them to a classic English pub, with a dark façade and multipaned windows facing the street. Victoria looked at the name painted in gold lettering above the windows.

"The Sherlock Holmes Public House and Restaurant." She laughed. "With all that's happened the last few days, I'd forgotten about this place. I looked it up on the Internet and really wanted to visit it while I was here. It has a replica of the sitting room and study Holmes and Watson occupied at 221-B Baker Street, doesn't it?"

"Except there never was a 221-B Baker Street. Or a Holmes and Watson, for that matter," he added, opening the door for her. "But we can see what it looked like in the mind of the author."

It being past the lunch hour, the place was nearly empty. They went into the main restaurant, where Victoria discovered to her delight that the famous apartments shared by Holmes and his sidekick Dr. Watson were indeed replicated in detail, furnished with authentic Victorian items and visible to diners through large glass partitions. Holmes memorabilia abounded, including a nostalgic collection of stills from movies and television programs featuring the famous sleuth and his trusty companion.

"For a Sherlock fan like me," she murmured, "this is the mother lode." After studying the replica for several minutes, she turned her attention to the souvenir display. "I need to take something back for Mike," she said, holding up a T-shirt. Then she spotted the most adorable teddy bear she'd ever seen. "Oh, look," she cried, picking it up. He was garbed in full Sherlock regalia—cape, deerstalker, and pipe. "I have to have one of those," she told Jonathan. "Let's eat first, and I'll come back for my goodies."

The young man who seated them explained that the Sherlock Holmes exhibit was purchased by Whitbread and Company from a special exhibit in 1957, and subsequently displayed here on the premises, which used to be the North-umberland Arms. "If you're familiar with the work of Conan Doyle, you'll recognize the Northumberland as the place where Sir Henry Baskerville stayed on his visit to London." He pointed out the mounted head of a fierce crea-ture he claimed was the Hound of the Baskervilles.

They ordered from a menu that featured courses such as "Mrs. Hudson's Steak and Ale and Mushroom Pie," which was self-explanatory; "Sherlock's Own Favorite," a grill of Scottish beef; and the "Sir Arthur Conan Doyle," roast beef with Yorkshire pudding and potatoes. Victoria opted for something lighter, an appetizer called "The Stockbroker's Clerk" that was comprised of avocado slices and prawns on greens.

As they were finishing their meal, they were startled to hear loud voices issuing from the ground-floor bar.

"Are you calling me a liar, sir?"

They couldn't hear the reply, but Victoria looked at Jon-athan, her eyes wide. "I could swear I've heard that voice before," she said, getting up and creeping down the stair-way, heading for the pub. He was right behind her.

They peered into the bar and saw two men at the far end of the room. The one who had his back to them was tall and thin. The other man who faced them was stout, and at the moment his face was the color of a ripe tomato.

"Well, I'll be damned," Jonathan said in a low voice from behind her.

"Reginald FitzSimmons." Victoria couldn't believe her eyes.

Jonathan took her elbow, and together they strode ca-sually up to the pair, and to Victoria's astonishment, when the second man turned she saw it was Alistair Huntley-Ames. He too looked thoroughly angry.

"Well, well. Looks like old home week," Jonathan said,

greeting the pair in an easy manner, although Victoria knew he was tense as a cat ready to pounce.

"Imagine finding the two of you here," she added. "Anybody seen Jack the Ripper around lately?" She ignored Jonathan's frown.

FitzSimmons's expression changed from anger to distress when he saw Victoria. "I hope all is well with you, my dear," he said, glancing from her to Jonathan. "Glad to see you are in good hands after that dreadful business."

"Do you know anything about that . . . dreadful business, Mr. FitzSimmons?" she asked.

His face darkened. "I know a great deal more than this gentleman is willing to admit," he replied. "I know who Jack the Ripper was."

"Old or new?"

"I beg your pardon?"

"Are you speaking of the original Ripper, or the copycat?"

"You know nothing, FitzSimmons," Huntley-Ames broke in. "Your claim is a blatant prevarication and could be harmful to . . . those in high places. You have no proof of your absurd contention." Victoria wondered what on earth he could be talking about. His words were derisive, but his tone was edged with what sounded like panic.

FitzSimmons glared at the other man. "Oh, but I do," he said, slowly raising his glass to his lips. "I have cold, hard proof. Proof I intend to bring forward soon, one way or another. You can't say you didn't have your chance."

Victoria didn't know what they were talking about, but it suddenly occurred to her that perhaps Reginald FitzSimmons was trying to blackmail Huntley-Ames in some way. Did it have something to do with the murder? "I'd be interested in seeing what you have, Mr. FitzSimmons," she said abruptly. "I don't suppose that whatever you're talking about is for sale?"

With that, she had FitzSimmons's full attention. "As a matter of fact, that's why I contacted Lord Chastain. He mentioned on Saturday he was a collector of Ripper memorabilia, and I just happen to have something in my bag of tricks that might be of interest to him, if he wasn't such a cheapskate. He knows I'm telling the truth. He just doesn't want to pay what it's worth."

"You're a phony, and I'm a busy man," said Huntley-Ames, preparing to leave. He turned to Jonathan. "I notice we have an appointment in the morning. Is it anything we can handle right now? I'm terribly booked, you know."

"No, I think it would be best discussed in private," Jonathan said, giving the man a confidential wink and nodding slightly in the direction of FitzSimmons.

He got the message. Important things were discussed in private, not in the presence of fools. "Very well, then, until tomorrow." Huntley-Ames looked at FitzSimmons. "You'd best not attempt to peddle your lies or you might find yourself in very hot water."

After the other man left, Victoria asked, "What is he talking about?"

Reginald Smythe FitzSimmons glanced around the room. The only other occupant was the bartender, but even so, he said in a stage whisper, "I should not have spoken so boldly in public. Come with me to my flat. I have something that I believe will be of great interest to you." He eyed her shrewdly. "If, that is, you are a bona fide buyer."

"I could be. But where is your flat?" Victoria asked. "It wouldn't by any chance be in Kent?" she added dryly.

He looked at her, not understanding at first. Then he smiled. "Oh, that. I registered that address because I don't want people to know where I really live. I've lots of valuables, you see, and you never know who you can trust. But you're Scotland Yard," he said to Jonathan, "and you're FBI," to Victoria. "If I can't trust the pair of you, who can I trust? Besides," he huffed, heading for the door, "after buying a round for the house last Saturday night, I need the money."

Victoria and the old man waited while Jonathan dashed upstairs to pay the bill for their lunches. The souvenirs were forgotten. Moments later, the trio emerged onto the sidewalk. "We'll take the Underground," FitzSimmons said. "Fastest and cheapest way to get to my place."

Then he stepped off the curb and directly into the path of an oncoming car.

Fourteen

It happened so quickly Jonathan had no time to grab the man's arm and pull him back to the curb. He hadn't even seen the car when he came out of the restaurant. He heard no squeal of tires, either. Just the roar of an engine and a dull thud when FitzSimmons's body engaged the metal of the oncoming vehicle.

Victoria screamed. The car vanished around the corner. FitzSimmons lay bloody and unconscious in the street. "My God," Jonathan swore, whipping out his cell phone to call the emergency number. Victoria ran to the old man's crumpled form and felt for the carotid artery. "I can't find a pulse," she cried.

Jonathan knelt beside her and tried again, but there was nothing. The man's face was blue, his eyes open but unseeing, his muscles slack. Jonathan caught the odor of urine and saw a dark stain against the fabric of FitzSimmons's trousers. "He's dead," he said simply, staring at the corpse in disbelief. "Did you get a license number on the car?"

Victoria clutched his arm. "No. It . . . it happened so fast . . ."

A crowd had gathered, and Jonathan wanted to take Victoria away from the gruesome scene. But they had been firsthand witnesses, along with one diner who had seen the incident from the restaurant. The paramedics arrived in only a few moments, as well as two constables from the nearby

Charing Cross Police Station. It took the medics only seconds to verify what Jonathan already knew. " 'E must 'ave died instantly," one of them said. "Looks like 'e took quite a blow to th' midsection. Probably crushed 'is 'eart."

Jonathan and Victoria gave their statements to the police, for what good it would do. "The car was a late model sedan, sort of gray or taupe, nondescript except that it was larger than most. Could have been a Japanese make." Jonathan wished he could do better than that. He was a policeman, for God's sake. But that was the best he had to offer. "It happened so fast, neither of us got a good look at it."

He took Victoria's hand as the two of them watched the ambulance take the body away. "Guess that narrows the list of suspects."

"Jonathan," Victoria said, turning to him, "was that really a hit-and-run accident? Or could someone have wanted the old man dead?"

"Someone like who?"

"Think about it. The taxi driver said he let FitzSimmons off close to where the murder took place on Saturday night. Because he was placed so near the scene of the crime at the time it was committed, we both thought of him as a prime suspect. But what if . . . what if he didn't commit the murder, but rather witnessed it?"

"And the killer has been following him around waiting for a chance to run him down? Seems like a bit of a stretch, but I suppose that's as plausible as anything at the moment."

"Here's even more of a stretch, but I think we have to consider it. What if the killer was Lord Chastain? What if FitzSimmons witnessed the killing and called him to come here today because he was trying to blackmail him?"

"You think Huntley-Ames ran him over?" The notion was absurd, and he was surprised Victoria thought it was possible. "Does Lord Chastain fit the profile you've been working on?"

"Only in that he may be an abusive personality type. I

don't think he's a serious contender for the perpetrator, but I'd check out his car at the very least."

Sobered, they made their way back to Jonathan's office where despite his skepticism about Lord Chastain's involvement in the hit-and-run, he assigned one of his men to look into Victoria's suggestion.

Later in the afternoon, he received a phone call from the detective inspector in charge of the case. "I thought you gave the victim's name as Reginald Smythe FitzSimmons."

"That's correct."

"Any reason he would have given you a phony name?"

"No, why?"

"We fingerprinted him. His name's not FitzSimmons. It's Brown. Burt Brown. We haven't confirmed it yet, but we believe he is a retired custodian once employed by the royal family."

The day after Reginald FitzSimmons was run down, Jonathan and Victoria led the team investigating the Whitechapel murder to a seedy flat in one of London's lesser neighborhoods where the man named Burt Brown had lived. According to his neighbors, who gave a positive ID on him from a photograph, he was a nice enough man, although they thought him a bit off his head at times.

The building was a shabby brown stucco-sided structure containing a beehive of tiny flats. Victoria wondered if Reginald FitzSimmons's reluctance to let anyone know where he lived had more to do with the rundown condition of the place than his concern about the theft of his valuables. She sincerely doubted he had any valuables worth stealing.

They found the front door secured by a chain lock, but rather than break it, they entered through the back with the help of the property manager. The door opened onto a postage-stamp–sized kitchen. The sink was filled with unwashed dishes, but otherwise the room was neat enough, if sparsely furnished. A squawk and a flutter of wings greeted them, along with the smell of a birdcage in need of cleaning.

"Oh, the poor little thing," Victoria exclaimed, going to the small cage in the corner and peering in at the frightened parakeet. "His food dish is almost empty, and he needs fresh water."

"Don't touch anything," Jonathan warned. "Not yet."

She scowled at him but did as he said, silently promising the little bird that he would soon be taken care of.

While she was fussing over the bird, Jonathan went into the small living room next to the kitchen, and moments later, she heard him say, "Well, I'll be damned."

"What is it?" As she went through the door, her chin dropped in amazement. Jonathan was standing across the room, laughing and shaking his head.

"Isn't this just the most peculiar thing?" he said.

The living room looked almost identical to the exhibit they'd seen the day before at the Sherlock Holmes Pub. It was 221-B Baker Street all over again. Reginald Smythe FitzSimmons, aka Burt Brown, appeared to be more of a Sherlockian than she'd ever dreamed. He'd literally lived in a world he'd re-created from the stories of Sir Arthur Conan Doyle. It was fascinating and sad at the same time. Did he fancy himself to be the famous sleuth?

"Inspector, I think you'd better come in here." One of the men beckoned from what she guessed was probably the bedroom.

Jonathan went into the room, and this time she heard him swear out loud. Hurrying to see what was the matter, Victoria passed from the genteel Victorian surroundings of FitzSimmons's fantasy living room to a house of horrors.

"Jonathan, what is this?"

"This is why he knew so much about the Ripper murders," he replied grimly.

Victoria felt sick to her stomach. From the walls, the mutilated victims of the original Ripper screamed silently at her from large posterized versions of the police photographs or sketches made at the time. They were all there, taped to the wall in a neat row, their names scrawled beneath each picture.

Mary Ann "Polly" Nichols. Annie Chapman. Liz Stride. Catharine Eddowes. Mary Jane Kelly.

A gallery of gore.

On another wall was an enlarged map of the Whitechapel area, with bold red X's to mark the murder sites. Jonathan went to it and studied it for a moment, then said, "Look at this." He pointed to the street where last Saturday's murder had taken place. It too was marked. "You said you thought the killer was delusional and might believe himself to actually be Jack the Ripper. Victoria, I know you don't believe he did it, but I think Burt Brown is our man."

Saddened, Victoria had to agree. This man's surroundings spoke volumes as to his mental instability. He was obviously a loner, alienated from society, delusional, and from what he'd used to decorate his bedroom, it was likely he hated women. There was a scrapbook on one nightstand containing photocopies of newspaper clippings of the original murders, and fresh, new ones about last Saturday's event. The man had been as obsessed with Jack the Ripper as he had been with Sherlock Holmes.

"He claimed Jack the Ripper was alive and well because he planned to be the new Ripper," she speculated reluctantly. "I guess he made up the address in Kent thinking it would somehow throw the police off."

"He swiped some stationery from the hotel and wrote that letter to the *Times,* probably over a glass of stout in the hotel bar," Jonathan said. "He might have mailed it as we left the hotel on our little excursion to Whitechapel. The post office is just around the corner."

"He was the one who urged us all to go to the Jack the Ripper Pub that night, but he stayed long after the rest of us had left." Victoria picked up the thread of Jonathan's thoughts. "Maybe he was faking his state of inebriation. The driver let him out just a few blocks away, and he found his victim."

"Whitechapel is only two stops from here on the Underground. It would have been easy for him to simply walk away, hop a train, and disappear into the night. He brought the piece of liver with him, wrapped it here, and went back briefly to the hotel to make his delivery."

Victoria looked up at him. "Do you suppose that's how the original Ripper escaped so easily? Was the Underground built back then?"

"It was. And some people believe that he used it to make his escapes. I even saw it in a movie once." Jonathan turned to one of his men. "Check the closets. See if there's blood on anything. Maybe we'll get lucky and find that poor woman's blood on his coat."

But they didn't. Although Burt Brown's meager wardrobe was shabby and in need of dry cleaning, there was not a spot of blood on any garment they found. Their search, in fact, turned up little, certainly nothing of any value that he might have sold to Huntley-Ames. Besides the furnishings and his personal belongings, the only thing of interest was a small lined writing tablet.

"This looks like the kind of paper the warning note was written on," Jonathan remarked, putting it into an evidence bag. They searched for but did not find anything, however, that provided a sample of FitzSimmons's handwriting. When he was satisfied that they had combed the old man's habitat thoroughly, he ordered his men to seal off the flat until the investigation was complete.

"Now I really wonder what Lord Chastain was so upset about yesterday at the Sherlock Holmes Pub," Victoria remarked. "If FitzSimmons was the killer, he wouldn't have been trying to blackmail him."

"He said Lord Chastain was a collector of Ripper memorabilia," Jonathan said. "Maybe he was trying to pawn off some of those posters."

But Victoria shook her head. "I don't think so. They aren't of any real worth. There must have been something else. Something much more valuable . . ."

They started to leave, but Victoria paused when she saw the bird in the cage. "We can't just leave him here, Jonathan. He'll die."

Jonathan frowned. "What are we going to do with a budgie?"

"Take him home?"

Jonathan and Victoria arrived back at his flat later that evening, Victoria toting the bird cage as she climbed the stairs behind Jonathan. She knew he was unhappy because they'd been unable to outplace the bird among his colleagues at the Yard.

"Mrs. Dunstan will have a fit," he growled as he unlocked the door.

"Maybe. Or maybe she'll be the one to take him."

"Don't hold your breath. She's a great one for neatness, and 'neat' is not the word to describe that bird." Victoria hid her grin, thinking of the drift of seed husks the bird had spit onto Jonathan's desk during the course of the afternoon.

"We couldn't just leave the poor thing to starve, Jonathan," she admonished, setting the cage on the kitchen counter. "I'm certain someone will adopt him soon. Maybe I'll ask Janeece Fairchild," she said, thinking aloud. "In the meantime, I'll make sure he's cared for."

Victoria had made Jonathan stop at a pet supply store, where she'd purchased seed and sanitary papers with which to line the cage. "Keeps it from smelling," the store owner had assured her. "Better than newspaper."

Hoping it wasn't a false claim, Victoria set about cleaning the cage, talking to the bird as if it were human, and ignoring Jonathan's grumbles. She pulled out the tray and removed the newspaper that FitzSimmons/Brown had used to line it, and blinked in surprise at what lay beneath.

"Jonathan," she said, "look at this."

Under the soiled newspaper in the bird cage was a key attached to a small chain. Jonathan picked it up and rinsed it before examining it closely.

"Looks like a key to a suitcase, or maybe a public locker somewhere. Old Burt Brown is just full of surprises."

Fifteen

London
Thirty-first August 1888

My dreams have been filled with crimson lust since the hunt earlier this month with Eddy, and when I awaken, my need for the bloodsport is excruciating. I sent guarded messages to Eddy, hinting at my agony and hoping he would join me, but either he never received them, or could not get away. I could wait no longer, and last night undertook the hunt alone. It was bittersweet without Eddy, and more dangerous, as there was no one to keep watch.

The whore I chose was coarse-looking, middle-aged, and staggering from drink. I followed her for over two hours, carefully watching the movement of the constables on duty. Opportunity came at last in Buck's Row. I accosted her and immediately engaged her for sex, requesting the back door, for it is easier and cleaner to strangle the prey from behind before beginning the work. Although I did not get the delight of seeing her fear, neither did she have the chance to cry out. She was dead before I laid her upon the ground, so when I cut her, the blood did not spurt in an uncontrolled gush as it did on our last hunt. It is not as exciting this way, but much safer. I found my thrill in sinking my dagger into her belly and carving away the vile essence of her.

As I sit at my desk reminiscing about the event, I am reminded of a tavern song I heard recently at the male brothel on Cleveland Street—

It was for her no fortune good,
That he should need to root his pud,
And chose her out of all the brood
Of Harlots of Jerusalem.
For though he paid his women well,
This syphilitic spawn of hell
Struck down each year and tolled the bell
For ten Harlots of Jerusalem.

Ten! I shall strike down ten times ten. Tonight's hunt has proven that with care, I can effect a kill in complete silence, enjoy the pleasure of the work afterward, and disappear without a trace. They will never catch me. I am free to kill into infinity.

He showered and shaved and dressed for the evening, his heart already thundering in anticipation. He'd chosen one of Phoenix's most exclusive country clubs for his venue. Not that he would share the Friday-night buffet with the elite of their smarmy little society. No, he would wait until one of them wandered outside. He'd already scoped it out, knew exactly where to park, and how he would get away before anyone had time to discover his work.

He stood, his gloved hands in his pockets, and watched as a woman stepped out of the building and onto a side patio, where she lit a cigarette. She was a tall blonde. He'd seen her through the windows from his hiding place, which afforded a view of the expansive dining room. She was stunning. A model, perhaps. He felt a familiar stirring in his loins. A model. The perfect whore. Selling her body for all the world to see.

"I don't blame you for escaping. It's stifling in there," he said, stepping around the hedge but remaining in shadow.

The woman jumped. "Oh, you startled me. I didn't know anyone was out here." She smiled at him. They always did.

"It's such a lovely evening. Thought I'd take a little walk. Maybe down to the first green. Want to join me?"

She hesitated, but he knew she'd come. She was curious about the mysterious stranger she'd discovered. "Sure. Why not? The party's a real bore." She dropped the cigarette and mashed it out with her shoe.

They reached the first green, which earlier he'd found ideal for his mission. Although the golf course was naturally wide open, a large thicket blocked sight of this particular green from the clubhouse.

"Look! There's a shooting star," he said, and when she turned to look up into the night sky, his hands encircled her neck. His fingers dug deeply into her flesh, and he could almost feel the breath damming up behind them. It turned him on. She struggled, but he was far stronger. In only moments, her futile flailing stopped and her body slumped, a dead weight against him. "Maybe I should have said 'fallen star,' " he said as he laid her out on the green. He slashed her throat one, two, three times, just for good measure.

Raising her skirt and pulling away her panties, he propped her legs open. This was his favorite part, for it brought him exquisite sexual pleasure. Inserting his knife just above the mound of pubic curls, he pressed until the blood flowed down her smooth, white abdomen like a river of red semen. His breath quickened as he felt his ecstasy grow. He cut her belly open clear to the rib cage, then made a horizontal slash and cut away the flaps of skin that barred his way to the prize. When he found what he was after, he carefully cut it from her body.

Holding her womb in his hands, he felt himself coming. It was a powerful ejaculation that left him quivering. He looked down on the woman. She was grotesque in the darkness. He spit on her, then took the organ and laid it carefully in the cup at the center of the green.

"A hole in one," he laughed, "or maybe I should say, a

whore in one." He wiped the bloody knife with a tissue and inserted it into its scabbard. Removing the surgical gloves he wore, he placed them and the soiled tissue in a zipper-type plastic bag he'd brought in his pocket. Although the master had worked bare-handed, he always wore gloves. What with AIDS and all, one couldn't be too careful.

He snapped two shots of his work, then headed swiftly through the shadows to where he had parked his car.

Saturday night passed without incident in Whitechapel. Not only were there no Ripper-style murders, there had not been so much as a domestic dispute reported in the area. "I guess the heavy police presence put off even the run-of-the-mill criminals," Jonathan commented over breakfast on Sunday morning.

"That, or they were terrified that such a murderer might be lurking in the shadows. The bad boys are often afraid of the really-bad boys," she replied with a yawn.

In spite of the lack of criminal activity that night, she and Jonathan had stayed at the Yard until dawn, just in case. When it appeared that no foul murder had taken place, they'd come back to Jonathan's flat, where he'd prepared a full English breakfast that she'd eaten with gusto, even though it was cholesterol city.

They sat in silence for a long moment, the only noise coming from the parakeet who made little grinding sounds with his beak from his cage in the corner. Victoria had dubbed him "Dr. Watson."

Finally, Jonathan spoke. "Sandringham is convinced that FitzSimmons must have been the Whitechapel killer," he said quietly. "He told me to tell you that you're free to return to the States."

Victoria's heart plummeted, and her throat constricted. She took a deep breath and exhaled slowly, trying to stifle the emotion that engulfed her. "We've both known that time would come," she managed after a long moment.

"Yeah."

"I'm still not convinced it was FitzSimmons, although

everything points to him." she said. "I wish we could come up with a sample of his handwriting to see if it matches the Ripper notes."

"We may have if Hensen can get an accurate trace of it from the impressions on the tablet we found in his flat."

"I'll bet they don't match. My money is still on Billy Ray. It might have been a murder of the moment for him, spurred by the symposium. He might never have planned to follow up with another. Maybe once was enough for him. Maybe it made him sick. That would explain why he got out of Dodge so fast."

"If he did."

"I think he was gone by the time we got around to interviewing the attendees, although we still have no proof. But if he did it, and if he keeps his mouth shut, he'll very likely get away with it, and poor old FitzSimmons will take the rap." She stretched. "At least with that scenario, there won't be another Ripper-style murder."

"It may have been FitzSimmons, but he's gone, and we'll never know for sure," Jonathan said. "Ironically, it's just like before, when the killings stopped as mysteriously as they began, leaving Scotland Yard unable to prove anything. Maybe the Ripper of old got run down by a carriage."

"Or drowned himself in the Thames," Victoria added, thinking about the young suspect named Montague John Druitt whose body was found shortly after the murders ceased. "I hate it when an investigation ends like this. Inconclusive."

Like Meghan's case.

"At least we can discount Lord Chastain. Although his alibi has changed from wife to mistress, he still has one, and his handwriting is nothing like that on the notes."

Victoria gave a small, derisive laugh, recalling the rather unpleasant interview they'd had with the man, when they'd learned he had left his wife's bed the night of the killing and gone to his mistress. He was uncomfortable revealing that, although he came clean about it. But she felt instinctively he was hiding something else. However, she did not think he was the killer.

Jonathan reached for the coffee carafe and started to re-fill her cup, but she covered it with her hand. "No more for me. I'm wired enough as it is, and we didn't get any sleep last night."

Jonathan set the pot on the table and went to stand be-hind her. She felt his hands begin to massage her shoulders. "I was hoping we could make up for that right now."

The desire underlying his suggestion was clear, and she forgot all about sleep. "Sounds like a good idea to me." She nuzzled the back of his hand, and a now-familiar sexual hunger rippled through her. Would she ever get enough of this man?

Leaving their breakfast things on the table, they went into Jonathan's bedroom where the bed lay unmade from their extended interlude the day before. "I see the maid didn't come," she teased. But when she turned to face him, he was not smiling. His eyes, in fact, looked haunted.

He unfastened the top button of her blouse. "It'd just be a waste of time."

It had been a week since he'd begun his work. Seven days and four hits. With each, he'd improved and gained con-fidence. But he still had a long way to go. He was not good enough yet . . . for her, although he'd done an excellent job on the bitch last night in San Francisco.

Strolling through the airport, killing time until his flight was called, he gazed at the headlines and grew angry be-cause not one newspaper had reported the sensational mur-der at Fisherman's Wharf. Well, that would change once the Phoenix *Sun* published the letter he'd sent from there. Then he'd be all over the news, in every city, on national TV. He could hardly wait.

He settled into a chair, took out a small map of Seattle, and contemplated the work he planned there the following night. Something nagged at him. In spite of his success, it had all been too easy. He must make it more of a challenge.

He was no longer afraid of being caught. With his plan, he doubted even the best of them could stop him, not unless he wanted to be stopped. He thought about Victoria Thomas, the FBI's hotshot profiler, and stifled a laugh. Surely she must have returned from London by this time. Had they called her in on the investigation yet? He was certain they would as soon as they began to connect the killings. Would she figure it out and call his hand before his grand finale? He didn't think so. She was a smart bitch, but he was smarter. A feeling of pure bliss spread through him. He was powerful. This was his life's work, his destiny, and no one, especially not Victoria Thomas, would stop him now.

He picked up the phone and dialed her number. It was fun to fuck with her mind. When she didn't answer, he left a short message. It didn't matter. He'd get to her soon enough.

It was Tuesday night. Victoria sat on the sofa in jeans and her soft green sweater. She wore no bra. Her feet were bare. She sipped a chilled Chardonnay and listened to Jonathan bustling about the kitchen. After their long vigil on Saturday night, he'd negotiated a few days off. Although Scotland Yard had released her, she'd decided to stay on a while.

She would have to leave soon, but when Mike had ordered her to come on this vacation, he'd insisted that she take two full weeks off. She hadn't been gone that long yet. For once, she would do as ordered. Her moments with Jonathan were too precious to cut short.

These past days had been like a dream, a fantasy that she never wanted to end. Jonathan had at last been able to show her around London as he'd promised the first day she'd met him, but mostly, they'd spent their waning time together in bed.

Jonathan entered the room, and she gazed up at him. He was shirtless and barefoot, wearing only a pair of jeans. Just the sight of him turned her on. Before she'd met him, her libido must have been not merely hungry, but starved, for her appetite for him seemed insatiable.

"Dinner won't be ready for another hour," he said.

She set her wine glass on the table and went to him. "That's plenty of time for a little appetizer," she said, no longer embarrassed at her boldness. She splayed her fingers across the breadth of his chest and ran her nails lightly over his skin.

"I wouldn't mind a little something," he said, running his hands beneath her sweater. She felt her nipples grow hard.

"Free samples in the bedroom," she whispered. A heated urgency claimed her. "Race you," she murmured, reaching for the top button on his jeans.

She didn't know who won, but in only moments they were lying naked beneath the covers. Jonathan's lips tasted hers, then traveled downward, leaving a trail of kisses along the way. She expected him to stop when he reached her breasts, but instead, after toying with her there unmercifully, he continued on his journey south.

"Jonathan." She gasped his name when he opened her legs and kissed the most intimate part of her. She'd never experienced the sensations that tremored through her as his tongue worked magic on her body. She lay back and opened to him completely, running her fingers through his hair. Her orgasm came in short, sweet lightning bursts, fulfilling and at the same time building her need.

Playing her body like a fine instrument, Jonathan once again began trailing kisses, this time traveling up until he reached her mouth. Victoria quivered with the most intense desire she had ever experienced. "Come inside me, Jonathan," she begged in an urgent whisper. "I can't stand it any longer."

She felt him slide into her, fitting as if they were two parts of one whole. They moved together, building the heat until the molten core of her very being glowed white hot. The earlier crescendo was like a tiny drop of rain compared to the hurricane force of the orgasm that shook her body in violent release.

She was slick with sweat and crying with emotion when she finally heard the telephone ringing.

"It's Mosier," Jonathan said, handing her the phone, dread striking like a fist in the center of his gut. There was only one reason her boss would be calling. He wanted her home.

He went into the bathroom, trying not to listen, but it was impossible.

"Oh, my God," she said, and he heard the horror in her voice. "When? Do you think it is the same guy?" She was silent for a long time, then said, "I see." Then, "You're kidding! He sent a letter?" More silence, followed by, "Yes, I suppose so. Scotland Yard no longer thinks I'm in any danger here. But it sounds to me like perhaps our perp moved his activities to the States. Did you find Billy Ray? Hmmm. I'd almost bet my life he's our man."

She rang off a short while later, and Jonathan came out of the bathroom. At the stricken look on her face, he knew their time had come to an end.

"You have to go home," he said.

She nodded, going into his arms. "It's horrible, Jonathan. Mike says we've got a Ripper-style killer working his way around the United States. We've been contacted by the police in four cities, and from their VICAP reports, he's certain the murders were committed by the same perpetrator. We're having a meeting at headquarters on Friday with law enforcement officers who are coming in from Chicago, Kansas City, Phoenix, and San Francisco, the places the Ripper has struck. He wants me there."

Jonathan's blood turned to ice as the truth sank in. "Our killer wasn't Burt Brown after all."

Her expression was grave. "I think not. I've felt all along that it was Billy Ray. Somehow he got back to the States and is carrying on his bloody business all over the country. I wish we knew more about him so we could build a profile.

Mike said nobody's been able to find out anything about him."

Jonathan didn't care about any profile. He cared about Victoria. He recalled the incident in the corridor of the hotel, when Billy Ray accosted Victoria, and he was struck with a sick, awful feeling that the man was just practicing on these other women, waiting for Victoria to return.

If she left, she was going to play right into his hands.

"Don't go, Victoria." A lump the size of a boulder caught in his throat. "If the killer is the same one who murdered here, he's also the sicko who sent you the liver. You'll be exposing yourself to danger all over again."

"You know I have to go."

He felt the nip of her teeth against his shoulder. "You could quit," he whispered hoarsely. "Stay here with me."

She didn't reply immediately. "It's tempting, Jonathan. But I can't do that. I've committed my life to stopping just this kind of killer. And I'm good at it. That's why Mosier wants me back."

"I could get you a job at the Yard." He lowered his hands until they cradled her buttocks. He felt hers caress the muscles of his back.

"Sex isn't everything, you know."

"This isn't about sex, and you know it."

He heard her let out a long sigh. "Then what is it about, Jonathan? It can't be anything else. We've only known each other a little over a week. We've had fun, and the sex has been great. But now it's time to get on with life."

His gut wrenched at her words. "Do you really mean that, Victoria?"

She didn't answer.

"You don't, do you?"

She shook her head. He raised her chin, forcing her to look at him, and saw tears in her eyes. "I love you, Victoria. Please don't leave me."

Her eyes widened. "Love?"

Jonathan had never thought it possible that he would fall in love with a woman, much less so hopelessly, irretrievably in love. "Yes. I love you. I didn't mean for it to happen. I don't know how it could happen so fast. But I fell in love with you almost from the moment I saw you."

Her lips tilted in a tremulous smile. "I love you, too, Jonathan. But that doesn't solve anything, does it? I still have to go home, and you have a life here."

He knew she was right, but he'd be damned if he'd let it end here. "I'm coming with you."

She gave him a skeptical look, but he saw a flicker of encouragement in her eyes. "How are you going to swing that?"

"Our murder case here is no longer resolved. With this turn of events, it would appear that our killer is now on the loose in America. I think I could convince Sandringham to let me follow it up there. Providing, of course," he added, kissing her full on the lips, "the FBI invites me in on the case."

Sixteen

London
Eighth September 1888

It is just past dawn, and I sit exhausted but unable to sleep, whilst Eddy lies in blissful slumber upon my bed. He read in the newspapers of the whore I killed last week and came to me in a rage, demanding to know why I would do such a thing without him. He never received my messages, which disturbs me, for I fear they have been intercepted by those who wish to keep me from him.

To appease him, and to satisfy my own growing need, tonight we made our way once again into the East End, going into Spitalfield this time rather than Whitechapel, which after my last two hunts has attracted too much attention by the police. After coaching Eddy on the technique of strangulation before incision, I offered him the honor of taking first blood, which he eagerly accepted.

While I stood watch, Eddy approached an old whore with a vile, consumptive cough, who was staggering against the wall of a tenement house. I followed them through a doorway at the side that led to a dark and uninhabited backyard. He followed my instructions to the letter, asking her to turn her back to him, whereon he attempted the strangulation. He being slight of build and she a pork pie, he was unable to choke her before she cried out, "No!" Before I could come to his aid, how-

ever, he had already applied the knife, killing her before she could make another sound. Unfortunately, her blood spurted and soiled his clothing. I have burned them just now in the grate. We must take no chances of discovery.

The souvenir of tonight's hunt sits before me on the table, sealed in a glycine bag. It is the womb of the old whore that I thought last night in my frenzy to serve up for breakfast, but seeing the disgusting thing now, I will feed it instead to the landlord's dog.

The air was cool and damp against his cheek as he walked along the quay, watching the fog settle around the luxury yachts berthed at one of the most exclusive marinas in the area. He wondered idly how many millions of dollars were tied up here, bobbing in the dark waters of the cove. Rich men's toys.

His eyes lifted to the bright lights of the adjacent clubhouse, where those rich men and their whores partied the night away, unaware that one among them would not see the light of another dawn. Like the other times, he had not chosen a specific one, but preferred to let fate deliver its choice into his hands at random. He did not have to wait long. A couple stepped out into the night, arguing furiously.

"I was not flirting with Arthur," the woman said in a high-pitched whine, "although he pays more attention to me than you do." She walked unsteadily and her speech was slurred.

"Shut up, bitch. You haven't been faithful to me one day since I've known you. As far as I'm concerned, this is it. The engagement's off. You can keep the ring. Hock it if you like. It's the last dime you'll ever get out of me." With that, the man turned and disappeared among the rows of expensive cars in the parking lot, leaving the woman standing alone and bewildered in the shadows.

He strolled up to her. "Rough night?"

She jerked around at the sound of his voice. "Who're you?"

"New kid on the block. Looks like you could use a friend. Want to take a walk?"

She sniffed, glanced back toward the parking lot, then with one hand tossed back the profusion of golden-red curls that crowned her head. "Sure. Who needs him anyhow? He was nothing but a royal pain in the ass." She studied his face. "Pretty cute. What's your name?"

"My friends call me Jack." He took her by the elbow and led her down the dock. "Any of these yours?" he asked, indicating the rows of yachts.

She shook her head. "Nope. But jerko owns the one down there near the end. Big sucker. Guess he had to buy a great big boat to make up for the size of his teeny-weeny pecker."

He frowned. He didn't like women who talked like this. He was glad the world would soon be rid of one more of her kind. Her boyfriend was right. She was a bitch. "Think he'd mind if we went on board and made out?"

She looked at him in astonishment, then threw her head back and laughed from her belly. "Do I give a shit if he minds? He's the one who left me. It'll serve him right. Come on, honey. And we don't have to stop at making out."

She ran down the dock, balancing precariously in high heels, and he was relieved when she finally stopped next to the biggest boat in the marina. Perfect.

"Any security alarms going to go off?" he asked as he joined her, trying not to act as if he were in any hurry, although he could feel his cock swelling in anticipation of the event.

He checked the other boats nearby to see if anyone might have seen them, but there was no one around and the boats all appeared unoccupied. He couldn't be too careful, however. This place was riskier than the others had been, because unless he wanted to swim, he would have to escape back down the dock after the deed. The heightened risk, however, only served to heighten the anticipation.

"No alarms. Not if we don't go below. But there's no need. The cockpit cushions will do nicely."

They climbed the short gangplank and went aboard and into the protective shadows of the enclosed cockpit. She turned to him and smiled seductively. "What'd you say your name was?"

"Jack."

"Well, come here, Jacky boy, and let me show you what that asshole gave up tonight."

He slid his hands up her bare arms, across her shoulders, and around her slender neck. He saw the expression in her eyes change from seduction to confusion to terror. It was the terror that lasted the longest, as he played with her, choking her until she was almost unconscious, then allowing her just enough air to revive and remember that he was killing her, a technique he'd learned from the master. She never made a sound, although her mouth was open in a silent scream.

At last he grew tired of the game and finished the kill and laid her out on one of the white canvas-covered cushions. He must be extra careful not to get any bloodstains on him tonight, for he wore white trousers with his blue blazer, the unofficial "uniform" of yachties.

His body heat began to rise as he slid the long, finely honed knife from its hiding place, raised it and slashed the blade across her throat in a clean cut. There was no great spurt of blood as he would have liked, as she was already dead, but he knew this way was safer. It was the master's design, and the master had never been caught.

He gutted her, thinking it not much different from gutting a large fish, and threw the entrails overboard to the fish as a midnight snack. Finding a large gaff hook secured to the roof, he swung it forcefully at her head, he hooked her through the jaw, then swiveled the instrument up to tear into the roof of her mouth, just to make sure she wouldn't get away.

He gazed down at his trophy, staring into eyes that were open and sightless as a dead fish. His breath became quick and erratic as he reached sexual climax, and he shuddered when the bloodlust at last released him from its demand. He felt a warm wetness trickle down the inside of his leg.

With shaking hands, he cleaned the knife on the victim's clothing and slid it lovingly back into its unique scabbard. He secured the plastic gloves in a zipper bag, as he had done each time, photographed his work, then made his way down the dock unobserved.

"He's not wasting any time," Victoria said grimly when she learned from Mike Mosier that the killer had struck again just the night before. She and Jonathan had come straight to Quantico from the airport when their flight landed. She was tired, but anxious to get on this case. She was not afraid of Billy Ray, but she was glad Jonathan had insisted on coming along nonetheless. For more reasons than one.

Mosier briefed them on the events that had taken place in the last week. "There have now been five murders that have so much in common, we can't dismiss the probability that they were committed by the same individual. All the victims were young women from the upper crust of society. All were strangled, then mutilated. In each case, the killer also made some kind of distinctive mark on the scene, rather like a sick joke."

"What do you mean?" Until that moment, Victoria had thought this killer was likely the same as the Whitechapel murderer, but he'd left no such mark on that scene.

"For example," Mosier said, "the victim in Chicago had recently been to the opera. Her body was found in a park several miles away, but the killer must have known where she'd been that evening, because he carved a large music note into her torso. The Chicago PD believes he killed her in the city, then moved the body to a more private place to finish his job.

"In Kansas City, the victim was a young beauty queen who had been at a fund-raising barbecue. Her body was found near the river not far from the site of the event, her body parts skewered on an iron pole."

"Oh, my God," Victoria murmured, sickened.

"In Phoenix, the murder took place on a golf course. The victim's womb was in the cup at the first green, like a golf ball. In San Francisco, the victim was the daughter of a prominent politician who had just announced plans to run for governor. Her mutilated body was found in a garbage can along Fisherman's Wharf, wrapped in newspaper like a dead fish. Her father's announcement was in that paper." He sighed and ran his hand through his hair. "And this morning, the Seattle police found a young woman on a yacht. In addition to strangling and eviscerating her, the killer gaffed her like a trophy fish."

"Did you find anything on the bodies of the victims that could identify the killer with DNA testing?" Jonathan wanted to know.

"Nothing yet, although the forensic reports won't be ready for a while. At first glance, there appear to be no fingerprints. No weapon left behind. No sign of sexual assault. No blood, except for the victims'. He's good, this one. He's bold, cold, and smart, and he wants us to know it."

"You said he sent a note to the Phoenix newspaper?" Jonathan asked.

"Yes." Mike passed a photocopy of the note that had been faxed to him across his desk to Jonathan, who read it aloud.

" 'Dear Boss, You thought I was an English bloke, but you was wrong. I'm an American pie now. Ha. Ha. There is so much work to do here, I might never finish it all. I will kill into infinity if I must, to play out the game. All the whores must die, especially Her. Yours truly, Jack the Ripper.' "

Looking over his shoulder, Victoria drew in a sharp breath. "It's . . . it looks like the same handwriting as was on the note that was sent to the London *Times*, doesn't it?"

"It could be. It's very similar," Jonathan said. "Could

we fax this to my men at the Yard? Even though it isn't a firsthand sample of the writing, the graphologist should be able to verify if it is in the same hand."

"Of course," Mosier said. He rubbed his chin. "Obviously, our subject is playing at being Jack the Ripper. You two think this guy is the same one who killed in Whitechapel?"

Victoria nodded slowly. "I think there's every possibility. It'll be interesting to see how the handwriting compares. But . . ." She hesitated a moment, then said, "Although the murderer in London had the same MO as Jack the Ripper, strangling his victims before mutilating them, there was no perverted twist at the scene of the crime. This killer's signature is different, more flamboyant. His territory is certainly larger. It's like he's trying to do the old Ripper one better."

"Good point," Mike said, noting her comment on the legal pad in front of him.

"The victimology is very different, too," Jonathan pointed out. "The Whitechapel victim was a prostitute, as were all of the original Ripper's. These victims all appear to be from the opposite end of the social spectrum."

"True. That's why we don't think this is a truck driver or some kind of transient salesman. This is somebody with a grudge against someone of a high social level. It could be he is from a society family, or perhaps considers himself to have been victimized by someone like that. Since there were no defense marks on any of the victims, it's possible he was somebody they knew. At the least, he must have appeared to fit in with them. I don't think our man wears denim or leather, at least not on the job. My guess is he is fairly sophisticated and has good social and verbal skills. And he has money. Airplane tickets are expensive."

Victoria thought of Billy Ray and found it easier to picture him in gymwear than a tux. He was good-looking enough, but he hadn't demonstrated any particular social acumen when he'd shown up at the costume ball in jeans and a polo shirt. But one never knew about people like

Billy Ray. Maybe he was the black sheep of a wealthy family.

"He's very aggressive," she noted. "Usually a killer like this will learn the neighborhood where he intends to strike to give him the greatest chance for escape. Sometimes he'll stalk his victim to learn her ways, so he can attack when she is most vulnerable. But he's committed five murders in nine days, over a great distance. That's one every other day. Is that part of the pattern?"

"I would say it is. Which means he'll strike again tomorrow night. But where?" Mosier turned to a large map of the United States, his face grim. "It's a big country. Because he's hit three times now in the western states, we think he may stay out there a while, although that's pure conjecture. My guess is that he'll try Los Angeles or Hollywood. He seems fixated on the rich and famous. What better hunting grounds than Southern California?"

"But his first two were in the Midwest. What's to keep him from hopping a plane back to see how his act plays in Peoria, Mike?"

He exhaled heavily. "Nothing. He could strike anywhere. We've alerted police departments in every major city in the country and asked them to warn those citizens who fit the killer's profile, but he'll be hard to stop. Maybe on Friday, when the investigators and profile coordinators come in from around the country, we can get a better handle on him. They're supposed to be bringing firsthand reports from the medical examiners in each case. Hopefully, that'll give us a leg up with the forensics, and we can come up with an accurate profile."

"What I want to know is where Victoria fits in his scheme." Jonathan's handsome face was marred by a scowl. "He went out of his way to terrorize her in London. I think she's in danger here."

Mosier looked across at Victoria. "Blake is right. If it's the same man who struck in London, you could certainly be at risk. He sent you a human liver, for God's sake. And what about those other messages you received? Were they also from the killer?"

Victoria shook her head. "Jonathan's forensic men were able to get an imprint from the tablet we found in the apartment of a man named FitzSimmons, aka Burt Brown, the man who was killed in the hit-and-run I told you about. He wrote the warning note on the tablet with enough pressure on his pen to leave an impression on the page beneath." She paced the room. "We both thought he could possibly have been the killer until we learned about these murders. Now we think he must have witnessed the murder and was trying to warn me, although I don't understand why he chose such an enigmatic way to do it."

Mosier stood up and came to stand next to Victoria, who was staring at the map on the wall. "You fit the killer's profile, Victoria," he said. "You come from the same kind of social background—"

Victoria cut him off. She didn't want to hear it. "If he wanted to kill me, why didn't he stay in London and finish me off there? I don't think he's after me at all. He must have sent the liver to me because he'd found out at the symposium that I was with the FBI. It was an attention-getting device, nothing more."

But her instinct told her there *was* more to it than that.

Yes, he'd done it to get attention. Her attention. It was a warning, as if she'd been put on notice that one day it would be her liver he wrapped in a gift box.

A wave of nausea washed over her as she acknowledged that Mike was right. She did fit the killer's profile. Her father was a prominent attorney, her mother a matriarch of Washington society. She came from wealth and privilege, the same as his victims in the United States. It chilled her to realize that a stranger had that kind of knowledge about her background. He must have spent a lot of time researching her personal life. Perhaps he'd even stalked her. She shivered. Had he followed her to London?

But that was impossible. How would he have known she was going?

Because she'd told him.

Victoria couldn't believe she was such a fool. The killer had known all about her plans because she'd shared them openly with other Sherlockians in on-line chats the week before she left. If he knew so much about her life, he'd probably managed to hack into her computer. Obviously, he'd been lurking and listening. Damn it all! She might as well have sent him an engraved invitation.

Victoria kept these thoughts to herself. No need exposing her stupidity to both her boss and her lover. And she might be wrong. Maybe she was just being paranoid.

"We don't want to take any chances," Mosier said. "Unless he has ESP, the killer doesn't know you have returned to the States."

"I haven't told anyone I was coming back. I haven't even been to my apartment yet. We came directly from the airport."

"Good. I don't want you to go home right now. If the killer is in Seattle, he can't be watching your place. But if you answered the phone when he called, he might be on the first plane back to D.C." He took another file from his desk. Handing it to Victoria, he said, "Go directly here. Don't even think about stopping by your apartment. You have what you took with you to London. Buy anything else you might need and send me the bill. I don't want to take a chance that the killer might learn of your whereabouts."

"What is this?" she said, frowning at the information in the file.

"It's a safe house. Stay there until Friday morning. I'll call you if anything comes up. Get some rest, and be here at ten A.M. for the meeting."

Seventeen

King's College, Cambridge
Twenty-fifth September 1888
  I have been watching with interest the newspaper accounts of our little forays into the East End, for it pleases me that we have managed our endeavors under the very noses of both police and populace. It does not please me, however, that the reporters are accrediting the murders to someone else. They say that our work is that of a Jewish shoemaker by the nickname of Leather Apron. I must set them straight, for no one must be given credit for the genius of our hunt. To that end, I have just composed a note which I will post this morning to the Central News. It was a lark to craft, and it identifies the real killer. Not me, of course, nor Eddy. I have given us a name. I believe the press will adore us.

  Dear Boss
    I keep on hearing the police
    have caught me but they wont fix
    me just yet. I have laughed when
    they look so clever and talk about
    being on the right track. That joke
    about Leather Apron gave me real
    fits. I am down on whores and
    I shant quit ripping them till I

*do get buckled. Grand work the last
job was. I gave the lady no time to
squeal. How can they catch me now.
I love my work and want to start
again. You will soon hear of me
with my funny little games. I
saved some of the proper* red *stuff in
a ginger beer bottle over the last job
to write with but it went thick
like glue and I cant use it. Red
ink is fit enough I hope ha ha.
The next job I do I shall clip
the lady's ears off and send to the
police officers just for jolly wouldnt
you. Keep this letter back till I
do a bit more work then give
it out straight. My knife's so nice
and sharp I want to get to work
right away if I get a chance.
Good luck.*

*Yours truly
Jack the Ripper*

Dont mind me giving the trade name

*wasnt good enough
to post this before
I got all the red
ink off my hands
curse it.
No luck yet.   They
say I'm a doctor
now* ha ha.

In the privacy of his hotel room, he cleaned the whore's
blood from his knife and surveyed his clothing. He had
been messy this time. Not only had he bloodied himself,
he'd come all down one of his pant legs. He placed the

white trousers and socks into a plastic laundry bag, then went to check on the condition of his shoes, which were soaking in a bathtub of cold water. He hoped he hadn't ruined them. They were his favorite Topsiders.

He twisted them gently beneath the water to ease the blood from between the narrow clefts in the soles that were designed to give safe footing on a boat. When he was satisfied they were clean, he set them on a table in front of the heater. They would be stiff when they dried, but unharmed. Boat shoes, after all, were made to get wet.

He considered what to do about the bag of bloody clothes. He couldn't just chuck them into a Dumpster somewhere. What if they were found? No, he needed to follow the master's plan. Bloody clothing must be burned. But there was no fireplace in this nondescript corporate hotel room.

Heaving a sigh, he turned to the map he'd laid out on the bed, and studied it carefully. A smile twisted his mouth. He would have to carry the clothing with him to his next stop, but he was sure he would find a cozy fireplace in which to dispose of them there.

It was all part of the design.

The master had not let him down.

As she drove, Victoria glanced across the car at Jonathan, who gave her a wry grin. She knew exactly what was going through his mind. A safe house. He was thinking about what he'd said he would do if they were confined to a safe house in London. Damn it all! She almost wished he hadn't accompanied her now. She didn't need the distraction. They were facing a horrific case, and she needed all her wits about her. How was she supposed to remain clearheaded when Jonathan Blake turned her mind to mush? This was a really bad idea.

Professionally speaking.

The safe house was a nondescript, low-slung rancher in a suburb south of D.C. "Are you certain this is the right address?" Jonathan asked, peering at the structure. "I thought a safe house would be in the city."

Victoria turned into the driveway and pressed the button on the garage-door opener. "Where better to become invisible than in suburbia?"

Mike had arranged for the car and provided the garage-door opener. He had called the woman who normally kept the house ready and alerted her that the premises would be in use for an undetermined length of time. He'd given them instructions on enabling and disabling the alarm system, and warned them to keep the blinds drawn and to stay out of sight.

"Lay low and get some rest," he'd told them. Rest sounded good to Victoria. And a hot shower. She felt like the queen of grunge after the long flight, followed by hours at headquarters. Jonathan dragged in their bags, and she hitched two sacks of groceries onto her hips. She was glad she'd insisted on picking up some supplies on the way. She doubted she would have the energy to go out again once she started to unwind.

The inside of the safe house was as plain vanilla as the outside. It was furnished with serviceable but unremarkable furniture. Just the usual. Sofa, chairs, tables, lamps, television . . . and a small surveillance camera winking at her from the corner.

Jonathan came out of the bathroom, zipping his fly.

"You might want to finish that before you come back in here," Victoria said curtly, pointing to the camera when he entered the room.

"They're spying on us?"

"I'm sure they wouldn't call it that. It's for security, but to me it's an invasion of privacy. Come on. Let's get out of here. This place is the pits." She waved into the camera before hauling the groceries back to the car. Jonathan followed but didn't bring their bags.

"You were ordered to stay here," he said. "It's for your own protection, Victoria. You can't just leave."

But Victoria wasn't about to give anyone who might be

monitoring the camera a firsthand view of what was likely to transpire between her and Jonathan. "Watch me," she said. "Bring our luggage, please."

"Victoria." Jonathan's voice was harsh as he stepped into the garage. "Don't be so bullheaded. Think about what you're doing. You can't go back to your apartment right now. What if the killer is waiting, watching for you to come home?" He drew her into his arms, his touch diffusing her temper somewhat. But she'd already made up her mind.

"Like Mike said, the killer can't be in Seattle and D.C. at the same time," she pointed out. "But don't worry. We're not going to my place."

"Where, then? A hotel?"

"Bring the bags and get in," she said with a grin. "I've got another idea."

Forty-five minutes later she pulled the car to a halt at the end of a long, private lane lined with trees whose leaves were burnished gold and red by the last rays of the setting sun. Before them stood a small but elegant red-brick house with white trim and black shutters, a house that had been in her family since the days of Thomas Jefferson. Victoria had forgotten how beautiful the place was in the fall.

"What's this?" Jonathan asked.

"My family's getaway place on Virginia's Northern Neck. Nobody lives here. We just use it for weekends and guests. I come here from time to time when I need a quiet place to think." She turned to Jonathan. "It's as safe as it gets, and . . ." she added with a wrinkle of her nose, "there are no snooping cameras."

They unloaded their gear once again, and Victoria ushered him into what her family termed "the cottage." She loved it here and immediately felt safe and secure. There was no way Billy Ray could know about this place. Mike would be furious that she'd disobeyed his orders, but he really couldn't force her to stay anywhere she didn't want to be. If she had to go into hiding, it might as well be someplace of her own choosing.

"It's chilly in here," she said, turning up the thermostat.

"We'll use the first bedroom to the right up the stairs if you want to stash our bags." Victoria felt a momentary hesitation. That was the room her parents had always used. The master bedroom. The one with the big fireplace. What would they say if they knew she was going to be romping around up there with her lover?

But they wouldn't know. And she had every right to be here. She legally owned half this property. It had been left to her and Meghan in her grandmother's will. Meghan's half was now in trust for future grandchildren. So technically, she supposed, it was more hers to use than her parents'. She looked around, seeing the old place with new, slightly possessive eyes.

And as for her lover, she thought, hearing his footsteps descending the stairs, that was nobody's business but hers.

"Quite some place you've got here," he said, coming to her and resting his hands on her shoulders. "How old is it?"

"My great-great-great-something grandparents built it just after the War of 1812," she told him. "It's been handed down through the generations. We're lucky it's never been sold outside the family."

He was silent for a long moment, and she wondered what he was thinking.

Her stomach growled. "How about something to eat?" she asked, troubled by the look on his face.

"Sure."

The kitchen was at the back of the house and had been renovated less than ten years before. It adjoined a large family room, and together the two rooms stretched from one side of the house to the other. A row of French doors opened onto a wide deck at the back. She flicked on the light, illuminating the china-blue floral wallpaper and bright white cabinets.

"I'm not much of a cook," she said, apologizing in advance for what would likely be a mediocre meal. Jonathan had managed far better in his kitchen than she could in her own. He'd made several wonderful meals for her during their too-short time together in London. "When I'm alone, I usually just pop a frozen dinner into the microwave."

"Sounds ghastly," Jonathan said, going to her and turning her to face him. "Let me do the honors."

For the first time since they'd become lovers, Jonathan felt ill at ease around Victoria. Coming here to this "cottage," a far grander house than he'd ever lived in, served to underscore the differences between them. She was American, he British. They lived thousands of miles apart. She came from the upper realms of society, he from the working class. She was wealthy, he lived month-to-month. The only thing they had in common was their career choice—law enforcement—and even in that they disagreed.

It was naïve to think that there was any hope for them in the long term. He shouldn't expect any such thing. He should put on some armor, do something to let himself down easy instead of setting himself up for the big fall he expected would inevitably come his way. And yet, when he looked at her, he was helpless. He loved her. He couldn't deny it, and he couldn't do anything about it.

The best he could do was try to protect her from the danger that presently threatened and hope for a miracle when it was behind them.

He could also feed her a decent meal.

While Victoria showered, Jonathan turned the items from the supermarket bag into a savory-scented supper of chicken breasts broiled in herbs and butter, roasted new potatoes with rosemary, sautéed artichoke hearts, and hot bread, accompanied by a crisp white Bordeaux.

"Where did you learn to cook like this?" Victoria asked, diving into the meal with relish. "The things you've made me have been more French than English by a long shot."

Jonathan laughed. "I learned by reading cookbooks written by an American," he confessed. "Julia Child. She's a wizard."

Victoria lowered her fork and stared across the table at

him, her eyes shining. "What did I ever do to deserve you in my life?"

Jonathan swallowed, his throat suddenly tight. "I'm the one who should be asking you that question."

Silence stretched between them. Then Victoria said quietly, "You're the best thing that's ever happened to me, Jonathan. I don't know what lies ahead for us, but I'm grateful for what we have right now. This moment. If it all falls down tomorrow, at least we will have had now."

Jonathan's heart constricted even more painfully than his throat. He didn't want it to fall down, tomorrow or ever, but he knew that it probably would.

They finished eating in silence, and Victoria insisted on cleaning up, since Jonathan had done the cooking. "Fair's fair," she told him. "And besides, I don't mind a bit. It took you half an hour to prepare things. It'll only take me five minutes to straighten the kitchen. I think I got the better end of the deal."

Jonathan sat on a nearby barstool and watched her bustle about the large, well-appointed kitchen, wishing with all his heart things could be different. He imagined them doing this together every night of their lives, sharing a safe, secure future in a beautiful home such as this. It was a dream he suddenly craved, but a dream that would never be.

The ringing of Victoria's cell phone broke through his gloomy thoughts. She dried her hands and gave him a rueful look. "The boss has found us out," she said in mock alarm.

"Agent Thomas here," she answered, making a face as if she were getting ready for a lambasting from Mike Mosier. But the voice on the other end brought an expression of shock and concern to her face. "Mother! What a . . . surprise . . ."

Jonathan could only hear one half of the conversation, but he could tell Victoria was nervous talking to her mother.

"I just got in this afternoon," she said rather defensively. "I haven't had time to call you. I'm at the cottage. No, no,

Mother, everything's fine. You know I love it here in the autumn. I just decided to spend the last few days of my vacation here. England's kind of cold and wet," she added, shrugging her shoulders at him apologetically. "How are you and Dad?"

She was quiet for a long time, then took the phone into the family room and slumped into a large chair. "When did this happen?" she asked quietly. "Are the police certain he's the one?"

At that, alarms went off in Jonathan's head. He didn't want to intrude, but Victoria's face had gone white. Something was wrong. He strode silently into the room and stood looking through the panes of the French doors into the gathering darkness, waiting for her to finish the call, on fire to know what was going on.

"No, I don't want to come home, Mother," she said, her words clipped. "Please, just leave me alone. I need some time to get used to this. I'll be fine here at the cottage, but please don't tell anyone I'm here. I don't want the media to find me. You of all people should understand that."

Disconnecting the call, she let the phone slip to the floor and covered her face with her hands. Jonathan was by her side in an instant.

"What is it, love?" he asked, dropping to his knees by her chair. "What's wrong?"

"They found him. The man who killed my sister."

Jonathan took her hands in his. They were like ice. "Who is it?"

"No one we knew," she answered, wiping her eyes. "He's the guy she ran off to meet at the motel. His name's Ferguson. Matthew Ferguson."

"How did they find him?"

"He left a suicide note." Her shoulders began to shake with the sobs she could no longer control.

"Good God." Jonathan drew Victoria out of the chair and held her as tightly as he could. He didn't ask anything further, but waited until she quieted enough to speak again.

"He . . . he was a married man, with two little children,"

she managed at last. "In his note, he confessed to his wife that he'd been having an affair with Meghan, and he said that he was responsible for her death. He wrote that he could no longer live with himself for the wrongs he had done. He begged his wife and children to forgive him." She sniffed and added bitterly, "Mother didn't mention whether he begged Meghan's family for forgiveness."

Jonathan was glad he had been here for her when she learned the awful truth. He couldn't believe her mother would tell her something that earthshaking over the telephone, instead of in person. But he surmised Victoria was not close to her parents. Maybe this was the only way they communicated.

At any rate, he was relieved that she finally had the answer that had eluded her for seven long years. Maybe now she could begin to heal from that terrible trauma. "Want some hot tea?" he asked after her sobs subsided.

She shook her head. "No. I only want you, Jonathan. Please," she said, looking into his eyes, "will you just hold me and make all this go away?"

Thursday morning dawned crisp and bright, with the reds and oranges of the autumn foliage stirring in the light breeze, their colors brilliant against a sapphire-blue sky. It was the most sensational fall leaf color Victoria could remember in years. She was up early, mainly because she had slept so fitfully. She'd dressed quietly so as not to awaken Jonathan, then brought a cup of coffee outside onto the deck at the back of the cottage, seeking an elusive tranquility. She could hear the trickle of the nearby creek as it worked its way toward the river. In the distance, a woodpecker drilled for breakfast. Overhead, a flock of birds headed south in formation. Everything seemed peaceful. In order. As it should be.

Except it wasn't.

She inhaled deeply of the fresh air, scented with the tart perfume of autumn, and tried to relax. She should feel some relief, she thought, some sense of satisfaction that at last they knew what had happened to Meghan. It was tragic and sordid, but over with at last. Grizzell must be relieved, she thought bitterly. Time, and Matthew Ferguson's guilt, had done his job for him. Now he could officially close the books, and no one would be the wiser about his gross incompetence.

Victoria sipped her coffee, turning everything over in her mind, as she had done for most of the night. Something about it didn't feel right to her. Maybe she was just in denial that her baby sister could have been involved in such an affair. But Meghan had been young and rebellious. What better way to get back at her strict and self-righteous parents than to have an affair with a married man? It didn't excuse her sister, but it was an explanation Victoria could understand.

She made a mental note to learn more about the young man who had committed suicide only a few days before. What had Matthew Ferguson been like? He must have been a charmer to get Meghan's attention. He'd been a liar for certain. Had he cheated before? Did he abuse his wife? Another question came to mind. Had he killed other women? Would his death resolve any other unsolved crimes in the area? Most importantly, was he the kind of man who could take a knife and butcher a woman as he had Meghan?

Killers were killers. They all took life. But some were more fastidious than others, preferring the distance and impersonality of a gun. To those killers, strangulation was too intimate and the knife a messy thing. Not every killer could do what Meghan's murderer had done to her.

Hearing the door open behind her, Victoria turned and saw Jonathan step out onto the deck carrying a cup of coffee. His hair was wet from the shower, and his shirt was not fully buttoned. The sight of him quickened her pulse and cheered her as nothing else could.

"Good morning," he said quietly, coming to her chair and taking her fingers in his.

"Good morning." She kissed the skin of his knuckles.

"Need a refill?" He indicated her nearly empty cup.

She shook her head. "Not right now. Thanks."

He squeezed her fingers. "Are you all right? You look as if you didn't sleep much last night."

She gave him a wan smile. "I'm all right. Not great, but all right. Mother's news was quite a shock, and I'm having difficulty getting used to it, that's all. I hope I didn't keep you awake with all my tossing and turning."

He shook his head. "No. I guess my jet lag was better than a sleeping pill. But I'm worried about you. You need some rest. Some quality sleep."

It warmed her that he was so concerned about her. "I know. But please don't worry about me. I'll get to it soon. Right now, I have other things on my mind, like how to stop all the other Matthew Fergusons of the world."

"You can't stop them all, Victoria."

"I can try." The image of Meghan welled in her mind. No one deserved to die like that. "I have to try."

"It's a crusade with you, isn't it?"

"I . . . I suppose so." She didn't want to pursue his line of thinking. She stood up, looking at her watch. "I'd better call Mosier and let him know where we are."

"I already told him."

She jerked her head up sharply. "You talked to Mosier? When?"

"Just now. I knew you weren't in the best of spirits, so I called him to check in. So far there haven't been any reports of another similar murder. Mike said he'll get back to us if anything earthshaking turns up. I told him we'd see him in the morning."

Victoria didn't have the energy to be angry with him for interfering. "Did you tell him where we were?"

"He already knew. Apparently he had a tail on us from the start, just for good measure."

She laughed. "I should have known. He doesn't trust me to do his bidding sometimes."

"I'm so surprised," Jonathan said, kissing her forehead.

"What if his bidding comes in the form of real orders? He is your boss, you know."

"Then I follow them. But this wasn't the same and you know it. Mike didn't really care if I stayed at the safe house. He just didn't want me to go to my apartment. And I didn't. Nobody knows where I am, except Mother and Mike, and the poor agent in the car at the end of the driveway."

Victoria went upstairs to make the bed, leaving Jonathan busying himself in the kitchen. Only minutes later, tantalizing aromas wafted up the stairs, causing her mouth to water. I could get used to this, she thought, but put the temptation out of her head. She mustn't get used to it.

There was no future for them.

Eighteen

London
Thirtieth September 1888

   My plan for regaining power over Eddy has succeeded
far beyond my dreams. By instilling in him the lust for
the blood of whores, I have discovered a lure powerful
enough to overcome his intimidation by those at Windsor
who would keep him from me. He has of his own accord
arranged with Lord Somerset to secure a coach whenever
he is able to steal away at night, and he has come to me
more frequently than he has since leaving Cambridge.
   We must be more careful than we were on tonight's
hunt, however, for we had a witness and barely managed
to escape detection. Eddy had scarcely got the whore to
the pavement when a man approached. I called out "Lip-
ski," our prearranged warning, and Eddy heeded the
alert, running away into the night. Such was my rage at
being interrupted, I chased after the man, who unfortunately eluded me. I fear he might have seen too much
and be able to identify Eddy.
   When I realized my pursuit was in vain, I gave up the
chase and began to look for Eddy. I worried that he was
lost in that filthy maze, perhaps bloodied and thus vulnerable should he be accosted by a constable or vigilante.
The thought terrified me, and I searched in near panic
until I came upon him, hatless and shivering in a hidden

*corner of Mitre Square. He shook, but not from fear. He
begged we try again, for the business was unfinished, and
his need had not been satisfied.*

*We found our next prey nearby, a whore so far gone
with drink she facilitated the job by passing out on the
pavement. We decorated her in her own intestines, and I
took her kidney as a souvenir. We were only a few short
blocks away when we heard the police whistles. We were
the hunted now, not the hunters. I had devised a ruse to
throw them off our trail, but it entailed remaining in the
area, a dangerous risk after our double event. Still, I
considered it worth the effort. I reached into the pocket
of my coat for the chalk I had brought along for this express purpose, and on the face of the black bricks edging
a nearby doorway, I inscribed:*

> *The Juwes are
> The men That
>   Will not
> be Blamed
>   for nothing.*

*Ha. Ha. Let them figure that one! Leather Apron is a
Jew. There are hundreds of Jews in that sewer. I want them
to believe that Jack the Ripper is also Jack the Juwe!*

He got off the plane in Denver and went straight to a news-
stand. Surely they would have figured it out by now, that
the series of brilliant murders all across the country was
the work of one man. He'd been keeping an eye on the
papers as he went along, and tuned in CNN every night,
but so far, there had been no mention of him as a serial
killer.

The vendor sold papers from major metro areas in the
West. He picked up one from Seattle and was gratified that
at least he'd made the front page. Gratified until he read
that the police were holding the woman's fiancé, considering him to be the prime suspect. He swore silently. He

should have thought of that. Damn it. He tossed the paper roughly back onto the shelf. Of course they would think it was that asshole. It was his boat. He'd had a fight with the girl. Shit!

The idea of someone else getting credit for his work infuriated him. He was the master behind the murder, not the dumb bastard who'd thrown the girl away.

A new sense of urgency burned in his belly. He was the one who had planned it all so carefully. He'd been the one who had orchestrated the entire tour with such brilliant precision. He would not allow someone else the glory. He would be, like the master, the most famous killer on earth.

Before renting a car, he purchased some stationery and a pen, and sitting with a cappuccino in the high-tech Denver airport, he wrote a note that should set things straight.

The rumble of thunder awakened Victoria from a sound sleep, and she rolled over and looked at the clock. It was nearly three in the afternoon. She frowned and got out of bed. She hadn't meant to sleep so long. It had cost her precious hours of what she believed would be her last private time with Jonathan.

She washed her face and brushed her teeth, wishing the picnic by the river they'd attempted hadn't been rained out. She had taken him to a place she'd often gone as a child, a secret grove just above the river, where she'd hoped they might share more than the picnic lunch. But the storm had abruptly changed their plans, and after their mad dash back to the cottage, her fatigue had nearly overwhelmed her. At Jonathan's insistence, she had gone to bed for a little nap, making him promise not to let her sleep too long.

Obviously, he had not kept his promise.

Turning off the water, she heard footsteps on the stairs. Instinctively she reached for her robe, but let it drop when she saw Jonathan enter the room. He carried an armload of firewood.

"I see Sleeping Beauty's awake," Jonathan said, his gaze sweeping slowly over the length of her body.

"You weren't supposed to let me sleep so long."

"You needed it." He laid the fire and lit it. The flames rose eagerly as the smoke trailed up the chimney, and warmth began to spread into the room. "I thought it was chilly up here. I didn't want you to be cold."

She crossed the room and leaned into his arms. "I know another way you can warm me up."

Their lovemaking began as a tender exploration, but like the fire, soon blazed with a heat that threatened to consume them. "Jonathan." Victoria breathed out his name, and on the intake, inhaled deeply of his scent, storing it in her soul. Her fingers roamed every inch of his skin, memorizing his body, never to be forgotten. Her tongue tasted him, savoring the slightly salty tang on her lips. A feeling akin to desperation overwhelmed her as she drew him inside of her. He completed her. He was part of her. And she never wanted to let him go.

She clung to him as together they rode the wave to its crescendo, and fought back tears when sometime later she returned to earth.

She had never known love could hurt this much.

Later, she heard the rain let up, and a stray ray of sunlight fell briefly across the bed where they lay entwined, holding on to each other and to the present moment, even as the clock ticked inexorably toward the end of their time together. A deep growl emitted from Victoria's stomach, and she laughed. "That wasn't very sexy, was it?"

"I see we've worked up an appetite." He grinned and kissed her, then rolled toward the edge of the bed. Reluctantly, she allowed him from her embrace, but to her surprise, he didn't leave the bed. Instead, he reached for something nearby, and when he turned to her, she was astonished to see he held the picnic hamper in one hand.

"Shall we finish what we started?"

She laughed and sat up. "Here?"

"Why not?"

"Let me throw on a robe."

He touched her shoulder. "No. Don't."

Victoria pulled the sheet up to her breasts, suddenly and irrationally self-conscious. "We're going to eat . . . naked?"

"Sure, why not? We'll have our picnic in front of the fire instead of by the river. It's warmer, and a whole lot drier."

Before she could protest further, he spread the laminated tablecloth over the bedspread, then brought out the sandwiches he had made earlier, along with fruit, some cheeses, a bottle of Merlot and two wine stems. "I'm surprised the glasses didn't get broken when we had to make a run for it," he remarked as casually as if they were fully clothed and seated across a table from one another.

Victoria shook her head and laughed softly. "Jonathan Blake, you are the most amazing man."

"Glad you aren't a prude."

"Me, too."

Opening the wine, he poured them each a glass and handed one to her. He raised his and clinked it against hers. "Here's to rainy days."

The wine was soft and mellow. Delicious. But when she bit into the thick chicken salad sandwiches he'd prepared, she forgot the wine.

"This is wonderful," she said. "I've never had chicken salad like this. What's in it?"

"I found some tarragon on the spice rack and some almonds in the freezer. I just chopped some of that celery we brought with us last night and threw in some mayonnaise."

Just.

"You *just* did that." She eyed him thoughtfully. "If I'd been making lunch, you would have had two pieces of cold chicken between two slices of bread. You'd have been lucky if I remembered the mayo at all."

"Then you'd better let me be in charge of our kitchen."

His words landed between them with an almost audible thud. "Our kitchen?" She turned to look at him. "Are we going to have a kitchen, Jonathan?"

To her surprise, he blushed. "That . . . just sort of slipped out."

He didn't take it any further, and Victoria swallowed her disappointment along with the bite of chicken salad. She knew theirs wasn't destined to be a long-term relationship, but God in heaven, she couldn't help it, a part of her longed for more.

She didn't have time to brood on it, however. Just as she was about to bite into an apple, she heard the front door open, and a familiar voice called, "Victoria? Victoria, are you here?"

"Oh, shit," she uttered, jumping off the bed and scrambling for a bathrobe.

Jonathan immediately worked into his jeans and shirt. "Who is it?" he asked in a hushed voice.

"Mother."

Victoria looked down to see Barbara Wentworth Thomas, as always elegantly dressed and adorned with expensive gold jewelry, standing in the foyer of the cottage, her expression a mixture of confusion and apprehension. She did not see her daughter when Victoria came out into the upper hall, clad only in a white terry robe. Victoria stared at her mother for a long moment, dreading the scene that was bound to ensue when she learned that Jonathan was staying here with her. Maybe she could find a way to prevent her from learning the full truth.

"Hello, Mother," she said. "What brings you out here?" Victoria came down the stairs and stiffly embraced her mother, giving her a peck on the cheek.

"Victoria, what is going on here?" Her mother's eyes were darker than Victoria's, and right now, they held a glint of anger. "I came all the way out here in the rain to make sure you were all right, and that man at the front gate almost wouldn't let me onto my own property! Who is he, and what is he doing here?"

"Don't know who got stuck with that assignment, Mother. One of our agents. And just to remind you, it's my property now."

Barbara sniffed and walked into the living area to the

left of the stairs. "It's family property. Why is that man there?" She said it as if "that man" were a leper.

Her disdainful attitude toward those she considered beneath her never failed to annoy Victoria, and she lashed out without thinking. "Oh, he's just somebody who's trying to save my life."

Her mother whirled around to face her. "What do you mean?"

Victoria saw the alarm in her mother's eyes and wished she hadn't been so cruel. She softened and gave Barbara a small smile. "Don't worry, Mother. I'm not in any immediate danger. Mike just wanted me to stay out of sight until we can get a handle on this creep who might be after me. I thought the cottage would be as safe a place as any. And," she added, bracing for the worst, "I'm not here alone. Besides the man at the gate, I have a . . . bodyguard."

"Bodyguard?" From the tone of her mother's voice, she could tell that Barbara Wentworth Thomas was thoroughly mortified at the notion. "Where?"

"Upstairs. I told him to give us a few minutes alone."

Barbara shifted her eyes to the landing, then looked at Victoria with a disapproving frown. "Why aren't you dressed? He isn't . . . I mean, are you sure it's safe for you to be alone . . . with a strange man?"

Victoria worked at controlling the blush that threatened to bloom on her cheeks. She didn't want to lie to her mother, but there was no need to tell her everything. After all, her relationship with Jonathan was only temporary.

"He isn't a stranger, Mother. He's a detective I met in London. He's here to help on the case and got stuck with the . . . uh . . . bodyguard assignment. As for the robe, I was just . . . taking a nap," she added, stretching the truth.

She explained about the murder in London, leaving out the parts about the killer being a Jack the Ripper copycat, and that he'd sent her a body part, and that he'd already struck again a number of times in the U.S. "I think that the killer was a young man named Billy Ray who was at the Sherlockian symposium. But the FBI has yet to locate him.

Until he's found, they want me to stay away from my apartment. Mr. Blake and the agent at the head of the lane are just insurance against anything happening."

"Oh, Victoria, that's just horrible. I couldn't bear it if—" She broke off, and Victoria knew exactly what her mother was thinking. They'd already lost one daughter to violent crime . . .

"Nothing is going to happen to me, Mother." She hoped she sounded reassuring. "That's why we're taking all these precautions."

Barbara reached into her purse, drew out a tissue, and wiped her eye dramatically. "I wish you would give up this FBI nonsense. A nice girl like you does not need to be chasing around after the scum of the earth. And those men you work with aren't of your class, Victoria. They're as hard as the criminals they go after. Let them run with the rats in the gutters. You get out of it."

Victoria's temper threatened to erupt. Her mother had never even met Mike Mosier or any of the others in their unit. They were nice people. Most of them were family men and women. But Barbara was prejudiced against a stereotype and did not care to know the truth, so there was no sense in pursuing it.

"What would I do if I quit, Mother?" she snapped. "Go back to law school so I could join Dad's law firm and run with the rats aboveground?"

"You mind your mouth, young lady."

"Mother, I'm thirty-three years old. Quit trying to run my life." She knew her mother meant well, but Victoria was sick of this same old diatribe that surfaced every time they were together. That's why she rarely went home anymore.

Suddenly, she got the feeling that someone was watching them and turned to see Jonathan at the head of the stairs. He was fully dressed, thank God, but he looked sexier than ever in his jeans and a blazer. She hoped she could manage to pretend he was nothing to her other than a bodyguard, but her mother would have to be blind and a damned fool not to suspect that something else was going on between her daughter and Jonathan Blake.

"Come on down," she said, waving her hand. "I want you to meet my mother." He approached, and she noted a curious, almost hurt look on his face. What had he overheard? "Mother, this is Detective Inspector Jonathan Blake of Scotland Yard. Mr. Blake, this is my mother, Barbara Thomas."

They shook hands politely, but she could almost feel the frost in the air.

"Scotland Yard?" her mother said. "Aren't you a long way from home?"

"Yes, Mrs. Thomas," Jonathan replied, his tone distant and professional. "I'm working on this case with Victoria because the first murder took place on my side of the pond."

"First murder? Have there been others?"

"Not that we can pin on this kid," Victoria broke in hastily, giving Jonathan a warning look. She didn't want to alarm her mother even more. "Like I said, we want to stop him before there are any more. Jonathan . . . uh . . . Mr. Blake came back to the States with me to help us with the case. He's a forensic expert."

Barbara looked from Jonathan to Victoria and back again. "I wish you would talk some sense into my daughter, Mr. Blake," she said. "Victoria has no business being in such a dangerous occupation."

"Mother—"

"Or running with the rats in the gutters," Jonathan replied evenly, not taking his eyes off the woman with champagne-blond hair and immaculately manicured nails.

"I see you understand me perfectly, Mr. Blake. Such a nice young man." She turned to her daughter, who wanted to go through the floor. "You listen to him, Victoria, if you won't listen to me." She looked at her watch. "I must run along now or I'll miss cocktail hour at the club. Take care of her, Mr. Blake. Her father and I would be very unhappy if anything were to go amiss with her life. After all, she's all we have now."

Jonathan watched as Barbara Thomas climbed behind the wheel of her honey-colored Mercedes, his stomach in a knot. He had barely been able to greet the woman in a civilized manner, for he'd clearly heard her opinion of law enforcement types. Like himself.

Hard. Like criminals. Not of her class.

The irony of it was that she was right, at least about one thing. He was not of Victoria's class. The encounter served as a reality check. He knew that Victoria did not share her mother's prejudice, but she came from the same mold nonetheless. He looked around the lovely old cottage that was nothing more to these people than a playhouse and wondered what kind of mansion the Thomases must claim as their primary residence.

He was flattered that Victoria had found him sexually appealing, but he felt sure her attraction ended there. What else did he have to offer her? An austere flat in London and a detective inspector's pay? He had a rather substantial sum set aside in savings, but nothing to match the wealth of these people.

What a bloody idiot he was. He should never have let things progress so far between them. He didn't know if he could backpeddle now, distance himself from her emotionally. But if he didn't, he could see that heartbreak was headed his way like a fast train.

"I suppose we ought to give Mosier a call," he said brusquely, looking at his watch. "He said he'd telephone with any new developments, but I'm accustomed to checking in from time to time when I'm in the field."

Victoria still stood at the front door, her back to him, looking out of the glass panes at her mother's retreating car.

"Don't let her get to you, Jonathan. She doesn't mean to be insulting. She has no idea how truly rude she just was."

He wasn't sure what to say. He'd met people like Barbara Thomas before, and he had no use for them. But she was Victoria's mother. "Don't apologize, Victoria. I'm not thin-skinned."

Neither was he stupid. He knew beyond certainty that if by some miracle he and Victoria managed more than a brief relationship, Barbara Thomas would never accept him. He didn't think he was imagining things when she'd warned him not to let anything happen to her daughter.

She didn't want Jonathan Blake to happen to her daughter.

Victoria turned to him, her face grave. "I'm sorry anyway. Mother often embarrasses me." She looked down at her robe. "Guess she sort of ruined the naked picnic, didn't she? I ought to get dressed."

She came to him and stood on tiptoe to give him a chaste kiss on the cheek. "Call Mike. Tell him we can come in any time he needs us. I'm feeling much better since my nap, and frankly, I'm getting antsy to be back on the job."

Jonathan watched her hurry up the stairs, feeling more desolate than he ever had in his life. Victoria's mother had put everything into perspective for him, and obviously for Victoria, as well, for in those few moments, she had changed, stiffened, grown more distant. She was suddenly all business once again, as she had been the first day he met her.

Perhaps it was just as well. It would give him a chance to regroup emotionally. He hoped Mosier would ask them to come in right away. He would gladly spell some other weary agent.

Otherwise, it was going to be a long night.

Nineteen

London
One October, 1888

My beloved Prince departed shortly after we returned to my quarters last night, pleading a headache and general malaise. His is a tender constitution, and I am sick with fear that he might suffer some illness after our hunt in the rain. He promised to return soon, and I pray he does. I began these hunts to recapture Eddy's love, but now I find I am myself a prisoner of the bloodlust. With each hunt, I seem increasingly driven toward another.

Earlier, possessed by a desire to learn firsthand what effect our work had had on the public, I dressed as the consummate gentleman I am and took a stroll into the East End. The havoc was a sight to behold. I was accosted at every turn by constables, uniformed and not, who warned me to leave the area immediately, saying it was not a fit place for a gentlemen such as myself.

The whole of the East End is in turmoil. People are panicked and the police struck dumb by the killer's boldness and invisibility. Their confusion warms my heart, and I left, scarcely able to contain my glee. But I have not seen my first little note published anywhere, and have heard no one refer to the homicidal maniac as Jack the Ripper. It would make the game far more interesting if

the reporters called us by name. To that end, before re-
turning home, I posted a second message, to wit:

> *I wasnt codding*
> *dear old Boss when*
> *I gave you the tip.*
> *youll hear about*
> *saucy Jackys work*
> *tomorrow double*
> *event this time*
> *number one squealed*
> *a bit couldnt*
> *finish straight*
> *off. had not time*
> *to get ears for*
> *police thanks for*
> *keeping last letter*
> *back till I got*
> *to work again.*
>
> *Jack the Ripper*

Surely they will not ignore these messages, but then, the
police are a curious lot. It almost seems as if they do not
want to catch the killer.

At ten o'clock on Friday morning, a group of solemn-faced
men and women convened in a large conference room in
the NCAVC headquarters at Quantico. They had come from
the cities in which the killer had struck during his lightning
blitz of murders in the past week. They were investigators
with local law enforcement agencies and the FBI's field
profilers. They joined the special agents at Quantico with
one purpose in mind—to find the killer and stop his bloody
rampage.

Victoria took a seat between Jonathan and Mike Mosier.
In spite of the grim business before them, she was glad to
be here, glad to have other things to occupy her mind than

the personal doubts that had tormented her most of the night.

She didn't know exactly why, but something about her relationship with Jonathan had shifted with her mother's intrusion. Although they had been quietly friendly during the course of the evening, the passion that had flared so easily between them seemed to have disappeared. Why? What had transpired in those few moments to so drastically change things? Did Jonathan dislike Barbara Thomas so much he would let that come between them? She couldn't imagine it. Was it something she had said or done?

She tried to focus her attention on the business at hand, but her mind kept going back over the events of the previous afternoon, seeking answers. She had known their time together would come to an end, but she had not thought it would end like this. In her mind, it was to have been a tearful farewell at the airport and a gradual slipping away over time. She had never imagined their affair would simply die on the vine.

Mike Mosier opened the meeting by thanking the law enforcement officers who had responded so efficiently to the crisis. "By entering the data on the murders into the new national computer network and sending it immediately to VICAP, you enabled our analysts to spot the similarities between these crimes at once. Not long ago, getting this kind of result would have taken weeks, not days. With luck, by the end of today's meeting, we'll have a profile of this killer and some suggestions for proactive intervention that will help this task force capture the bastard."

Victoria had earlier explained to Jonathan that VICAP was the Violent Criminal Apprehension Program, designed to be a clearinghouse for information on crimes committed in various parts of the country. VICAP analysts made daily computer comparisons of all the cases submitted by local law enforcement agencies, and as in this instance, were often able to find matches between crimes committed in different locales. By linking the disparate agencies, VICAP facilitated communication and cooperation between them, often resulting in the quick resolution of the crimes.

"Let's get down to business," Mike said, and called on the investigator from Chicago to make the first presentation. He distributed photos and the crime-scene report, along with the notes he'd made at the autopsy. "The victim was twenty-nine years old. Name: Candace Malone. Occupation: Part-time fund-raiser for a local charity. Her father told us she had no need for any other pursuit. Apparently she lived off the income from investments he'd made for her. She'd gone to the opera alone, as she had recently broken up with a long-time boyfriend. We've checked him out. He was out of town the night of the murder.

"The autopsy showed the cause of death was manual strangulation. She was not sexually assaulted. We believe she was killed near where her car was parked, and that the killer then drove her car to the park at the edge of the city and finished his work there. Other than the victim's blood, the car was clean—no fingerprints except the victim's. Forensic is still working on it, but so far, we haven't found any foreign fabrics, hair, blood, or semen."

Victoria studied the grisly photos while she listened to the discussion about the Chicago killing. Oddly, she was able to somewhat detach from the horror of it when it came to her work as a profiler. Staring at the pictures, she tried to visualize what had happened that night, and when it came her turn, she shared her thoughts with the others.

"Despite the fact that there was no sexual assault," she said, "this is a sexually motivated murder perpetrated by a highly organized killer. Because he is so organized, I would say this is not his first murder, but he is still in the early phases of his career. I'm certain he did not plan to drive her car from the city to the park, but rather that it was a decision based on the situation at the moment. For whatever reason, strangling her didn't sufficiently gratify him. Otherwise, he would have left her on the street. But the strangulation did not fulfill his fantasy. This creep gets off on the mutilation, not the murder. His need was so strong that he put himself at considerable risk by taking her body to the park, because he hadn't planned a safe getaway."

"He must have walked back to the murder site to pick up his own vehicle," Mike Mosier interjected. "I doubt he would have risked taking public transportation. His clothes must have been bloodstained."

"If he had a vehicle. It could be that he had a room in a hotel near the murder site. Maybe somebody saw him come in that night but hasn't come forward," she said to the members of the Chicago team. "It's a long shot, but you might try checking around the hotels in the area. My guess is this guy has the money to stay in nice places. He wouldn't be caught dead in a Holiday Inn."

The investigators from Kansas City were up next. Their story was similar.

Natalie Jenkins had been a younger victim than Candace Malone. Barely twenty, she was a beauty queen, reigning for a day over a celebrity barbecue cook-off. Her father was a state senator, her mother head of the Women's League. Natalie was in college, studying finance. Her nude body, or what remained of it, was found by a creek in a wooded area near the site where the event had been held. Stuck into the ground next to it was a long metal pike onto which various internal organs had been skewered. From the lack of defense or restraint marks on the body, the Kansas City investigators believed she had willingly accompanied the killer to the murder site.

The victim in Phoenix was thirty-three. Shelley Langham was a model, and the daughter of a wealthy family. The killer had become bolder, for he had committed the crime in a relatively open area at a time when the nearby country club was filled with people. "He's getting better," Mike commented. "Faster. More confident. Therefore more daring."

"Let's hope he gets overconfident," Victoria remarked. "That's when he'll start making mistakes."

The first sign that the killer was doing exactly that came from the Seattle police. "He got a little sloppy this time.

We found bloody footprints on the dock. We're hoping that we can find a match for the shoe."

Victoria leaned forward. It wasn't much in the way of forensic evidence, but it was the first the killer had left for them. She listened carefully as the man went on.

"The imprint left by the soles of the shoes was that of a common type of boat shoe, brand name Topsider, approximately size ten. We took the fiancé in for questioning. He wears a size nine and a half and presented us with his own sets of boat shoes. No match, but that doesn't prove anything. He probably deep-sixed the shoes some place where we'll never find them."

Victoria hoped they did find the shoes. But she knew when they did, they wouldn't belong to the fiancé.

It was nearing noon by the time they had listened to the presentations of all the visiting investigators, and one thing had become crystal clear to Victoria. This killer was not only brutal, he had a warped sense of humor about his work. His MO had changed slightly from victim to victim, but his signature—some sort of twisted joke relating to each crime—was stronger than ever. So far, the police had managed to keep this aspect of the killings from the media, but it was only a matter of time until some creative reporter figured it out and broke the story. Then, the Ripper copycat would become known as the most sensational serial killer of all time.

Which was what he wanted most.

The door opened and a grim-faced man entered the room, bearing a computer printout. "This just came in from the Boulder PD," he said, handing it to Mosier.

Victoria's stomach clenched. She knew without being told the killer had struck again. Without thinking, she reached for Jonathan's hand.

Jonathan was startled when he felt Victoria's touch. She had remained distant since her mother's visit, and he had not encouraged her to be otherwise, even though their evening had been awkward. It was better to start easing away

from what he considered to be an impossible situation before it destroyed him. But now, feeling her pulse and the
warmth of her hand, he lost the control he'd struggled so
hard to maintain for the past eighteen hours. He squeezed
her hand, and she returned the squeeze, but without looking
at him.

Special Agent Mosier looked up from the paper, his expression grave. "They found the body of a young woman
this morning in a Jacuzzi at a ski resort just outside Boulder," he reported. The others took notes. "Her name was
Helen Manders. Twenty-five years old. From California, a
guest of the resort. Details about her are sketchy, but she
has been identified as the daughter of Jeff Manders, one of
Hollywood's film moguls."

"MO?" asked Ed Champion, another profiler in the unit.

"Manual strangulation from behind, like the rest. The
body was viciously mutilated before being thrown into the
water. The deck was saturated in blood."

"What about the signature?" Victoria asked. "What little
joke did he attach to this one?"

Mike shook his head in disbelief. "He poured a jar of
crab boil into the hot water and left the container on the
edge of the pool. No prints, of course."

"Oh, jeez," he heard one of the men say. Others swore.
Victoria said nothing, but her hand was tense.

Jonathan had never witnessed this kind of investigation
before. He was used to working with a small team, with
their efforts focused solely on hard evidence, such as the
bloody shoes. Until now, he had discounted the value of
psychological profiling, but seeing Victoria and the others
in action had changed his mind. Over the course of the
morning, he had developed a mental image of this madman
he simply would not have been able to conjure only from
the scanty forensic evidence.

"There's more," Mosier said, and the general commotion
in the room died instantly. "He's sent another letter, this
one to the Denver *Post*." He passed the paper to Victoria,
and she read it for them all to hear.

" 'Dear Old Boss, I wasn't codding when I said I will kill into infinity. Haven't you figured it out yet? I laughed when I read the Seattle police think they've caught the killer. I laugh at their stupidity, for they haven't caught me, and I'm the one who gaffed the girl. Think I'll stir up a little stew in your neighborhood tonight. Hoping for a double event after that, just for fun. I won't stop ripping until I get buckled. Ripping is my destiny. It is my heritage, it is in my blood. My knife is sharp and I love my work. Can't wait to show it to Her. Yours truly, Saucy Jacky.' "

Victoria looked up at the others. "Some of this wording is taken from one of the original Ripper letters. I'd have to look it up to know exactly which words are the same, but the tone and content are carefully copied. I wonder what he meant by 'Ripping is my destiny . . . it is in my blood . . .' "

Jonathan stared at the now familiar handwriting. "There's no doubt this is the same killer that sent the note in London," he said.

" 'Stir up a stew . . .' " Mike said. "That must refer to the Boulder case. He must have planned all along to throw the crab boil in the hot tub. Very organized at this point."

" 'Hoping for a double event after that . . .' " Victoria repeated the words, her voice sounding haunted, and Jonathan saw her shudder.

"The original Ripper murdered two women in the same night, and sent a letter to the Central News Agency warning of it in advance," he explained to the others.

"He's going to commit a double murder, tomorrow night if he keeps to his pattern." She said it in a matter-of-fact tone, but her face was ashen. "We have to stop him."

"It would help if we knew where he will strike next," Mosier said, sounding discouraged.

Ed Champion spoke up. "A double event might mean he'll strike in twin cities, like Minneapolis–St. Paul or Dallas–Fort Worth."

"Or he could have twins on his hit list," suggested another profiler.

"There's something else about the letter that bothers me," Mosier said, rustling through a file. He withdrew another paper and studied it briefly. "That's what I thought. This is the photocopy of the note he sent to the Phoenix paper. Listen to this: 'Dear Boss, You thought I was an English bloke, but you was wrong. I'm an American pie now. Ha. Ha. There is so much work to do here, I might never finish it all. I will kill into infinity if I must, to play out the game. All the whores must die, especially Her. Yours truly, Jack the Ripper.' "

He raised his head. "He refers to 'Her' in both letters. 'Her' with a capital *h*. He talks about killing into infinity, but I think he has a destination in mind. Her. The rest may be random victims, but I believe he is driven by his desire to kill a specific victim."

"His mother maybe?" Ed suggested.

"Perhaps. It will be a woman whom he perceives to have misused him at some point in the past," Victoria said. "It could be a relative or other parental figure, or it could just be a 'type,' like the type of girl who wouldn't have anything to do with him in school. In that case," she added, "he will likely kill into infinity unless we stop him, because 'Her' doesn't exist as an individual. 'Her' is a composite of all the girls who rejected him."

Jonathan was afraid there was another possibility.

"I'm not a psychologist, nor am I given to speculation," he spoke up, surprising himself, "but I think we need to consider something else." He quickly explained what had happened in London, and told them about the killer gifting Victoria with the victim's liver. "If this is the same fellow, then 'Her' could be Victoria Thomas."

The room grew silent. Mike Mosier made the only sound, tapping his pen end over end on a yellow legal pad in front of him. Victoria withdrew her hand from Jonathan's and steepled her fingers on the table in front of her. Her face had lost all color. Jonathan hadn't meant to frighten her, but if they were to consider all possibilities, then they must consider this one.

Taking a deep breath, Victoria spoke. "Mr. Blake's supposition is valid," she said. "But let's deal with that in a moment. First, let's take a look at the profile that is emerging here. I see the subject as a young male between twenty and thirty who comes from the same level of society as his victims and moves easily among them. He is well educated, well financed, but most importantly, well organized in his crimes, which leads me to believe he's an analytical thinker, a careful planner. By profession, he could be an accountant, a consultant in strategic planning, or on the other end of the spectrum, a computer hacker.

"On the Zodiac he's likely to be a Virgo, because he's someone who must have all the details in order. But he must also have some Leo in his chart, because he's bold and impulsive and seeks notoriety for his crimes. That points me in the direction of a man who has never felt valued by anyone. He has grown up in the shadow of someone who has manipulated and controlled him until now he is impotent, both psychologically and physically. Symbolically killing the person whom he perceives to have victimized him restores his manhood and gives him a sense of power. But it is a fleeting sense of power, and he must kill again and again to try to get it back.

"I'm convinced our subject was at the Sherlockian symposium on Jack the Ripper," she continued, "and that his participation in it triggered the first murder, which was in Whitechapel. I first thought he sent a piece of the victim's liver to me as a sort of taunt, because he knew I was with the FBI. He was daring me to come after him. But after consideration, I don't think that was it at all. I must represent, either physically or in some other manner, that person toward whom his rage is directed. Maybe I look like the mother who abused him, or the schoolgirl who wouldn't give him the time of day. For whatever reason, he fixated on me in London, and his fantasy of killing me has grown with each murder. I agree with you, Mike, that he has a definite destination in mind, and that he won't stop killing until he kills me."

Jonathan's blood ran cold. She, on the other hand, seemed unperturbed.

Mosier's brows furrowed. "In that case, we'd better sequester you in that safe house—a real safe house, Victoria—until we take him out."

Victoria shook her head. "Wrong move if you want to save lives, Mike. Use me as bait."

"You're out of your mind!" Mike Mosier almost shouted at her.

"It makes sense, Mike. This killer is going to keep taking lives until he gets what he wants. If it's me he wants, let me face him before any more innocent people die."

"No way. We're not about to set you up like that."

But Victoria knew in her gut this was the most expedient way to take out the killer, and she was not going to be put off, even by her boss. She leaned forward. "Let me go back to my apartment. Let things appear normal. If he calls me, I'll talk to him. Make a date even. You can put an electronic tracer on me and have a team on our tail, ready to strike if I need help."

Mosier bolted out of his chair and struck the table with his hand. "No. It's out of the question, Victoria. So drop it."

Victoria stood up, as well, furious. "I won't drop it, Mike. It's the right thing to do. I'm not afraid. Unlike his other victims, I know what to expect. I have a gun, and I know how to use it. And as for self-defense, you of all people know about my martial arts skills." During her training, she'd managed more than once to throw her heavyset boss to the floor and disable him. "If it's who I think it is," she continued, "he isn't a large man, although he is muscular. I can probably disarm him before backup even gets there."

"And if you don't, you'll be dead."

Victoria straightened and nailed him with her gaze. "Then he'll have what he wants and quit killing."

"You're willing to sacrifice yourself to this maniac?"

"I won't get hurt."

"And how do you know that, Agent Thomas?"

She didn't blink. "The same way I knew to look for an older perpetrator when we caught William Coleman. I just know."

Twenty

King's College, Cambridge
Fifteenth October 1888

Dark dreams assail my nights, and melancholy enve-
lops me by day as I await a message from Eddy. I have
heard nothing from him since our hunt, and I fear for his
health and safety. At the same time, I am in agony with
fear that he may not have held his tongue with regard to
our work. It would be our undoing. I try to control the
need to kill again, but it grows painful, and I do not
know how long I can hold out for him.

My only consolation is that my letters have made their
way at last into the newspapers. We are famous beneath
our pseudonym. Jack the Ripper! A brilliant deceit, if I
do say so. But there has been no mention of my chalked
message, blaming the murders on the Jews. Surely it has
been discovered. I suspect the police are playing games,
but I cannot guess their reason. I must not let them think
we have ceased our endeavors, however, even though it
has been over two weeks since our last hunt. So today I
posted a little present, not to the police, but rather to Mr.
Lusk, who heads the Mile End Vigilance Committee. My
gift to him was the kidney, or rather half of it, which I
took as my latest souvenir, and this note:

> From hell
>
> Mr Lusk
> > Sor
> > > I send you half the
> > Kidne I took from one women
> > prasarved it for you tother piece I
> > fried and ate it was very nise I
> > may send you the bloody knif that
> > took it out if you only wate a whil
> > longer
> > > signed   Catch me when
> > > > you can
> > > Mishter Lusk

*Playing with the coppers like this is an engaging dalliance,
but my heart is wrenched by Eddy's silence. I must hear
from him soon, or I shall go mad.*

Jonathan could scarcely believe what had happened at the
end of the meeting at Quantico. In spite of all of Mosier's
objections, in the end Victoria had had her way. He could
not comprehend how her boss could allow one of his top
agents to put herself in such a treacherous situation. But he
of all people knew how strong-willed Victoria was. Maybe
Mosier knew it was pointless to try to change her mind and
just got tired of arguing.

At least there was a plan in place, carefully worked out
with a group of special agents Victoria knew and obviously
trusted. And he was grateful he was part of that plan, even
though it meant he would remain as Victoria's "bodyguard"
until it was all over.

Filled with foreboding, he stared out the window of the
car that was taking them back to the cottage to get their
belongings, and which then would drop them at Victoria's
apartment. The two agents in the front seat would never be
far away, and a surveillance van had been dispatched to her
neighborhood with agents who would monitor her every
move. He recalled her anger when she'd seen the security
camera in the safe house and was glad she hadn't pitched

a fit about these arrangements. The stakes now were considerably higher.

Victoria lived in a complex of red-brick town houses in a quiet suburb just outside of the nation's capital. The driver pulled into a parking space marked "Visitor," shifted into park and turned to Victoria. "Mosier's right, you know. You're nuts."

"Thanks for the lift, Grady," she said, ignoring his comment. "If you want to be inconspicuous, I suggest you park on the street. My place is just a couple of doors away." She touched the device that would allow their ears to hear everything she said and track her every move. "I'm not as big a fool as you think. I'll expect you to come running if you hear me screaming bloody murder."

Dismayed, Jonathan wondered if it would come to that.

Taking the suitcases from the trunk, he followed her up the walk that was lined with bright yellow chrysanthemums. Autumn leaves blew from the many trees incorporated into the pleasing landscape. Although not pretentious, Victoria's two-story apartment was a far cry from his own modest flat. While she unlocked the door, he noted that the mullioned windows across the front were sealed, but saw two double-hung windows on the second floor. If an intruder wished to gain entry from the front, other than by the door, he'd have to do so by ladder.

Once they were inside, he was glad to see Victoria throw a heavy dead bolt into place.

"I have to make a pit stop," she said, and headed up the stairs, leaving Jonathan to become acquainted with his new surroundings. The apartment was tastefully and expensively furnished, as he had expected it would be. A blue velvet sofa faced the brick fireplace and was flanked on both sides by armchairs upholstered in a floral pattern. Bright pillows picked up the colors from the chairs and splashed them around the room in accent chairs and on the hearth. In one corner, a bentwood rocker was covered by a throw woven in a large blue and white plaid. Artwork covered the walls and magazines smothered a low table by the sofa, completing a scene that although richly done, looked homey and comfortable rather than elegant. He wondered how Mother liked it.

Jonathan picked up the mail that had been slipped through the slot in her door and stacked it neatly on the small desk in the hall. He noticed the message light was blinking on her answering machine. A framed photo on the desk caught his eye, and he picked it up. He recognized two of the three people in the picture. Trey Delaney was in the center, his arms around two women. Victoria was on the right and on the left was a redhead.

Meghan?

He heard Victoria's footsteps on the stairs and his thoughts returned to the moment and the crisis they faced. "Is there a back door?" he asked when she reached him.

"Straight ahead." She pointed down the hall. He strode to the door and saw that it too was secured by a dead bolt, although the paned windows could give relatively easy access. He didn't like what he saw beyond the door, either. The small garden area behind the apartment was enclosed by a tall fence, which would give a would-be intruder privacy. In the garden was an outdoor table and chairs, some empty flower pots, and a bicycle.

"What's beyond the gate?" he asked.

"Covered parking."

"Garage?"

"Carport."

"Maybe we should have the men park back there. It's closer."

But Victoria shook her head. "It's bad enough that they can hear everything we say and know our every move," she said, pointing to the bug she was wearing. "I couldn't stand it if they were peering in my windows, as well."

Jonathan considered what she had just reminded him of. He was not as jealous of his privacy as she was, but he did not wish the agents who would be monitoring them to hear anything personal that might pass between them. "Can you turn that thing off?"

She grinned and pressed a button on the device. "Yes. I'm not supposed to, but there might be times . . ."

He heard a catch in her voice and looked up to see the question in her eyes.

"Jonathan, what's wrong?" she asked.

He knew what she meant, but he didn't want to deal with it. "I don't like this business of you being set up to lure the killer."

She came to him and laid her palms lightly on his chest. His skin seemed to burn beneath her touch. "That's not what I meant."

He took her hands in his. "I know."

"It's about Mother, isn't it? Did she really put you off so badly that you've changed your mind about me?"

Jonathan thought his heart would break. Nothing could ever change his mind about Victoria. He loved her. He always would. But . . .

"No, it's not about your mother. It's . . . nothing. This is a difficult time, that's all. I'm worried about you."

Her eyes searched his for a long moment, and he saw the pain in her expression. She did not understand why he'd withdrawn from her. He didn't understand it fully himself. He wanted her. God knew he wanted her. And she wanted him. But other than his body, he had so little to give her. He must resist the temptation to think it could work out for them, because it wouldn't. He had to keep his distance. In the long haul, it was for the best.

"I don't believe you," she said. "But I won't push it right now." She turned away from him. "But when this is all over, I want some answers."

If Barbara Thomas, with her haughty ways and overt prejudice, had destroyed her daughter's relationship with the only man she had ever loved, Victoria would never forgive her. She didn't know what was going on with Jonathan, but she'd begun to suspect that Barbara had succeeded in "putting him in his place," so to speak. She burned with fury at her mother, and no small measure of anger at Jonathan himself. Why was he buying into all that crap?

She went to the phone stand in the hall and picked up her mail. Among the bills and junk mail were five Express Mail packets. Her heart nearly stopped beating when she saw the handwritten labels. "Good God, Jonathan, look at this."

If there had been any doubt before that Victoria was the killer's intended destination, the overnight deliveries put an end to that. Both she and Jonathan recognized the hand-writing as being the same as on the modern-day Ripper notes. The packages were postmarked in Chicago, Kansas City, Phoenix, San Francisco, and Seattle. Inside were Po-laroid photos very similar to the crime-scene photos they had studied earlier in the day. The quality wasn't as good, but the blood was fresher in these, for they had been taken by the killer.

Clipped to each photo was a note.

"And so begins the game. Follow my work closely if you wish to guess the secret. If you don't it won't matter. When I pass GO, you'll be gone. Ha. Ha. Sincerely, Jack the Ripper." These words accompanied the photo of the woman's body that was splayed across the hood of a white Mercedes, a musical note cut neatly into her torso.

"A juicy tidbit for you to consider. Can't wait for a taste of you. Yours truly, Jack the Ripper," came with a photo of the beauty queen and her skewer. "A whore in one here. I'll stroke you off soon as well. Love, Jacky," accompanied the photo of the gore on the golf green. The other two photos were sent with equally chilling messages, written with grotesque coy references to the signature of his slay-ings.

Victoria shuddered, and for the first time questioned her decision to try to attract the killer to her. He was cold, brutal, and crass. And for some reason, she was the focus of his hatred.

Jonathan grasped her by both shoulders. "Victoria, are you sure you want to go through with this?"

She was beginning not to want to, but she knew it was

the only way. "This guy has to be stopped. Look at those poor women. What did they ever do to deserve that?"

"What did you ever do to become his target?" he asked. She saw fear in his eyes.

"I don't know why he's after me, Jonathan. But clearly he is. We've got to find a way to let him know I'm back. We have to bring him in. Soon."

A knock on the door interrupted them, and she jumped. "Who is it?" she demanded, her heart in her throat.

"O'Brien. Something's wrong with your audio transmitter. We're not getting anything."

She peered out of the peephole before opening the door. "Sorry. I turned it off for a minute. Is the van set up yet?" she asked, darting a glance over the shoulders of the two men on her doorstep.

"They're just down at the end of the street. Y'know, that bug isn't going to do you any good if you don't leave it on."

"I know, I know." She turned the device on again. "Listen," she said, carefully slipping the photos back into their original mailing packets, trying to avoid contaminating any fingerprints that might be on them. "Get these to Mike ASAP. And don't touch them." She went to the coat closet and brought out a paper shopping bag. Holding them by the edge, she placed the packets into the bag. "Likely, the only prints on those will belong to postal workers," she added, handing it to Grady O'Brien. "But you never know."

After the agent left, Victoria turned to Jonathan. "He got sloppy in Seattle. Maybe he got careless when he was taking the photos. Right now, I could go for a good set of fingerprints, the hard evidence you prefer, that would lead us to this butcher."

She reached to press the button on her answering machine and noticed that her hand was shaking.

The machine whirred and spoke to her. "Tori, it's Trey. Just checking to see if you're back yet. Call me." The message was dated over a week ago. There were several messages from her mother and one from her father, all asking her to call them right away, saying that something urgent had come up. Those calls had been made four days ago. She already knew the urgent news . . . that they'd learned the identity of Meghan's killer.

Then came another one from Trey, who sounded impatient this time. "Tori, where the hell are you? I called the hotel in London, but they said you'd checked out. Call me when you get home. I'm worried."

"I'd better give him a call right away," Victoria said, surprised that Trey was so concerned about her.

There were two more messages from Trey on the tape, along with several from other friends, a reminder from her dentist that she was due a checkup, and a call from the library to let her know a book she'd ordered from interlibrary loan had come in. "It's been a slow couple of weeks," she commented, waiting for the last message to play.

The cold male voice that curled out of the speaker raised the hair on her neck and arms.

"Victoria Thomas, you conniving, publicity-hungry cunt, you are going to die for taking him away. I know where you live, and I'm watching you. It may be today, or tomorrow. Or maybe I'll wait until next year. But I will get you, and when I do, I'll cut you to pieces, just like Jack the Ripper."

Victoria's knees gave way, and she fell into the small chair that sat by the desk. She felt sick to her stomach. "That's him. That's what our man sounds like." She fumbled for the replay button.

After the second time, Jonathan asked, "Did you recognize the voice?"

"No. It sounds sort of familiar, but . . . I can't say." Blood was pounding so furiously in her ears she could scarcely hear at all.

"Is it Billy Ray?"

She inhaled a deep breath, trying to calm herself. She could not afford to let fear gain control of her reason. She wouldn't be any good to anyone and might end up getting herself killed. "Probably. But I can't remember what he sounded like exactly."

"Too bad your men never found him."

She nodded. "Yes, it is. They tried everything. The address he used to register for the symposium was that of a large chain restaurant in Fairfax. There was nobody named Billy Ray on the personnel records, and the manager was new and didn't recall anyone who fit his description. If Ray worked there at one time, he didn't make much of an impression.

"Mike passed his description along to the state troopers and local area law enforcement agencies in Virginia, but nobody's been able to locate him. Even the fingerprints your men found in his hotel room led nowhere. Obviously, he doesn't have a record. And Billy Ray must be a phony name."

"What did he mean 'you are going to die for taking him away'?"

Victoria shook her head. "I can't imagine. But it throws a new angle into the profile. It sounds like this guy is out for revenge, so there is a motive. Unfortunately, it may be a terrible case of mistaken identity. I never saw Billy Ray before in my life. Why would he want to take revenge against me?" And then she recalled that Billy Ray had accused her of wrongly convicting William Coleman. Was there a connection between these killings and the Coleman case?

"Grady," she said, directing her voice into the device at her waist. "Have you guys left for Quantico yet? If not, swing by here again and pick up this tape. I want Mike to hear it."

His plane was late landing at DFW. He'd grown irritable as the pilot reported again and again that their flight was in a holding pattern, and that they would be landing as soon as he had clearance from the air traffic controllers. The drill had gone on for more than forty-five minutes now, turning his irritation into alarm. What if the damned thing ran out of fuel and crashed?

His anxiety was amplified by the tight schedule to which he had committed himself. This was to be a big night, and a dangerous one. In his last note, he'd given the cops an enormous clue, and unless they were too dim-witted to get the implication, he expected to find security in both Dallas and Fort Worth rather tight, especially around the country clubs, theaters, opera, and charity events. That's where he'd struck before, and that's where they would expect him to strike again.

He toyed with the swizzle stick that had come in his drink and smiled. They were so wrong. Tonight, he would kill another kind of whore. The kind the master had killed. Two of them, in fact.

It was a big order, but he could fill it. And move his piece along one more space on his game board.

He was getting closer to the end, the grand finale. But he was troubled. By now, his name should have been splashed on every newspaper and television across the country. Instead, he remained unheralded and ignored. It was probably her fault. Damned controlling bitch. He would not complete the game without attaining the fame he deserved. He had already surpassed the master in number, distance, and ingenuity. Yet no one had heard of him.

The pressure of his thumb snapped the stir stick with a pop.

The country dance hall in Fort Worth was in full swing by the time he arrived. Cowboys and yuppies alike, dressed in tight jeans and cowboy boots, sipped on longnecks and tried to score with the whores in even tighter jeans.

He wouldn't have minded the scene if they'd all been for real. He had great respect for the working man. But the phonies really got to him. They were easy to spot. Their jeans said Eddie Bauer instead of Levi's. Their hats were neat, not battered, and they showed no soil. On their carefully manicured hands, their diamonds were bigger. They were slumming, and so was he. But one of them would pay for her social hypocrisy.

It didn't take him long to spot her, a busty redhead in a glitzy purple shirt that was soaked with sequins, more likely purchased at an exclusive boutique than at J.C. Penney. She was trying to look with-it and thirty-something, but he'd bet she was ten years older than that.

That was fine. He hadn't killed an old whore yet.

She sat alone, watching the dancers, drinking a beer, and looking distinctly forlorn. When he sat beside her, she turned unfocused eyes on him and tried to smile. "Hi, cowboy," she said. He could smell the beer on her breath.

"Howdy, honey. You here with anybody tonight?"

She shook her head. "Nope. It's just me and my Lone Star." She hiccoughed. "You're pretty cute."

"Want to dance?"

"Um, sure."

They made their way onto the crowded dance floor, but she was too drunk to do the two-step. "How about we go out for a little fresh air?" he suggested. They were all alike, he thought with contempt. So easy.

He guided her through the parking lot to where he'd left the rental car. He'd chosen a spot out of the glare of the floodlights that illuminated the lot for safety. He slipped on a pair of plastic gloves as he walked behind her. The music filtered faintly from the bar. "Now would you like to dance?" he said, feeling a sudden urgency to finish the work.

She hiccoughed again. "Where? Here? Are you crazy or something?"

He turned on her in fury, grabbing her arm. "Why not, bitch? You think you're too good for me?"

He hadn't meant to lose control, but he'd had a bad day, and the words spilled out before he could stop them. Her eyes widened, and she tried to pull away. "Oh, no, you don't," he hissed.

"Help!" she managed to cry out before his fingers encircled her neck.

Damn her to hell, he thought, panicking. What if she'd alerted someone? Hastily, he finished the job, not finding the fulfillment that he so desperately needed, not even when he cut her neck. It was the only slash he took the time to inflict, for he heard voices nearby. Shit. He wiped the knife on her jeans and secured it, then ran for his car, leaving her buxom body crumpled on the asphalt.

He drove around the deserted streets of downtown cowtown, as they called it, trying to recover from the disappointment. His hands shook, and he stopped at a 7-Eleven for an ice-cream bar. He preferred the sugar from alcohol to calm his nerves, but he needed to be clearheaded tonight. Ice cream would have to suffice.

He returned to his car and sat behind the wheel, thinking. He should have finished the job. He should have made the old whore pay with more than her life for her rejection of him. Bitch. Cunt. Mother . . .

His rage burned out of control. He had to go back. He had to finish the job. Maybe nobody had found her yet.

But about a block from the dance hall, he heard sirens. He pulled to the curb. Police cars and an ambulance raced past him and careened into the parking lot of the nightclub. He pounded the steering wheel.

Damn it. Too late.

Then he paused as an idea struck him. This could be fun. If he wasn't yet famous on the national news, he was sure to be the talk of the parking lot. They wouldn't know his name, of course. Or that he was the killer. But he would be able to hear what they said about him. He would see the terror his work instilled in the rest of the whores. It wasn't what his body craved, but it was a fulfillment of a different sort.

He locked the car and walked toward the parking lot. He heard a man's voice as he approached the scene. "He damned near cut her head off,"

"Oh, this is gross," said a young female. "I think I'm going to be sick."

He pushed as close as the police would let him. The

whore in the purple shirt lay about thirty feet away, looking like a dead cow.

"What happened?" he asked casually to the man standing next to him.

"Somebody murdered her. Cut her throat, I heard."

His date looked up at him, fear etched on her face. "I saw the news on CNN tonight, Davy," she said, her worried words drawn out with a heavy Texas accent. "There's a killer traveling across the country, slashing women, just like Jack the Ripper. Maybe he's right here in Fort Worth."

She immediately had his full attention. "What's that?" he asked her.

"On the news. They're calling him Traveling Jack, because he's been traveling around the country, killing women, ripping them like I said." She turned anxious eyes to her date. "I'm scared, Davy. Can we go home now?"

He watched them leave, a glow of deep satisfaction suffusing him. Traveling Jack. Not the name of the master, but not bad.

Traveling Jack.

He liked having a name of his own.

Twenty-One

London
Tenth November 1888

    I can scarcely put pen to paper, even though a full day has passed since the bloody night's work that surpassed all others. I had no plan for this one until Eddy knocked upon my door yesterday morning, his face haggard, his eyes wildly tormented. He had just escaped from the asylum where he has been held prisoner since our last quest by Dr. Gull, the Queen's physician, at the old Whore's own request. He was in tears and cried out for vengeance against the women who control his every move. I held him in my arms, soothing him and rocking until he calmed. My poor, poor Prince. My heart filled with rage and my loins grew hard with dark passion. I wanted to kill the old Whore Queen for reducing my beloved to this state.

    He too was overcome with rage and demanded we return to Whitechapel. He screamed he would kill every whore he saw, but I soothed him at last and insisted one would suffice. At nightfall, we made our move. It was our luck that the whore dwelt in a private room, a room we had all to ourselves for as long as the night would cover us. Working by the blaze of the fire, which we kept burning brightly using her clothing as fuel, we cut the whore into pieces.

My hands are bloody still, and I cannot seem to re-move the stain from beneath my fingernails. I fulfilled my need early on, but Eddy cried and slashed at the body in a frenzy, cursing the old Whore Queen and MotherDear with every stroke. I have never seen him in such a state, and I could only wonder what infernal medications that doctor had forced upon him. His strength was like that of two men, his stamina far outstripping mine.

When at last he had satiated his bloodlust, he turned to me, his eyes feral and shining in the firelight. He was clearly mad as he dashed out into the graying light of predawn, and although I followed in quick pursuit, he outstripped me and vanished into the thick fog. I know not where he went, but I fear our secret is no longer safe, and that soon our Jack himself will be ripped.

He checked into the high-rise hotel in Dallas and wasted no time in tuning into CNN *Headline News*. It was ten till the hour, and he nearly went insane while waiting for the sports news and the Play of the Day and what seemed like an endless stream of commercials to run before the main news was repeated. It was the top of the hour at one A.M. on Sunday morning.

"Top agents with the FBI have joined forces with police in major metro areas in search of a man they're calling 'Traveling Jack,'" the announcer said. "According to sources, he is suspected of viciously killing and mutilating six women, one each in Chicago, Kansas City, Phoenix, San Francisco, Seattle, and Boulder. Here's more . . ."

And there she was. Victoria Thomas was speaking into a microphone at a press conference. She looked regal, although a little on the severe side, he thought, with her hair all pulled back and her face pale. She wore a tasteful, expensive-looking navy suit and a white blouse and looked every inch the ice queen. The supercilious bitch. Rage boiled in his gut. He couldn't wait to get his hands on her.

"This man kills in the style of Jack the Ripper," she was saying. "He is delusional and may even think he is that famous killer, although he's only a copycat."

"Cópycat!" he screamed at the television. "Fuck you, bitch. You don't know anything. I have the blood of the master in my veins, and nothing, nobody, not even you, can stop me." He lowered his voice, hoping he hadn't been heard by whoever occupied the room next door.

He mustn't let her get to him. He must maintain control. But what came next nearly sent him over the edge.

The announcer returned to the screen. "A national manhunt is under way for the killer, who is believed to be a white male in his mid- to late twenties who has been known to go by the name of Billy Ray." The camera cut to a police sketch of the suspect, and he stared at it, fury mounting like an inferno.

"No," he growled, his hands shaking. "No. She can't do this to me. That fucking bitch . . ."

It was nearly dawn when he returned to the hotel, shaken and spent. He went in by the most remote door and climbed the stairs to his eleventh-floor room, because his clothes were covered with blood, and he didn't want to take the chance of encountering somebody along the way.

He couldn't remember leaving his room earlier, or how he had arrived at the club where the dancer worked. It was a shithole of a place on the east side of Dallas, but he didn't care. He had promised himself that he would make this stop a double event, and he had, although this whore was even worse than the bitch he'd had to ditch in the parking lot. He felt degraded for having sunk so low. He hadn't even enjoyed it when he finally came. The only good part about this one was that he'd had some privacy. She'd taken him to a stinking motel room next door to the club where he'd met her, and he'd taken his time. Somebody would find her body in the morning. But would they know it was his work?

Once in the safety of his room, he changed his clothes and wadded the bloodied ones up and stuffed them into a bag. He'd have to find another fireplace.

Before going to bed, he gazed at the photo he'd taken

of his latest work, stared at it long and hard. His work had been so vicious, so complete, the woman was scarcely recognizable as a human. Suddenly, the image shifted. The scene became a scene from another time, the carnage the remains of another woman, and it brought back memories he didn't wish to see.

He crumpled onto the couch and wept.

Victoria watched her image on television late Sunday night. CNN had been running the story steadily since early Saturday afternoon, and she knew it had by now made headlines in newspapers all across the country, if not the world. She hated the publicity, but it had been necessary for her to be the presenter at the news conference, because the killer needed to see her face and know she was not only home from London, but was on his case, as well. If that didn't flush him out, she didn't know what would.

It had come too late, however, to save the lives of two women, one in Dallas, the other in Fort Worth. The killer's double event. Their bodies had been found, one late Saturday night, one early this very morning. The police weren't sure it was the same killer, because neither of the women had come from high society.

Neither was there a twisted joke left at either of the crime scenes. But Victoria was convinced that the Ripper copycat had struck again. Perhaps he'd been interrupted the first time. The victim had been found in a rather public place, a parking lot at a nightclub, and she'd been seen in the club earlier. That meant he'd killed her on the spot, not somewhere else, and he'd likely had to make a run for it when someone came out to the parking lot.

The second murder reflected the pent-up rage he must have felt at not being able to complete his butchery the first time. The police described a motel room smeared with blood and gore, very reminiscent of the original Ripper's murder of Mary Jane Kelly. These were crime photos she didn't relish seeing.

The phone rang, and she went to answer it. "Hello."

"Tori!" Trey almost shouted her name. "Thank God I caught you. I've been worried sick about you since I saw you on the CNN news story about that serial killer. What the hell's going on?"

Victoria heard the anxiety in his voice. "We're trying to catch the guy. That's all."

"He's crazy, Tori. You shouldn't be getting this involved. It's too dangerous."

"Crazies are my business, Trey. You know that. This is nothing new."

"I don't know, Tori. There's something really weird about this guy."

"There's something weird about anyone who murders, Trey. Get over it. It's my job."

"Is this the same one who killed that prostitute in Whitechapel while we were there?"

"We think so." Victoria heard him swear softly.

"The same one who sent you the liver?"

"It's likely."

"Jesus, Tori, why you?"

She'd been asking herself that same question for over two weeks. "I don't know, Trey. It could be someone I helped put behind bars, maybe someone out on parole and looking for revenge." Or a total stranger, like Billy Ray. It didn't make sense, and she didn't want to think about it. "Where have you been?" she asked, changing subjects. "I've tried several times to call you since I got back from London."

"I'm still in training for my job. In fact, I'm in Vegas right now, at the tail end of our sales conference, but I should be home in a few days."

"Well, give me a call when you get in. Hopefully by that time, we'll have this slimebag in jail, and you can buy me a celebration drink."

"You're on. But in the meantime, lock your doors. I mean it, Tori. Don't take this thing lightly."

"Believe me, Trey, I'm not. Gotta run now. Ciao, baby."

She hung up the phone and saw Jonathan watching her

from across the room. His face was grim, and he looked distinctly unhappy. She wondered for a fleeting moment if he might possibly be a little jealous of Trey Delaney. She hoped that was the case, as unwarranted as it was. At least she'd know he still cared.

"That was Trey. Just checking in. Says he's worried about me." She picked up the remote control and clicked off the TV set.

"He has every reason to be," Jonathan growled. Victoria caught his eye and saw the anguish in his expression. He was worried, too. He was probably also sick of being cooped up. Unlike her, he hadn't left the apartment since Friday afternoon, and he might not be able to surface again for days, depending on how things went.

As the inside man, it was his job to remain out of sight, so that anyone watching would not know there was extra firepower inside. If the killer should somehow manage to break into her apartment, he would meet with a surprise attack from Jonathan. That was the plan, anyway.

But Victoria had gone about her life as if nothing unusual was taking place. The monitor she wore allowed the agents in the van to track her, and there were now two cars staked out nearby, one in the street, the other in the alley behind the carport. One or the other would follow her if she went out. She was double-covered. She was safe.

She'd proceeded to go about her daily life, going out to her favorite gourmet grocery to pick up food, dropping some clothes off at the dry cleaner, checking out the book at the library. Although she'd been a little edgy, she'd seen no sign of Billy Ray. The only tail had been the familiar white car driven by Grady O'Brien.

The only thing that was out of the ordinary for her was Jonathan's attitude toward her. He had remained remote, aloof, and at arm's length ever since they'd arrived. It tore at her every time they spoke.

"Guess we'd better turn in," she said, wishing they could discuss what she considered to be their most unsatisfactory sleeping arrangements, but not willing to share her personal unhappiness with the boys outside via the monitor.

Jonathan had taken up residence in her spare bedroom, which also served as her office, so he'd ended up sleeping on a fold-out couch across from the computer table. He had claimed that he'd slept well, but she'd tossed restlessly for both nights they'd been under the same roof but not in the same bed. She longed for the warmth of his body next to hers, and her heart ached because he had remained so distant. It was almost as if their affair had never happened.

"Think I'll stay up a while," he said, rising and going to the telephone stand in the hall. He picked up a notepad and wrote, "I miss you."

A small noise escaped her throat before she managed to stifle the words she wanted to say to him. He handed her the pad and pen.

"I miss you, too. Terribly," she wrote, and underscored the last word.

They stood an arm's length apart, and she wanted more than life to go into his embrace. But his arms remained at his side, and she saw him clench his hands into fists. She scribbled on the notepad, "Come to me in a little while. I'll turn off the monitor." Then she added, and again underlined, "Please!"

He gave her a slight nod, and her spirits soared. If there was one place they could communicate, it was in bed.

Twenty minutes later, showered and naked, she lay between the covers, hoping, praying, he would do what he'd said. The monitor was on the nightstand, turned off. She hoped the boys in the van would think things were quiet because they were sleeping. She'd turn it on again later, after she and Jonathan worked through a few difficulties that threatened her life in a different way.

He came to her silently in the darkness, smelling faintly of soap and aftershave. She drew back the covers and welcomed him into her arms, so relieved to have him there she thought she might cry.

"Jonathan," she whispered, and he answered by taking her lips in a kiss fierce with passion. They did not speak, but wasted no time rediscovering the magic that they had somehow lost over the past few days. Theirs was not a tender reunion, but rather one of fierce desperation. Neither had time for subtleties or explanations.

Victoria's body raged with the need for Jonathan to become part of her once again, and when she threw one leg around his waist, she felt his own need pressing against her. Only when he entered her did she begin to release the terror she had not known she held. Terror that he did not love her after all. That he did not want her. That he would leave.

He did not leave, not even when their passion was spent and they lay quietly in each other's arms. Victoria wouldn't let him. She clung to him with arms and legs and will. She did not know why he had left her emotionally a few days ago, but she wasn't about to let it happen again.

Jonathan lay spent and breathing hard, more afraid than he'd ever been in his life. Maybe he had little to offer Victoria Thomas, but he knew he couldn't live without her. The past few days had been sheer hell.

Was he being selfish, wanting her so much that he would ask her to spend the rest of her life with a detective inspector from Manchester? Perhaps. And perhaps she would turn him down flat. He would understand if she did. But it would cut his heart out. Did he dare risk it?

Lying next to her, still intimately joined, he knew he had no choice. He could no longer run away, no longer avoid the truth. His life wasn't worth living if she wasn't in it.

"I love you," he whispered.

She nestled even closer to him, if that was possible. "I love you, too, Jonathan. I don't know what that standoffish nonsense was all about, but don't ever do that to me again."

"Marry me."

There, he'd said it. She did not answer right away, and his heart nearly stopped beating.

Then he heard a whispered, "Yes."

He couldn't believe his ears. "You mean it?"

"With all my heart. Why wouldn't I?"

Jonathan closed his arms around her tightly. "I . . . I didn't know if . . . I don't know how—"

She cut off his doubts with a kiss. "Shhh," she murmured. "We'll figure it out. Tomorrow. Right now, I'd like to make up for lost time."

The first thing Jonathan became aware of when he awoke the next morning was an unusual sense of peace, a happiness that pervaded every cell of his body. Victoria had said she would be his wife.

The second thing was that she was not in the bed next to him.

He sat up, blinking in the early morning light. How could he have slept so soundly that he didn't sense her leaving? He slid out of bed and into his shorts and jeans. She was probably downstairs with the coffee pot perking.

But she was not downstairs. She'd left a note. "Gone for doughnuts. Back in a flash."

She had left the coffee ready for him. He poured himself a cup and looked out at the overcast skies. It had rained during the night, and many of the glorious leaves that had crowned the trees lay in a soggy carpet on the ground.

He wandered into the living room and flicked on the television. The story about Traveling Jack was still major news. The copy editor had changed the words around, but the sensational tone was stronger than ever.·

God, he'd be glad when this was all over. He was worried sick about Victoria's safety, and although he trusted her judgment and respected her abilities as a law enforcement officer, she was still the only woman he had ever loved, ever would love. He could not stand it if something happened to her. He wanted her out of this mess and in his life forever. He did not know if he could share her with the FBI.

The phone rang. He didn't answer it, for no one was supposed to know he was there. He listened to the caller's voice as it came across the answering machine..

"What's going on in there? Pick up. This is Grady."

Jonathan lifted the receiver. "What's up?"

"That's what we want to know. Did she turn the monitor off again? We haven't heard squat from you guys since midnight."

The monitor. Yes, she'd turned it off. And he was damned glad she had. Last night. But this was today, and she should be wearing it. "Just a minute." He set the receiver on the table and raced upstairs, a cold premonition washing over him. Had she forgotten to put it on this morning?

As he feared, the small black electronic device lay on the nightstand on her side of the bed. He picked it up and turned it on, then ran back down the stairs to the telephone.

"She turned it off last night before she went to bed," he told them. "I just found it in her room."

"Well, tell her to put the blasted thing on and leave it on. What does she think we're going to do out here, get off on listening to her snore?"

"She's not here."

Dead silence for a long moment. Then, "Tell me you didn't say that."

"She's not here. She must have left a little while ago. I just got up. There was a note on the counter that said she was going out for doughnuts."

"Shit."

"Didn't you see her leave?" Jonathan's skin prickled in alarm.

"We changed shifts just before six-thirty. It's possible she left when we were shuffling cars. We didn't think anything about it. Her car's still under the carport."

Jonathan looked out the back windows into the garden. He could see the reflection of the car's shiny paint between the slats of the gate. He also noted something was missing from the small enclosure. "She took her bike."

Twenty-Two

London

Nineteenth November 1888

The world has turned to ashes since our last fearful hunt, for I have neither seen nor heard from Eddy. I must find him! I fear for his very life, and my own.

After hiding here in rented lodgings for nearly a fortnight, today I dared to move out into the world again, seeking information about my beloved Prince. I called at Windsor but was told that Eddy was not in residence and was swiftly shown the door. I sought out Somerset, Eddy's friend who supervises the stables, who confirmed my fears, telling me he'd heard the Prince had fallen ill and had been taken to a private asylum to recover. Gull again!

It was with forced restraint that I called upon that doctor, and although my reception was more polite than I had received at the palace, it was cool nonetheless. Gull confirmed Eddy's illness, but would not describe its nature. Neither would he reveal the Prince's whereabouts. It seemed to me that he gave me an odd appraisal, as if he were suspicious of me. Has Eddy talked? If he has, it will be my ruin. I must find that infernal asylum and rescue him. I must be assured of his love, for my life is pure hell without him. I would rather be dead.

The game board lay in front of him, but today he had no enthusiasm for it. After the bloodbath in Dallas, something had changed. He had no more spirit for the game. He was tired and drained, but he had to push on. There was one more whore he must bring down before he put away the knife. Her. The high-and-mighty one who had managed to steal away the only person in his life who had ever mattered.

Her. Victoria Thomas.

He had jumped three spaces ahead on the board as a reward for the grueling work in Texas. He was home now, and it was time to exact his final punishment.

Victoria guessed the battery was dead. When she'd tried to start the car to make a quick run for fresh doughnuts from a nearby shop, the engine had not even tried to turn over. A click from the ignition was the most response she'd roused from the vehicle that had not been used in a couple of weeks. She thought about walking the four blocks, but then remembered her bike.

The cool, rain-washed air felt good as it streamed past her cheeks and through her hair, which she had not bothered to put up. Never had she felt so good, so happy. Jonathan's proposal had surprised her, but she'd hesitated only long enough to make sure she'd heard him right. She didn't know how they were going to rearrange their lives to accommodate their marriage, but she was not worried. They would work it out. All she knew was that she never wanted to be without him again.

The scents wafting from the doughnut shop made her mouth water. She parked the bike by the front window and hurried inside, where she selected two each of her favorites, wondering if Jonathan would like them, as well. They had so much to learn about each other. "Please put them in a carry-out bag with a handle, would you, Steve?" she asked the proprietor, who knew her well from her frequent visits to his shop. "I'm on the bike today."

Her order in hand, Victoria jumped on the bicycle again

and pedaled down the parking lot and into the street, her mind on Jonathan and what changes his proposal would bring to their lives. The car was upon her before she became aware of it. All she could remember later was hearing a thud and the scrape of metal against metal, feeling herself being catapulted onto the pavement where she landed painfully on one shoulder. The sound of a car door slamming. Approaching footsteps. And a blow to the head that turned the world black.

Pain glistened on the shards of what once must have been her brain as Victoria struggled for consciousness. Behind her eyes, bright lights looped and swirled like in a carnival ride, bringing with it a nausea that turned her skin clammy. A cool breeze from somewhere brushed against her cheeks. She shivered.

"Good. You're awake." A male voice seeped through the murkiness. "I didn't want to have to carry you."

Victoria managed to sit up and open her eyes. She was in the front seat of an old car that smelled rather like dirty socks. Her hands were bound in front of her, and a gag was tied so tightly around her mouth it cut her skin. Slowly, coming out of the pain, she turned her head toward the sound of the voice.

To her right, lounging against a low wall just outside the open car door, Billy Ray gazed complacently at her. His arms were crossed in front of his bulky chest, looking like meaty cudgels.

Victoria's heart sank. How could this have happened? Where were Jonathan and Grady and the rest? They should be on this guy's ass right now.

And then she remembered. The monitor. She'd forgotten all about it. She'd broken the rules one too many times, and now, it appeared she was about to pay the price.

"Uhhhhhumnnh." She tried to speak, but the gag only cut tighter.

Billy Ray laughed, his lips twisting in a cruel smile. "You won't have the last word this time, Miss Big-shot

FBI Agent. Miss Rich Bitch. Miss Know-It-All."

Victoria looked into his eyes, refusing to show the fear she felt shooting through every nerve in her body. She knew those eyes. She'd seen those eyes before, on someone else.

He pulled a long hunting knife from a scabbard on his belt and flashed it in the sunlight.

"I'm gonna use this on you, bitch. And I'm gonna go real slow, so you'll know what it feels like to die."

"Mmmghrump."

Go to hell. She struggled to speak, but her words were drowned by a mouthful of cotton.

"You want to talk, bitch? Well, maybe in a little while. Let's you and me go for a walk first."

He pulled her roughly from the car and held her by both arms until she got her balance. She glanced around. They seemed to be in some kind of a park. She could hear the sound of running water in the distance. But there were no people in sight.

Victoria didn't want to take a walk. Not here. Not anywhere with this creep. Visions of the crime-scene photos of his handiwork rose in her mind, and she wondered wildly what sick joke he had in mind to leave with her body when he was finished with her.

Another vision came to mind. Her mother and father. Oh, dear God, how would they endure losing both their children to violent killers like Matthew Ferguson and Billy Ray? She felt a sudden pang of remorse for putting herself in this position, not for her own sake, but for them. Her decision to join the FBI and catch all the bad guys had been purely selfish, driven by anger and a need to avenge Meghan's death. She'd never thought that as a consequence, she might cause her parents even more grief.

But then, she'd never thought she would fall into the hands of a killer like Billy Ray. She wasn't that damned stupid.

But she had been.

"Walk," he commanded, pointing down a leaf-strewn

path. She felt the needle of the knifepoint between her shoulder blades.

Victoria did as he said, her mind now racing furiously, groping for some kind of strategy that would set her free. She could use her martial arts skills, but she'd only be able to use her feet. With her hands tied securely, the chances of overpowering him were slim. He wasn't a tall man, but he was stocky and muscular. And he had a knife.

She stumbled, and Billy Ray jerked her up. "Don't even think about it. I'm not going to carry you. You're going to walk to your death, just like he's going to soon, and all because of you."

He? What was he talking about? Then Victoria remembered the message that had been left on her machine. She was sure it was the same voice. *You are going to die for taking him away.* Was he talking about William Coleman? Why would Billy Ray care about William Coleman?

They reached a cliff overlooking a river that raged below them. She didn't know how long she'd been unconscious, or how far they'd driven, but this place seemed familiar. She guessed they were somewhere along the Potomac above D.C.

At the cliff's edge, she turned and glared at him, unafraid and wanting to know why she was going to die.

"Garupmpghp!"

Billy Ray blinked, startled at her boldness. "What?"

"Garupmpghp!" she repeated. *Untie me, you asshole.*

"You're a pushy broad," he snapped. "I'm going to loosen your gag, but only because I want to hear you beg." He touched the knife to her neck. "You scream and you're dead meat."

"I'm dead meat anyway," she said when he removed the filthy kerchief and she regained use of her voice. She quivered, but more with anger than fear. "Why are you doing this?"

He slid the knife blade ever so lightly across her throat, raising the hair on her arms and neck. "I'm going to pay you back for taking my old man away. He is innocent."

"Your old man?"

But Billy Ray grew silent. He stared at her intently. "You think you're so damned smart, but I'm smarter," he said at last. "I know all about you, Ms. Victoria Thomas. I know where you live, what you eat, practically when you go to the bathroom. I know your e-mail address and have hacked into your computer almost daily for the past six months. That's how I knew you were going to London. I followed you there, thinking I would kill you then, but I wasn't ready. I . . . I had to wait."

"Why?" She meant, why was he going to kill her, but he told her why he had to wait to do so.

"I didn't know my way around there. It was safer to wait until you got home." He gave her a menacing smile. "But I'm glad I spent the money to go there. I learned a lot. I'm going to use what I learned to kill you and slice you all up, just like Jack the Ripper did to the whores he killed. They'll find your body all cut to pieces, just like your sister's."

Some of Victoria's courage deserted her at the mention of Meghan. "How do you know about my sister?"

He smirked. "Like I told you before, I know all about you, and I follow all the big murder cases. They never found the guy, did they? Just like they'll never find me."

"You're wrong, Billy. They did find him." Well, sort of—after the fact, she thought grimly. "They'll find you, too. And you'll pay for what you've done. But I want to know what I've done to piss you off."

Without warning, he backhanded her across the cheek with a blow so hard it knocked her to the ground. "Cunt!" he screamed, leaning over her. "Don't you ever talk to me like that."

Victoria's head rang again in pain, and her jaw throbbed fiercely. She was certain she didn't have much time left before he came in for the kill. She must think of something. If her profile of this guy was right, he had likely grown up with a domineering mother, someone who had reproved him at every turn, belittling him, emasculating him. She decided to become his mother figure. It was a dangerous move, because if he'd killed all those other women in an effort to kill Mother, her taunting might likely invite the knife sooner. But it could also be that he'd killed those women because he couldn't kill his mother. If she became his mother, then he couldn't kill her.

"That's right, Billy Ray," she said, leaning on one elbow and raising her head haughtily. "Your mother always said that nice girls don't talk like that."

He hovered over her, breathing hard. "What do you know about my mother?"

Good. She'd gotten his attention. "Your mother loves you, Billy. She wants to be proud of you. But she won't be proud if you kill me."

"Fuck my mother!" His face was nearly purple with fury. "I hate my mother. It was her fault my old man went away."

"I thought that was my fault." Victoria didn't know where her nerve was coming from, but she was ready to push Billy Ray to the limits, even if it cost her her life. Maybe, just maybe, by yanking his chain, she'd get him to make a mistake.

"It *is* your fault. You sent him to death row. But my mother sent him away, caused him to do all those bad things."

"Who's your father, Billy?"

He was panting, and she could see large beads of sweat ringing his forehead, despite the autumn cool. "William Coleman," he hissed. "My old man is William Raymond Coleman. You were the one who convinced the judge he ought to die."

William Raymond Coleman. Billy Ray . . . Coleman.

Good God. She looked into the eyes of the man standing over her, and she knew where she'd seen them before. Like his father's eyes, they were filled with hatred and rage. And like his father, Billy Ray wanted to kill her. Would kill her, if she let him. She had to force his hand.

"Your father is a cold-blooded murderer, and he deserves to die. I suppose you're trying to fill his shoes now. Well, good luck, sonny boy. You're just a two-bit Jack the Ripper wannabe. You're no good, Billy Ray. You'll never be famous like Jack the Ripper. You won't even be as famous as your father. I'll see to that. I'll make sure your picture never gets in another newspaper. Certainly not on CNN."

She watched his fury mount, and she was ready when he roared out and lunged at her. She rolled onto her back, feet in the air, and met his midsection with the soles of her shoes. The momentum of his attack and his weight pushed her painfully back onto her neck but took Billy Ray on over her head. She heard him scream and jumped to her feet, ready to do whatever she could to kick away the knife. She crouched, but Billy Ray was nowhere in sight.

"Oh, my God," she uttered, realizing that in front of her, the terrain dropped straight down to the rocks and the river below. She scrambled to the edge of the precipice, and her breath caught in her throat.

Below, thirty feet or more, Billy Ray Coleman lay crumpled on the rocks.

Jonathan was beside himself with guilt and worry. He should never have gone to Victoria's bed last night. He had allowed his personal interests to override his professionalism, and it might have cost Victoria her life.

He paced the floor of her small apartment, his gut churning. They'd found her bicycle and a box of spilled doughnuts about four blocks away, just a short distance from the shop where she'd purchased the sweets. There was no blood at the scene, but it was obvious she'd been hit by a car. Grief sliced through him like a laser, made worse by his overwhelming sense of helplessness. She was in the hands of a killer, and he could do nothing.

Nothing but follow orders and stay put. Mosier had insisted that Jonathan remain at Victoria's apartment, in case she somehow managed to escape and called for help. He prayed for that miracle, but his heart was like lead. The owner of the doughnut shop had told Grady that he'd seen a small, rather beat-up blue Toyota sedan drive by slowly as Victoria had peddled away. The description he'd given of the driver had fit that of Billy Ray.

At ten fifty-seven, the telephone rang. Jonathan jumped, spilling his fifth cup of coffee, and ran to answer it, hoping Mike Mosier had some news. Some good news.

"Hello."

Her voice was weak, and she sounded on the verge of tears, but he recognized Victoria immediately. "Jonathan, it's me, Victoria. I'm okay."

Relief flooded him, and his heart pounded. "Where are you? I'll come for you."

"No. I've already called Mike. I'm at a state park north of D.C. The police should be here shortly. I'll need to finish things up with them before I can leave."

"What things?" Terrible images ran through his mind. Images of Victoria having been raped, nearly murdered. Still in danger.

"I think Billy Ray is dead."

"You think?" He listened as she told him what had taken place on a high cliff overlooking a raging river, and his stomach turned to a rock. He could not picture the petite woman who had agreed to become his wife in a life-and-death struggle with a man much larger than she, and winning.

"I have to go now," she said. "The police are here."

"Victoria . . ."

"I love you, Jonathan," she said, and hung up, leaving him staring at the receiver. She was alive; she sounded shaken but she was in one piece. But again he was helpless. He had no way to go to her, even if he knew where she was. Damn it to hell.

He hit the disconnect button and got a dial tone, then feverishly pressed the numbers he'd written earlier on the pad by the phone. "Grady. Blake here. Have you heard—" .

"Just got the call from Mosier. We're on our way."

"Not without me."

"Be ready in two minutes."

The remote park was decked in the bright leaves of fall, or what was left that had not already filtered to the forest floor. A police car was blocking the road to normal traffic, and a helicopter had just landed on the highway about a block away. Several police cars with lights flashing were parked at the ranger station, alongside an ambulance. Jonathan was out the door almost before the car came to a halt. "Where's Victoria?" he demanded of an officer who was standing near the ambulance. "Is she okay?"

"I presume you're speaking of Special Agent Thomas?" Jonathan turned and looked into the worried face of Mike Mosier, who had just arrived on the scene via the helicopter. The FBI agent flashed his badge at the police officer. "Where is she?"

The officer pointed down a narrow lane. "Hop in. I'll drive you. It's a ways."

Another pack of police cars and a second ambulance were parked about a mile down the lane, at the head of a secluded path. "He fell down a cliff at the end of this path," the officer said, letting them out of the car. Jonathan tore off at a run, followed closely by Mike Mosier. Around a slight curve in the path, he saw figures ahead.

"Victoria!" He called her name before he even saw her. The clutch of police officers who stood in the clearing moved aside, and a small, mud-smeared woman in jeans and a sweatshirt looked up. Her face broke into the most beautiful smile Jonathan had ever seen, and she ran into his arms.

"Oh, God, thank God," he cried, holding her for dear life, tears burning his eyes. "If anything had happened—"

"It did, Jonathan," she said with a slight sob.

Her words stabbed him in the gut. "Did he . . . hurt you?"

"Only a bump on the head and some bruises."

"Then what happened?"

"We got him, Jonathan. We got our man."

Twenty-Three

King's College, Cambridge
First January 1889

    I am filled with despair and have not left these rooms at the Devil's house for the majority of the holiday season. Anxiety and fear have become my constant companions, although it seems doubtful that Eddy has told anyone of our activities in Whitechapel. Otherwise, I would already be a dead man. I have heard nothing from Eddy, and have lost hope that I will unless by some miracle he manages to escape Gull's clutches once again.

    My brother Harry has tried often to rouse me from my melancholy, but I am unable to find any spirit. Then today he came bearing the news that our friend Montague John Druitt was found drowned in the Thames yesterday at Chiswick. The private word is that Druitt was fired from his teaching position at Blackheath for becoming involved with one of the boys, and overcome with despair, threw himself in the river with his pockets full of rocks. But Harry does not believe that, for he learned there was a return ticket from Chiswick on his body that would indicate he had planned to return to London, and not via the Thames.

    Harry then told me he had learned the police considered Druitt a primary suspect in the Ripper murders. Why? I wondered. Why Druitt? And then it came to me.

Druitt looked like Eddy! He was slender in build, with large, heavy-lidded eyes, and a mustache styled in the same fashion. Had he been accused of the murders by someone who had actually seen Eddy instead? Did he take his own life, knowing how keen the public is to punish the killer? Did he prefer drowning to the humiliation of a public trial, followed by an engagement with the hangman?

Whatever happened, this ends it neatly enough for the real Jack, whose bloodlust after the last hunt seems sated, at least for the moment. Perhaps it is best to end it here, for without Eddy, there is no joy in life, no reason to go on. I shall let Druitt take the blame, and for now, let Jack lie. I am drained of desire, filled with dark despondency, and without my beloved Prince, I have no energy to pursue the game further.

The time she had dreaded was upon them, and as she maneuvered her car through traffic, headed for Dulles, Victoria worked at controlling the tears that threatened.

Several days had passed since she had been abducted by Billy Ray, and during that time, they had learned much about the young man who had tried to kill her. Although he didn't fit the profile as precisely as she'd thought, mainly because he didn't appear to be well financed, the rest was close enough to suit her.

It bothered her, however, that he couldn't be traced to the cities where he'd murdered those women. Somehow, he'd managed to completely cover his trail. The task force was still scratching its head over that one. He must have created a new identity for each plane ticket he purchased, for they had not found the name of Billy Ray Coleman, or any consistent alias, on the airline records.

But it was clear that Billy Ray suffered from low self-esteem at the hands of a domineering woman. Victoria and Jonathan had interviewed Mrs. William Coleman, Billy's mother, who had proven to be a most malignant woman with delusions of grandeur despite the meager conditions under which she lived. She was not unlovely, if rather painted, and she greeted Victoria and Jonathan at the door to her rundown trailer wearing a long, dramatic dressing gown and gaudy jewelry. The tiny living quarters were covered with magazines about the rich and famous.

Sally Coleman was rude, haughty, and showed not a hint of grief over her son's tragedy. "He was no good, just like his daddy," she said, spitting out the words with venom. "Never did like him. A pig of a boy." Ironically, the only room in the small apartment that was not cluttered and filthy was the bedroom Billy Ray had occupied. It was neat as a pin, with his computer still running. The only filth surrounding him was on the porn sites bookmarked on his Internet software.

They confiscated the computer and other items of Billy Ray's effects as evidence, for they'd quickly found files that proved he had stalked Victoria and had carefully planned her murder. She was chilled, but as they left the mobile home, she glanced at Sally Coleman, and a part of Victoria felt deeply sorry for the tormented young man.

And she began to better understand where the monsters came from.

To Victoria's relief, there had been no more Ripper-style murders since Billy Ray's death, and everyone in the unit began to breathe easier. Once again, they were left without definite closure on the case, for Billy Ray had never confessed to being the Ripper copycat, but everyone, including Victoria, believed that the beefy young man was the killer.

He fit the profile well enough—right gender, right age, even the right sign of the Zodiac—a Virgo, highly organized and fastidious. Although he hadn't technically lived at the level of society she would have expected, his mother's delusions that she was from high society and her domineering ways would explain his hatred for women of that type. He was also surprisingly well educated. His mother told them that he'd put himself through night school and had achieved an A.A. degree from the local junior college. They also learned how he'd financed his education, and his computer, and his killing spree. Sally Coleman admitted that her son was an accomplished thief,

Billy Ray had been at the Sherlockian symposium, he'd had motive, or at least believed he did, revenge against Victoria for her role in William Coleman's conviction and death sentence. He'd tried to kill Victoria, and the murders had stopped after his death. Considering all that, the team felt that Billy Ray was their man.

Only occasionally did she get the feeling they were wrong. She told herself it was nothing more than residual paranoia.

With the case concluded, there was no more reason for Jonathan to remain in the States, and his boss had recalled him to duty. She'd pleaded with him not to go, but his reply reminded her why she loved him so.

"Sandringham is a fine and fair man, Victoria. He insists he needs me to wrap up the hit-and-run. He has been good to me, and I can't let him down. But I promise, as soon as that affair is resolved, I'll tell him about us. About our plans."

Which were still uncertain. They had spent the past week trying to resolve the issues of real life that faced them, but they'd arrived at no definite plan.

"I don't care where we live," he'd said, relieving her somewhat, because she really did not want to live in England. "But what would I do? I can't be a kept man, Victoria."

"You could join the agency."

He'd shaken his head. "I'm too old. I probably wouldn't survive the academy."

Victoria hadn't told him, but she was experiencing an agonizing ambivalence about staying with the agency herself. It was not that she'd lost her commitment, but the day she'd thought she might die at the hands of Billy Ray, she'd had sort of an epiphany when she'd suddenly understood that it wasn't just about her. It was about family. Her family. Jonathan. The family they would have together. She was torn, because she believed her work as a profiler made a difference. But she was needed on other fronts as well now.

She parked the car in the short-term lot and turned off the ignition. Then she looked across at Jonathan, and the tears threatened all over again.

"How long do you think it will take?" she asked bleakly, trying to turn her thoughts in a more professional direction.

Jonathan reached for her hand and entwined her fingers in his. "Too long," he said, kissing her fingertips. "But maybe it will go faster than I think. Sandringham told me an informant tipped us off that Lord Chastain's car was being repaired in an obscure body shop in Banbury. He claimed he hit a deer when he was driving in the country-side, but forensic is checking the blood they found on the front fender to see if it matches Burt Brown's. If it does, we'll have a nasty little case on our hands, and I'll likely have to stay through the prosecution."

Victoria closed her eyes and swallowed hard. It might be months before she saw him again. Without a thought of the public eye peering at them in the busy parking lot, she scooted across the seat and into his lap.

"Jonathan," she whispered, kissing him hungrily. "I love you so much. No matter . . . what happens, I will always love you."

His kiss in return was fierce with passion and grief. "I'll come back to you, Victoria. Soon. I promise. Wait for me."

Victoria managed to restrain the tears until Jonathan had boarded his plane to London. Only when she watched the big jet take to the sky did she allow herself at last to cry. It was a quiet storm, witnessed only by the clouds she stared at through the plate-glass window.

What lay ahead for them?

This was the tearful farewell at the airport she had an-ticipated. Would it be followed by the gradual letting go she feared?

*   *   *

Deplaning at Heathrow the following morning, Jonathan was like the walking dead. He tried to work up some enthusiasm for the task that lay ahead, but without Victoria, the hit-and-run and Lord Chastain and Burt Brown just didn't matter. Nothing seemed to matter.

He was on autopilot as he claimed his bag and went through customs, going through the motions, acting normal. But nothing was normal. His life could never be normal without Victoria.

He shuddered when he thought of how close he'd come to losing her. And although Billy Ray's death had brought an end to the copycat murders, he was still afraid for her safety. Something just didn't feel right. He wasn't used to listening to his intuition. Before he'd met Victoria, he hadn't really believed in it. But something in his gut told him that the danger had not passed.

He connected with the Underground and rode into the city feeling desolate and cursing himself for the fool he was for leaving her. Yes, he owed Sandringham a great deal. The man had made Jonathan's career. But he owed Victoria more. His love, his life, his protection. He would never forgive himself if they'd let down their guard too soon.

But he'd returned to London, his loyalty to Richard compelling him to finish working his cases. After that . . . ? He didn't know exactly. He wanted a life with Victoria so much it hurt. But he had to make his own way in that life. Call him old-fashioned, but he could not, would not, live beneath the shadow of her family's wealth and her own brilliant career. Maybe this sojourn back to England would give him time to come up with a plan.

In his office, a mountain of messages awaited him. He did not bother to look through them on his way into Richard Sandringham's office. Although his emotions were in a muddle, he had a job to do. The sooner he got it behind him, the sooner the rest of it could be resolved.

"Welcome back, Blake," the older inspector said, rising and extending his hand.

Jonathan shook his hand. "Thank you, sir."

He must have looked dreadful, for his supervisor frowned and peered at him intently. "Are you sick?"

"Just tired from the trip, that's all."

Sandringham looked skeptical. "Well, have a seat and I'll bring you up on things. It was Burt Brown's blood on Lord Chastain's vehicle, but we've had a bit of a complication. Lord Chastain has disappeared."

Jonathan wasn't surprised. "He's a coward, sir, if I may be blunt. He ran down an innocent pedestrian, then fled the scene. Now that he was to be made accountable for his actions, he's fled once again."

"Are you sure Burt Brown's death was accidental?" Sandringham asked, surprising him. "Or is there reason to believe that Alistair Huntley-Ames might have struck him down intentionally?"

Jonathan rubbed his forehead. That had been Victoria's initial suspicion, when she'd thought that perhaps Brown had witnessed the murder and was blackmailing Huntley-Ames. But they now knew that Lord Chastain was not the Whitechapel murderer. There was no reason to believe the incident had been other than accidental. "I can't imagine it. Burt Brown was a nobody."

"Yet the two were seen arguing violently at the Sherlock Holmes Pub just before the accident."

"True. We got in on the tail end of it. Seems Brown believed he had something of value that he was trying to peddle to Huntley-Ames, who thought Brown was just trying to rip him off."

"Any idea what he wanted to sell?"

Jonathan shook his head. "There was nothing in Brown's flat worth much of anything." Suddenly, he thought of the key Victoria had found in the bird cage and wondered if his men had located the locker it opened. "Is the flat still secured?"

"Yes, but the property manager is screaming for us to release it. The company that owns the complex is missing the income. I don't think there's much there that we need, but I didn't want to turn it over until you were back on the case."

"I'll get to it today. What about his belongings?"

"We've attempted to find the next of kin to claim his things, and his body for that matter, but so far, no one has come forward."

Jonathan felt a twinge of pity for the old man who'd lived a life of charades and died in anonymity. "I heard he used to work for the royal family."

"He did. He was a caretaker at Windsor for years. Much loved, although he was considered an eccentric. They had no record of his next of kin, though. In fact, the personnel office knew little about his personal life. Pretty frightening to think about, actually. He could have been a spy or in some other way a threat to the queen. But the personnel man believed he was harmless enough. Apparently he'd been hired as a boy because his father worked there."

A thought niggled at the back of Jonathan's mind. Forensic had proven that the warning note that Victoria had received had been written on the tablet they'd found in Burt Brown's flat. Accompanying the note was another, much older letter, and Erik Hensen had thought it was an authentic piece of correspondence from Queen Victoria to an unknown person.

Burt Brown had worked at Windsor. Could he have stumbled across some old letters of the queen's and stolen them? Was that what he'd been trying to pawn off on Huntley-Ames? Jonathan recalled Lord Chastain's pride in being related, even if remotely, to the royals. It was a long shot, but perhaps there was a connection that would lead to an answer to Sandringham's question—was the hit-and-run accidental or intended?

"I'll get right on this," Jonathan said when they were finished. "I've got a few ideas."

"I thought you might," Sandringham said with a smile. "You're one of our best. We'd hate to lose you."

Now why did he say that? Jonathan was troubled as he returned to his office, not about what Sandringham had said, but because soon, he would have to tell his supervisor and friend that he was, indeed, leaving.

He called a brief meeting of his team, who had located the locker to which the key from the bird cage belonged. "What was in it?" he asked.

His deputy shrugged. "We didn't open it. We thought you'd—"

"Does the world come to a stop just because I'm out of town?" he said irritably. "What if there's something in there relevant to this case?"

"Inspector Sandringham sort of tied our hands on this one, sir. He kept thinking you'd be back soon."

Jonathan shook his head. He hadn't realized that Sandringham relied on him so heavily. He hadn't considered himself all that important to this case. Hadn't, in fact, really thought it was much of a case. "Sorry."

One of his investigators held up the key. "CC 36," he said, tossing it to Jonathan. "The lock box is at Charing Cross Station."

Jonathan pocketed the key and briefed his men on the outcome of the Whitechapel murder. "The FBI believes it was a young man who attended the Sherlockian symposium. He'd registered as Billy Ray, but his real name was William Raymond Coleman. Can one of you dig out the rosters of airline passengers you checked out?"

One man went for his files, and in a few minutes, they confirmed that a William R. Coleman had been on an early afternoon flight out of Gatwick the Sunday after the murder. "Although we were unable to get a confession because the suspect was killed in the act of trying to commit another murder, there is enough evidence to convince most of the investigating team that he was the copycat killer. The FBI has not closed the case, but is considering it cold."

Even as he said it, he was struck by uneasiness. The outcome of the case still didn't satisfy him. Inconclusive, as it had been when they thought FitzSimmons was the Whitechapel murderer. They had been wrong then. They could be wrong now. But Victoria and the FBI knew their business. He had to go with their call on the matter. He pushed aside his apprehension. "Now, about Lord Chastain . . ."

Sandringham had put out a country-wide police alert for the missing MP, but stopped short of using the media. Alistair Huntley-Ames was, after all, a member of Parliament. There were certain things even Scotland Yard did not pursue publically when it came to England's better families. That was probably why Sandringham had wanted him back on the case. Jonathan understood the politics involved.

Later, Jonathan glanced at the pile of messages on his desk and decided they could wait one more day. "See you in the morning," he told the clerk as he left. "I'm mobile if you need me," he said, indicating his cell phone.

He headed toward the Underground, on his way to Burt Brown's depressing little flat, wishing Victoria was with him.

Victoria arrived home from work early the following day, for Jonathan had said he would try to call around six o'clock, D.C. time. It had been more than twenty-four hours since she'd said goodbye to him, and she longed to hear his voice again. The telephone was ringing when she unlocked the back door, and she dashed for it.

"Hello, Jonathan?"

"Jonathan?" She heard a familiar male voice give a short laugh, but it wasn't Jonathan. "No, Tori. It's me, Trey. Remember me? Or has the intrepid inspector stolen you away from me?"

Disappointed, Victoria sagged into a chair, breathing deeply to calm her heartbeat. "Hi, Trey. When did you get back in town?" She was glad to hear from him, but she didn't want to linger on the phone, because she didn't have call waiting.

"Last night, but too late to call you. What's the latest on your case?"

"We caught our man a few days ago. Just after you last called me."

There was a long silence, and Victoria thought maybe they'd been disconnected. "Who was it?" he asked at last.

"The man whose sketch you must have seen on television. He went by Billy Ray, although that was not his full name. Didn't you recognize him? He's the creep who sat at lunch with us the first day of the Sherlockian symposium."

"I thought he looked familiar. Is he in jail?"

"He's dead." Victoria told him what had happened.

"God, Tori, you could have been killed. When are you going to give this up?" he demanded.

"Trey, don't—"

"Okay, okay. Let's change the subject. How's your love life?"

Victoria would rather have continued talking about her recent triumph. "My love life is none of your business."

"Ah, then the inspector must still be in the picture."

"Jonathan Blake is in London, Trey."

"Your mother told my mother you were shacked up with him down at the cottage."

Victoria's chin dropped. Then her cheeks blazed in indignation. "What? When did you hear that? I thought you weren't speaking to your mother."

"We're getting along a little better these days. I called her to let her know I was back in town, and as usual she was full of juicy gossip."

"Shit."

"Tsk, tsk. Such language," he said, and she was irritated at the amusement in his voice.

"We weren't . . . shacked up." It was a lie, but she wasn't about to admit the truth to her little brother.

"This is Trey, remember? You can tell me anything."

"Why should I? You're as bad a gossip as your mother. For your information, Jonathan . . . uh . . . Inspector Blake was here on business. He was working on the Ripper case."

"Whatever you say. Your mother seemed to think it was funny business, not crime detection, that was going on down there in the cottage."

"Like I said, Trey, it's none of your business."

"Okay, I'll lay off." There was another long silence, then he said, "Mother also told me that they finally found out who killed Meg."

"Yes," she replied, her voice suddenly thick. "Can you believe it?"

"I didn't at first," he said in a low tone, then his voice rose. "But now I see what Meghan really was. She wasn't the bad girl wannabe that you always claimed. She was bad. And she had it in for all of us." Bitterness edged his words. "She did it to hurt you, Victoria, and your parents, and even me. Maybe she got what she deserved."

Victoria was shocked. She'd never heard Trey speak of Meghan in anger. She knew that Trey had been in love with Meghan, but Meghan had not felt the same toward him. She'd once confided in Victoria her dilemma, that she wanted to keep Trey as a friend, but wasn't romantically interested in him, and Victoria had advised her not to do anything that would lead him on or give him the wrong signals. "Tell him straight out what you want," she'd said, "and what you don't want." And Meghan had, and it had broken Trey's heart, but only for a short while. Trey never took anything too seriously. But maybe he had been angrier than she'd thought, and only now was allowing his true feelings to surface.

"Meghan was young and stupid, Trey. She didn't do it to hurt us. And she wasn't bad. She did it because it was . . . naughty. She was tired of being forced to be the good girl all the time."

Trey snorted. "You were the good girl, Victoria. Not Meghan. Meghan knew plenty about being naughty."

"I don't want to hear it, Trey. Meghan is dead, her killer is dead, and it's time to put it behind us."

"Yeah, right."

Something in his tone chilled her to the bone. "Leave it alone, Trey. It's behind us."

Twenty-Four

It was nearly midnight before Jonathan reached his flat. He was exhausted, hungry, and missing Victoria. He was also wired with excitement. Although he had not accomplished much toward his aim of solving the hit-and-run, he had hit pay dirt as a Ripperologist, if everything that had come his way proved authentic.

He laid his many parcels on the table, including the Sherlock Holmes teddy bear and souvenir T-shirt he'd bought for Victoria on a stop in at the Sherlock Holmes Pub. Then he went straight to the phone and dialed her number. He was on fire to talk to her. The line was busy. He emptied his pockets onto the table, then tried the number again.

Busy.

He carried the groceries to the kitchen, stashed them where they belonged, opened a beer, and tried again.

Busy.

Damn it. He was anxious to tell her about all that had transpired today, but more than anything he just wanted to hear her voice. Wanted to hear her say, "I love you, Jonathan."

He studied the treasures that lay on the wooden table. And treasures they were, indeed, although he wasn't quite sure what to make of it all.

After going to Burt Brown's flat, where he removed the

remaining Ripper memorabilia that had not been previously confiscated, he'd stopped by Roger Hammersmith's shop, as it was on his way to his next destination.

"Jonathan, old boy," Roger had greeted him enthusiastically. "Where the hell have you been? I've had a little package waiting for you for an age. Don't you get your phone messages anymore?"

"I've been out of the country," Jonathan said, his curiosity whetted. "Another package from my mysterious benefactor?"

"The same." He brought out an envelope similar to the first one, only thicker. "She asked me again not to reveal her identity," Hammersmith said with a devilish smile.

"She?"

"Oh, did I say 'she?' Sorry. The person wishes to remain anonymous."

Jonathan knew it was no slip of the tongue. So the owner of the papers, or the thief who had stolen them, was a woman. He grinned at Roger. "And I suppose, like the last time, she—I mean, this person wants them returned in three days."

"From the time you receive them. I will notify her that the delivery has been made."

"Very good. The last bundle was quite interesting. I can't wait to see what's inside this one." His friend was waiting with an eager expression on his face, hoping Jonathan would share the secret. But he wasn't ready to, not just yet.

"How is Janeece?" he asked, tucking the envelope under his arm and changing the subject.

Roger's face fell, but only momentarily. Then he brightened again. "Janeece? Oh, she's fine. We have, in fact, struck up quite a relationship. A wonderful woman, that."

"And interesting. I seem to recall her telling me she was a distant relation of Virginia Woolf's." Jonathan was only making small talk, but he saw that he'd lit a spark somewhere inside of Roger Hammersmith.

"Now that you bring it up, we've had some exciting

developments in her search for that connection. Have you got a minute?"

He didn't, but Jonathan was deeply indebted to his friend. "Sure."

Jonathan glanced around the cluttered shop and spotted the little parakeet, "Dr. Watson," in his cage in the corner, busily talking to himself and spitting bird seed onto the floor. He looked comfortable here, sort of scruffy, like the shop itself. Victoria had chosen his new home well.

In a few moments, Roger bustled back into the main room of the shop and motioned for Jonathan to come to the table at the rear. "I found this among a shipment of books I received recently from a dealer in Cambridge."

It was a Bible, large and old but not ancient. Roger opened the cover. "There's nothing particularly valuable about this per se. It was printed in the twenties. But look at this."

He retrieved a paper from inside the cover and showed it to Jonathan. It appeared older than the Bible. It was brown, creased, and the handwriting had faded. "Families Venn and Stephen" was written across the top.

Following was a list of names, to the side of which were notations about each person. The birth and death dates. Marriage dates and names of spouses, followed by any progeny.

"A family tree?"

"Of sorts," Roger said. Quickly he ran his finger down the list until he came to a name near the bottom. "Let's see. Harry L. Stephen. Herbert Stephen. J. K. Stephen. There. Adeline Virginia Stephen. Daughter of Leslie Stephen, also a distinguished writer. Married in 1912 to the journalist Leonard Woolf. She was the niece of Sir James Fitzjames Stephen, who became a famous judge until he screwed up at the James Maybrick trial."

Jonathan remembered Maybrick for two reasons. James Maybrick had been a merchant from Liverpool in the same era as Jack the Ripper. His wife, Florence Maybrick, an American, was convicted in 1889 of poisoning her husband with arsenic, but was later pardoned and returned to America. More recently, almost one hundred years exactly after the Ripper murders, a mysterious diary surfaced, purported to be the diary of James Maybrick. The "author" claimed to be none other than Jack the Ripper. Although it made a good tale and added yet another dimension to the already convoluted theories concerning the Ripper mystery, it was considered by most serious Ripperologists to be a hoax.

"How did the judge screw up at the Maybrick trial?" Jonathan asked Roger.

"He told the jury that Mrs. Maybrick was an adulteress, and that an adulteress was by nature inclined to commit murder."

Jonathan laughed out loud. "Was she an adulteress?"

"The good judge had not a shred of proof. He just didn't like women in general. The upshot of it all was that his prejudice against women caused a terrible public outcry, and the judge was forced to resign from the bench."

"There's a theory that Maybrick was an arsenic eater," Jonathan said, recalling part of the diary. "His wife may have killed him inadvertently by not giving him his daily dose. Once you are addicted to arsenic, you literally can't live without it."

"Could have happened. Nobody knew much about the side effects in those days. And arsenic was commonly used to treat certain diseases, such as syphilis and impotency. Me, I'll take Viagra." He squelched a self-conscious little laugh. "Or Janeece."

"I'm happy for you, Roger."

"Thanks," his friend replied, red in the face. "Now, to get to the meat of the matter we were looking at . . ." He turned to the next page in the Bible. "This appears to be a continuation of the old list," he said, pointing to the first entry that was actually inscribed into the book, which duplicated the last entry on the inserted sheet. "We think someone in the family copied out records from an older Bible to keep with the new one when it was started. Now, following down from here, we get to Janeece's family, the

Fairchilds. See?" He pointed proudly to the entry.

But Jonathan's eye caught on another name farther down the list.

Delaney.

"That's interesting," he murmured.

"What?"

"This entry here toward the end. The youngest Swanson daughter, Marilyn, married an American named James Winston Delaney the Second in the late fifties. Victoria's friend who was with her at the conference was named James Winston Delaney the Third. Wonder if he could be their son?"

"Serendipity," Roger said. "If he is, he's distantly related to Janeece. Wouldn't that be a jolly coincidence?"

Jonathan didn't find anything jolly about it. He didn't like Trey Delaney, if for no other reason than that Trey had been Victoria's long-time and intimate friend. Jonathan didn't like to think he was jealous, but he recognized the emotion when he saw it, even in himself.

Bringing his thoughts back to the moment, Jonathan drew on his beer and dialed Victoria's number again, and his heart leapt when he heard the phone ring.

"Jonathan, oh, it's so good to hear your voice." Victoria took the portable telephone and nestled into the cushions on the sofa where only days before she had nestled with Jonathan. "How was your trip?"

"Long. I miss you, sweetheart."

Her heart tripped over itself much like it had the first day she'd laid eyes on his sexy grin. She could see it now in her mind's eye. "I miss you, too."

"Anything exciting happened since I left?"

"Nothing. I've just about finished my report on the Traveling Jack case. And tomorrow I've promised to go to dinner at my parents' house. I dread it, but Mother is giving a surprise birthday party for Trey, and I don't know how to get out of it. I'm supposed to hijack him and bring him to the party. That's about the extent of the excitement here.

What's happening on your side of the pond?"

"A lot. Some of it you won't believe. I wish you were here." He sounded both tired and excited.

"Well, tell me. Hurry! These calls aren't cheap. My nickel next time."

"For starters, I stopped in to see Roger this afternoon. He had another package for me from our mysterious donor. He hinted that they're coming from a woman, although he didn't say who. This one was far more interesting than the last."

Victoria's interest sharpened at the eagerness in his voice. "What was in it?"

"More of the missing police files. But these held some major new material. It seems a hat was found at the scene of the Berner Street murder, the first of the double event the Ripper pulled off that night."

"A hat?"

"Not just any hat. The prince's hat. It was identified by the hatmaker as being made specifically for Prince Albert Victor Edward."

"Well, I'll be damned. So it was the prince. What became of the hat?"

"Whoever is sending these materials claims she has it."

Victoria was astounded. "Oh, my God, Jonathan. There's your hard evidence."

"If I can lay my hands on it. If there is a hair or other testable material on it. If we can find something to match it with. If these files are authentic. There are a lot of 'ifs' here."

"The last files checked out. Is there any reason to believe these won't?"

"We'll find out tomorrow. But there's more. I have no doubt the prince was in on the killings. But he may not have been working alone."

"He had an accomplice? Was it Dr. Gull?"

"Dr. Gull was an accomplice of sorts, in that he covered up the prince's involvement. But he didn't participate in the killings as some people previously believed."

"How do you know all this? Was it in the police files?"
She heard him let out a breath.

"You remember the key you found in the bird cage? Well, it fits a storage locker at Charing Cross Station. My men located it, but didn't open it. They were waiting for me. So when I left Roger's shop, I went there, and you'll never guess what was in that box."

Victoria was now sitting on the edge of her seat. "No, I never will. So tell me, damn it!"

"It's Dr. Gull's diary. Victoria, I have it right in front of me. It's a small black ledger with notes dating from the day after the double event. The notes are exclusively about his treatment of Prince Eddy during the last couple of years of his life."

"My God! Is it for real?"

"If it isn't, whoever wrote it knew a lot about the royals in those days. This is how it starts: 'Letter from V.R. today informing that my previous speculation concerning the heir has been confirmed and directing me to take immediate action as we had discussed.' "

"Jonathan, those are almost the same words as were written on that old note FitzSimmons sent with the warning."

"Dr. Gull may have just received that same note when he wrote this."

"Or a forger wrote them both."

"Could be. But I don't think so. I just feel this must be authentic."

Victoria laughed. "Don't tell me you're using your intuition these days."

Jonathan cleared his throat and said, "You can learn a lot from your gut feelings."

The warmth of his words and the love behind them flowed through her, and she whispered, "I love you, Jonathan." She swallowed the emotion that tightened her throat, and said, "Go on with what you were telling me."

"The doctor was ordered not to keep any official record of his treatment of the prince. He notes here: 'H.R.H. has

forbidden me to keep medical records of my work henceforth in regard to Prince Albert Victor Edward, but as a
conscientious physician I must make note of my treatment
program for my own use.' "

"That explains the missing medical records. They were
never missing. They never existed. The prince's complicity
was covered up from the start."

"According to this, Prince Eddy returned to Windsor the
night of the double murder, covered in blood and shrieking
at the top of his lungs. Dr. Gull was summoned, and he
sedated the prince and removed him to an asylum, but he
escaped again on November 9, the day of the last Ripper
murder.

"Listen to this: 'H.R.H. is furious that the prince escaped
my care, and I fear that the demon that lives inside his
syphilitic mind will cause him to kill again. Accompanied
by a discreet guard of muscular fellows, I went directly to
the quarters of the prince's known preferred consort, J. K.
Stephen, for in his madness, he had raved about that gentleman of dubious repute. Stephen was an ill choice for the
prince's tutor, and I fear his perversions have swayed the
prince's already fragile psyche. The prince was not where
I had expected him to be, however. In fact, no one was in
residence. I returned home, nearly sick with apprehension,
and rightly so, for only hours later, I was summoned by the
Prince of Wales to make haste once again for Windsor
Castle.

" 'This night, it was even more terrible than before. The
Prince was wearing bloodstained women's clothing and
crying inconsolably, sobbing that he had killed his Mother
Dear. Since Princess Alexandra was in residence, hale and
hearty, I can only presume the Prince had murdered another
in her place. His is a sickness of mind that I cannot comprehend. Once again, I sequestered him in the asylum, this
time with double the guard, for the Prince of Wales threatened my ruin should his son escape again. I must not fail
in my duty, for God and the Queen both look to me to
prevent his madness not only from taking more lives, but

also from bringing down the monarchy should his complicity be discovered by the social democrats. These are uneasy times, and the royal family is under considerable criticism by those who would topple our way of life as we know it.' "

"Dr. Gull knew and covered it up." Victoria inhaled deeply. "And the prince got away with murder."

Twenty-Five

After saying a reluctant good-night to Victoria, Jonathan sat up into the small hours, reading the words written by Dr. William Gull more than a hundred years before and trying to imagine the ambivalence he must have felt about the orders he'd been given by his queen. He did not dare disobey, and yet he knew the prince had brutally killed those women.

Most of the notebook was filled with shorthand notations of medications and dates, but some of it was recorded diary style. One such passage caught his eye:

The Prince is experiencing spells of delusion that are becoming more frequent as his syphilitic madness progresses, and it is difficult at times to discern if he is lucid when speaking of certain things. Tonight, for instance, before I sedated him at bedtime, he began to cry. He told me he was sorry for what he had done to those women, and promised he would never do such a thing again. At first I thought this was a ploy to persuade me to release him, but it turned into something else altogether. He pleaded with me to stop the killer!

I thought he was referring to himself, for I know beyond a shadow of a doubt that he was behind the Whitechapel murders. But he kept crying and begging me to stop his erstwhile tutor, J. K. Stephen, from killing again. 'It would not be fair for him to continue to hunt without me,' he sobbed at one point. I asked him to which hunt he was referring, and he told me the most ghastly tale, I know not whether to believe it. According to his story, Stephen, with whom I believe the Prince has had a long-standing homosexual relationship, lured the Prince into the East End where they engaged in a "hunt," with the prey being the prostitutes who walked the darkened streets. Once these adventures began, they were unable to give them up. He vacillates between remorse and a desire to kill again, for he does not want Stephen to hunt without him, and he said Stephen had vowed to "kill into infinity."

Jonathan laid the book in his lap and rubbed his eyes. J. K. Stephen. He'd heard the name before. In fact, if he wasn't mistaken, that name had appeared on the family tree in the old Bible Roger had shown him. Virginia Woolf's maiden name had been Stephen. Had she been related to Prince Eddy's tutor? Small world.

Of course he'd heard about the tutor before, although he had forgotten his name. Indeed, some Ripperologists held that it was the tutor, not the prince, who had been Jack the Ripper. But from what he'd read in these documents, he now believed the Ripper was the two men working together, much like the famous duo Leopold and Loeb in the twenties.

He went to his briefcase and shuffled through it until he found photocopies of the note the copycat murderer had sent to the *Times* and the two he'd sent to the U.S. media. He laid them side by side on the table and studied the messages carefully.

I will never finish my work. I will kill into infinity.

Infinity. Did the killer believe he was invincible? Or did this refer to something altogether different?

I will kill into infinity if I must, to play out the game.

What game?

I wasn't codding when I said I will kill into infinity. Haven't you figured it out yet?

Figured out what? His game?

His game was pretty clear. *Ripping is my destiny. It is my heritage, it is in my blood.*

Jonathan was troubled by something he couldn't quite put a finger on, but it was late and he was too tired to think about it any more tonight. He laid the book aside and went to bed.

His was a fitful sleep, filled with dreams of someone being chased by a madman with a bloody knife. Someone, he couldn't tell who, was in deadly danger, and he was running, running, trying to pursue the killer, but his feet were not carrying him anywhere. Then a woman screamed and his blood ran cold. Victoria. The madman was after Victoria.

Jonathan bolted upright in his bed, his body drenched in cold sweat. It was just a dream, he told himself. Only a dream. But he was uneasy as he drifted off to sleep again.

The specter of the dream followed him into the next day, and he was tempted to call Victoria just to make sure she was all right. That was a foolish notion, of course. The dream was nothing more than his subconscious recalling his terror when Victoria truly was in grave danger.

He finished reading Dr. Gull's notebook before leaving for work, and once in his office, he undertook the chore of photocopying both it and the old police reports before entrusting the treasures to Erik Hensen in the forensic lab. "These are for your eyes only," he told the man, whose eyes grew to the size of saucers when he saw what had come his way. "I don't want it known that they exist. For now, it's our little secret. They may be phony, and I don't want to look like a fool, you know what I mean?"

Jonathan left with a smile on his face, knowing that the curious and highly efficient little man would put aside everything else to find out if those materials were authentic. Knowing Hensen, he'd probably started on it the minute Jonathan had left the office.

In his own office, the message pile still awaited him. He poured himself a cup of coffee and sat down, determined to wade through them and get it over with. But his mind tripped back to the intriguing police records and the incredible little diary. To J. K. Stephen and the prince's plea for Dr. Gull to stop him from killing again. To the phrase "kill into infinity."

Kill into infinity.

That expression had not been used in any of the notes sent to the media by the original Ripper, but the copycat had used it three times. The coincidence of coming across it in the diary, in reference to J. K. Stephen, the man he thought had likely been the real Ripper, was too great to ignore, although it was impossible that Billy Ray had read Dr. Gull's diary. But Coleman had known a great deal about the old Ripper murders. It was possible he might have stumbled across some other mention of the term, but Jonathan could not recall having seen the phrase in any of the considerable research material that he had read on the subject.

Jonathan tried to ignore the misgivings that stirred in his gut. Billy Ray was dead. Why was he suddenly so concerned about Victoria's safety? Just to set his mind at ease, he picked up the phone to call her, but realized it was only four A.M. in D.C. He'd wait a couple of hours.

During that time, he forced himself to return the phone calls that had come in for him while he was away. As he talked, he doodled on a yellow legal pad, and when he hung up, he realized he'd been drawing the infinity sign—a figure eight turned sideways—over and over again.

Kill into infinity.

Infinity. A pattern? A game? A game board?

Haven't you figured it out yet? Curious, Jonathan left his office, and minutes later in the reference room, he was poring over a map of the United States. He laid a piece of tracing paper over the map and marked an X over each city where the Ripper copycat had struck.

Chicago. Kansas City. Phoenix. San Francisco. Seattle. Boulder. Dallas–Fort Worth. And finally, Washington, D.C. He figured that Billy Ray had begun his journey of death from his home just outside of D.C., so Jonathan used that as both starting and ending point. With a pencil, he connected the dots, so to speak, moving from D.C. to Chicago and on along the killer's route. The result was loosely the image of an infinity sign.

"Well, I'll be damned," he muttered. "There *was* a pattern." If they'd guessed his game from the note he'd sent to the Denver *Post*, they might have saved the lives of two women in Texas. And Victoria might have been spared the hours of terror when she'd been held captive by Billy Ray.

Jonathan returned to his office, pleased at himself, but still vaguely uneasy. How had Billy Ray come up with the pattern of the infinity sign? It could only be ... that the original Ripper had murdered in a similar pattern.

He called the evidence custodian and requisitioned a photocopy of the rough map of Whitechapel that had been pinned to the wall of Burt Brown's bedroom. The map that was marked with the Ripper murder sites. Going through the same "follow the dots" motions, he saw another, fatter infinity sign appear before his eyes.

Jonathan pursed his lips, letting out a low whistle as he leaned back against his chair. He hadn't thought Billy Ray was that smart. He must have observed the same thing, that the original Ripper had killed in the pattern of an infinity sign, and decided to copy him on a grander scale. Had the Ripper of old been that organized? He doubted it. From all he had read, the original Ripper, although an organized killer to some degree, had relied a great deal on chance and opportunity. And yet, according to Dr. Gull's diary, J. K. Stephen had vowed to kill into infinity. Had it been coincidental that he'd struck in those particular spots, or was it part of a predetermined pattern?

His thoughts were interrupted by an incoming call.

"Blake here."

The receptionist told him he had an international call. When she put the call through, the voice on the phone was young and female, heavy with a French accent. "Inspector Blake," she said in a hesitant manner. "You may not remember me. My name is Chantal Dupres. I was at the Sherlockian symposium with my friend Nicole."

Remember them? How could he forget that pair? "Yes, Miss Dupres. What may I do for you?"

She paused, then told him, "My friend and I have been talking, and we feel bad about somezing. We . . . uh . . . did not quite tell your men all ze truth ze day after ze murder."

From the moment she got out of bed, Victoria dreaded the evening to come. Why her mother insisted on something like this was beyond her. She knew that Trey had been estranged from his parents for years and had only lately shown signs of mellowing. Why was she trying to force a reconciliation between them? It was bound to backfire. Victoria wondered at her own stupidity in agreeing to more or less kidnap Trey and deliver him to the doorstep of her parents' mansion. He'd be royally pissed at her.

On the other hand, he had seemed more open to reconciliation. Only yesterday he'd told her he'd called his mother to let her know he was back in town. *And his mother had told him that her mother had said she was shacked up with Jonathan at the cottage.*

She had a major bone to pick with both women. But she wouldn't do it tonight.

Tonight, she'd be there for Trey. She'd made a dinner date with him, ostensibly to pay him back for going to London with her. She'd just failed to mention where she planned to take him. She would tell him before they arrived. If he truly didn't want to go, she wouldn't make him.

Victoria dressed for work with an eye to the evening's party, for she wouldn't have time to come home and change. She chose an elegant tailored dress rather than a suit, and higher heels than she normally preferred. She wasn't exactly dressing to satisfy her mother, yet she knew her mother would be pleased. She didn't know why she cared. But being suitably dressed when she broke the news to everyone that she'd decided to marry Jonathan Blake would at least give her some psychological armor. Her announcement would cause a shitstorm, and she didn't plan to broach the subject this evening unless it came up. But between Barbara and Marilyn, she knew it would come up, and she wasn't going to lie anymore about her feelings for Jonathan, or their plans for the future. Whatever they were.

She had hoped to spend the day sorting out her desk and doing other housekeeping chores around the office that had been ignored during her vacation and the ensuing case with the copycat Ripper. But when she arrived, she found a group of dignitaries in the main office, including two congressmen, members of a "watchdog" committee that was supposed to police the police. She never made it to her desk, as Mike invited her to join him in giving the group a tour of the headquarters of the National Center for the Analysis of Violent Crime. "We sometimes refer to this as the National 'Cellar' for the Analysis of Violent Crime because of its underground location," she joked, trying to sound at ease, but in fact, these people made her nervous. They could never understand fully what went on here, and she suspected their visit had something to do with funding.

She did her job well, however. Too well, it would seem, for they became fascinated with the new computer system and took their time learning its capabilities. "We're getting kind of close to Big Brother here," one remarked skeptically.

"There is a fine line sometimes between criminal investigation and protection of privacy," she said in agreement. "But this system is not about invasion of privacy. It's about communication between law enforcement agencies. Because we had this system in place, for example, we were able to assist police departments across the country in resolving the recent series of brutal murders you may have read about."

"Traveling Jack?" asked one of them.

"That's right."

"But I read that you never got a confession out of the man before he was killed," remarked one of the congressmen. "How do you know you got the right man?"

The question was fair, and Victoria didn't mind answering it. But as she began to tick off the reasons the agency had concluded that Billy Ray was Traveling Jack, something in the pit of her stomach turned over. By all reason and logic, Billy Ray had to have been the killer. But the evidence, other than the fact he'd tried to kill her, just wasn't there. They had no proof that he had so much as looked at those other women, much less been at the crime scenes. She wasn't going to tell this to the assembled group, however.

"It's difficult sometimes," she admitted. "In this case, particularly so, because the perpetrator left no evidence at the crime scenes such as bodily fluids, hair, fingerprints, that could give us a genetic match with the man we believe committed the murders. The case has not been closed, but it's gone cold."

It was mid-afternoon before the group left, and Victoria hoped she'd answered their questions satisfactorily. It wasn't that she didn't believe in watchdog committees, but even with completely altruistic motives, they had the power to interrupt the valuable work being done by the profiling unit at Quantico, as well as by their agents in the field.

"I'm starved," she said, plopping down on a chair in Mike Mosier's office after they'd left. "Want to buy me lunch?"

"Yeah. Let's get out of here. That's enough for one day."

Two square white boxes tied with identical red ribbons sat on Jonathan's desk, and huddled in chairs to one side, Chantal Dupres and Nicole St. Germain looked miserable and contrite. They'd called him from Paris that morning. They had read the continuing stories about the Whitechapel murder and begun to realize they might have withheld some pertinent information. They had insisted on driving to London to speak with him in person. It was late afternoon by the time they'd arrived, having driven through the Chunnel, the tunnel beneath the English Channel. The story they were laying out for him chilled him to the marrow.

"We . . . we should have thought about this from the start," Chantal said, biting her nails.

"But . . . but we were afraid."

No one could be more afraid than Jonathan was at the moment. Afraid they had all made a terrible mistake in thinking that Billy Ray Coleman was the Ripper copycat. Afraid that Victoria was in more danger now than either of them had ever conceived possible. He struggled to remain outwardly calm, but inside he was trembling.

"Let's see if I have this straight. You say on the night of the Whitechapel murder, Trey Delaney left you for an extended period of time. When was that?"

"About . . . well, it was right after we got to ze nightclub. We left ze Jack ze Ripper Pub about ten o'clock and took a taxi to a new dance place out in ze Docklands. He said he had to go out for a little while, that he wanted to give us a present. He bought us drinks, gave us money to buy more if we finished those before he returned, and was gone before we could say anything. Soon, he came back with flowers for us, in those boxes." She pointed to the boxes on the desk.

"How long was he gone?"

"About . . . thirty minutes. Forty-five at ze most. He must have known a place open late at night to buy ze flowers. He was such a gentleman. We do not believe he would have done anyzing else, so when your men asked us if Mr. Delaney had been with us all night, we said yes. We thought he meant . . . well, you know . . . with us in bed all night. Which he was."

Jonathan was reeling. Thirty to forty-five minutes! Trey Delaney had left them for that long right around the time the coroner estimated the murder had occurred. It was enough time to hop a train back into London—a train that went almost directly back to Whitechapel for that matter, it wasn't that far—commit the murder, and return, flowers in hand. There was probably one of those all-night shop-ettes in the neighborhood of the nightclub that sold flowers.

The timing was tight, but it could have happened.

But most damaging were the gift boxes in front of him.

"You say the next day when you were packing, you noticed one of the gift boxes was missing."

"Yes, but we were in a hurry. We did not think anything of it. I could not remember if I'd brought mine back from ze club," Chantal admitted. "I'd . . . had quite a bit to drink by zat time."

They had brought one of the boxes with them from Paris that morning, thinking it might somehow be cogent to the case. Jonathan had retrieved the other from Scotland Yard's evidence custodian. It was the box in which the murdered woman's liver had been delivered to Victoria's door.

Two rooms away from Trey Delaney's room.

The boxes were identical in every respect. When the young women had learned what the missing box had been used for, they were horrified.

Jonathan did not know Trey Delaney well, but he had instinctively disliked him from the start, feelings that he had chalked up to jealousy. Maybe his intuition had been operational all along, and he'd chosen to ignore it.

"Did he leave the room any time during the night?"

They shook their heads in unison.

"But as I said," Chantal reminded him, "we'd had a lot to drink. Strange," she said reflectively, "he didn't seem to want to . . . you know, have sex with us. We just curled up together and went to sleep. He could have . . . left the room, and we wouldn't have known it."

Nicole began to cry. "Zis is so horrible. I am so sorry."

Jonathan felt sorry for them, for they were in deep trouble. But he felt sorrier for the women who had died because these two had protected the man whom he now fully believed was the real Traveling Jack.

Trey Delaney.

Victoria's childhood friend.

How could she have overlooked him as a suspect? he wondered. She never once considered him at all. Maybe it was because she knew him, was his friend, and could not believe it was possible for him to be the killer. But he fit her profile much better than did Billy Ray. *A young male between twenty and thirty*—Jonathan would guess that Trey was in his late twenties—*who comes from the same level of society as his victims and moves easily among them . . .* Trey Delaney would have had no trouble meeting his victims in social surroundings. *Well educated.* Yes. *Well financed.* Yes. *Well organized in his crimes, a careful planner.* Yes. He must have planned the Whitechapel murder carefully. Otherwise, he would have become bloodied from the act. He had had to plan ahead, for he must have taken some kind of receptacle along with him to store his bloody souvenir. Where had he come by the zipper-lock plastic bag? He had also had to find a way to obtain the gift box he wanted in which to deliver Victoria's present.

Victoria.

Ignoring the two frightened young women, Jonathan dialed Victoria's office number. He got her voice mail and left a message for her to call him on an important matter. He wanted to tell her his suspicions directly, not leave what surely would be a devastating message on a recording. And what if he was wrong? He would be accusing her friend of the most heinous of crimes. Would she ever forgive him?

But he had to press the issue. The French women's story was too important to ignore. He called Victoria's apartment but the phone there was also answered with a recording. His apprehension mounted. He had to talk to her, to warn her before she innocently opened her door to a man who might be the killer, thinking him a friend.

And then dismay washed over him as he remembered that she'd said she was taking Trey to a surprise birthday party at her parents' house. Tonight.

Oh, God.

He looked at his watch. It was four o'clock Greenwich time. That would make it only ten A.M. her time. He had to get through to her before she made what could be the worst mistake of her life. Maybe the last.

He turned Chantal and Nicole over to two of his best

CID men, who were to tape formal depositions from the women and question them further. He returned to his office and paced the floor, telling himself this was madness. There was no way Trey Delaney could be the Ripper copycat. Perhaps the young women had made up their story. But why? What motive did they have for that? None. They had, in fact, put themselves at considerable risk by coming forward. They could have kept quiet, and no one would have known the difference.

Trying to convince himself that Trey could not be the killer, Jonathan considered the issues of Trey's motive, means, and opportunity in the Whitechapel murder.

Motive. What motive did he have for the killings? None that he knew of. But then, psychopathic killers needed no real motive. They were driven by madness. But Trey Delaney did not seem mad in the least.

Means. Did Trey Delaney carry a knife? Did he know how to use it? Again, it seemed unlikely. He'd gone to Whitechapel that night dressed like a young lord of the realm, complete with top hat, spats, and cane. Where would he have secured a knife?

Opportunity. If the French women's story was true, he did have the opportunity. It was the only element that fit. But even so, the window of opportunity was narrow.

Jonathan glanced down at his yellow legal pad filled with doodles of the infinity design. He recalled the notation from Dr. Gull's diary. *He will kill into infinity.* Who would kill? Jack the Ripper? J. K. Stephen? Prince Eddy? Trey Delaney?

Suddenly, he recalled his visit to Roger Hammersmith's bookshop the day before, and the family tree that was in the old Bible. J. K. Stephen was a cousin of Virginia Woolf. Janeece Fairchild's family was descended from that bloodline.

And so was a family named Delaney.

Coincidence?

Renewed alarm washing through him, Jonathan raced to the telephone again and placed another call to Victoria's office. This time, instead of leaving a message on her voice mail, he dialed the operator, who told him Ms. Thomas and Mr. Mosier were both tied up with members of an important Congressional committee and wouldn't be available for the rest of the day. Damn! He slammed the phone down, his stomach knotting painfully. He felt helpless and frustrated, knowing that thousands of miles away, Victoria might be in terrible danger.

Running his fingers through his hair, Jonathan tried to decide what to do next. Call the police in Virginia? What, and quite possibly make a complete ass of himself? Trey Delaney was, after all, the son of a very powerful family there. On the surface, he seemed an unlikely candidate for being a serial killer. Would the police even listen to him? And again he considered the ramifications if he was wrong. Scotland Yard was sensitive to libel suits.

Maybe he was overreacting, he thought. But something in his gut told him he must take action. Now. He couldn't just stand around and wait. As crazy as it seemed, he had to go to her. He had a substantial stash of money saved— for what, he had never known. He'd just never had much to spend it on. Now, he could think of no better use for it than to spend it to get to Victoria as quickly as possible. If he was wrong about Trey, so be it. But if he was right . . .

He picked up the phone again and in moments had secured a seat on the first available flight of the Concorde headed to the U.S.

Twenty-Six

It was nearly seven o'clock when Victoria arrived at Trey's town house in Georgetown. She'd had a light lunch with Mike late in the afternoon and was not one bit hungry, either physically or emotionally, for the evening that loomed in front of her. She lucked into a parking place not far from Trey's front door, and drew in a deep breath as she turned off the ignition, praying everything would go smoothly.

"Hi," she said, kissing Trey's cheek when he opened the door. "I brought you something." She handed him a bottle of his favorite single-malt whisky, which she'd stopped to purchase after leaving Mike. "Happy birthday."

Trey lived in a gracious old town house and had spared no expense in renovating it to suit his bachelor tastes. Most of the walls were painted in subtly contrasting shades of off-white, beige, and taupe that could have set the room up for the blah so common with neutral tones, but Trey's designer had offset the vanilla with generous splashes of black and red and other vivid colors in contemporary furnishings, artwork, and accents. To Victoria's eye, it was wild and frenetic. She could never relax in this place. But Trey had always been on the daring side, and she supposed it suited his nature.

"I'm flattered you remembered my birthday," he said, looking a little surprised when she handed him the bottle.

"Of course I remembered your birthday. We've always made a big deal out of birthdays."

Odd. It sounded like he'd forgotten his own.

He took the whisky to the bar in the large, spacious living area and opened it eagerly. "What's your pleasure? Want to share some of this mother's milk, or would you prefer wine?"

Victoria rarely drank hard liquor, and not at all when she was driving. "Got a nice white vintage something lurking in there somewhere?" she replied, indicating the built-in refrigerated unit designed specifically for maintaining wine at the proper temperature. It was an extravagant device, but Victoria knew Trey had installed it to impress the women he entertained here.

He poked around until he came up with one that pleased him. "Let's see. Ah, yes. Will Pouilly Fuiseé suffice?"

He sounded like the Trey she'd always known, a trifle arrogant, decidedly flippant, untouchable except by a few—of which she was one. But Victoria thought he looked haggard, and she noted he had taken to walking with a cane, although he didn't seem to lean into it. It looked like the cane that was part of his costume at the ball in London.

"Are you feeling all right?" she asked as she accepted the wine. "You look tired. Hard trip?"

"Just the usual strain of a new job," he said. "I'm fine. Cheers." They clinked glasses, and he quaffed his double shot in a single swallow, then poured himself another.

He was lying when he said he was feeling all right, and she knew it. Dark circles bruised his face beneath the eyes, and his skin seemed paler than ever. He looked, in fact, as if he hadn't slept since she saw him last. She saw that his hands shook when he raised his glass, and she wondered how much whisky he'd been drinking lately.

He most certainly did not look up to an evening with the senior Delaneys and Thomases.

"So, what's the scoop on Inspector Clouseau?" he asked, taking a seat on the sofa across from where she sat on a cushy leather chair.

She smiled over the top of her wine glass. "His name, as you very well know, is Jonathan. Jonathan Blake."

He lit a pipe and crossed one leg over the other. "You make it with him?"

Since when did Trey smoke a pipe? "None of your damned business."

He laughed caustically. "You did. And Mommy doesn't like it."

"It's none of her damned business either." She sighed. "I wish she wasn't such a snob. Jonathan's a good man. An excellent law enforcement officer. I'm in love with him, and . . . I'm going to marry him, Trey."

His glass slipped from his hand and shattered on the polished hardwood floor, jolting Victoria. He stared at her in disbelief. Then a cynical smile turned up one side of his mouth. "Oh, I doubt that, Tori."

Jonathan looked out the window as the massive supersonic jet descended into New York's JFK airport. It had been less than four hours from when he'd departed London, but it seemed he'd been in the air for an eternity. He set his watch to the local time. Six P.M. Had Victoria already left for the party with Trey, or had she picked up one of the many messages he'd left on both her home and office answering machines, placed from the airphone, warning her not to go out tonight, to stay put until he arrived?

After clearing customs, he tried again to reach her from a pay phone, to no avail. He cursed himself for not arguing with that receptionist at FBI headquarters and insisting that Victoria be pulled out of the meeting with the Congressional committee. But he hadn't, and his failure might cost Victoria her life.

All he could do at the moment was make sure he didn't miss his connection to Dulles. And pray.

Victoria was pissed at Trey as they left the town house, although she tried to cover it with a polite veneer. It was his birthday after all. But she was disappointed in his sardonic response to her announcement that she planned to marry Jonathan. He'd told her she didn't have the balls to go against her parents' wishes, and he was certain that they would be against such a marriage. But she sensed that at the moment Trey himself was being as big a snob as her mother at the moment, and she felt betrayed because her lifelong friend would not support her in this.

She pulled her car onto the beltway and headed toward the exclusive suburb where the Thomases and the Delaneys lived in neighboring mansions. Suddenly realizing the direction she had taken, Trey asked, "Where are we going?"

Before, she had been willing to let him off the hook if he didn't want to go to his birthday party. Now, it would be a little payback for his disloyalty.

"Surprise."

But when she turned down the lane that led to the two properties they both knew so well, he snarled, "What the hell are you doing, Victoria? Get me out of here."

"Sorry." She smiled at him sweetly as she pulled up to the front portico of her parents' palatial home. "It's a surprise party, for your birthday, Trey. You may not like it, but people are trying to be nice to you. So behave."

She got out of the car and hurried up the steps and into the house, not at all sure Trey would follow. But he did. And when he caught up to her, there was thunder in his expression.

"Thanks a lot," he growled under his breath as they entered the drawing room. He shook his elegant walking cane in her direction. "I'll get you for this."

Their parents rose from their seats when they entered, and Victoria saw anxious expressions on their faces. It had been years since Trey had spoken directly to his parents. Victoria couldn't remember the last time he'd been face-to-face with hers. Meghan's funeral perhaps. Apprehension knotted her stomach. These people meant well. She hoped he would behave himself.

"Happy birthday, son." His father, James Winston Delaney II, stepped forward and extended his hand. "We're glad you could make it."

Trey glared at his father, but eventually took his hand in an unenthusiastic handshake. Marilyn Delaney hurried over to him. "Happy birthday," she said, touching his cheek in a motherly fashion. Trey jerked back as if he'd been burned. Although Victoria did not like Marilyn, at the moment she felt sorry for her, for it was apparent that her only child hated her.

"Good evening, Mother," Trey said stiffly. "Good evening, Mr. and Mrs. Thomas." He nodded toward her parents. "Whose idea was this little shindig anyway?"

"We thought it was time for you to come home," Marilyn said in a tone that brooked no argument. She'd always been like that. Bossy to the extreme. "You've spent enough time licking your wounds. It's time you grew up. Fulfilled yourself as a man."

Trey went to the bar and poured himself a stiff drink, tossed it back and refilled the glass. His back was to the rest of them, and Victoria saw James Delaney frown at his wife and shake his head, warning her not to nag Trey. Victoria agreed with him. If Marilyn didn't shut up, she'd drive yet another wedge between them and their son.

"We've missed you, son," his father said, sounding uncharacteristically conciliatory. Victoria had seen this man shout at Trey and berate him in front of others for real or perceived transgressions. Was he going to apologize now? Had he really changed that much? She couldn't see it.

Trey whirled and faced them all, drink in hand, his face contorted with fury. "Missed me? You've missed me? That's a good one, old man. You never missed me a day in your life. Out of sight, out of mind, it was, as I recall. Unless you needed something from me."

"That's not true," Marilyn protested. Her British accent always got thicker when she was upset. "Your father and I have always enjoyed your company."

Trey gave her a scathing look. "Like you are enjoying it at the moment? You're a lying sack of shit, Mother."

"Now see here. Don't talk to your mother like that."
Trey's father advanced toward him as if to strike him, but
he stopped when Trey took a step in his direction, holding
his cane like a weapon.

"You can go straight to hell, old man," Trey said, glaring
at his father with pure hatred in his eyes. "You and Mother
dear never gave a damn about me. All you cared about was
your social standing and prestige. I was an accident, but
you graciously allowed me into your lives as long as I
didn't fuck up. But I did fuck up, didn't I, Mother?"

Victoria watched the scene in horror. Trey's eyes had
taken on the glint of a madman. His face was filled with
anger so vile it appalled her. What was going on here?

Her father went for the phone. "I'm calling the police,"
he said. "Sorry, Delaney, but your son is no longer welcome in my house."

Trey threw his whisky glass at Victoria's father, who
ducked barely in time. The fine crystal shattered against the
wall. "Don't touch that phone. This is a family affair, is it
not? We wouldn't want our dirty laundry hung out for the
rest of the world to see, now would we?"

Victoria knew he'd hit a nerve with both her parents.
They deplored public exposure. No police would be called
into this domestic dispute.

"Trey, please," she said, finding her voice at last. "Come
on, let's just go."

But he ignored her. He strode to where his mother, for
once, stood speechless. "You don't like me, do you, Mother
dear? You never have. But you know what? You made me
what I am. It's your blood that taints my veins and drives
me to the work I do."

Marilyn turned a ghastly white. "Don't, Trey. Don't . . ."

Victoria frowned. What was he talking about?

Trey took his mother's wrists in his hands. "What,
Mother? What don't you want me to do?"

Victoria had never seen Marilyn Delaney reduced to the
quivering, frightened woman she was at the moment.
"Don't do this to yourself," she said after a moment. "Don't

do it to us. We never meant to hurt you, James."

"James!" He spat the name as if it were poison. "You didn't even have the decency to give me a name of my own." He released her wrists. "I despise you, Mother. I hope you rot in hell."

His anger seemed dissipated, at least for the moment, and Victoria tried again to undo the horrible mistake she'd made in bringing him here. "Trey, let's go."

Her voice at last seemed to penetrate the insanity that had come over him. His eyes shifted to her.

"I told you not to bring me here." Something in the way he looked at her filled her with misgiving. But she did not look away.

"I'm sorry," she said. "It was a mistake. Let's go."

Outside, Victoria reached into her purse for her keys, but Trey snatched them from her. "Get in," he ordered. "I'm driving."

Knowing he'd had ample to drink, Victoria hesitated. "I'd better drive, Trey."

He grabbed her roughly by the arm, opened the passenger door, and threw her down on the seat. "I said get in." She barely pulled her legs inside the car before he slammed the door.

"Trey," she said, touching his arm when he got behind the wheel. "This is dangerous."

He glared at her, his lips curling into a vicious smile. "You have no idea just how dangerous."

He peeled away from the house, and the car fishtailed around the curve at the end of the drive. Victoria screamed. "Stop it, Trey. Don't take your anger out on me."

He didn't answer. Neither did he slow down. At the corner where the private drive intersected the lane, he turned left instead of right.

"Where are you going?" But she already knew. There was only one other house on that lane. His parents'. Victoria's stomach knotted. Something terrible was going on between Trey and his parents, something deep and dark and secret. Something that had caused him to go over the edge.

She wished she'd brought her gun, for friend or no friend, Trey was clearly dangerous. But the only weapon she had was her cell phone. Quietly, she reached inside her purse and felt for the number pads, hoping the roar of the engine would drown the tiny beeps when she dialed 911.

"Trey, let me go," she called out moments later, hoping she'd dialed correctly and that someone on the other end of the line was listening. "Stop this car right now. Heritage Lane was never meant for fast traffic. You're going to kill us."

"Not us, sweetheart. Just you."

Victoria hadn't thought she could be much more frightened, but her fear turned to terror as she suddenly realized Trey's anger went far deeper than a temporary fit against his parents. If she wasn't able to calm him, she fully believed he might kill her.

"Trey, don't do this. Let me help you."

"What? You think I need counseling? Been there, done that." He drew the car to a screeching halt in front of the looming mansion where he had grown up. "My dear parents threw me into a private mental hospital after Meghan died. You never knew that, did you? That story about me taking off for the wild west was just so much bullshit. She and Father didn't want their friends to know about their lunatic son."

"Why did they do that?" Victoria asked, astonished.

"Because," he said, twirling the knob on his walking stick as if he were unscrewing it, "I came home all bloody that night." He pulled the knob away from the cane, and with it came a long, slender knife. The steel of the blade glinted in the moonlight.

Victoria drew in a sharp breath. She didn't know what he was talking about, or why he had pulled a knife on her, but she wasn't about to hang around to find out. She jerked the door open and tried to run, but Trey was faster. He tackled her and knocked her to the ground. His face was in hers, his body pinning her to the pavement.

"Trey, get off me," she yelled, pushing against his chest. But he was much larger and more muscular than she.

"I fucked up that night." He was breathing heavily as he spoke the words next to her ear. "I fucked up the whole thing with Meghan. I loved her, but she wouldn't have me. Not after you told her to ditch me."

"I never—"

"Oh, yes you did. Meghan had told me she would marry me. Did you know that, Tori? She promised me. She even fucked me to seal the promise. Bet you didn't know that, did you, Miss Prude? Well, she did. She fucked me a lot. Until you told her to leave me. It's all your fault she died, Tori. All your fault!"

"No!"

"Yes. If you hadn't interfered, she would have been safe with me, instead of running off to meet her lover. What was his name? Ferguson?" In the moonlight, his eyes glittered with malice.

Victoria's heart slammed furiously against her ribs, half in fear and half in shock at what he was telling her. What did he mean, he came home all bloody that night?

"She was a whore," he went on. "Nothing but a bloody whore who thought she was too good for me. Just like you think you're too good for me. But I got even. Oh, yes, I got even. And I'll get even with you, too, for betraying me." He rolled off her but kept a tight grip on her wrists and brought her painfully to her feet.

Victoria fought to keep her mind clear. This was incomprehensible. Surrealistic. A dream. Or rather, a nightmare. Trey twisted her arms behind her and forced her to walk toward the house. She felt the knifepoint against her throat. She prayed that one of the servants was home, but the house was dimly lit inside.

"Trey . . ." she said, trying to plead with him to let her go.

"Shut up."

"What are you going to do? Take it out on me because Meghan betrayed you? I never told her to leave you. She just didn't feel for you what you felt for her. I told her to be honest with you."

"I said shut up!" He shoved her into the door while he pressed the opening code into the alarm system. Victoria's mind raced. What had he meant when he'd said he had gotten even with Meghan? Had he killed her? If so, why had Matthew Ferguson confessed to the murder in his suicide note? If she was to die tonight, she was determined that she'd go to her grave with some answers.

Inside the house, Trey dragged her into the main living room where a low light burned from recessed lighting above the mantel. It was an elegant room but inhospitable and had always made Victoria uncomfortable. Above the fireplace, a portrait of Marilyn Delaney glared down at them.

Mother.

Victoria called upon all of her knowledge of psychology to try to come out of this alive. "This isn't about Meghan, is it, Trey? It's about your mother."

"Don't try to pull that psychological shit on me, Tori." With his knife, he sliced the silken tiebacks from the brocade drapery and bound her hands painfully behind her back.

Victoria was beside herself with fear and desperation, but she pressed her point that Trey had been a victim, hoping to gain his sympathy. "You hate your mother because she's always dominated you. I know she has because I've seen her do it. You were innocent, Trey. You were her victim."

He slammed her into a chair and stared at her, panting. "Yes, goddammit, I was her victim. Every time I turned around, she was in my face. I was never good enough. I was never good enough for her, or Meghan. I was Meghan's victim, too. Whores! Both of them! All of you!" he shrieked, picking up a fire iron and waving it at the portrait of his mother. "Fuck you!" With that he skewered the painting right in his mother's belly.

Victoria managed to pull herself out of the chair and

started to run, but he grabbed her again and forced her to the floor, facedown. To her surprise, he sat on her. "Keep quiet," he warned. She could scarcely breathe, much less cry out.

Strangely, Trey suddenly turned chatty. "I'm going to kill you, Tori. Just like I killed the rest of the whores. But I want you to know how you are going to die." She heard a snap, like a rubber band, and could feel his body moving, as if he were arranging something with his hands. "You know that business trip I was on? Well, guess where I went on my new job? I started in the Midwest. In Chicago. Just after the opera. Then I made a stop in Kansas City for barbecue. Played a little golf in Phoenix." He laughed. "A whore in one there. But you didn't get my pun. My jokes never made the newspapers."

Victoria went cold. No, those details never made the news. The sick, twisted jokes that the Ripper copycat had played at the scene of his murders had never been revealed to the media. There was only one way he could know about those.

Trey Delaney was Traveling Jack.

And he'd just put on surgical gloves to execute his next murder. Victoria rested her head against the floor and closed her eyes, holding back tears. How could she have been so stupid? So blind? But she had known Trey. They had been friends for a lifetime. It couldn't be . . . And yet it was. He was continuing his litany of death, accurately describing each crime with details only the killer would know.

"Why, Trey? What made you do it?"

"I would have been called to the work sooner or later, but it was divine intervention that you invited me to that symposium. When I listened to your boyfriend prattle on about Jack the Ripper, I realized my time had come. I knew more about that case than he ever did, understood what drove the man who was the most brilliant killer of all times. I got the story from the master's own hand, you see."

She didn't see, but she didn't press him about it. He was

clearly mad. Her time was short, and she wanted an answer to only one question. "Did . . . did you kill Meghan?"

He rolled her over onto her back so he could look into her eyes. She knew what he wanted to see there. Fear. Terror. He needed to see that, because it put him in control. This time, she could not hide her fear, for she knew soon she would lose everything to the killer she'd called friend.

"Did I kill Meghan?" He repeated her question with a sneer. "Yes, I killed her. I was away at law school, but I couldn't get her off my mind after she broke off our affair, so I came home unexpectedly that night. She told me to leave, said she had a date. I left, but I followed her. I wanted to know who she was meeting that she considered better than me. I followed her to that sleazy motel. I saw what room she went into. I knocked on the door, thinking they were both in there humping it. I was ready to kill both of them." Sweat beaded Trey's forehead as he went on.

"But she was alone. She answered the door wearing nothing but a smile. But it wasn't for me." His face filled with anguish as he relived that night. Victoria listened in sickened astonishment to his confession.

"She had to be punished for her betrayal. So I took this"—he held the knife beneath one of Victoria's ears— "and did this . . ." She felt the keen-edged steel trace a stinging line across her throat to the other ear, and she choked trying to draw in a short breath.

"I punished her," he said, holding the dagger up and tasting her blood from the tip of the blade.

"You didn't punish her. You murdered her," Victoria cried at him, anger overcoming her fear. "You butchered her."

"Yes, I butchered her," he said in a low growl. "I took my time, just like the master did. I cut her into little pieces so she could never hurt me again. And I watched later from the parking lot as the little prick who thought he was her lover went into the room and discovered my handiwork. Ha. You should have seen the bastard run. He never called the cops. He never told anyone."

In an instant, Victoria understood what had happened that night. She glared up at Trey. "You sorry son of a bitch."

His face contorted with fury. He dropped the knife and lunged at her, his fingers encircling her neck.

"She was a whore," he screamed. "She deserved to die. And so do you."

His fingers tightened around her neck. She gasped for air and found none. Blood sang in her ears, and her vision faded.

Her last conscious thought was of Jonathan, the man she loved and would never see again.

Twenty-Seven

Jonathan's plane landed at Dulles shortly before eight P.M., and he was the first one off. During the short second leg of his journey, he'd grown increasingly anxious, until now he was a walking bundle of nerves. He shot down the concourse like a madman, headed for the bank of telephones. He dialed Victoria'a apartment for what seemed like the hundredth time, and for just as many times, he got the answering machine. Mosier. He had to get in touch with Mosier. He could send the police to the Thomases' home faster than Jonathan could get there. Frantically, he searched the fat D.C. metro area telephone directory for Mike Mosier's number, but there was none listed that was even remotely close. Beads of sweat popped out on his brow. Christ Almighty, he had to find her!

He looked at his watch. Surely she and Trey had arrived at her parents' house by now. He racked his brain, trying to remember her parents' names. He clearly remembered Barbara. But what was her father's name? Recalling that she'd said he was a prominent attorney and a partner of Trey Delaney's father, he thumbed furiously through the Yellow Pages and ran his finger down the long list of law firms until he came to one called "Thomas and Delaney." That had to be it. Although he suspected the offices were closed at this hour, he dialed the number anyway, hoping some clerk might be working late and pick it up. Such was not his fortune, however. The system answered automatically, giving the office hours and other information about the practice.

Jonathan was about to hang up when the recorded voice said, "In case of extreme emergencies, you may dial . . ." and gave another number. Repeating the number aloud again and again so as not to forget it, he dug in his pocket and found enough American coins for one more call. The line rang six times before someone answered.

"Hello. This is Detective Inspector Jonathan Blake of Scotland Yard. Please, I must speak to Mr. Lloyd Thomas. It's urgent."

The female voice on the other end of the line was unimpressed. "Mr. Thomas is unavailable. May I have him call you?"

"No, you don't understand." Panic nearly took Jonathan's breath away. "Mr. Thomas's daughter, Victoria, is in grave danger. Can you find him? I must speak to him immediately. Please!" He almost screamed into the phone.

The woman was clearly surprised. "Victoria? One moment please." She put him on hold, and he waited for an agonizingly long time. After what seemed an eternity, a man's voice came across the wire.

"Mr. Blake? This is Lloyd Thomas. What's going on here? My assistant said something about Victoria being in danger."

"Yes, sir, she may be. Where is she?"

"She's . . . just left."

"With Trey Delaney?"

"Why, yes. What's this all about, Blake?"

With as much control as he could muster, Jonathan explained the situation to Victoria's father, praying that he would believe the story, as wild as it sounded. "She's his next victim. I'm certain of it. Where did they go?"

"Good God! I . . . I'm not sure where they went. But they couldn't have gone far. They only left the house a short while ago."

Jonathan got directions to the Thomases's home, then

told Lloyd to call the emergency number and alert the police to be on the lookout for the vehicle they were driving.
"And if you know his home number, call Mike Mosier and
get him on it."

Jonathan had brought only one small carry-on bag, so
he was at the taxi stand in a matter of minutes, trying not
to think about how precious few minutes Victoria might
have. He gave the taxi driver the address of the place where
she had last been seen—her parents' house—and told him
there was an extra fifty dollars in it for him if he got Jonathan there in less than half an hour. Then he held on for
dear life as the man careened the cab through the traffic,
bent on earning his bonus.

It wasn't hard to find the action once they turned into
the sedately elegant suburb where the Thomases lived. Several police cars sped through the quiet streets just ahead of
them, sirens blaring. "Follow them," he instructed the
driver. His gut twisted in terror. Would any of them get to
Victoria in time?

The cars all converged at the same time on the grounds
of an impressive mansion, in front of which was parked
Victoria's car. "Dear God," Jonathan growled as he yanked
the taxi door open. He raced to the front door, ignoring the
shouts of the uniformed policemen who followed him.

"Victoria!" he called, and pounded on the door. Not
waiting for an answer, he pressed the large brass lever and
pushed his way inside. "Victoria!"

The house was dark except for lights coming from the
nearby living room. Jonathan rushed toward the room, but
at the doorway froze in horror at the sight that met his eyes.
Trey Delaney knelt astraddle Victoria's inert figure, his
hands around her neck and a look of twisted ecstacy on his
face.

"You bastard!" Jonathan cried out and lunged at Delaney. He lost all reason, ignored all caution. His only
thought was to rid Victoria of this false friend once and for
all. He slammed his entire body against Trey's, knocking
him to the floor, stunning him, but only momentarily. With

brute strength, Trey pushed Jonathan away and scrambled for a knife that lay nearby on the floor. The knife he had planned to use to carve up Victoria after the kill.

"Oh, no you don't," Jonathan said, kicking his hand as he reached for the weapon. But Trey's determination overcame the painful blow, and he rallied, clutching the knife and advancing toward Jonathan.

"So, Inspector," he hissed, breathing heavily, "you think you've come to her rescue. Well, too bad. You're too late. She's already dead. The stinking whore is dead, although I didn't get the pleasure of cutting her."

"Drop it, Delaney!" A familiar voice came from somewhere nearby, and Jonathan glanced in the direction of the sound. Behind Trey, Mike Mosier and two uniformed policemen stood poised and ready to shoot.

But Trey did not drop the knife or alter his stance. Instead, he gave forth a hideous laugh and, blade raised, charged full force at Jonathan. The crack of gunfire exploded in the room, and Jonathan saw Trey halt in midstride, a surprised look on his face. He fell first to his knees, and then crumpled into a heap on the floor.

Dazed, Jonathan dashed to where Victoria lay unconscious on the carpet. He knelt beside her, touching her tenderly but desperately, searching for a pulse, a breath, any sign of life. "Don't leave me, Victoria," he pleaded, his voice hoarse over the ache in his throat. "Please don't leave me."

The paramedics moved in, and reluctantly he left her side to give them room to work. His vision was blurred with tears, but he was aware that the room was filling with people. From somewhere nearby, he heard a woman's scream.

Victoria's eyelids felt as if they were made of lead. She struggled to open them, wondering why it seemed so difficult to wake up. She managed at last to peer out into the world, a world that was mostly white. She closed her eyes again. Was she dead? A dull pain registered in her throat when she swallowed. Dead people didn't feel pain, did they? She opened her eyes again, wider this time, and turned her head slightly to one side. There, dozing by her bedside, was Jonathan Blake.

She frowned, confused. What was Jonathan doing here? Wasn't he supposed to be in London? But where was "here" anyway?

"Jonathan?" She tried to speak, but found no voice. He must have heard her stir, however, for he woke up immediately and leaned over her, taking one of her hands in his.

"I'm here, my darling," he murmured and bent to kiss her cheek. "Don't try to talk now. Everything's going to be all right."

The tears in his eyes and the emotion in his voice only confused Victoria more. What the hell was the matter?

And then it all came rushing back. The disastrous birthday scene, Trey's confession of the murders, his vicious assault on her. Her eyes widened at the memory. Trey had tried to kill her! Her lifelong friend had tried to kill her. Just as he had killed her sister. Her fingers tightened around Jonathan's as the monstrous truth washed over her. She began to tremble, and then her whole body began to quake violently, and tears flooded down her cheeks. Tears of horror, and anger, and grief. Not Trey! He could not have done this to her!

Jonathan sat on the bed and enfolded her in his arms, rocking her gently. "Shhh," he whispered, soothing her. "It's over, darling. It's all over. Everything's going to be all right now."

Victoria wondered how anything could ever be all right again. She felt so . . . betrayed. Nothing was as it seemed anymore. How could she believe anything or anyone ever again? And yet, feeling the warmth of Jonathan's arms around her, hearing the tenderness in his voice, she knew she could believe in him. He was real, and honest, and somehow had managed to be here for her when she needed him most. He restored her faith, and her soul. She brought his fingertips to her lips, grateful beyond words for his love.

Gradually, she pulled herself together again. Her throat and head throbbed with pain, but she needed answers. She forced herself to speak. "What happened?"

"Don't try to talk now," he urged again. "Your throat is severely injured."

But she had to know. "Trey . . . ?"

"He's dead. I came on the scene just as he thought he'd strangled you. He attacked me, and the police shot him."

Dear God. Victoria closed her eyes and felt another hot tear trickle down her cheek. Jonathan brushed it gently away.

At that moment, the door opened, and Victoria looked up to see her mother and father peering in at her with anxious expressions. "She's awake," Lloyd said, a relieved smile softening the lines of his face. Her mother rushed to her bedside, and Jonathan stood up. Barbara Wentworth Thomas, with reddened, puffy eyes and smeared mascara, looked more disheveled than Victoria had ever seen her, and more beautiful, for suddenly she appeared human after all. Barbara took her in her arms, and Victoria didn't resist.

"Oh, sweetheart," her mother murmured, sitting on the side of the bed, holding her daughter and crying openly in a display of emotion Victoria had never before experienced from her reserved mother. "The doctor says you will be fine. You'll be fine," Barbara repeated, as if to reassure herself.

Victoria glanced over her mother's shoulder, and to her amazement, she saw that her father was crying. And in that moment, Victoria understood at last the depth of the love her parents had for her. They weren't demonstrative people, but she knew without a doubt they loved her nonetheless. She straightened to look her mother in the eye and over the bruises in her throat she rasped out the words she'd rarely said to her. "I love you, Mother." She turned to her father and whispered, "And I love you, too."

Her mother took both her hands and looked into Victoria's eyes. "I'm so sorry. I've been a miserable mother. I drove both of you away, you and Meghan, and . . . and I

almost lost you both because of it." Her grief was so deep
it sliced through Victoria, too. She drew her mother back
into her arms and held her until Barbara shed all the tears
she had withheld since Meghan's death. It had been a horrible seven years for all of them, but Jonathan was right.

Now it was over.

Now it was time for the healing to begin.

Three days later, Victoria prepared to accompany Jonathan
and a team of special agents and local law enforcement
officers to Trey's town house in Georgetown, where they
were to undertake a careful search of his belongings, looking for answers to explain the inexplicable. Her external
injuries were healing quickly, and she had almost regained
her voice, but inside, she was still painfully in shock over
all that had come to light since that horrible night when
Trey had tried to kill her.

After Trey's death, Marilyn Delaney had become hys-
terical and had confessed to the police the whole story of
what had happened the night Meghan was murdered. She
said her son had come home, covered with blood, ranting
hysterically. He had broken down and told her what he had
done. She gave him a tranquilizer to calm him down. Then
she threw him in the shower, took his clothes and burned
them, and the next day put him in the hands of a psycho-
therapist.

Always able to intimidate Trey, she'd told him he must
never let anyone know the truth, that the scandal would be
their ruin, and that he would go to the gas chamber for
what he'd done. Her threats, and her domineering manner,
were sufficient to keep his mouth shut. Eventually, a few
weeks after the murder, he was institutionalized for nearly
a year. The family covered the truth by saying that he'd
gone out west to "find himself."

But the deceit had not stopped there. Victoria had
learned that the Delaneys had both known what had happened and had taken steps to cover it up. Marilyn Delaney,
in fact, confessed that she had paid off the officer investi-

gating the case to "lose" certain evidence, including the crime scene photos and case notes.

Marilyn and James were both in jail now, as was Grizzell, but that offered Victoria little comfort. At times, she wished she would awaken to find it was all a bad dream. She wished that the murderer had in fact been Matthew Ferguson. It would be so much easier to accept. In his suicide note, Ferguson had written he felt "responsible" for Meghan's death, but he hadn't said he'd actually killed her. It must have been the guilt and pressure of keeping that terrible secret to himself that caused him in the end to take his own life. In some respects, Victoria felt sorry for him, for he too was a victim of that crime.

The one happy outcome of the whole affair, other than the reconciliation with her parents, was that Jonathan was by her side, and he'd promised never to leave her again. They'd told her parents of their plans to be married, and she'd been delightfully surprised that even Barbara had welcomed him openly. He was a guest in their home, although they hadn't gone so far as to put him in the room where Victoria had spent a few days recuperating.

That was okay. There was time enough for that later, when she was fully recovered. For now, she wanted some answers to the tragedy that had befallen them all.

Mainly, she wanted to know what had made Trey become a killer.

Trey's first murder had been a crime of passion, although he had mutilated Meghan in the same style as Jack the Ripper. Then seven years had gone by, during which to her knowledge he had refrained from killing. He'd babbled something at the end about it being "divine intervention" that he'd gone to the symposium, which apparently had triggered him to kill again, but she had no clue what he'd meant about having received the story from "the master's own hand."

When she entered Trey's town house with the other agents, she shivered, remembering coming here just a few nights ago, totally trusting, not knowing the deadly secrets

this place held. "I'd like to take his bedroom," she told
Mosier as the team began to divide the responsibilities of
the search. "If there is anything that will give us some answers, it'll likely be among his personal belongings."

She and Jonathan started at opposite ends of the room,
Jonathan in the closet, Victoria at the exquisite antique desk
of which Trey had been so proud. The mahogany of the
wood gleamed in the morning sunlight. He'd claimed it had
been in the family for generations, handed down from his
mother's British ancestors. It was late Victorian, and Victoria wondered if it might once have belonged to the man
Jonathan had told her he believed to have actually been
Jack the Ripper, or at least part of that persona, J. K. Stephen.

She opened the top drawer. Inside lay a battered tome,
covered in faded green cloth. "What's this?" She lifted it
gingerly from the drawer and laid it on the desktop, running
her fingers over the cover. Something niggled at the back
of her mind, and she had the sudden feeling that she had
seen this book before. But she could not recall when or
where.

Victoria opened the book. Inscribed on the flyleaf was
a name and a date: "J. K. Stephen. 1876."

"Jonathan! Look at this!"

Jonathan peered at it over her shoulder. "It looks like a
diary."

"It is a diary," she said, turning the pages carefully but
with growing excitement. "Listen to this." She read aloud:

*Eton, Twentieth September, 1876—Visit from the Devil to-
day.*

> *Oh, James, James, the Devil thou art,*
> *Sneaking up from behind, stabbing my heart,*
> *Oh, James, James, James Fitzjames,*
> *How James Fitzjames doth shame.*

*Father had not the decency to limit his tirade against me
to the privacy of my rooms, but burst upon me with full*

force within view of Wilson and the others. He demanded
I work harder, said I was a disgrace to the Stephen family.
I laughed in his face, but my innards wretched in shame.
Even now, though the shame has subsided, I am consumed
with rage. If I had a dagger, I would thrust it through his
cold, hard heart.

Victoria shuddered involuntarily. She'd seen James
Winston Delaney II, Trey's father, do this very sort of thing
to his son. If J. K. Stephen, the author of this diary, had
suffered such degradations, and if that abuse had led to
murderous impulses, it was easy to see how Trey would
relate to the feelings recorded here. She wondered what else
the book would reveal about the killer's background, his
mind and motivation, and how much of it would mirror
Trey Delaney's own torment.

She looked up at Jonathan, who had laid his hands gently on her shoulders. "If you are correct that J. K. Stephen
was involved in the old Ripper murders, this could be the
diary you have been hoping would turn up."

"But how on earth did it come into the hands of Trey
Delaney?"

"You told me about that family tree that Janeece Fairchild was researching. Didn't you say that the name Delaney was on it?"

"At the very bottom. It showed that a daughter of the
Swansons, Marilyn, married an American, James Winston
Delaney II, in the late 1950s."

"Marilyn Delaney." In her dislike for Trey's mother,
Victoria had always considered the woman's British accent
to be artificial and affected. But it had been real. Victoria
had never asked her mother about Marilyn's background.
Now, she didn't have to.

"I've seen this book somewhere before," she murmured,
stretching her memory, reaching into the nether reaches of
her mind. She closed her eyes, concentrating, and she saw
three children in an attic. Playing dress-up. Saw one of
them open a large trunk, searching for more old clothes

with which to costume themselves. Saw a boy reach in and bring out . . . a fancy walking cane. Victoria realized with a start it was the same walking cane Trey had used the night he'd tried to murder her. It was in the custody of the police now. An ingenious device, sheathing the long, deadly knife the old Ripper had used to kill at least five women in Whitechapel more than a century ago. Which Trey had used to kill her sister and eight other women in recent weeks in cities across America. Which he had nearly used to kill her.

She searched her memory for more and saw the boy take a pipe from the trunk. The pipe! It now lay on a table downstairs, where Trey had placed it as they left for the birthday party. She squinted her closed eyes, looking further. She saw the boy strut across the large space with the air of a gentleman, swaggering with the cane and pretending to puff on the pipe. She heard the two girls giggle. Then suddenly, she saw the book in the boy's hands.

And the memory faded. "He found this in the Delaneys' attic," she said quietly, opening her eyes again, "when he was just a kid. We were playing up there one rainy day, and we came across this big chest with tons of old clothes in it. We had a lark, dressing up in things that were probably priceless in terms of historical value. But we didn't know that. I couldn't have been more than thirteen, which means Trey and Meghan were around eight or nine."

Jonathan picked the book up and turned the pages to the dates of each of the Ripper murders, and the gruesome story unfolded as he read. Interspersed among the personal narrative, which revealed the wrenching tale of forbidden love and the psychological decline of the author, were detailed descriptions of each murder, how they were executed, what mistakes had been made and what he had learned from them. A virtual how-to murder manual.

"Unbelievable," he said. He shook his head when he got to the last inscription, a poem. "Listen to this:"

I have no time to tell you how
I came to be a killer

But you should know, as time will show,
That I'm society's pillar.*

Jonathan let out a low whistle and handed the book back to Victoria. "If this proves to be authentic, it is the written record left by the man who was responsible for those old murders," he said quietly, massaging her shoulders. "Unfortunately, it must have served as a textbook for the man who committed the recent ones."

"He's had this book all along," Victoria mused. "He's been studying it. He called it the work of the 'master.' When he killed Meghan, he copied the style of the old Ripper, but it was a crime with a different motivation than his recent killings. The recent spree was surely triggered by the Ripper symposium. And I asked him to go." Grief and regret washed through her.

After a few moments, Victoria rose, thinking to take the book to the agent who was charged with securing any evidence they found in Trey's home, when something fell from between the pages and drifted to the floor. She knelt and picked up a delicate ring of what appeared to be a thin braid of hair.

"What on earth?" she asked, holding it up for Jonathan to inspect.

"You know what that looks like?" he said as she laid it in the palm of his hand. "A mourning bracelet. During Victorian times, lovers used to braid strands of their hair which they exchanged as tokens of their affection. You don't suppose this was a gift to J. K. from the prince?"

Victoria brought out a large magnifying glass from her purse and began to examine the hair. Jonathan laughed. "Do you always carry that thing around?"

"Comes in handy sometimes, like now. A little trick I learned from Sherlock. Jonathan, I think you're in luck here. These hairs appear to have been pulled from the head, not clipped. There are root follicles."

"Which means they carry genetic information."

They looked at each other, stunned by the possibility of

what the braid of hair might reveal. Then they each let out what sounded like a native war whoop and gave one another a high five before celebrating their find with a kiss that left her breathless.

Mike Mosier came into the room on the run. "What's wrong?"

Victoria opened her eyes but didn't withdraw from their heated embrace. With a wave of her hand, she let Mike know nothing was wrong.

Nothing at all.

Twenty-Eight

Three weeks later, Jonathan and Victoria were in his office at Scotland Yard, clearing his personal belongings from his desk and shelves. She had resigned from the FBI, albeit reluctantly, and he from Scotland Yard, after together they'd made the decision to open their own private criminal investigative agency in Virginia.

Upon returning to London, they had tried to wrap up the hit-and-run before Jonathan submitted his resignation, but Lord Chastain had seemingly disappeared from the face of the earth. On a visit to Lady Chastain, they'd learned that her husband had transferred most of their funds to an account in the Grand Caymans, and none of them expected him to surface again in England. Lady Chastain, in a bid to set her finances in better order, had surprised them by offering for sale the items she had earlier routed to Jonathan through Roger Hammersmith—the missing police records concerning the original Ripper murders. In addition, she had a hat she'd claimed had belonged to the Duke of Clarence, Prince Eddy, that together with the police records would prove beyond a doubt he was Jack the Ripper. The items apparently had been in Lord Chastain's family for generations, handed down for safekeeping from an ancestor who was in Queen Victoria's secret service. It was he, she claimed, who removed the evidence from Scotland Yard at the queen's own direction to protect her grandson from becoming implicated in the murders. "Alistair has this crazy notion that he too is in the queen's secret service," she'd said with a bitter laugh, "but that's just so much jolly rot."

Giving her a substantial sum for the lot, Jonathan and Victoria had then had Erik Hensen in the forensic lab check out the hat. He'd discovered several strands of hair, one of which still retained the follicle, and he'd come up with a DNA match with the hair from the mourning bracelet. There was no doubt that Prince Eddy was involved in the original Whitechapel murders. He had lost his hat during the double event, as recorded by J. K. Stephen in his diary.

The evidence was incontrovertible—together, J. K. Stephen and Prince Albert Victor Edward had become the Whitechapel murderer known as Jack the Ripper.

As they packed books and mementos of Jonathan's career at the Yard, he and Victoria discussed how best to present the truth about Jack the Ripper to the world. Jonathan had shared his find with the commissioner, who had shown a keen interest in the various items of evidence in the Ripper case that had been unearthed during the past few weeks. He had insisted that Jonathan put everything under lock and key in the Crime Museum.

"We've just recovered all this," he'd said. "We wouldn't want it to get into the wrong hands again."

They both jumped at the sound of a brisk knock on the door. A woman handed Jonathan an interoffice memo. "You're to take action on this right away," she said, then turned and walked briskly away down the corridor.

"What part of 'I quit' don't these people understand?" Victoria asked with a smile.

"I'm not taking on another thing," Jonathan assured her. But he was curious as to what he'd been sent. He read the official summons aloud to her:

" 'The queen requests your appearance at two P.M. today in the private conference room of Specialist Operations. Please bring with you all items which have recently come into your possession concerning the Whitechapel murders of 1888, as it is of the greatest interest to Her Royal Majesty.' "

"The queen?" Victoria looked astounded, but not as astounded as he felt.

Jonathan glanced at his watch, then down at his rather rumpled suit. He didn't have time to go home and change. "I've never met the queen before," he said. "Wish I looked a little fresher."

Victoria came over to him and straightened his tie. "It's one-thirty now. Just go to the men's room, splash a little water on your face, comb your hair, you'll look fine." She tweaked his cheek. "If all else fails, grin at her. She'll go for the dimple. I did."

At two o'clock, Jonathan and Victoria, laden with the items they'd been requested to bring along, entered the conference room of the division of Scotland Yard that was its most secret. Specialist Operations was charged with crimes of a most serious nature, such as international and organized crime. They provided protection duties to the royals and other political VIPs. Forensic science was under their direction. And then there was something called the "Special Branch." Even Jonathan did not know what went on in that division.

He'd expected the assistant commissioner in charge of this division to be present, but he was not. Neither was the queen. Instead, two burly strangers greeted them, and once they were inside the room, one of them moved to stand between them and the door.

"You can deposit the items over there," the other man said, indicating the far end of the conference table. Jonathan was alarmed to see a paper shredder perched there.

He didn't deposit any items anywhere. "Where's the assistant commissioner?"

"He had to step out for a while."

"Who are you?"

"Friends of the queen," one of them said with a cynical grin.

The door opened, and a tall, thin man in a dark suit

entered. Jonathan heard Victoria's involuntary intake of breath. He turned to the man, who gave him a cold smile.

"Good afternoon, Inspector Blake," said Alistair Huntley-Ames. "Ms. Thomas. The queen thanks you for coming. Did you bring the materials she requested?"

"What the hell is going on here?" Jonathan stepped slightly in front of Victoria, acutely aware of the truly strange circumstances in which they found themselves and suddenly concerned for their safety.

Lord Chastain laughed and threw his hat on a chair. "Relax, Blake. No need to get in a dither. All we want is what you have in your hands."

"Who is 'we'?" Jonathan clutched the old police files possessively.

"My wife made a little mistake in giving you those," he said, nodding toward the envelopes in Jonathan's hands. "She asked me to apologize. You see, she wants them back."

Jonathan knew better and hoped Elizabeth hadn't suffered when her husband had learned that she'd turned the historical documents over to him. "I don't believe you. Besides, they don't belong to her," he said, scowling. "Or to you."

"You're quite right," Huntley-Ames replied mildly, removing his gloves. "They belong to the queen. They did then, and they do now."

"They belong to the people of Britain," Victoria snapped. "To the world."

He regarded her with cold gray eyes. "The matters revealed in those archives are considered a risk to national security. As a member of the queen's secret service, I demand that you turn them over at once or stand accused of treason."

"Treason!" Jonathan had never heard of anything so preposterous. And he didn't believe for a minute that Huntley-Ames was in the queen's secret service. His wife certainly hadn't. "I'm not turning over anything until I talk to the head of this outfit."

Lord Chastain let out a heavy, impatient sigh. "I'm afraid that will be impossible. You see, he was called away on an important assignment today. In Scotland."

He went to Victoria and glanced at the materials she had in her hands. Materials they had so foolishly believed were of interest to the queen. Jonathan was furious at himself. They'd walked into a trap.

"May I?" Huntley-Ames asked, indicating he wanted her to turn the precious items over to him.

"You sure as hell may not!" she lashed out, backing away from him. But she ran into the wall of one of Lord Chastain's henchmen who easily wrestled the goods from her and handed them to queen's would-be protector. He set the hat on the conference table and proceeded to peruse the two diaries with interest.

"So the old man did have Gull's diary," he commented. "I thought he was just blowing smoke. Too bad he met with such an untimely end. I hadn't planned on running him over, but the opportunity presented itself, and it seemed the thing to do at the time. Prevention, you know. Being dead, he couldn't cause trouble."

He fanned the pages of the other diary. "Interesting. I didn't know about this one. Hmmm. Supposedly written by J. K. Stephen. A hoax, I'm sure. But we mustn't take chances."

He rose and took the two small books to the shredder.

"No!" Victoria shouted and dashed after him. But the second man intercepted her, wrapping his arms tightly around her while she flailed her fists at Lord Chastain.

Jonathan attempted to bolt to Victoria's rescue but was himself restrained by one of the goons. "Let her go," he demanded.

But Huntley-Ames only smiled blandly. "Relax, both of you, and you won't get hurt."

"You're insane to even think about destroying those artifacts," Victoria cried desperately. "What possible harm could come of finally resolving the Ripper murders?"

The self-styled operative turned on the machine, tore a

few pages from the green diary and fed them into the teeth of the beast. Despair tightened Jonathan's stomach. He hardly heard the man's explanation.

"I'm an old man now," he told them. "Ready to retire. I have things all set up in the Caribbean. But I could not leave until I secured this secret forever. It is a duty that has been handed down in my family for generations. But I have no heir, and therefore no choice but to destroy the evidence that has been in my charge all these years. I must thank you for providing that second diary, as well. I doubt if J. K. Stephen kept a duplicate anywhere. We should have all the evidence in our possession now." More pages went into the shredder. When he was finished with the content of the diaries, he took an elegant gold lighter from his vest pocket and set fire to the board covers of each, watching them burn in a metal trash bin. When the flames rose brightly, he added the hat to the mix. The odor of scorched fabric filled the room. Jonathan hoped the smoke would set off the alarms, but it didn't.

Huntley-Ames turned to Jonathan. "Now, may we please have your set of documents, or are you going to make these lads earn their keep?"

Jonathan looked at him with contempt. "These documents are priceless. They belong in a museum."

"They belong in the shredder. I should have destroyed them years ago."

With that, the older man strode to Jonathan and tried to wrench the manila envelopes from his grasp. Jonathan was able to shrug off the man who had been restraining him, and managed to give Huntley-Ames a rough shove in the stomach. But he was outnumbered three to one, for both of the henchmen were on him in an instant, one of them delivering a blow to his chin that sent him crashing to the floor. The three manila envelopes went flying across the room.

"Jonathan!" He heard Victoria cry out angrily and turned in time to see her race across the room and kick one of the bullies between the legs from the rear, effectively rendering him useless. But the other one whirled and grabbed her securely.

Finding his footing again, Jonathan lunged at Lord Chastain, knocking him off balance. The two men tumbled to the floor, skirmishing for control. Jonathan became aware in his peripheral vision that someone else had entered the room. He glanced around and saw the woman who had delivered the summons to this insanity hurrying through the room, gathering up the precious documents.

"Shred them, Penelope," Lord Chastain called out to her.

"No!" Jonathan cried, but his protest was silenced by the blow of something heavy against his head.

When he came to, the room was quiet. Victoria knelt over him, stroking his forehead. The three men and the woman had gone. The conference table was empty. There was no sign of the shredder or the trash bin.

All that remained as testimony to what had taken place here was the faint scent of smoke and Jonathan's splitting headache.

Later that day, Victoria pressed a cold cloth across the ugly lump on Jonathan's forehead. He lay on the bed in his flat, looking more forlorn than she'd ever seen him, and she had to admit that she too had never felt so defeated.

After the men had left, Victoria had run into the adjoining offices, calling out for help. But the entire wing of the building was curiously deserted. Worried about Jonathan, she'd returned to care for him just as he was regaining consciousness.

"We have to report this," she'd insisted when he sat up, but he'd simply shaken his head.

"No. There's no point. I don't know if Huntley-Ames is in the secret service or not, but he managed to pull off his hijacking in the offices of some very powerful people here at Scotland Yard. I don't think he did it on his own."

When he'd managed to get to his feet, they had returned to Jonathan's office, picked up the rest of his belongings and left. Jonathan had walked in silence, while Victoria searched for some way to lighten his disappointment.

"We have photocopies of everything," she'd pointed out.

"Nothing that could be forensically proven as authentic. We'd just be laughed at as creating yet another hoax."

She hated to admit it, but he was right.

"I'm sorry things turned out this way," Victoria said, changing the compress tenderly.

Jonathan rolled over on the bed and tugged her into his arms. "It doesn't matter," he said, grinning and running his hands through her hair. "I have all I want in my arms right now."

Historical Notes

The Whitechapel murders of 1888 ceased as abruptly as
they began. With the death of Montague John Druitt in
December 1888, many at Scotland Yard believed that the
man who called himself Jack the Ripper was gone.

J. K. Stephen continued his tormented existence, doing
all in his power to thwart the demands of his overbearing
father while sinking ever deeper into madness. He saw little
of his beloved Prince Eddy in the two remaining years of
his life.

Prince Albert Victor Edward was sent to India by his
parents after recovering from the "illness" that kept him
confined in Dr.Gull's asylum for several months after the
Ripper murders ceased. Upon his return, the queen announced his engagement to Princess Hélène, a Catholic, the
daughter of the Comte de Paris, the pretender to the French
throne. The engagement was later canceled, ostensibly for
religious reasons. The royals chose another bride for him
the following year, his cousin Princess May of Teck, a Prot-
estant. The wedding was to be held on February 27, 1892.

On November 21, 1891, J. K. Stephen was admitted to
St. Andrew's Hospital, Northampton, where he lived until
his death. Admitting diagnosis: "Extreme depression, almost mute. Has had episodes of depression lasting some
weeks followed by periods of unusual excitability. This
morning (at home) threw a looking glass into the street and

stood naked in the window. Believed there was a warrant out for his detention."

Hospital records describe him as a "tall, well built, rather stout man in good physical health." His condition generally improved and by January 1, 1892, he was described as being more cheerful and joining in activities.

On January 7, 1892, Prince Albert Victor Edward, "Prince Eddy," the duke of Clarence, became fatally ill at Sandringham after participating in a vigorous hunt the day before despite the fact that he was suffering from influenza. The following day after lunch he was taken seriously ill with abdominal pains and dizziness. He suffered a high fever and a rattling cough, and was diagnosed with incipient pneumonia, although the gastric attacks continued. For the next week, he slipped in and out of consciousness and became delirious. He died on the morning of January 14, 1892.

Curiously, no records concerning the medical treatment of the prince have ever been found. From the description of the last days of his life, however, it is believed that Prince Eddy died in the advanced stages of syphilis, which he contracted during a shore party in the West Indies years before.

On January 15, 1892, J. K. Stephen, unaware that his beloved prince had died, suddenly began refusing all food and had to be tube fed. This circumstance remained until February 2, when his physical condition collapsed. He died on February 3, 1892. Cause of death is listed as "Mania, refusal of food, and exhaustion."

The identity of Jack the Ripper has never been proven.

Even the deepest secrets will be revealed on…

THE

ISLAND

JILL JONES

A young English woman from an isolated island off the coast of Cornwall is killed, her body found in a London hotel, in what looks to be a murder/suicide. Jack Knight, an American private investigator, arrives on the island in search of the killer. And on his journey he meets Keely Cochrane, a young woman torn between two very different worlds. But a conspiracy that has existed for centuries threatens their every move—and someone is stalking them…watching them at every step…and waiting to stop them dead in their tracks.

"This fast-paced story deftly combines modern suspense with ancient ritual and lore."
– *Library Journal*

"A magical escape into a realm steeped with legend."
– *Bookpage*

A Curse.

A Mystery.

A Love Story.

A Legend.

All come Full Circle in…

CIRCLE OF THE LILY

JILL JONES

Claire St. John has the gift to see into the very heart and soul of others, but when American Michael Townsend rents her guest cottage, she sees a man whose tormented soul is as dark as midnight. Together they challenge mysterious and sinister forces to solve a century-old mystery, break a damning curse, and discover that the most powerful force of all is love…

"CIRCLE OF THE LILY is almost impossible to put down, so plan accordingly."
—*Rendezvous*

AVAILABLE WHEREVER BOOKS ARE SOLD
FROM ST. MARTIN'S PAPERBACKS

COTL 3/00

THE SCOTTISH ROSE

JILL JONES

Jaded TV host Taylor Kincaid works on a top-rated series that debunks everything supernatural. But her beliefs are challenged when she travels to the Scottish coast, and searches for Mary Queen of Scots' jeweled chalice, The Scottish Rose. For there she meets Duncan Fraser, a man who helps her to find what she seeks—and to understand the magic of love...

TSR 3/00

Do you believe in destiny? One hundred and fifty years ago, two lovers disappeared on the same night. Today, two lovers find each other again, but they are sworn enemies because of a wrenching betrayal. Together they must search for the ultimate element of love. They must search for the essence of a perfume known only as "My Desire"…

JILL JONES

ESSENCE OF MY DESIRE

A delightful new romance from the bestselling author of
THE SCOTTISH ROSE,
MY LADY CAROLINE and EMILY'S SECRET

AVAILABLE WHEREVER BOOKS ARE SOLD
FROM ST. MARTIN'S PRESS